Twin Star Exorcists

O N M Y O J I

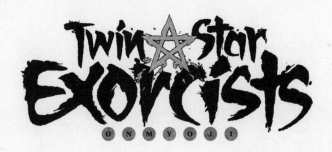

Twin ★ Star Exorcists

O N M Y O J I

15

STORY & ART
YOSHIAKI SUKENO

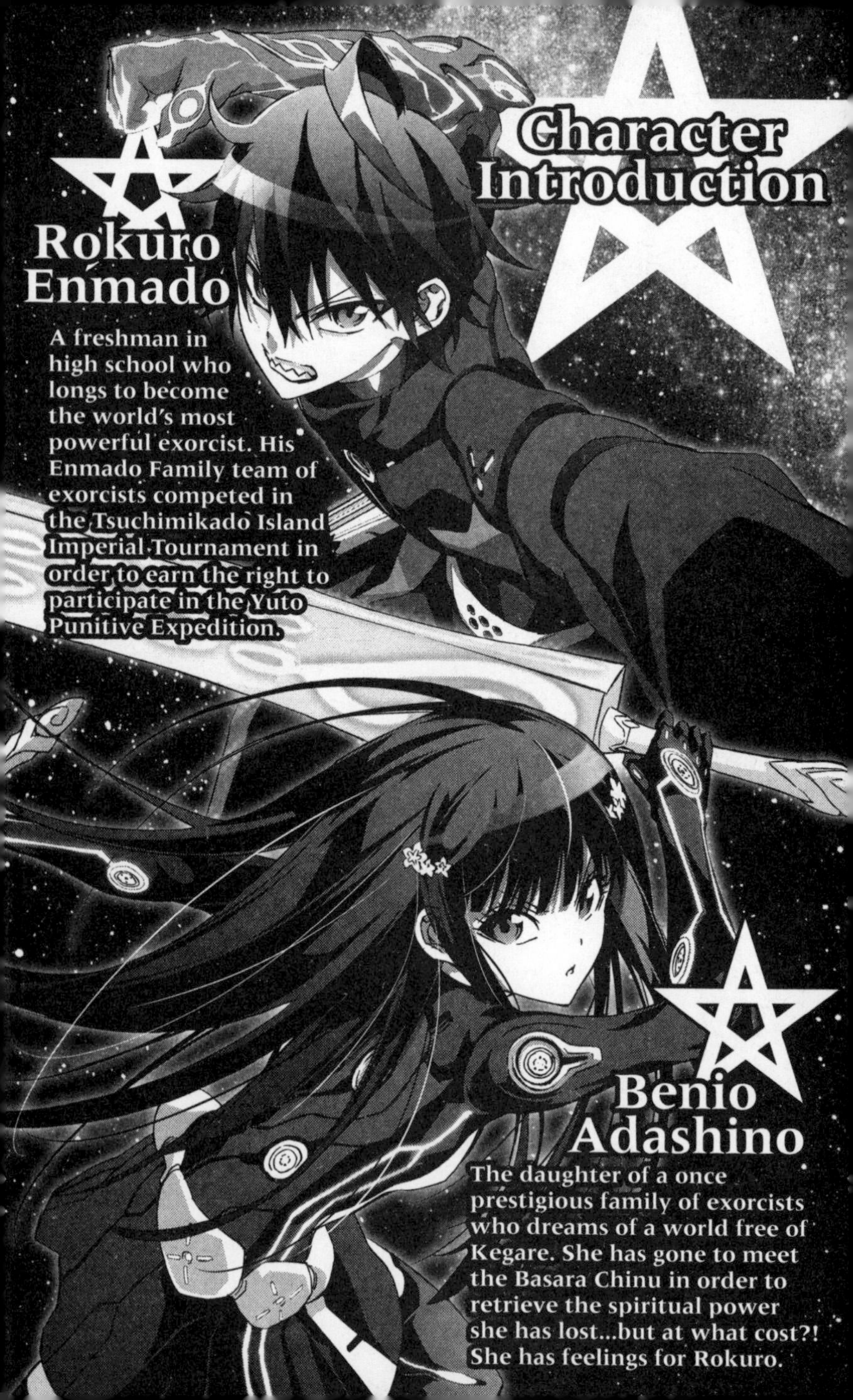
Character Introduction
Rokuro Enmado
A freshman in high school who longs to become the world's most powerful exorcist. His Enmado Family team of exorcists competed in the Tsuchimikado Island Imperial Tournament in order to earn the right to participate in the Yuto Punitive Expedition.
Benio Adashino
The daughter of a once prestigious family of exorcists who dreams of a world free of Kegare. She has gone to meet the Basara Chinu in order to retrieve the spiritual power she has lost...but at what cost?! She has feelings for Rokuro.

Mayura Otomi

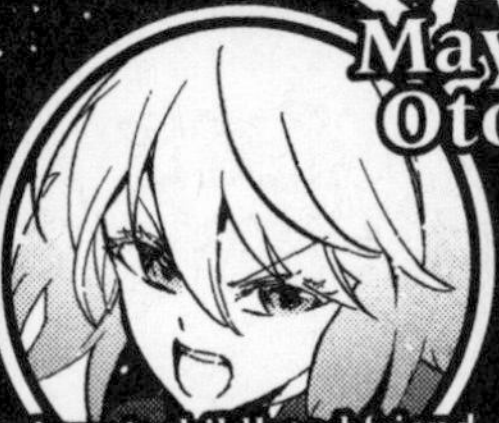

Rokuro's childhood friend. During a fierce battle in Magano, her commitment to protecting others earned her the spiritual protector White Tiger. She has become the new head of the Amawaka Family.

Kamui

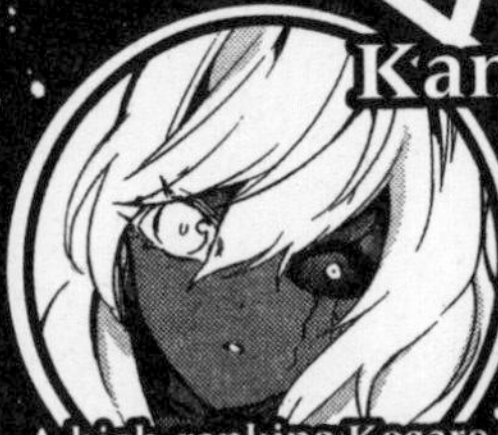

A high-ranking Kegare called a Basara who has the ability to communicate in the human tongue. Kamui killed Benio's parents.

Yuto Ijika

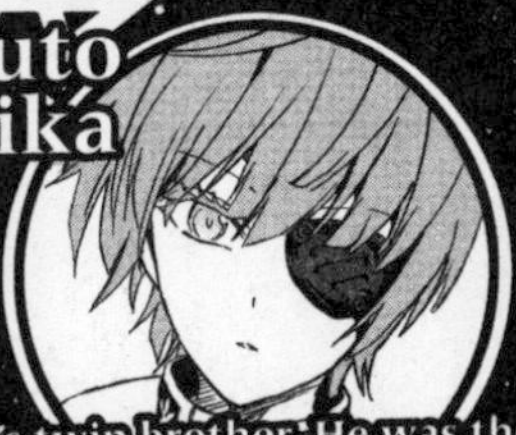

Benio's twin brother. He was the mastermind behind the Hinatsuki Tragedy. He awaits Rokuro in the layers of Magano beneath Tsuchimikado Island.

Chinu

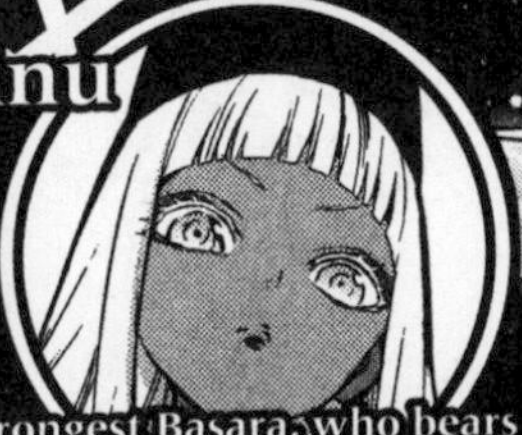

The strongest Basara, who bears a striking resemblance to Abeno Seimei. She is the only one who can perform the ritual that will bring back Benio's spiritual power.

Kaguya

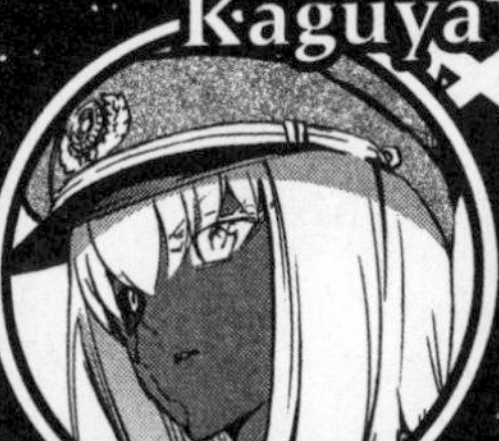

Sixth-ranked Basara. She pursued Benio inside Magano beneath the mainland and has just attacked Kamui...

Ashiya Doman

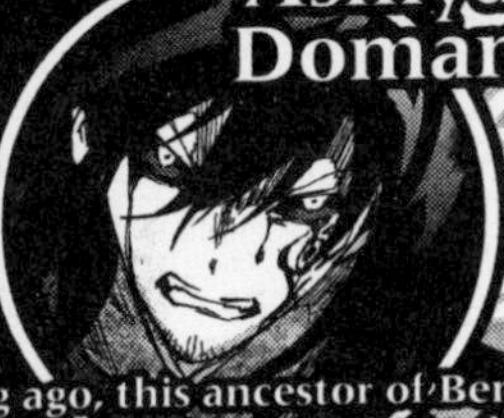

Long ago, this ancestor of Benio went to extreme lengths to defeat the king of the Kegare. His experiments led to the creation of hybrid human Kegare.

Story Thus Far...

Kegare are creatures from Magano, the underworld, and it is the duty of an exorcist to hunt, exorcise and purify them. Rokuro and Benio are the Twin Star Exorcists, fated to bear the Prophesied Child who will defeat the Kegare. Their goal is to go to Tsuchimikado Island to get revenge on Yuto, who is the mastermind behind the Hinatsuki Tragedy and Benio's brother.

After two years, Rokuro qualifies to go to the island, but Benio loses her spiritual power in battle. Leaving her behind, Rokuro instead moves to the island with his childhood friend and newbie exorcist Mayura. Having proved their mettle at the imperial tournament, Rokuro's team is allowed to join the Yuto Punitive Expedition, where he hopes to avenge his murdered dorm mates. But during the last match of the tournament, Tenma critically injures Shimon. Meanwhile, under the guidance of Kamui, Benio travels through Magano to meet the mysterious Chinu. Benio is shocked to learn that to regain her spiritual power she will have to become her true self, a human Kegare. Nevertheless, she decides to go through with Chinu's ritual and undergo the transformation...

Twin Star Exorcists

O N M Y O J I

EXORCISMS

15

ONMYOJI have worked for the Imperial Court since the Heian era. In addition to exorcising evil spirits, as civil servants they performed a variety of roles, including advising nobles by foretelling the future, creating the calendar, observing the movements of the stars, measuring time...

#53: Kamui and Benio

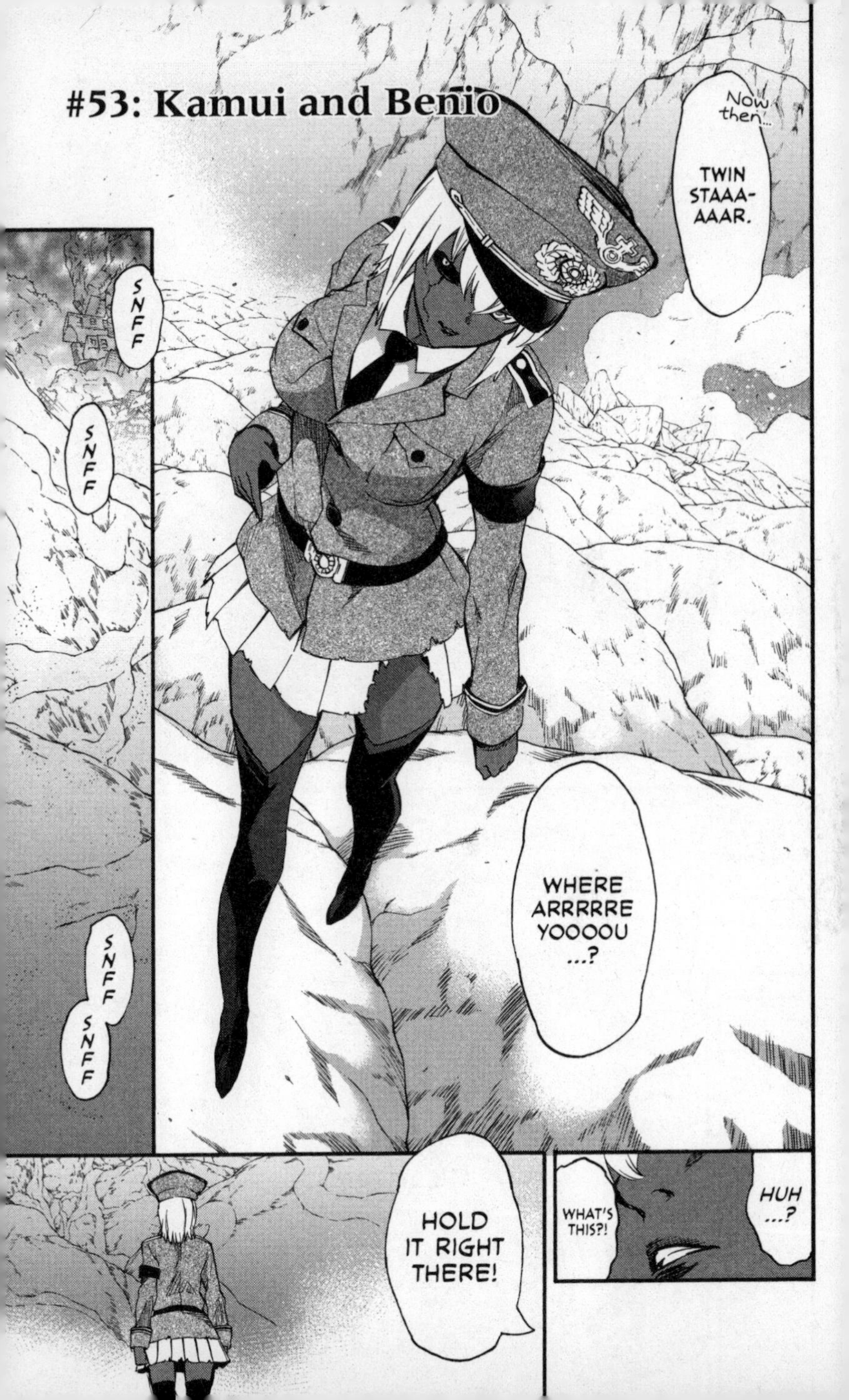
Now then...
TWIN STAAA-AAAR.
WHERE ARRRRRE YOOOOU ...?
SNFF
SNFF
SNFF SNFF
HUH ...?
WHAT'S THIS?!
HOLD IT RIGHT THERE!

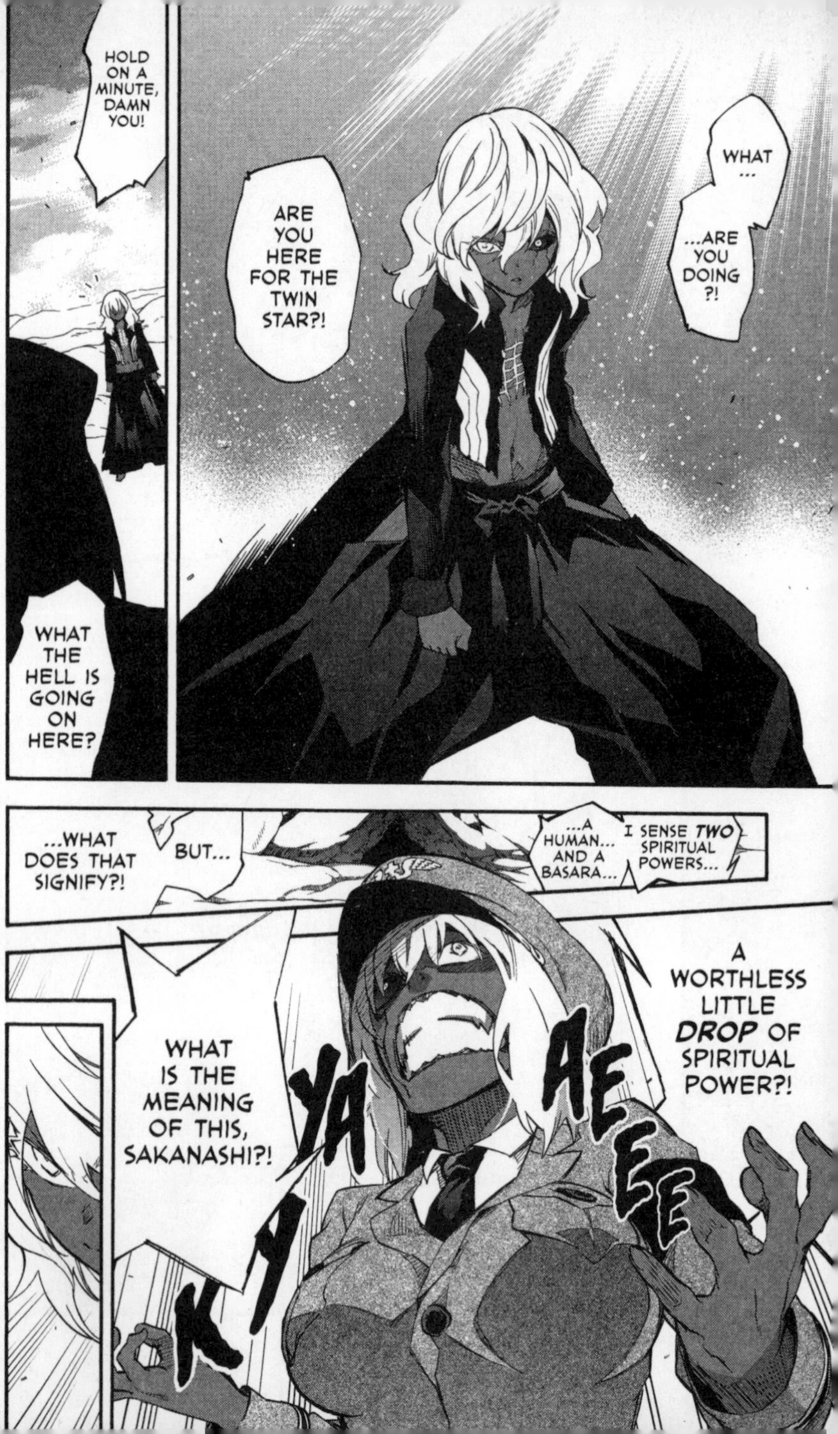
WHAT ... ...ARE YOU DOING ?!
ARE YOU HERE FOR THE TWIN STAR?!
HOLD ON A MINUTE, DAMN YOU!
WHAT THE HELL IS GOING ON HERE?
I SENSE *TWO* SPIRITUAL POWERS...
...A HUMAN... AND A BASARA...
BUT...
...WHAT DOES THAT SIGNIFY?!
A WORTHLESS LITTLE *DROP* OF SPIRITUAL POWER?!
KAYAAEEE
WHAT IS THE MEANING OF THIS, SAKANASHI?!

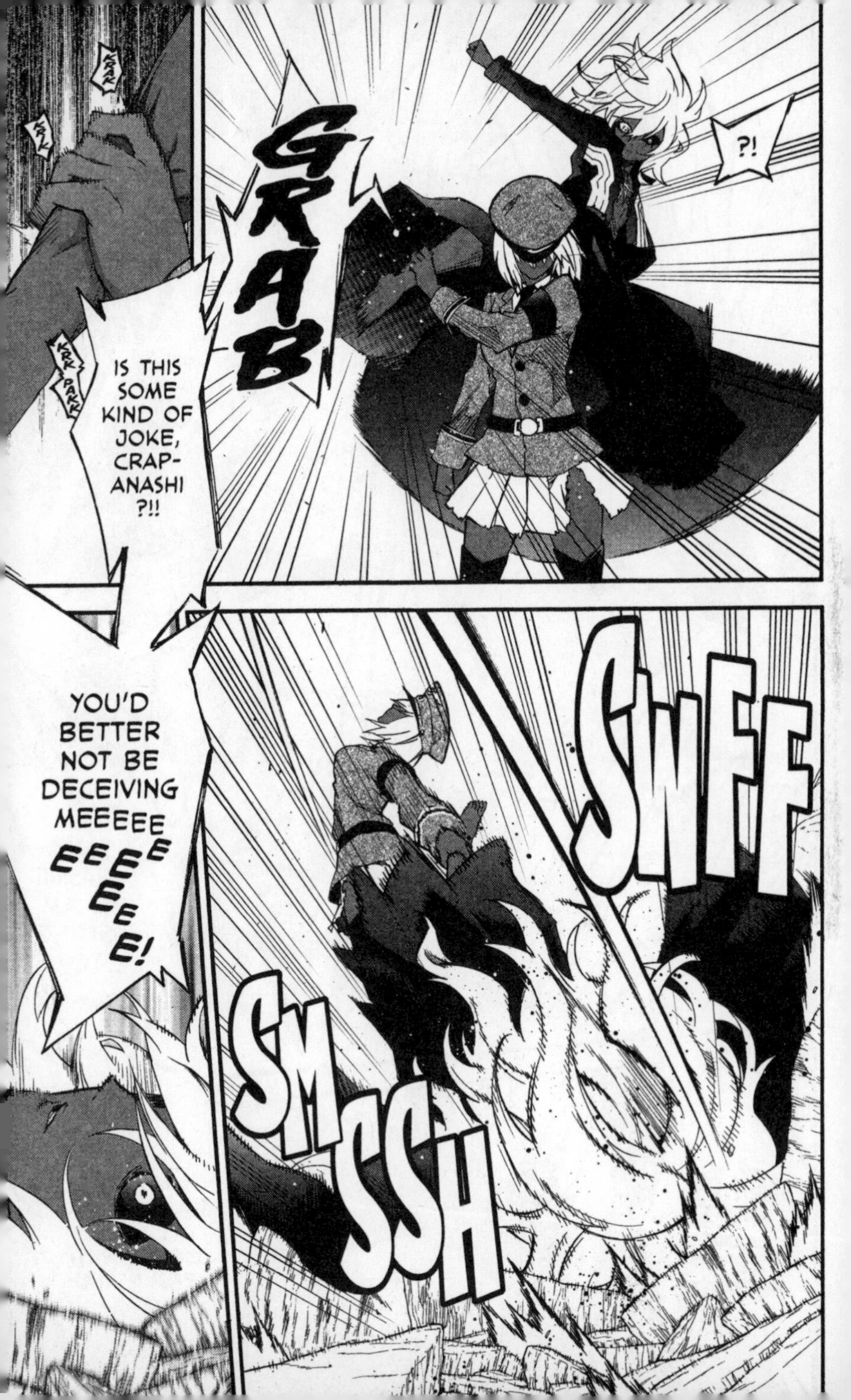
?!
GRAB
KRAK
KRK
IS THIS SOME KIND OF JOKE, CRAP-ANASHI?!!
KRK
PAKK
SNFF
YOU'D BETTER NOT BE DECEIVING MEEEEEEEEEEEE!
SMSSH

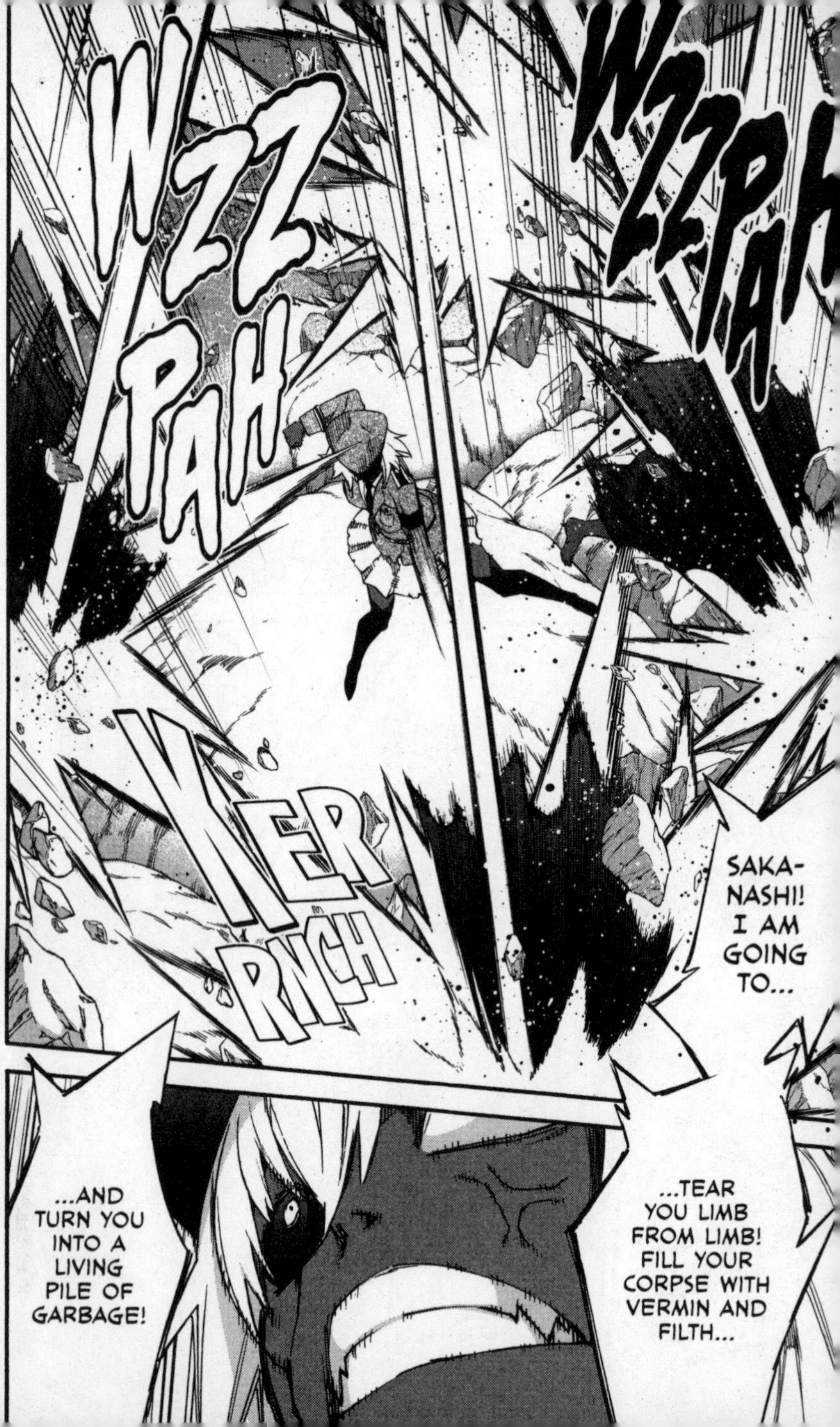
WZZPAH
WZZPAH
SAKA-NASHI! I AM GOING TO...
KERRNCH
...TEAR YOU LIMB FROM LIMB! FILL YOUR CORPSE WITH VERMIN AND FILTH...
...AND TURN YOU INTO A LIVING PILE OF GARBAGE!

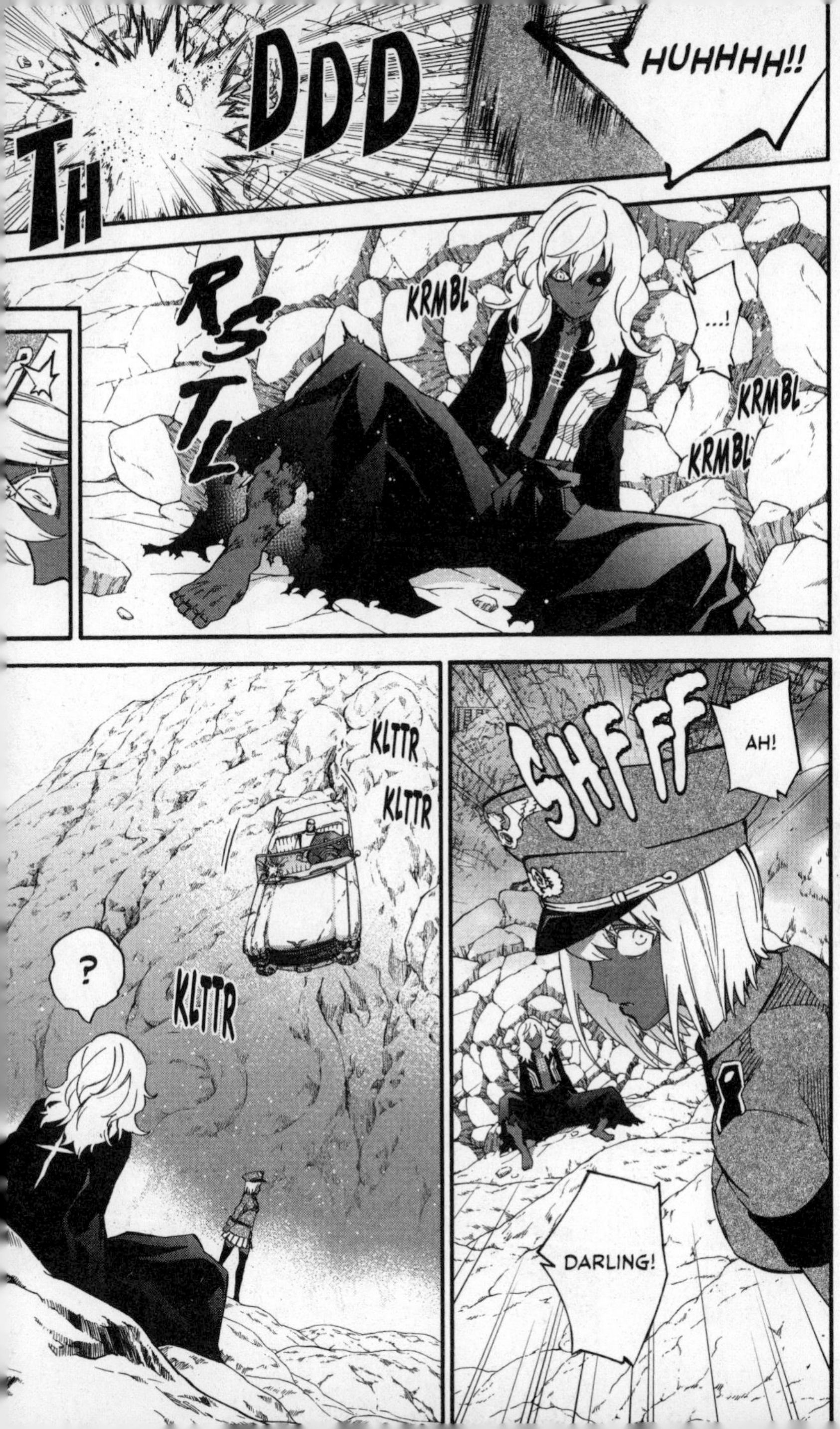
HUHHHH!!
THDDD
...!
KRMBL
KRMBL
KRMBL
KRMBL
RSTL
AH!
SHFFF
DARLING!
KLTTR
KLTTR
?
KLTTR

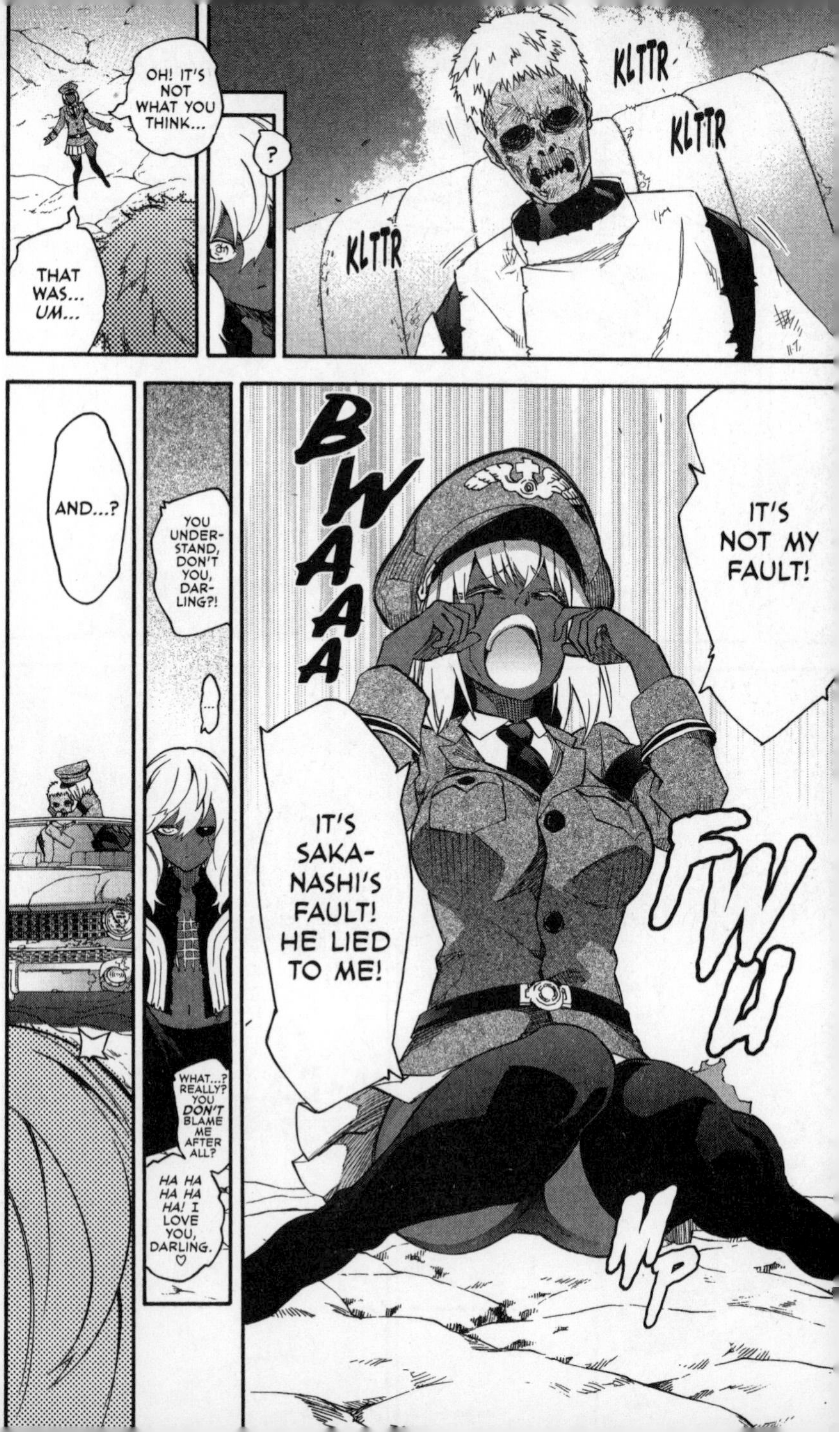
KLTTR
KLTTR
KLTTR
?
OH! IT'S NOT WHAT YOU THINK...
THAT WAS... *UM...*
BWAAAA
IT'S NOT MY FAULT!
IT'S SAKA-NASHI'S FAULT! HE LIED TO ME!
FWUMP
YOU UNDER-STAND, DON'T YOU, DAR-LING?!
...
WHAT...? REALLY? YOU *DON'T* BLAME ME AFTER ALL?
HA HA HA HA HA! I LOVE YOU, DARLING. ♡
AND...?

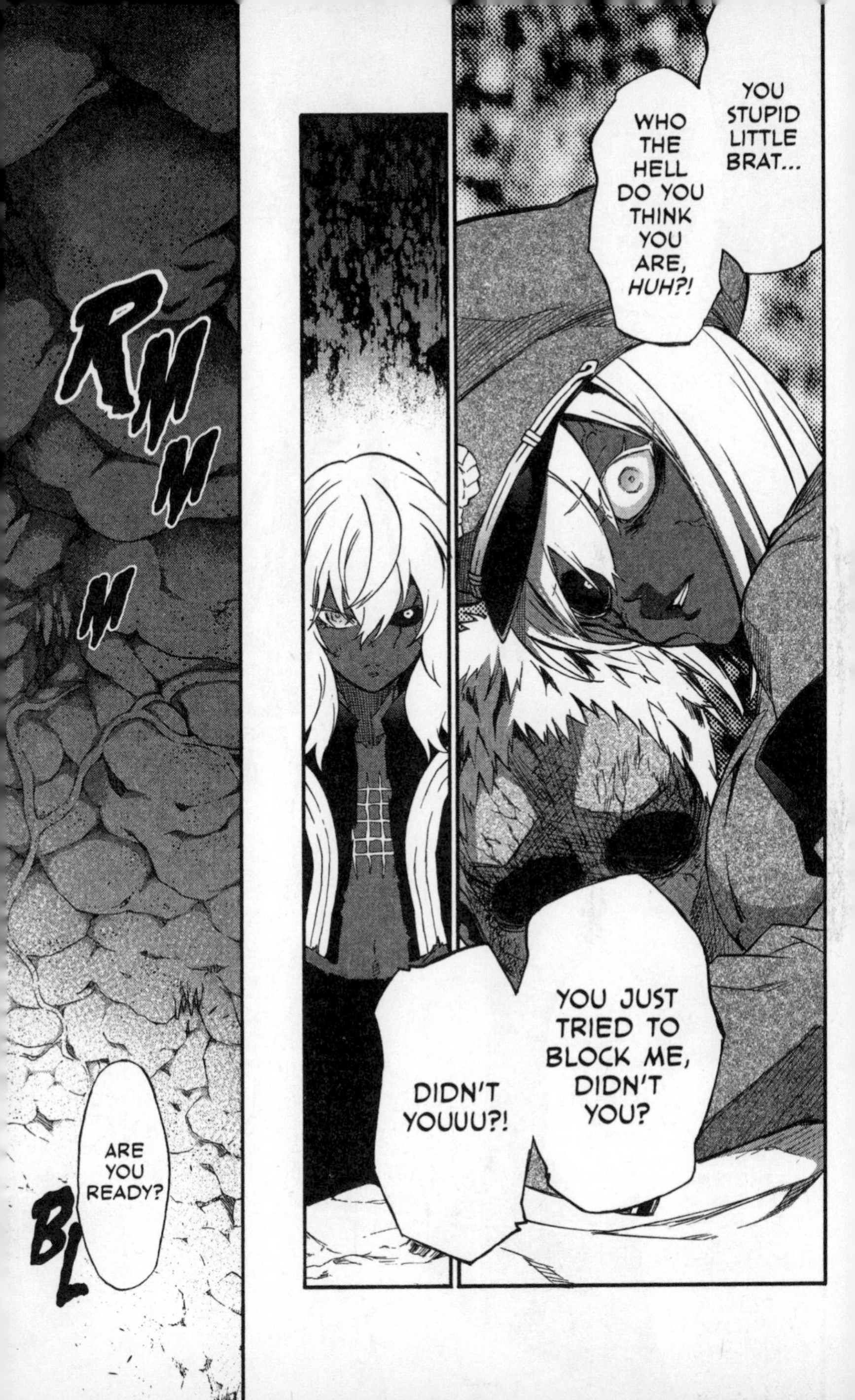
YOU STUPID LITTLE BRAT...
WHO THE HELL DO YOU THINK YOU ARE, *HUH?!*
YOU JUST TRIED TO BLOCK ME, DIDN'T YOU?
DIDN'T YOUUU?!
RMMM
ARE YOU READY?
BL

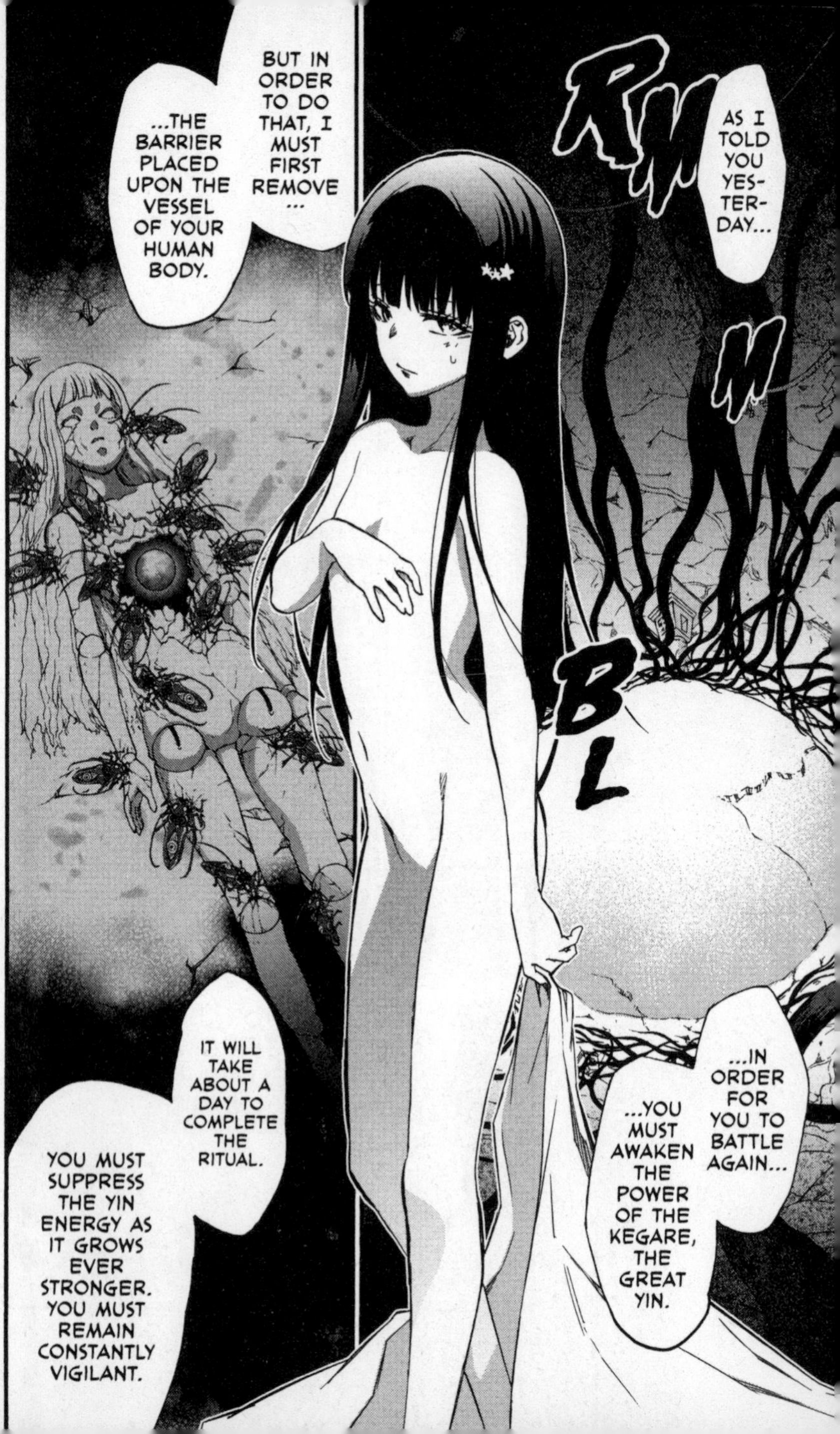
AS I TOLD YOU YESTERDAY...
RMMBL
...IN ORDER FOR YOU TO BATTLE AGAIN...
...YOU MUST AWAKEN THE POWER OF THE KEGARE, THE GREAT YIN.
BUT IN ORDER TO DO THAT, I MUST FIRST REMOVE...
...THE BARRIER PLACED UPON THE VESSEL OF YOUR HUMAN BODY.
IT WILL TAKE ABOUT A DAY TO COMPLETE THE RITUAL.
YOU MUST SUPPRESS THE YIN ENERGY AS IT GROWS EVER STRONGER. YOU MUST REMAIN CONSTANTLY VIGILANT.

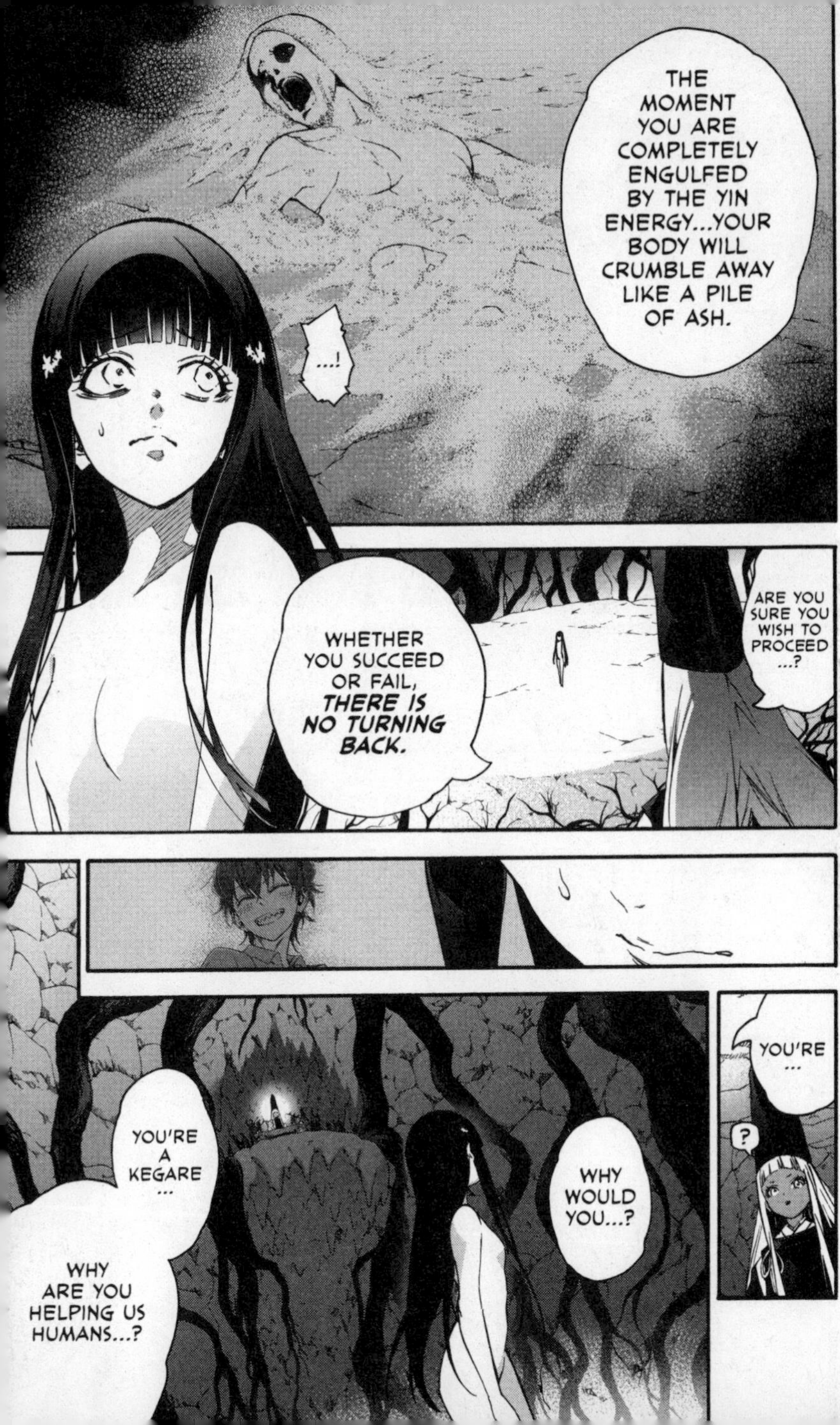
THE MOMENT YOU ARE COMPLETELY ENGULFED BY THE YIN ENERGY...YOUR BODY WILL CRUMBLE AWAY LIKE A PILE OF ASH.
...!
ARE YOU SURE YOU WISH TO PROCEED ...?
WHETHER YOU SUCCEED OR FAIL, *THERE IS NO TURNING BACK.*
YOU'RE ...
?
WHY WOULD YOU...?
YOU'RE A KEGARE ...
WHY ARE YOU HELPING US HUMANS...?

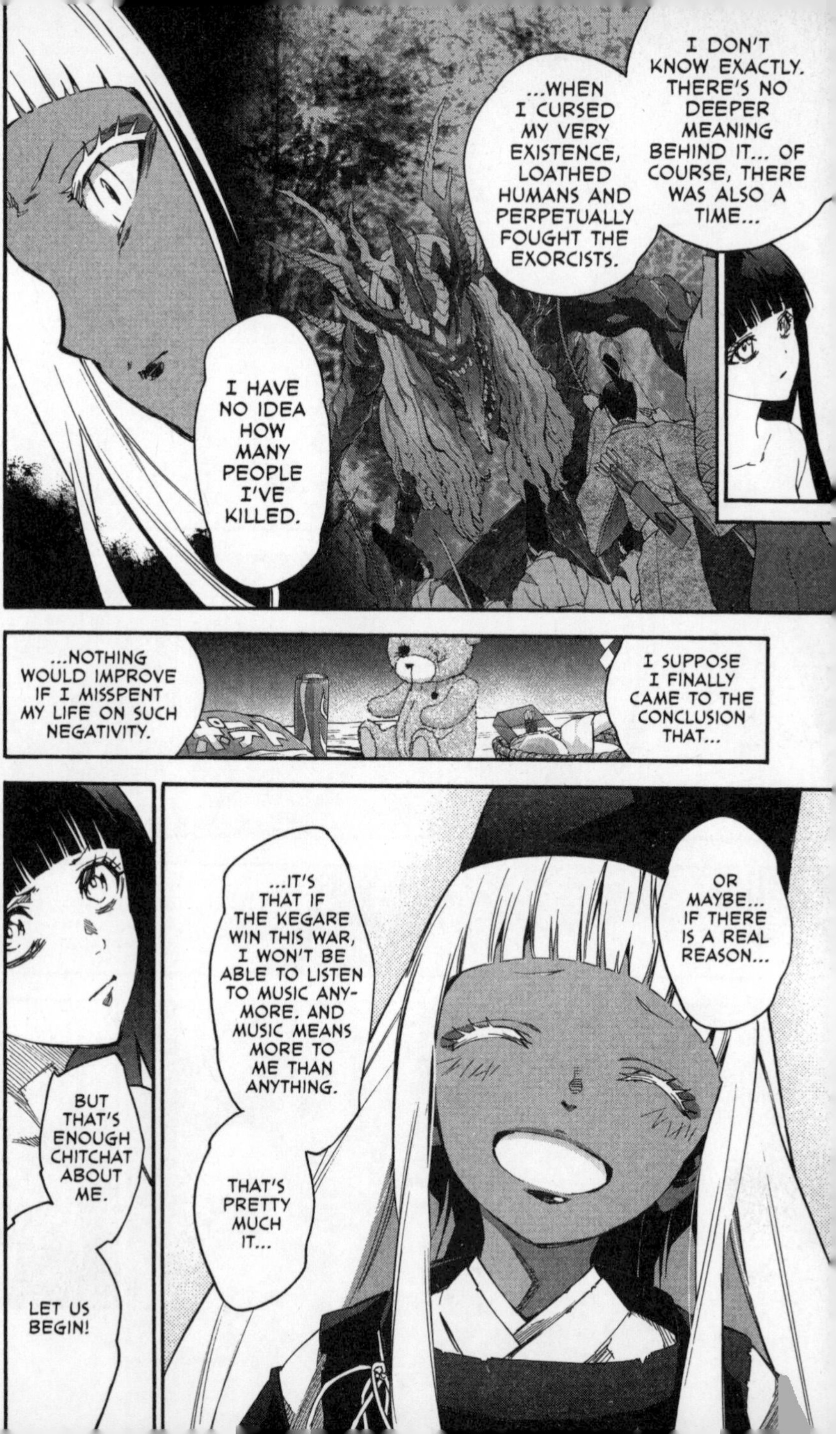
I DON'T KNOW EXACTLY. THERE'S NO DEEPER MEANING BEHIND IT... OF COURSE, THERE WAS ALSO A TIME...
...WHEN I CURSED MY VERY EXISTENCE, LOATHED HUMANS AND PERPETUALLY FOUGHT THE EXORCISTS.
I HAVE NO IDEA HOW MANY PEOPLE I'VE KILLED.
I SUPPOSE I FINALLY CAME TO THE CONCLUSION THAT...
...NOTHING WOULD IMPROVE IF I MISSPENT MY LIFE ON SUCH NEGATIVITY.
OR MAYBE... IF THERE IS A REAL REASON...
...IT'S THAT IF THE KEGARE WIN THIS WAR, I WON'T BE ABLE TO LISTEN TO MUSIC ANY-MORE. AND MUSIC MEANS MORE TO ME THAN ANYTHING.
THAT'S PRETTY MUCH IT...
BUT THAT'S ENOUGH CHITCHAT ABOUT ME.
LET US BEGIN!

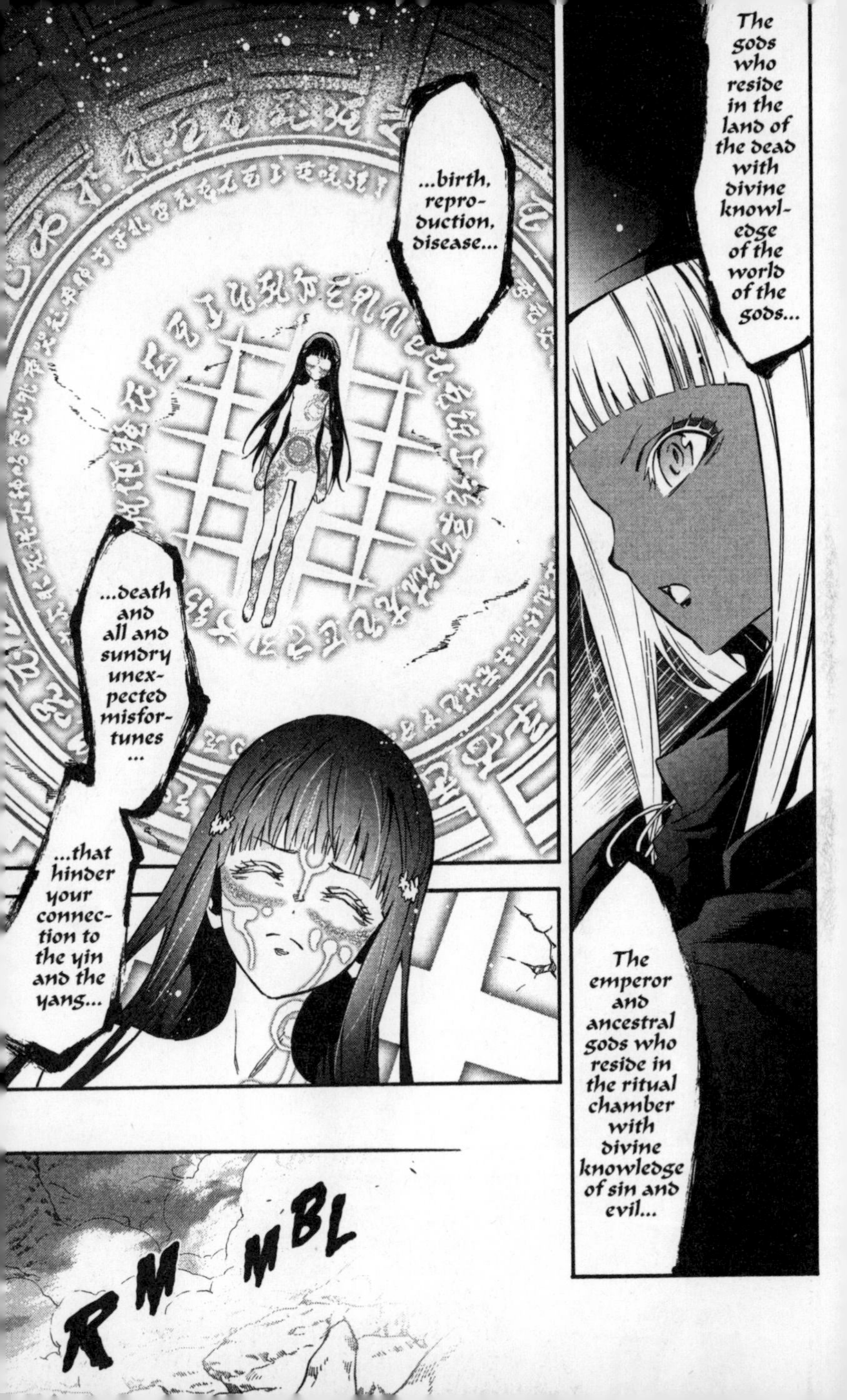
The gods who reside in the land of the dead with divine knowledge of the world of the gods...
The emperor and ancestral gods who reside in the ritual chamber with divine knowledge of sin and evil...
...birth, reproduction, disease...
...death and all and sundry unexpected misfortunes...
...that hinder your connection to the yin and the yang...
RMMBL

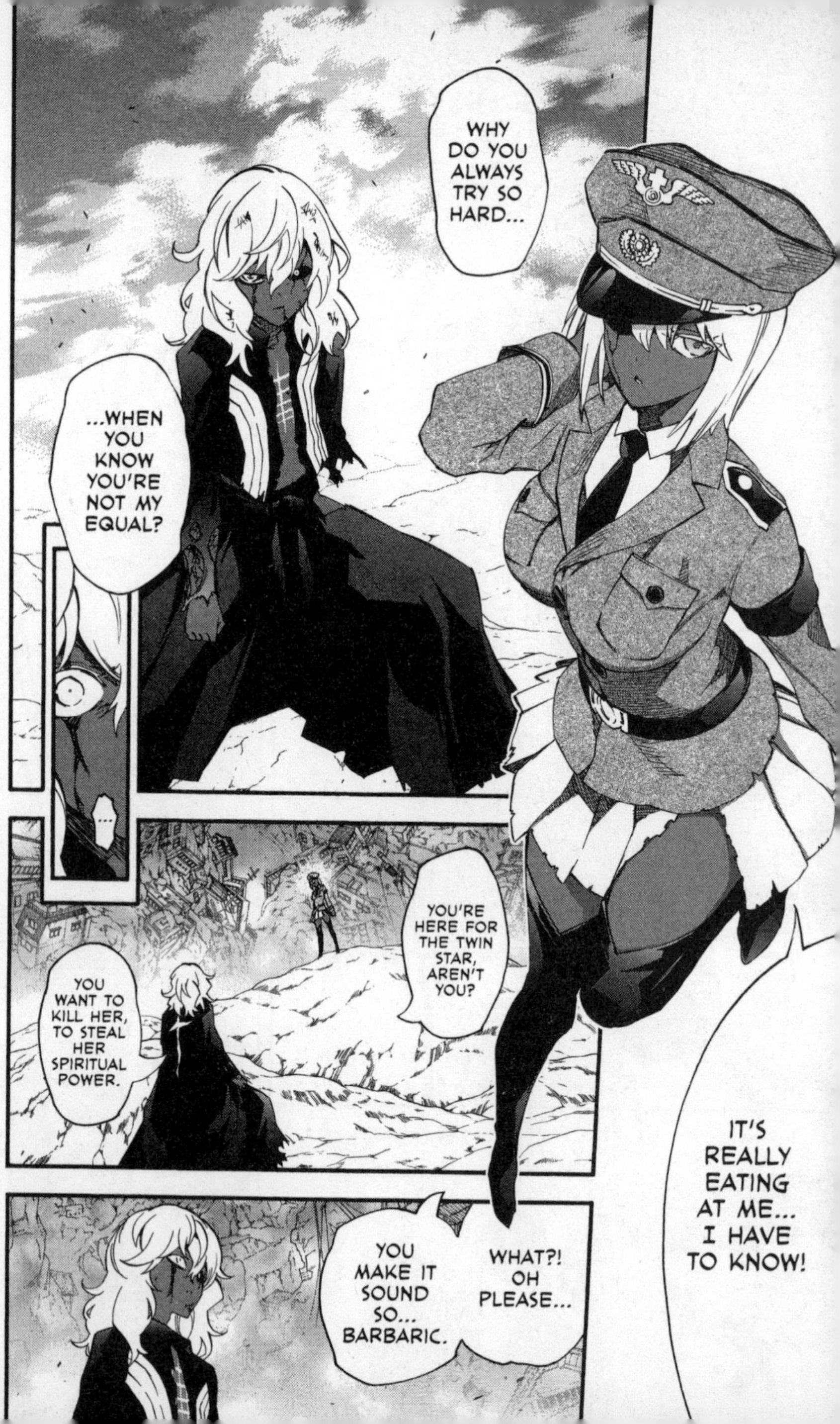
WHY DO YOU ALWAYS TRY SO HARD...
...WHEN YOU KNOW YOU'RE NOT MY EQUAL?
IT'S REALLY EATING AT ME... I HAVE TO KNOW!
...
YOU'RE HERE FOR THE TWIN STAR, AREN'T YOU?
YOU WANT TO KILL HER, TO STEAL HER SPIRITUAL POWER.
WHAT?! OH PLEASE...
YOU MAKE IT SOUND SO... BARBARIC.

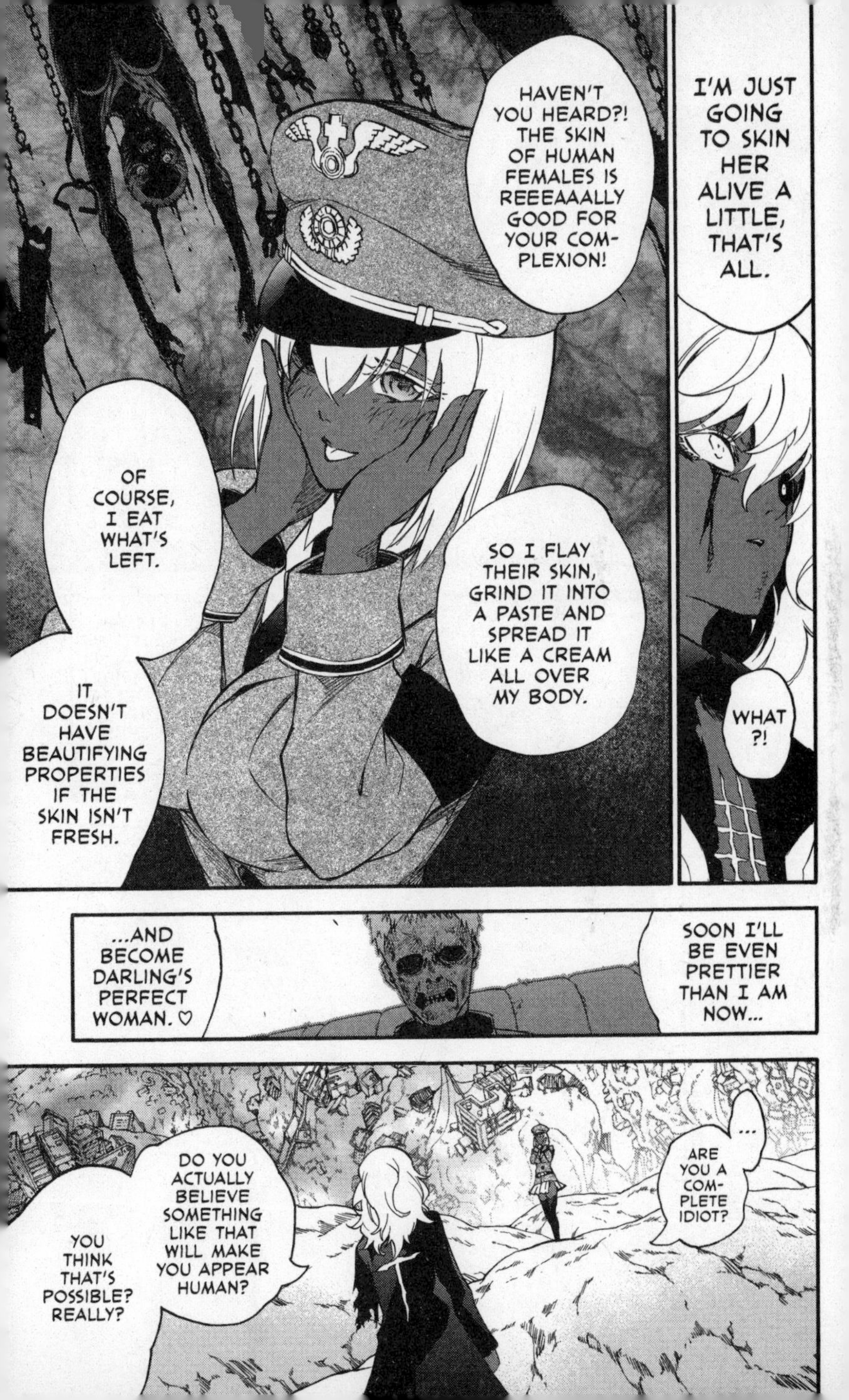
I'M JUST GOING TO SKIN HER ALIVE A LITTLE, THAT'S ALL.
WHAT?!
HAVEN'T YOU HEARD?! THE SKIN OF HUMAN FEMALES IS REEEAAALLY GOOD FOR YOUR COM-PLEXION!
SO I FLAY THEIR SKIN, GRIND IT INTO A PASTE AND SPREAD IT LIKE A CREAM ALL OVER MY BODY.
OF COURSE, I EAT WHAT'S LEFT.
IT DOESN'T HAVE BEAUTIFYING PROPERTIES IF THE SKIN ISN'T FRESH.
SOON I'LL BE EVEN PRETTIER THAN I AM NOW...
...AND BECOME DARLING'S PERFECT WOMAN. ♡
...
ARE YOU A COM-PLETE IDIOT?
DO YOU ACTUALLY BELIEVE SOMETHING LIKE THAT WILL MAKE YOU APPEAR HUMAN?
YOU THINK THAT'S POSSIBLE? REALLY?

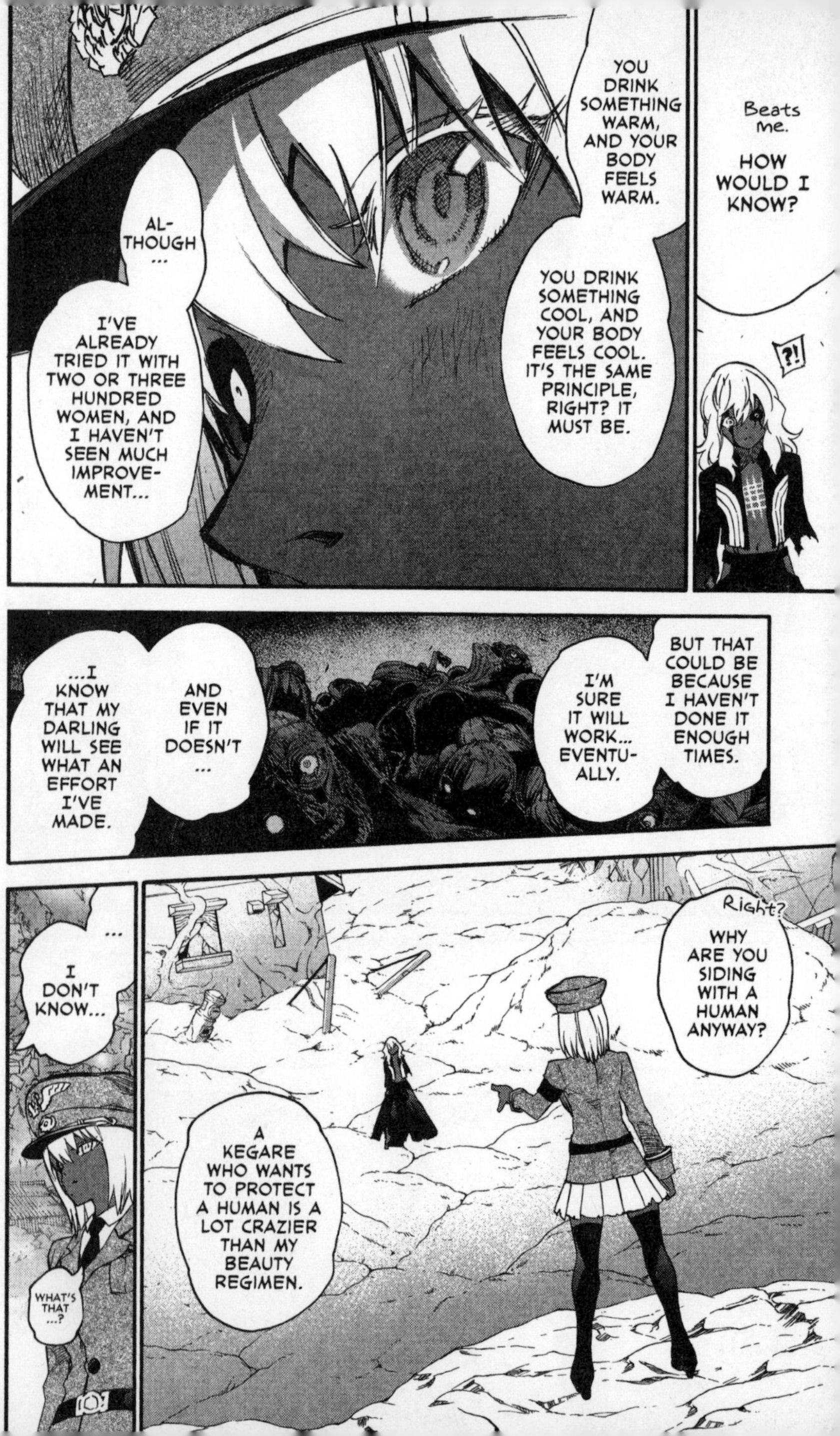
Beats me.
HOW WOULD I KNOW?
?!
YOU DRINK SOMETHING WARM, AND YOUR BODY FEELS WARM.
YOU DRINK SOMETHING COOL, AND YOUR BODY FEELS COOL. IT'S THE SAME PRINCIPLE, RIGHT? IT MUST BE.
ALTHOUGH...
I'VE ALREADY TRIED IT WITH TWO OR THREE HUNDRED WOMEN, AND I HAVEN'T SEEN MUCH IMPROVEMENT...
BUT THAT COULD BE BECAUSE I HAVEN'T DONE IT ENOUGH TIMES.
I'M SURE IT WILL WORK... EVENTUALLY.
AND EVEN IF IT DOESN'T...
...I KNOW THAT MY DARLING WILL SEE WHAT AN EFFORT I'VE MADE.
Right?
WHY ARE YOU SIDING WITH A HUMAN ANYWAY?
A KEGARE WHO WANTS TO PROTECT A HUMAN IS A LOT CRAZIER THAN MY BEAUTY REGIMEN.
...
I DON'T KNOW...
WHAT'S THAT ...?

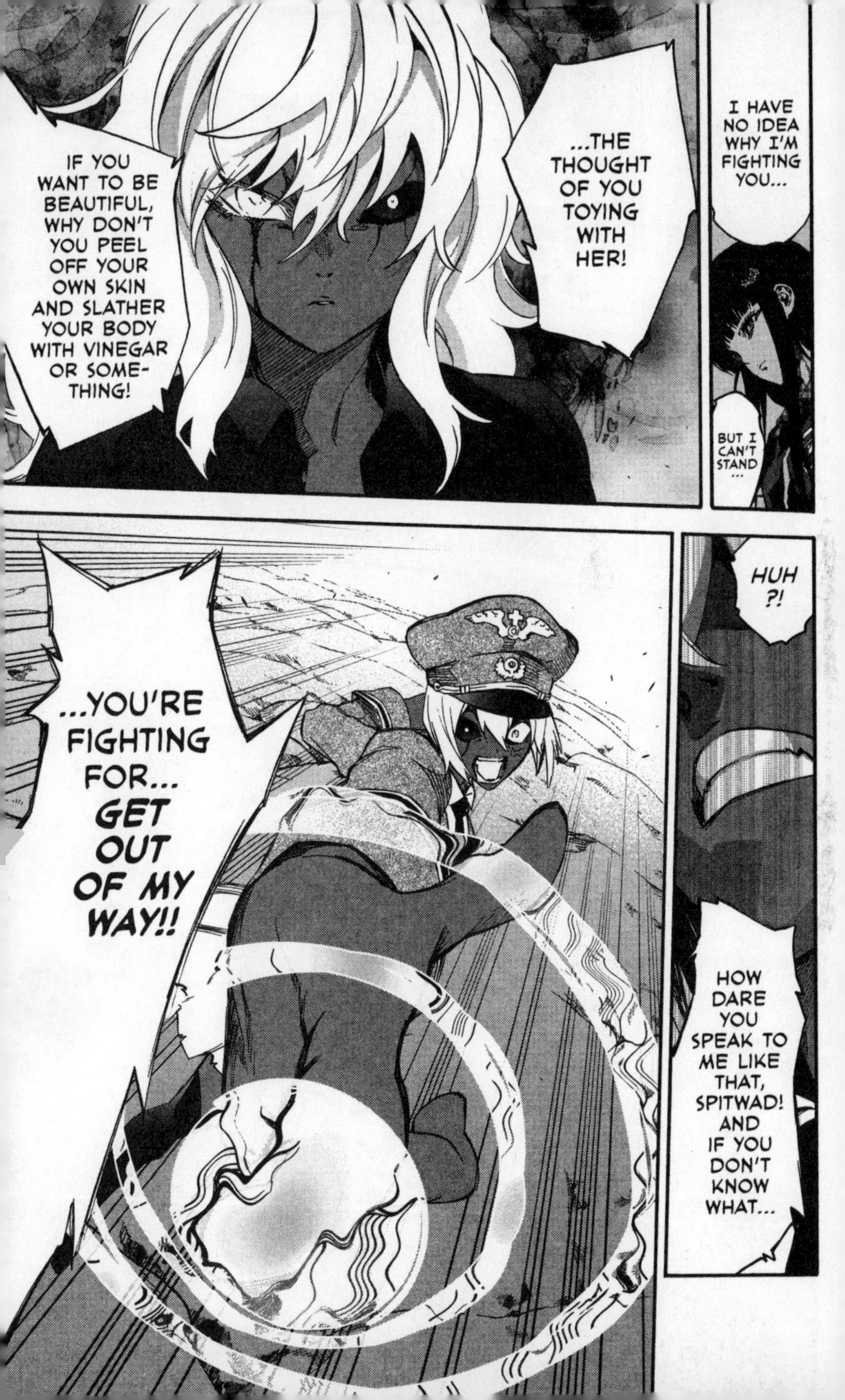
I HAVE NO IDEA WHY I'M FIGHTING YOU...
BUT I CAN'T STAND ...
...THE THOUGHT OF YOU TOYING WITH HER!
IF YOU WANT TO BE BEAUTIFUL, WHY DON'T YOU PEEL OFF YOUR OWN SKIN AND SLATHER YOUR BODY WITH VINEGAR OR SOMETHING!
HUH?!
HOW DARE YOU SPEAK TO ME LIKE THAT, SPITWAD! AND IF YOU DON'T KNOW WHAT...
...YOU'RE FIGHTING FOR... GET OUT OF MY WAY!!

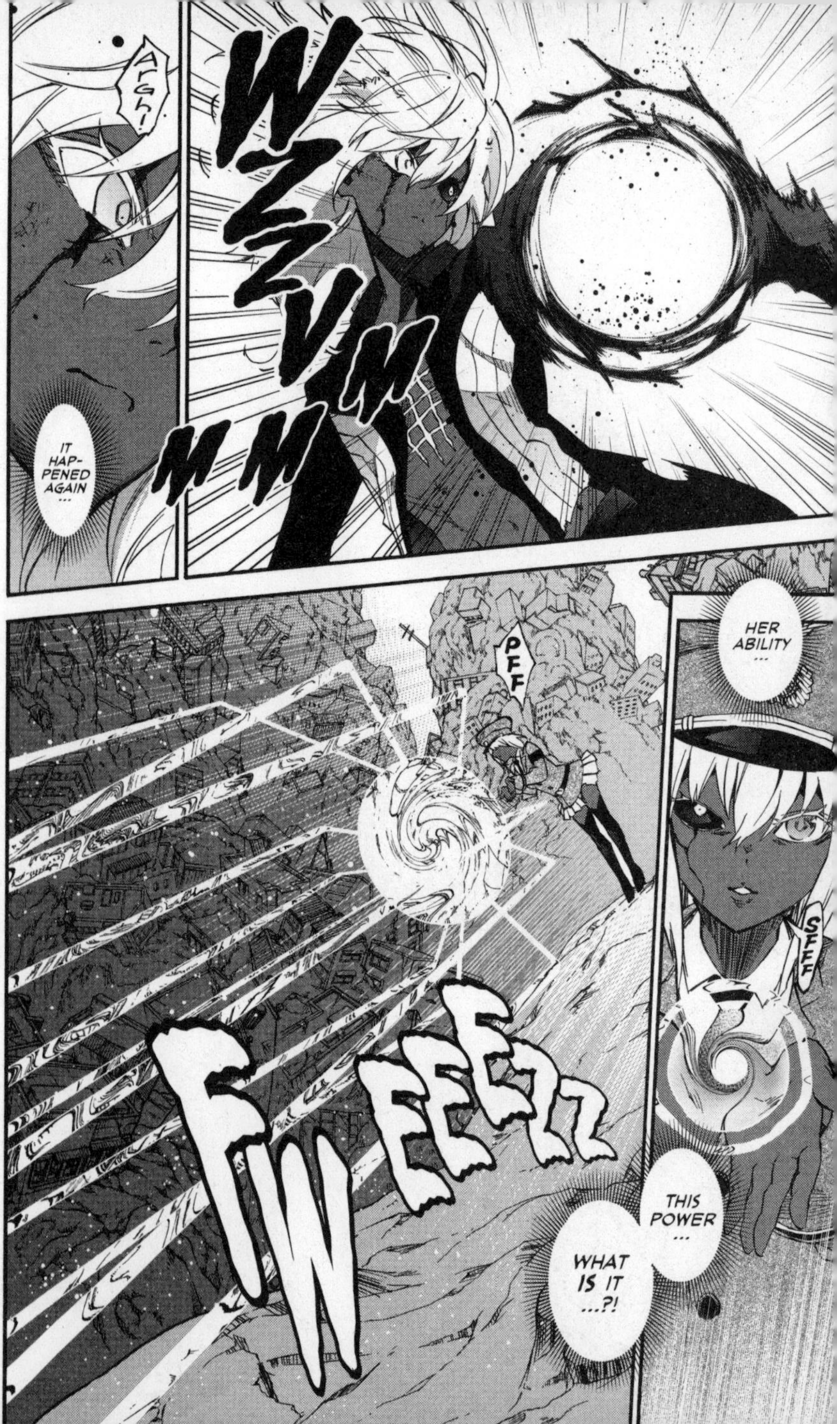
WZZVMMM
Argh!
IT HAPPENED AGAIN...
HER ABILITY...
SFFF
THIS POWER...
WHAT IS IT...?!
PFF
FWEEEZZ

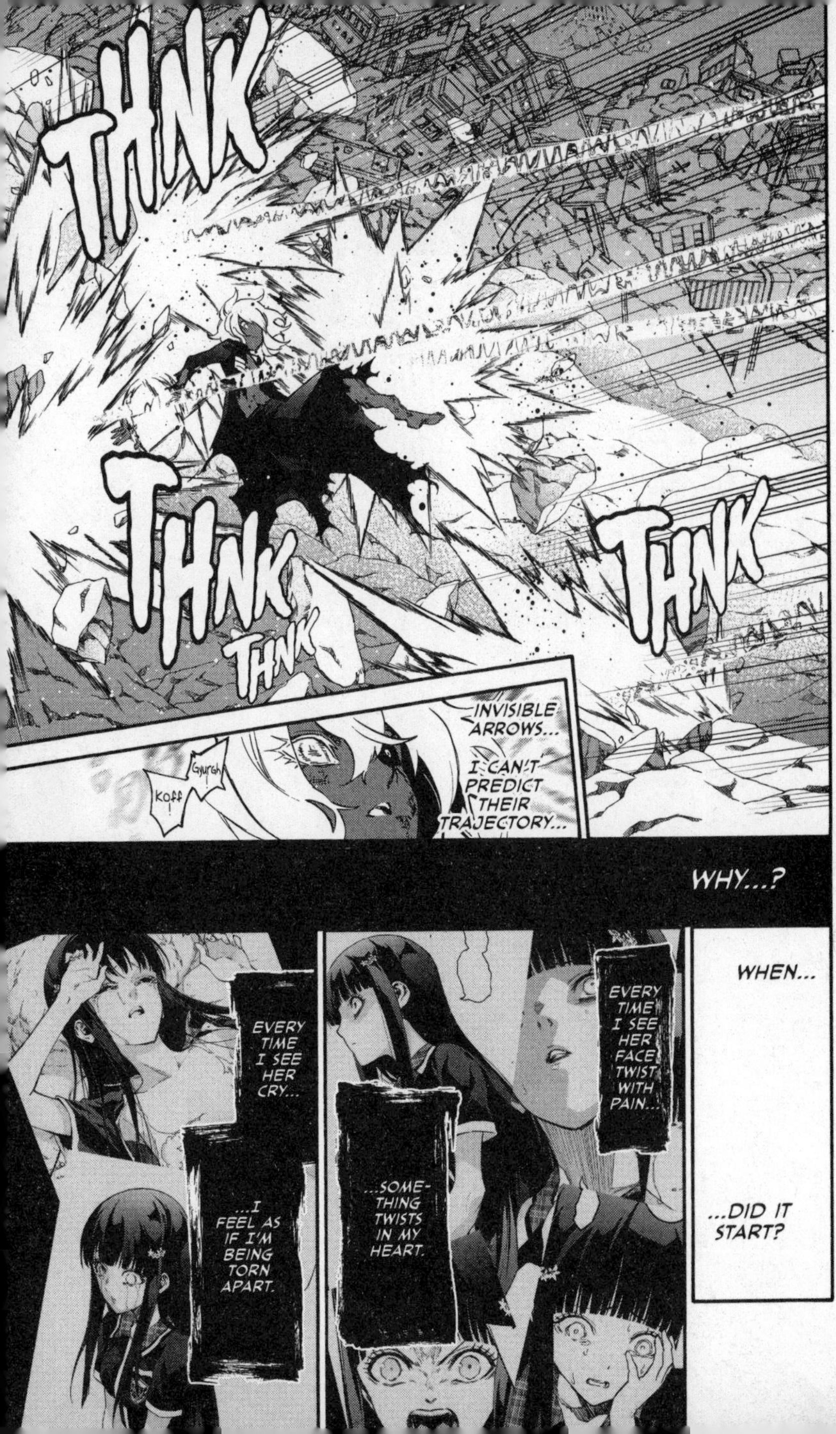
THNK
THNK
THNK
THNK
INVISIBLE ARROWS... I CAN'T PREDICT THEIR TRAJECTORY...
Gyurgh!
Koff!
WHY...?
WHEN...
...DID IT START?
EVERY TIME I SEE HER FACE TWIST WITH PAIN...
...SOMETHING TWISTS IN MY HEART.
EVERY TIME I SEE HER CRY...
...I FEEL AS IF I'M BEING TORN APART.

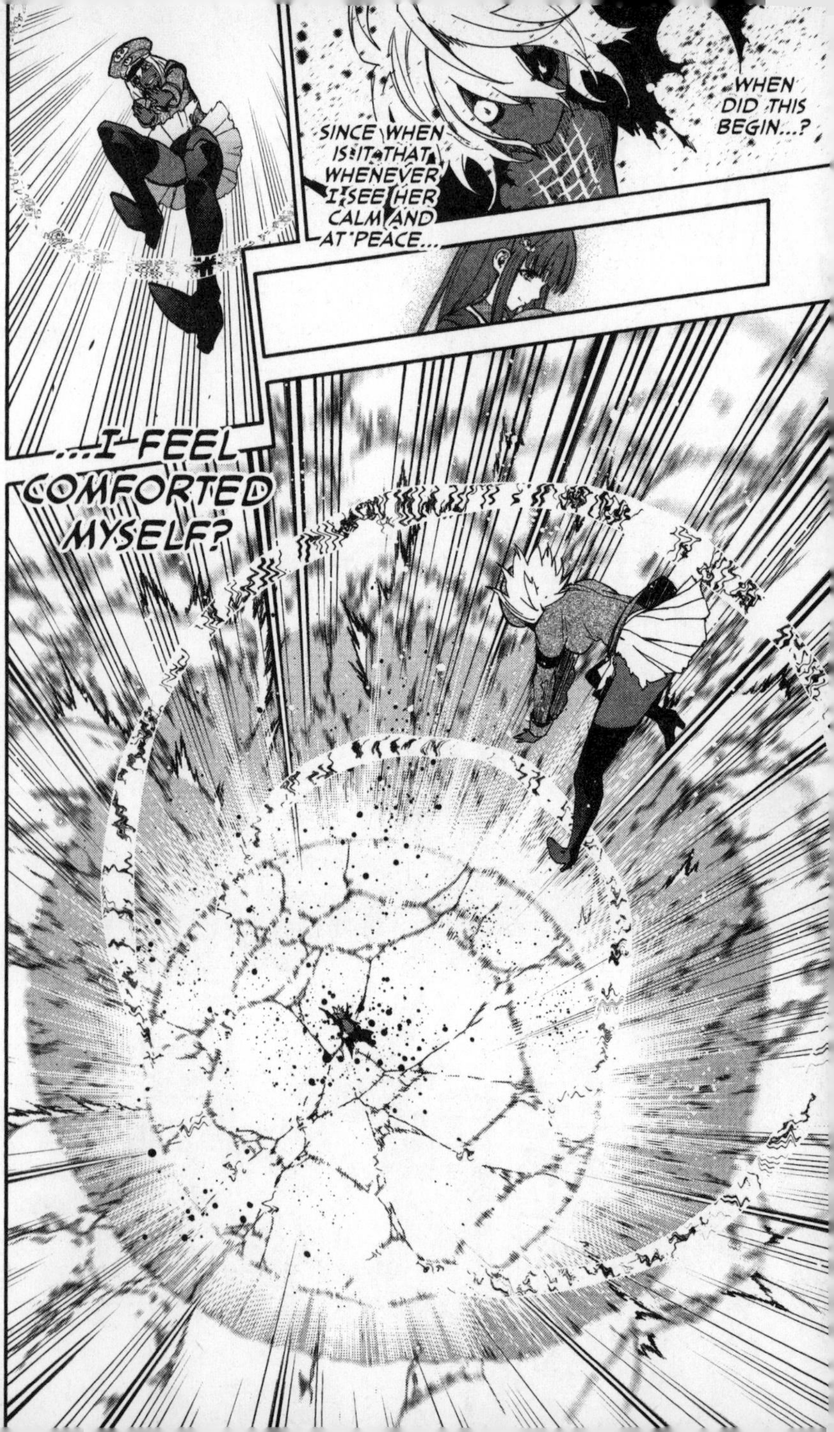
WHEN DID THIS BEGIN...?
SINCE WHEN IS IT THAT WHENEVER I SEE HER CALM AND AT PEACE...
...I FEEL COMFORTED MYSELF?

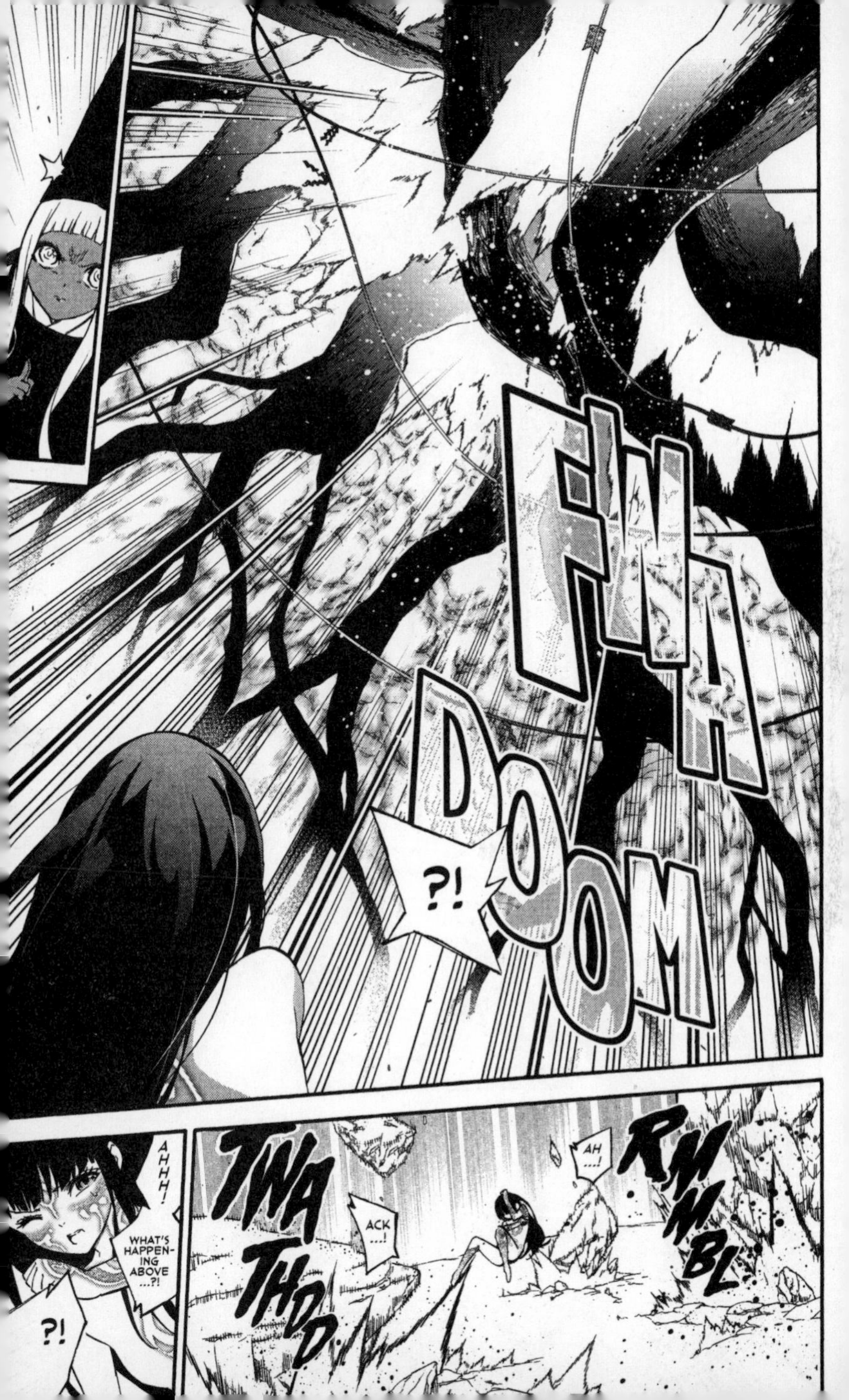
FWA
DOOM
?!
RMMBL
AH ...!
ACK ...!
TWA
THDD
AHHH!
WHAT'S HAPPENING ABOVE ...?!
?!

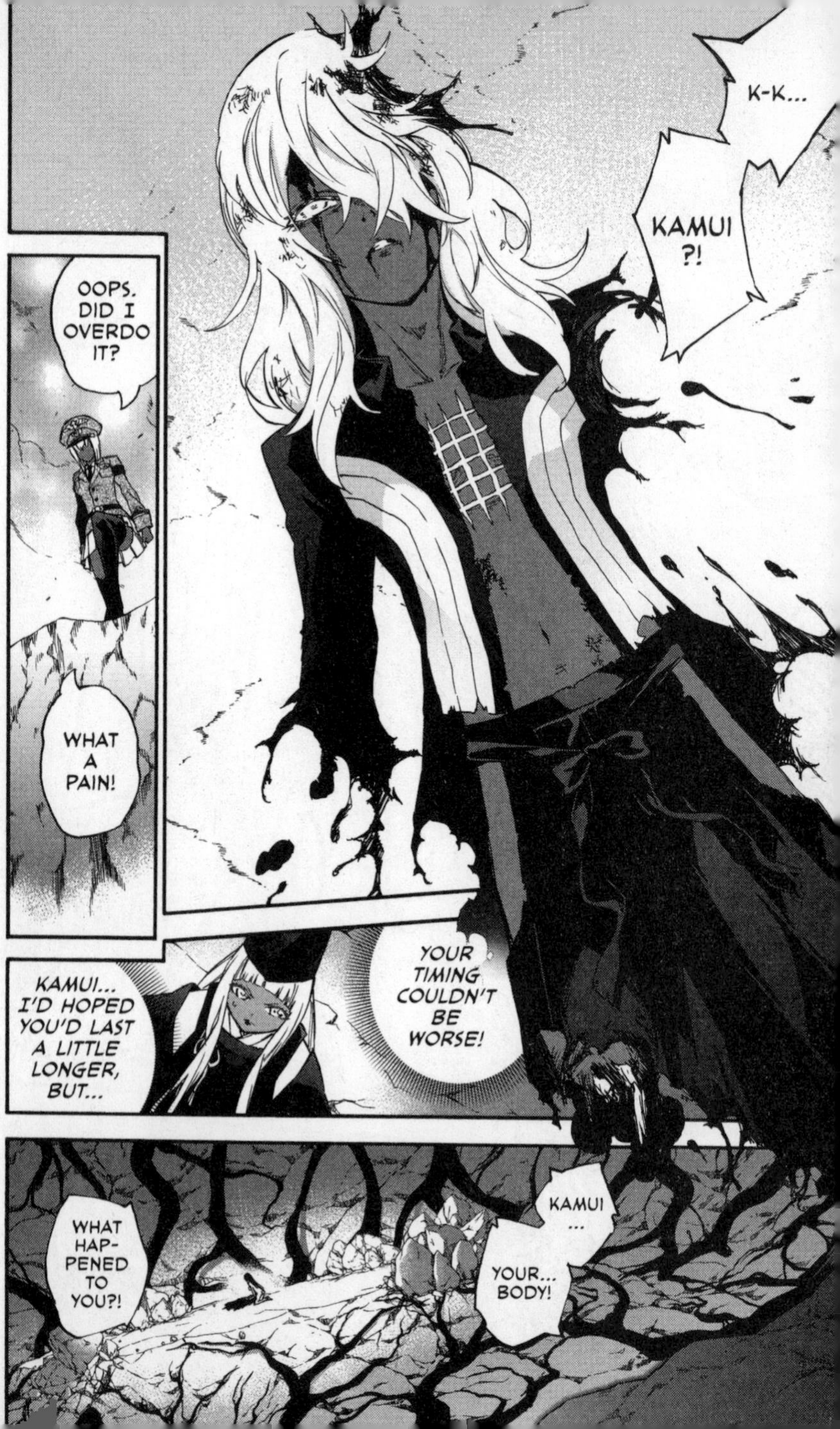
K-K...
KAMUI ?!
OOPS. DID I OVERDO IT?
WHAT A PAIN!
YOUR TIMING COULDN'T BE WORSE!
KAMUI... I'D HOPED YOU'D LAST A LITTLE LONGER, BUT...
KAMUI...
YOUR... BODY!
WHAT HAP-PENED TO YOU?!

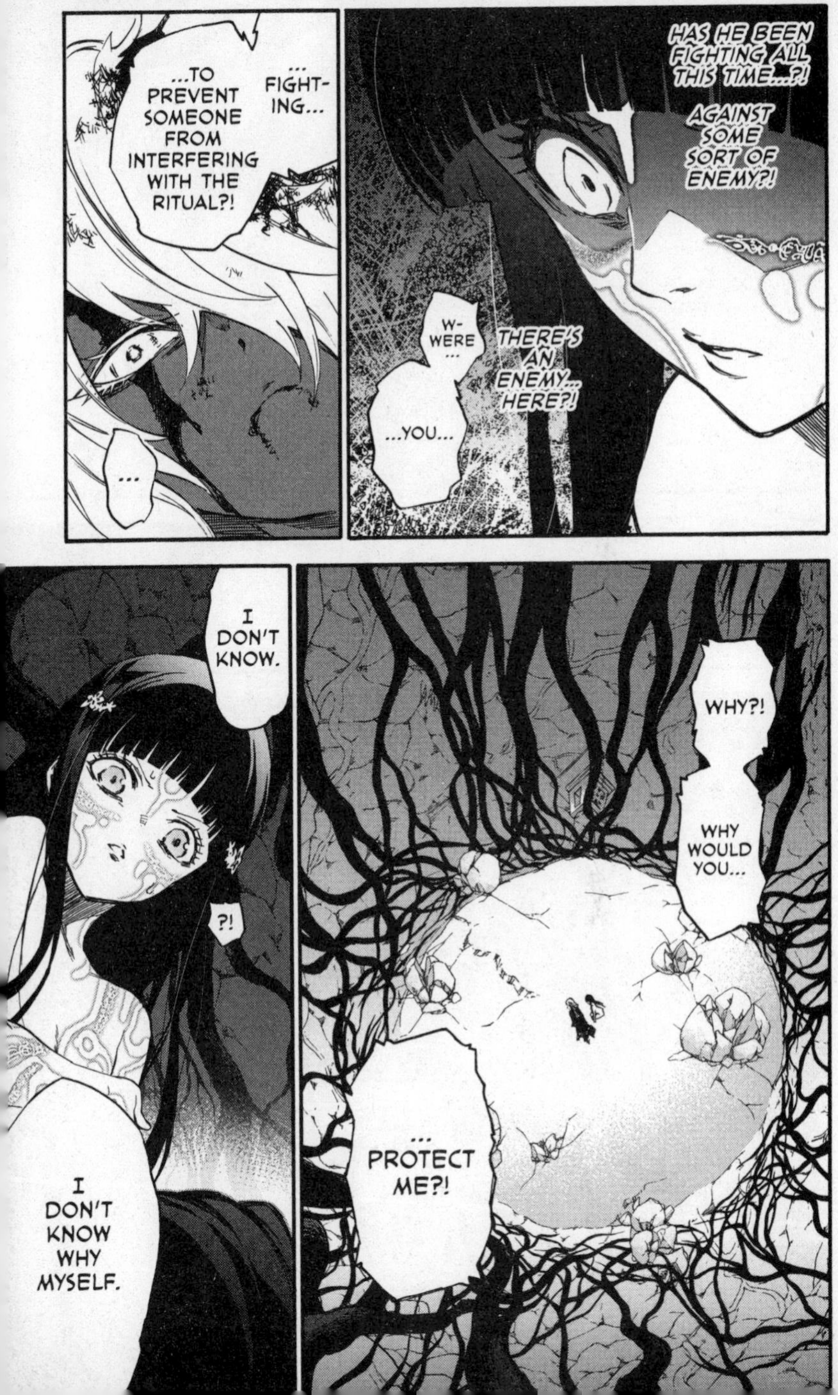
HAS HE BEEN FIGHTING ALL THIS TIME...?!
AGAINST SOME SORT OF ENEMY?!
THERE'S AN ENEMY... HERE?!
W-WERE ...
...YOU...
...FIGHTING...
...TO PREVENT SOMEONE FROM INTERFERING WITH THE RITUAL?!
...
WHY?!
WHY WOULD YOU...
...PROTECT ME?!
I DON'T KNOW.
?!
I DON'T KNOW WHY MYSELF.

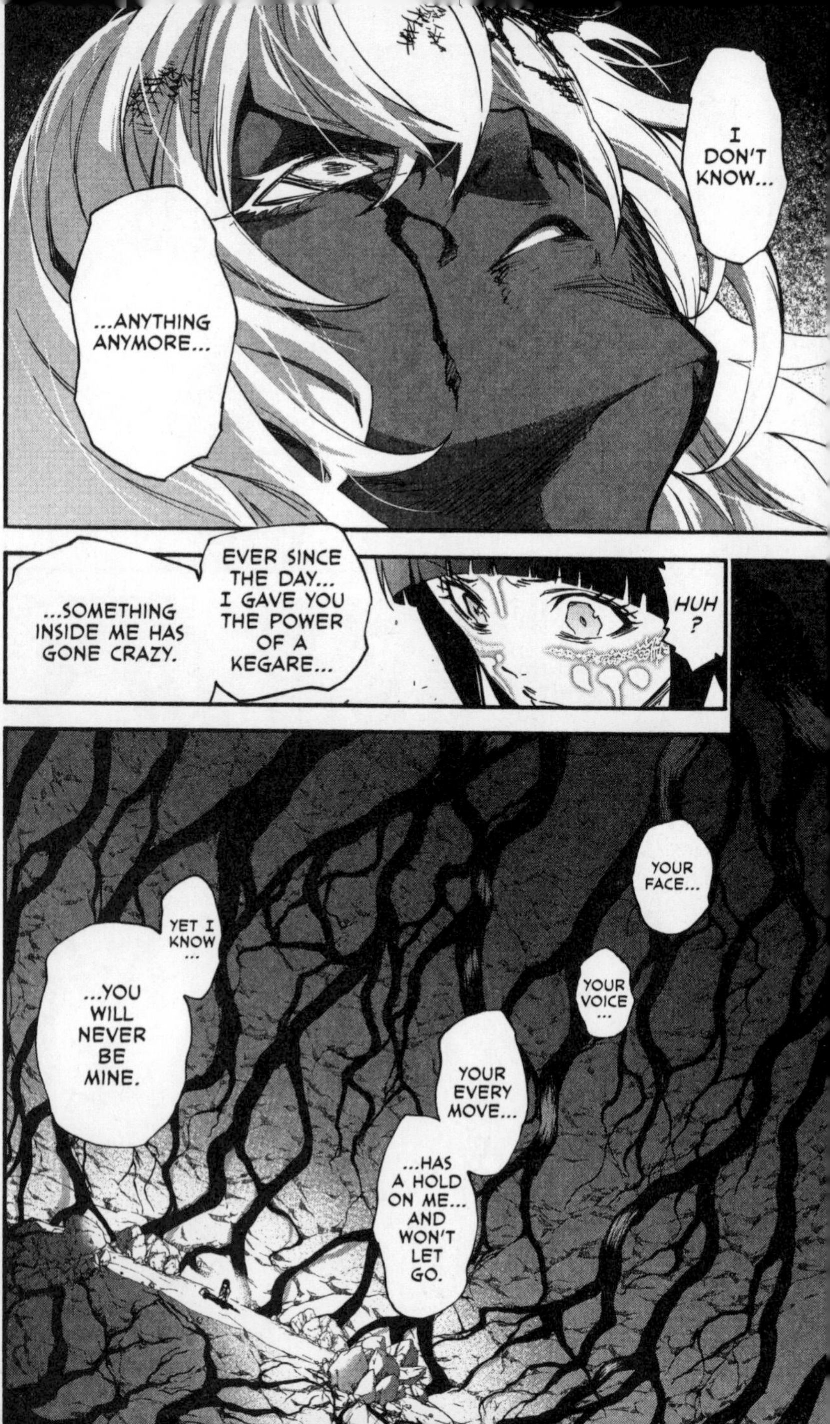
I DON'T KNOW...
...ANYTHING ANYMORE...
HUH?
EVER SINCE THE DAY... I GAVE YOU THE POWER OF A KEGARE...
...SOMETHING INSIDE ME HAS GONE CRAZY.
YOUR FACE...
YOUR VOICE...
YOUR EVERY MOVE...
...HAS A HOLD ON ME... AND WON'T LET GO.
YET I KNOW...
...YOU WILL NEVER BE MINE.

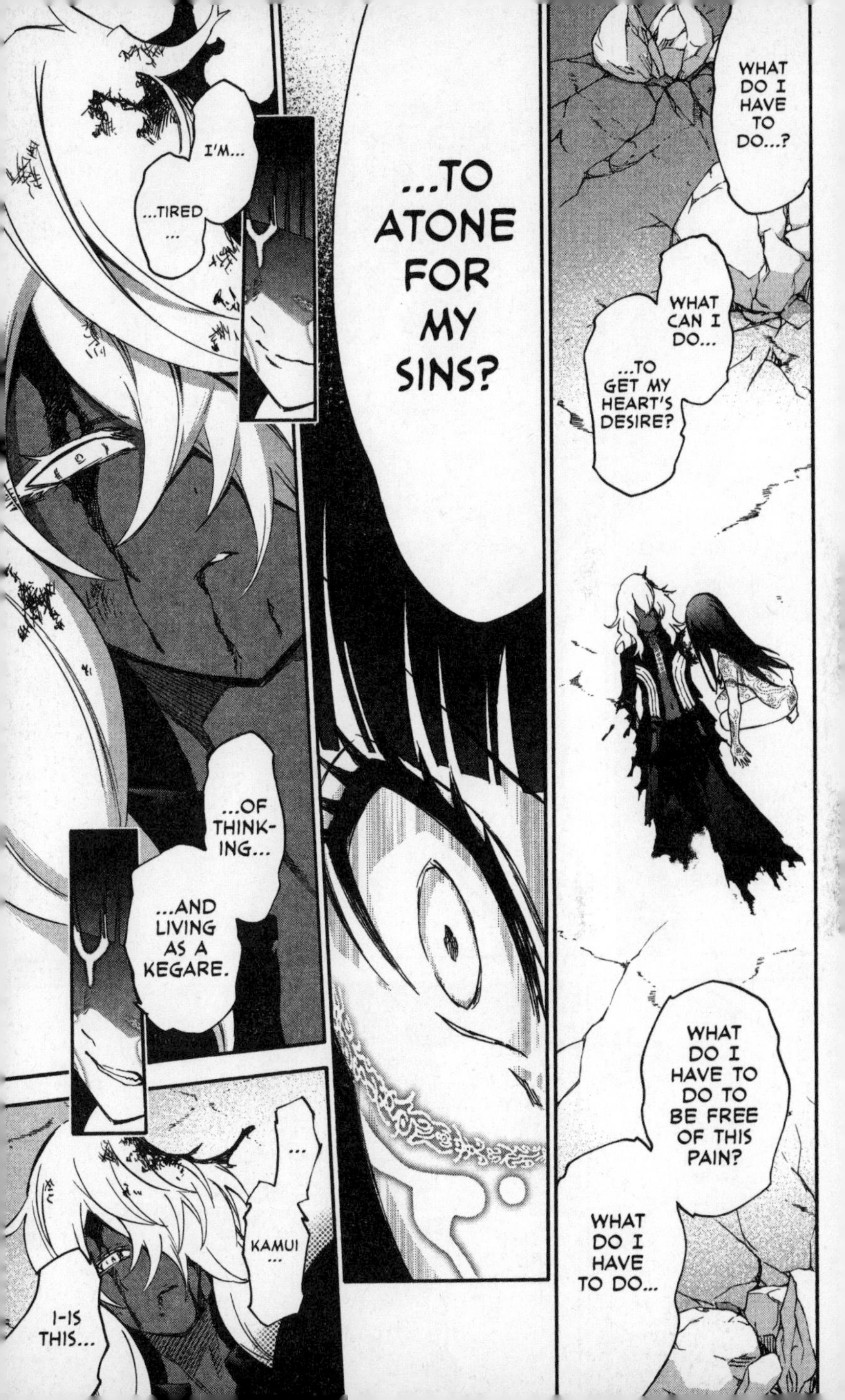
WHAT DO I HAVE TO DO...?
WHAT CAN I DO...
...TO GET MY HEART'S DESIRE?
WHAT DO I HAVE TO DO TO BE FREE OF THIS PAIN?
WHAT DO I HAVE TO DO...
...TO ATONE FOR MY SINS?
I'M...
...TIRED ...
...OF THINKING...
...AND LIVING AS A KEGARE.
...
KAMUI ...
I-IS THIS...

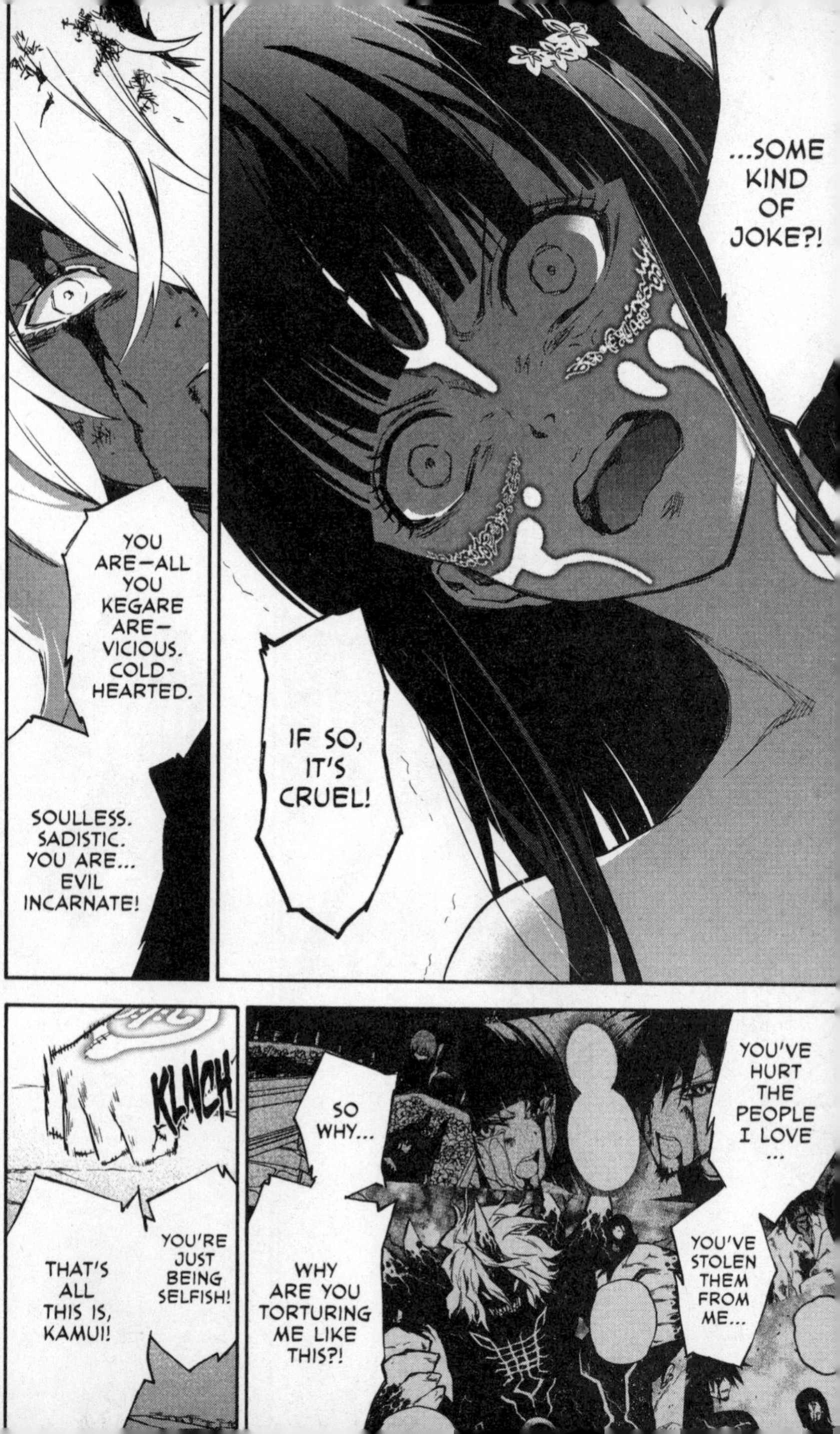
...SOME KIND OF JOKE?!
IF SO, IT'S CRUEL!
YOU ARE—ALL YOU KEGARE ARE—VICIOUS. COLD-HEARTED.
SOULLESS. SADISTIC. YOU ARE... EVIL INCARNATE!
YOU'VE HURT THE PEOPLE I LOVE ...
SO WHY...
YOU'VE STOLEN THEM FROM ME...
WHY ARE YOU TORTURING ME LIKE THIS?!
KLNCH
YOU'RE JUST BEING SELFISH!
THAT'S ALL THIS IS, KAMUI!

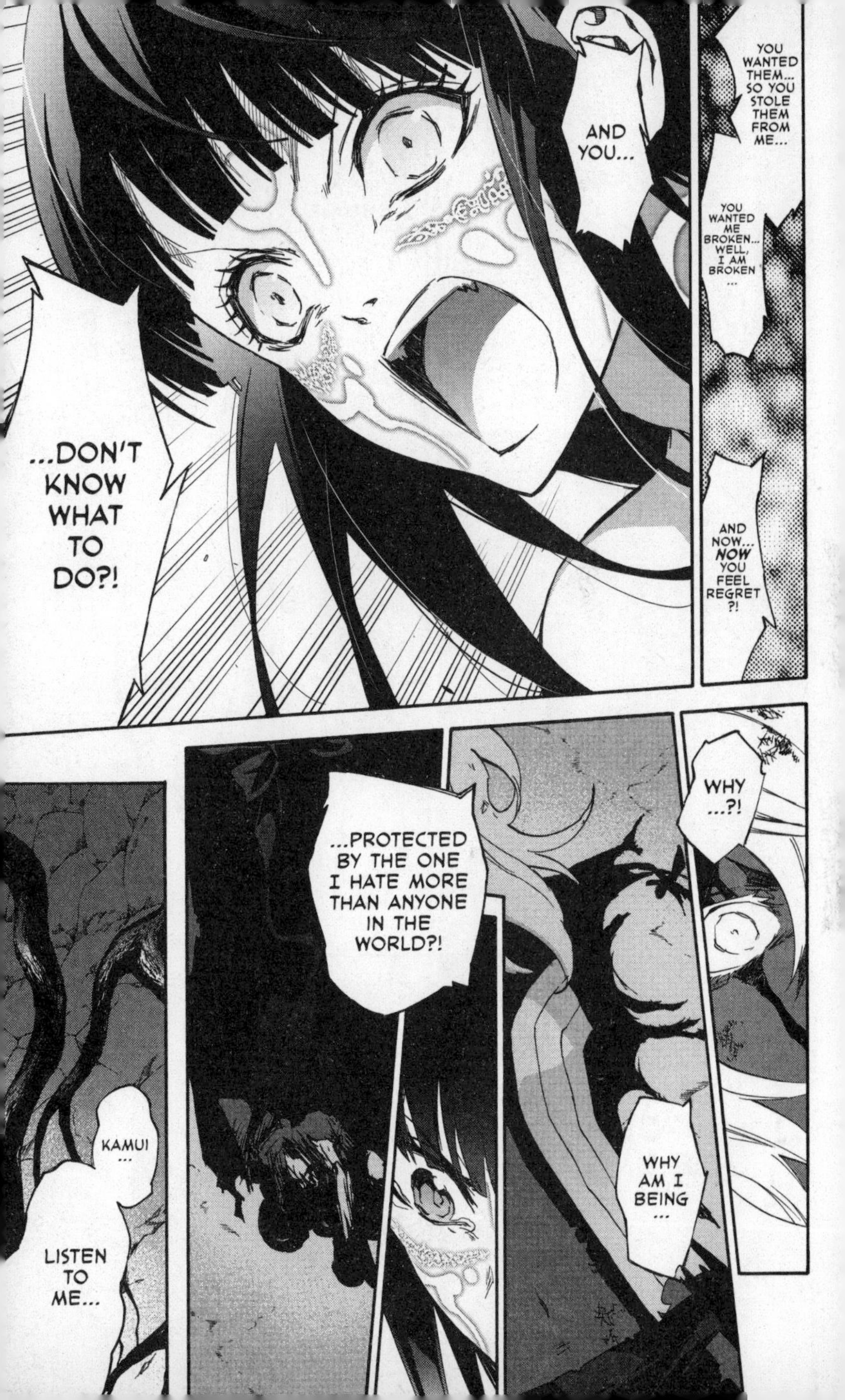
YOU WANTED THEM... SO YOU STOLE THEM FROM ME...
YOU WANTED ME BROKEN... WELL, I AM BROKEN ...
AND NOW... *NOW* YOU FEEL REGRET ?!
AND YOU...
...DON'T KNOW WHAT TO DO?!
WHY ...?!
WHY AM I BEING ...
...PROTECTED BY THE ONE I HATE MORE THAN ANYONE IN THE WORLD?!
KAMUI ...
LISTEN TO ME...

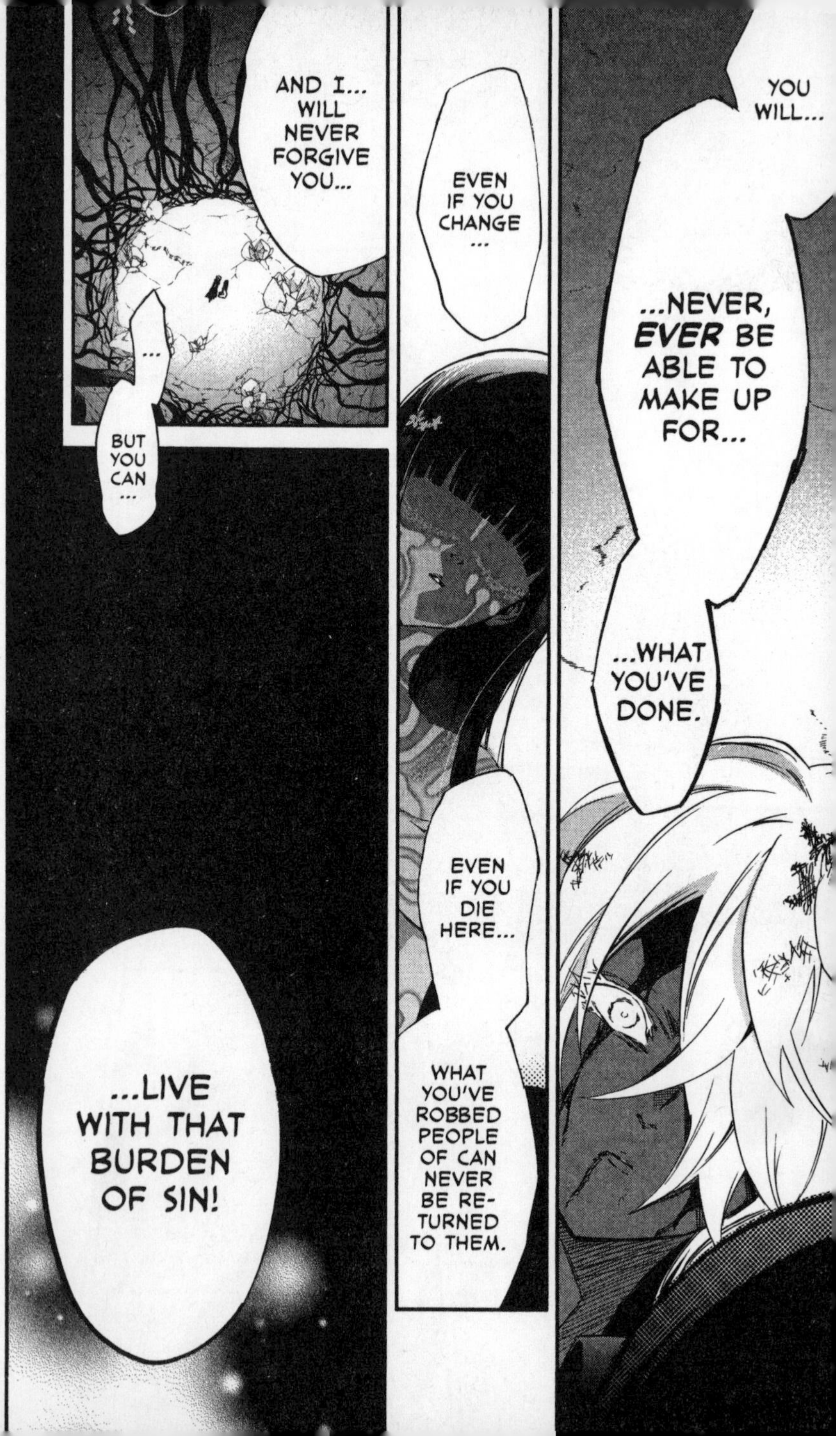
YOU WILL...
...NEVER, ***EVER*** BE ABLE TO MAKE UP FOR...
...WHAT YOU'VE DONE.
EVEN IF YOU CHANGE ...
EVEN IF YOU DIE HERE...
WHAT YOU'VE ROBBED PEOPLE OF CAN NEVER BE RE- TURNED TO THEM.
AND I... WILL NEVER FORGIVE YOU...
...
BUT YOU CAN ...
...LIVE WITH THAT BURDEN OF SIN!

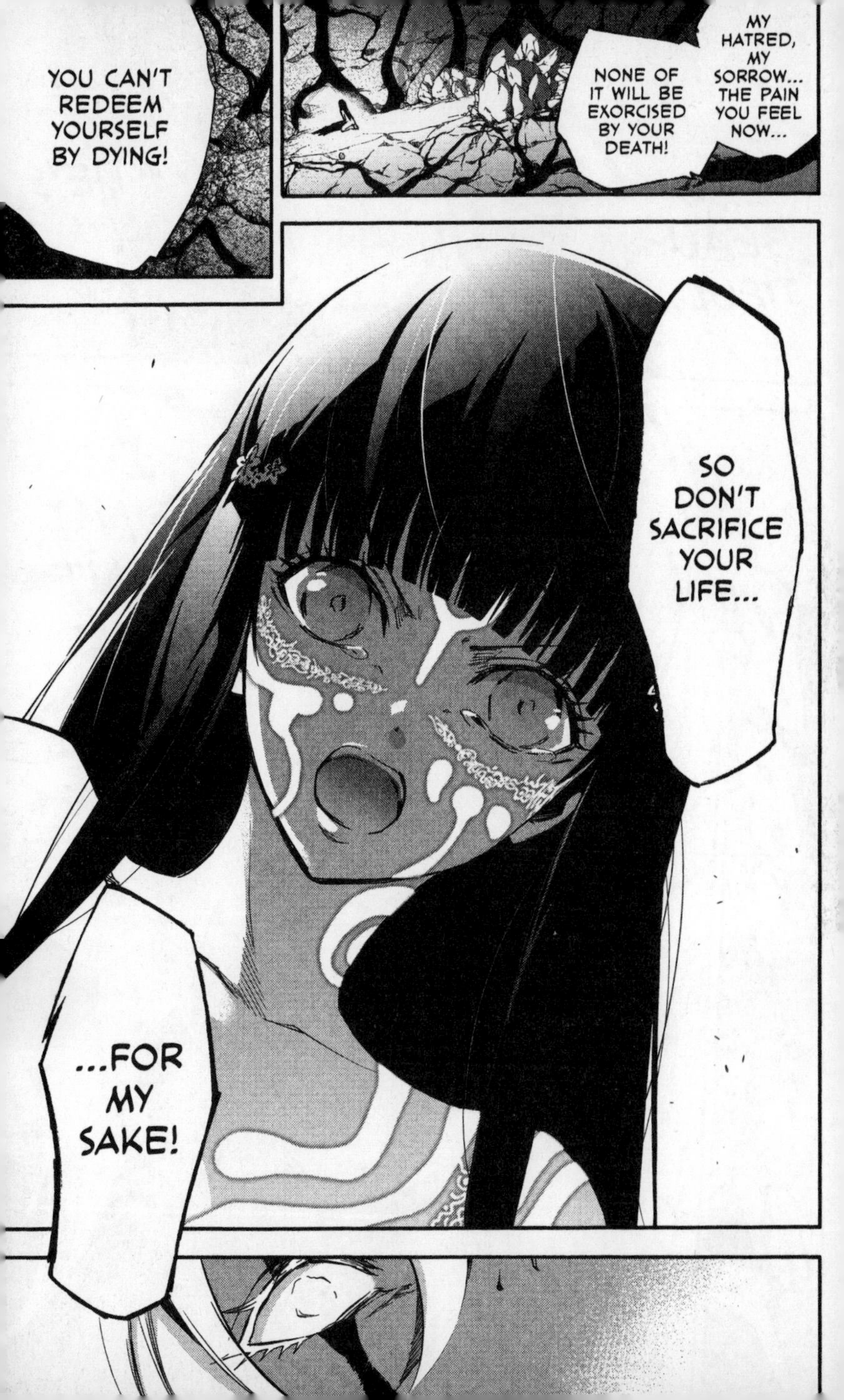
MY HATRED, MY SORROW... THE PAIN YOU FEEL NOW...
NONE OF IT WILL BE EXORCISED BY YOUR DEATH!
YOU CAN'T REDEEM YOURSELF BY DYING!
SO DON'T SACRIFICE YOUR LIFE...
...FOR MY SAKE!

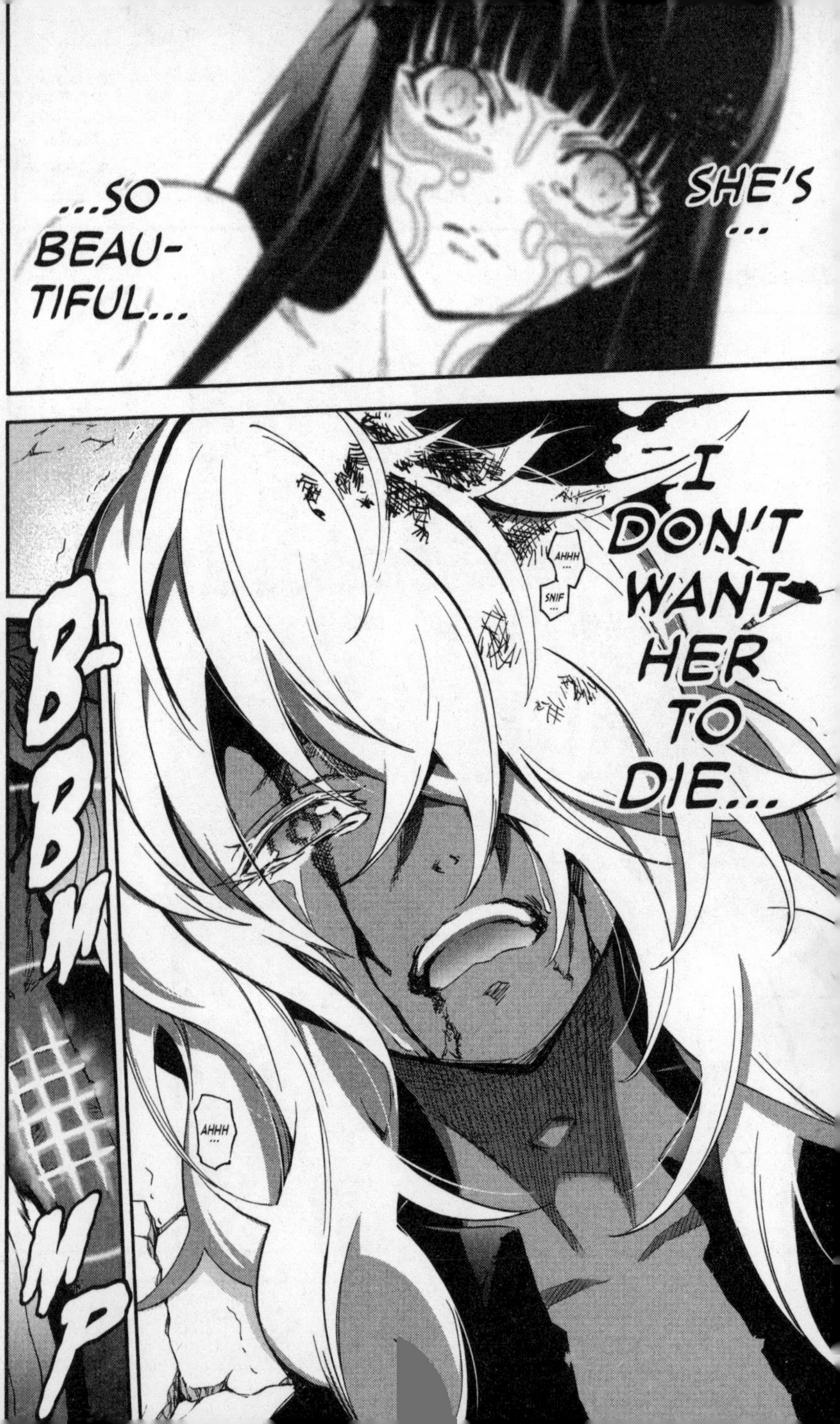
SHE'S ...
...SO BEAU-TIFUL...
I DON'T WANT HER TO DIE...
AHHH ...
SNIF ...
AHHH ...

W-WHAT...

...IS THAT?!

I SEE NOW...

I CAN'T FIGHT THIS URGE TO PROTECT HER!

FA A

WHAT DROVE ME MAD IS...

...THAT BEFALLS HUMANS.

...A CURSE...

OH, BUT...

...WARM CURSE IT IS?

...WHAT A GENTLE!..

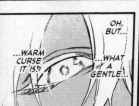

SH

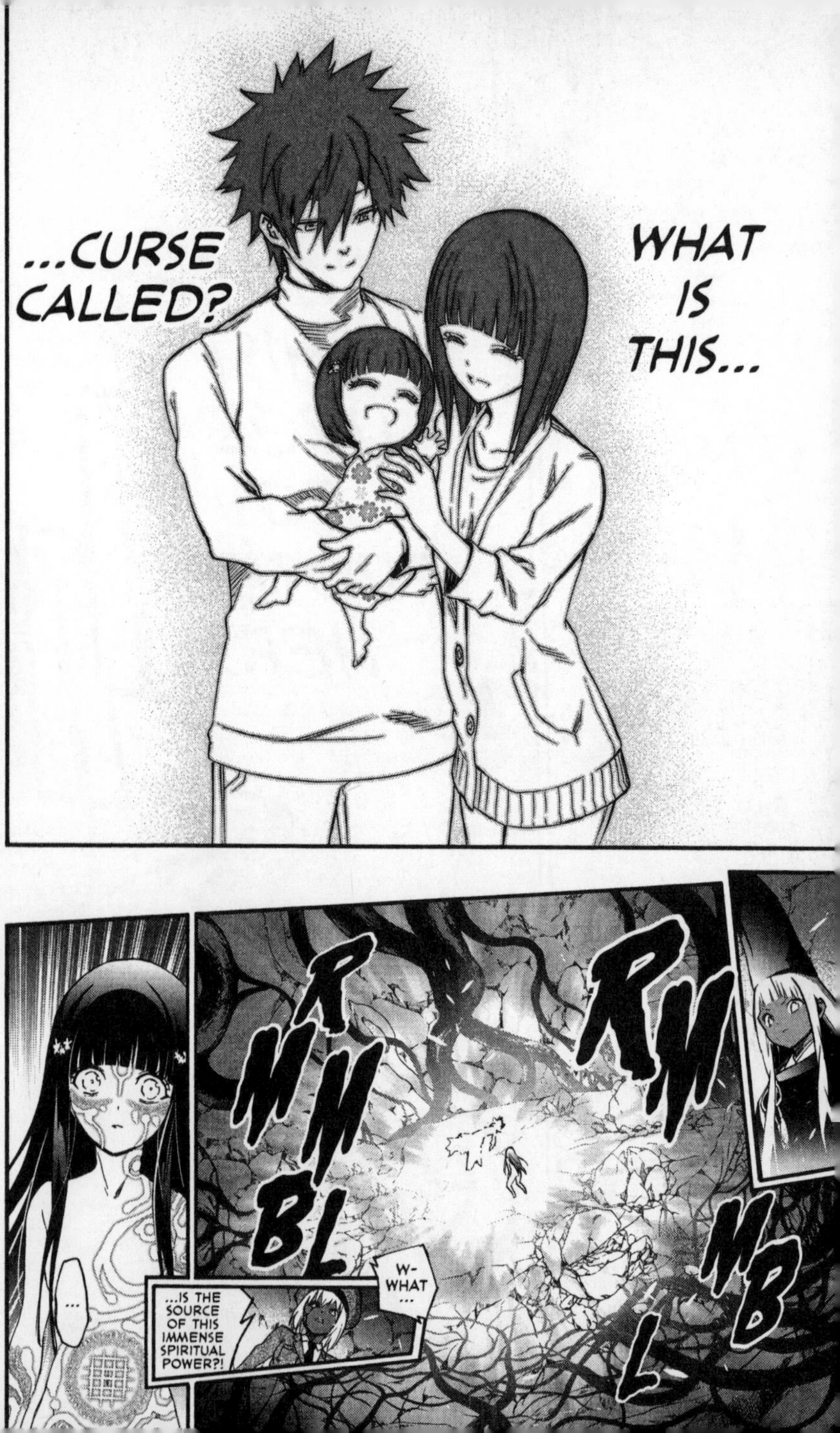
WHAT IS THIS...
...CURSE CALLED?
RMMBL
RMMBL
W-WHAT...
...IS THE SOURCE OF THIS IMMENSE SPIRITUAL POWER?!
...

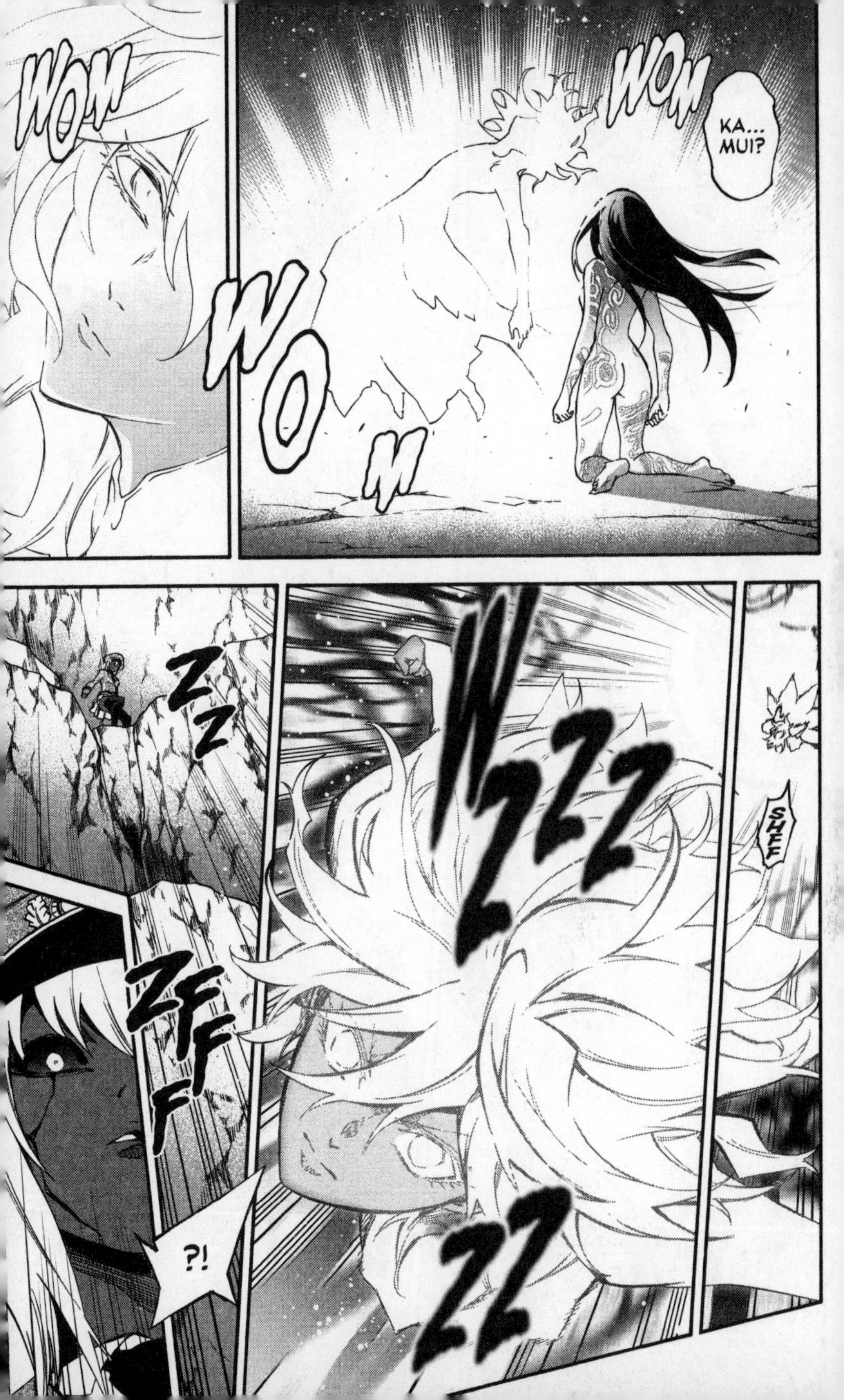
WOM
KA... MUI?
WOMM
WOM
SHFF
WZZZZ
ZZ
ZZ
ZFFF
?!

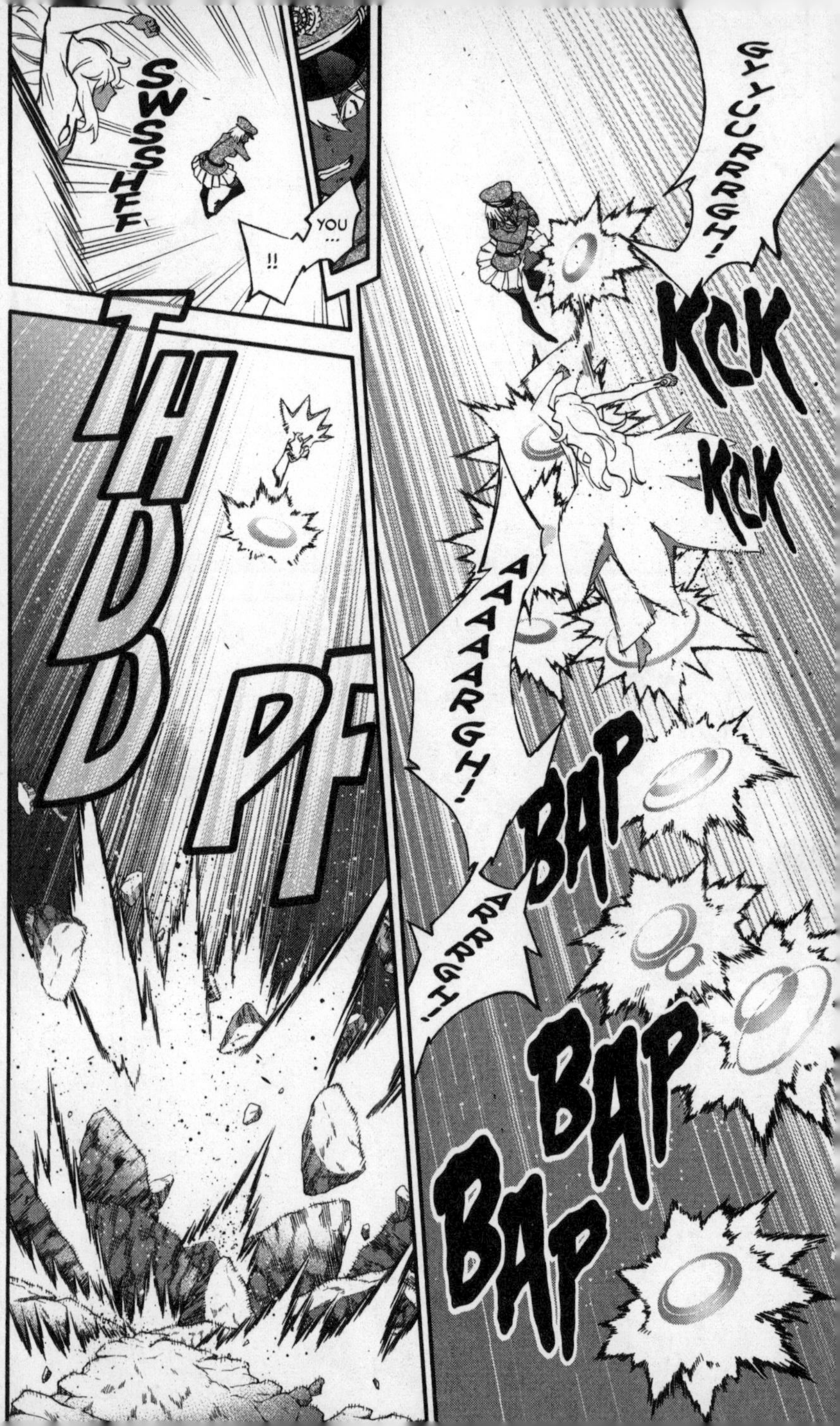
GYYURRRGH!
KCK
KCK
AAAAAARGH!
ARRRGH!
BAP
BAP
BAP
BAP
YOU...
!!
SWSSHFF
THUDDPF

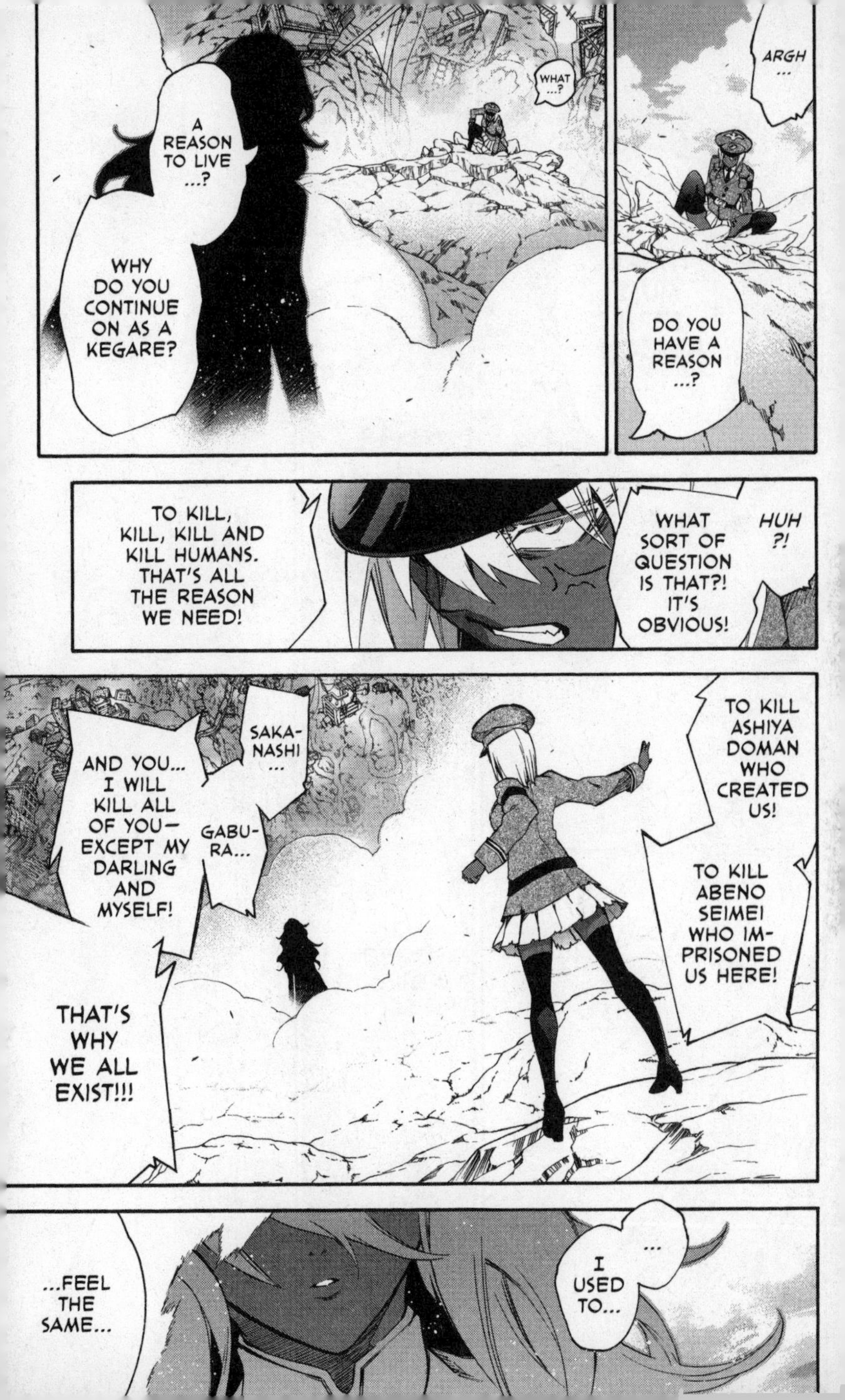
ARGH ...
DO YOU HAVE A REASON ...?
WHAT ...?
A REASON TO LIVE ...?
WHY DO YOU CONTINUE ON AS A KEGARE?
HUH ?!
WHAT SORT OF QUESTION IS THAT?! IT'S OBVIOUS!
TO KILL, KILL, KILL AND KILL HUMANS. THAT'S ALL THE REASON WE NEED!
TO KILL ASHIYA DOMAN WHO CREATED US!
TO KILL ABENO SEIMEI WHO IM-PRISONED US HERE!
SAKA-NASHI ...
GABU-RA...
AND YOU... I WILL KILL ALL OF YOU— EXCEPT MY DARLING AND MYSELF!
THAT'S WHY WE ALL EXIST!!!
...
I USED TO...
...FEEL THE SAME...

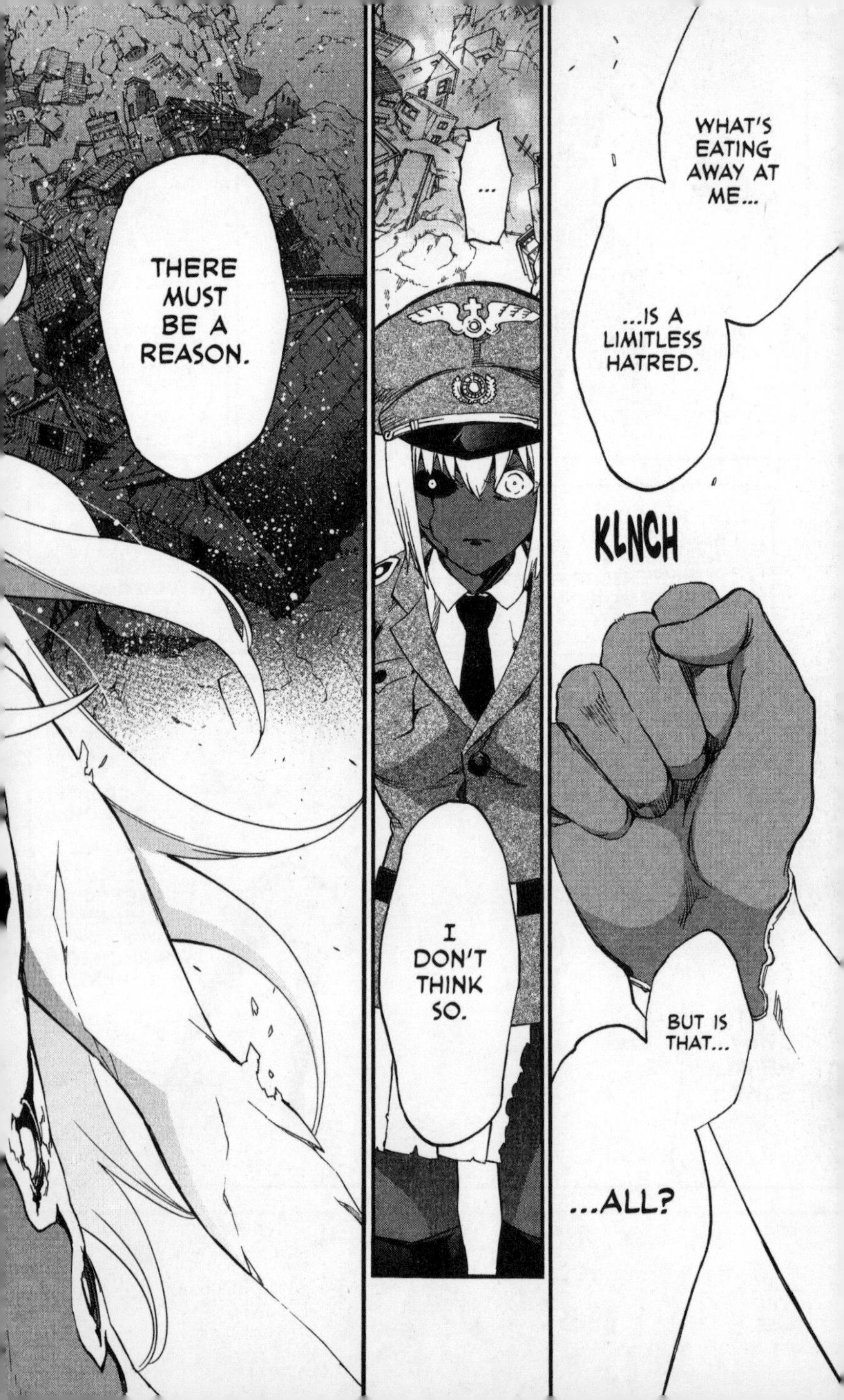
WHAT'S EATING AWAY AT ME...
...IS A LIMITLESS HATRED.
KLNCH
BUT IS THAT...
...ALL?
...
I DON'T THINK SO.
THERE MUST BE A REASON.

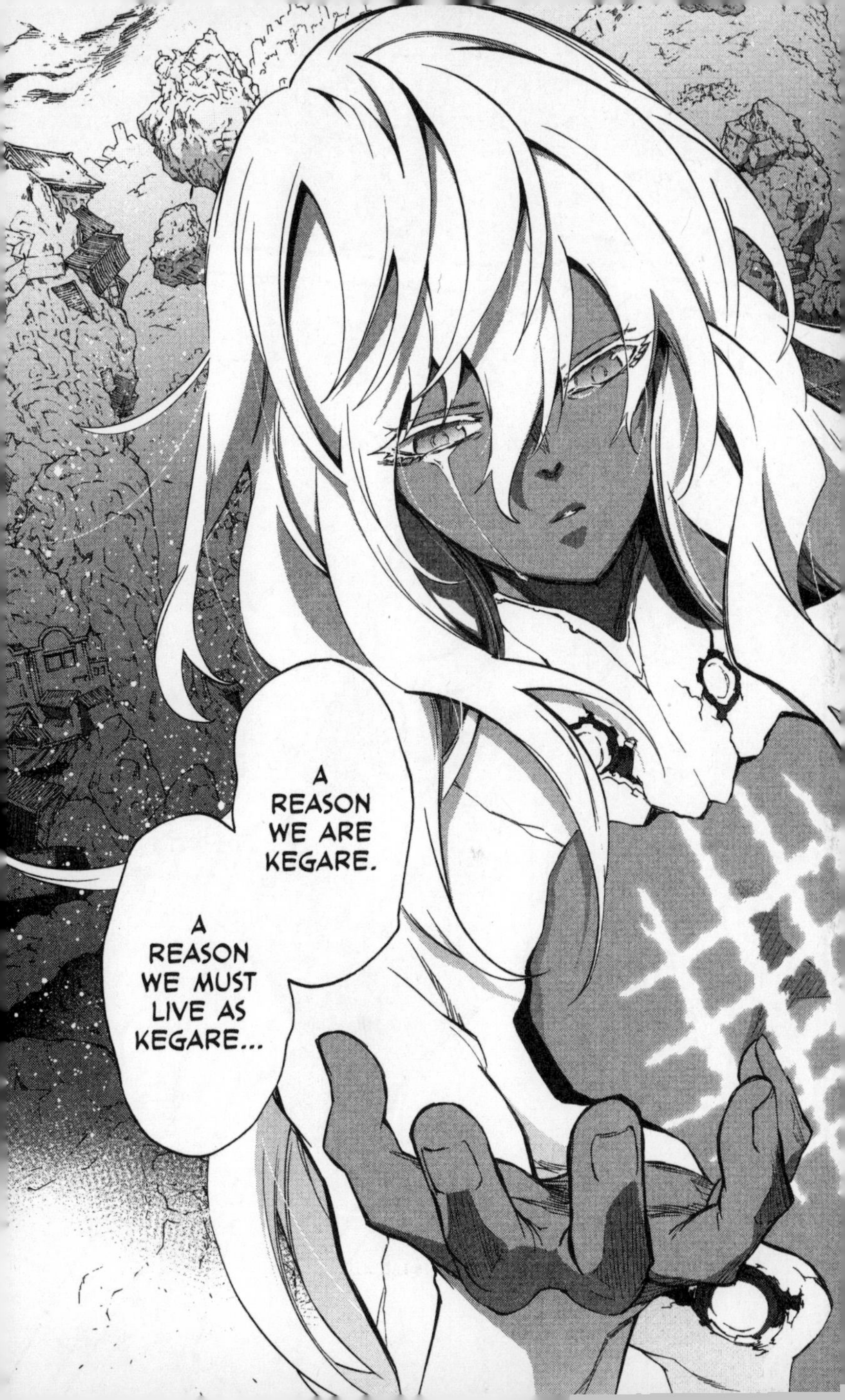
A REASON WE ARE KEGARE.
A REASON WE MUST LIVE AS KEGARE...

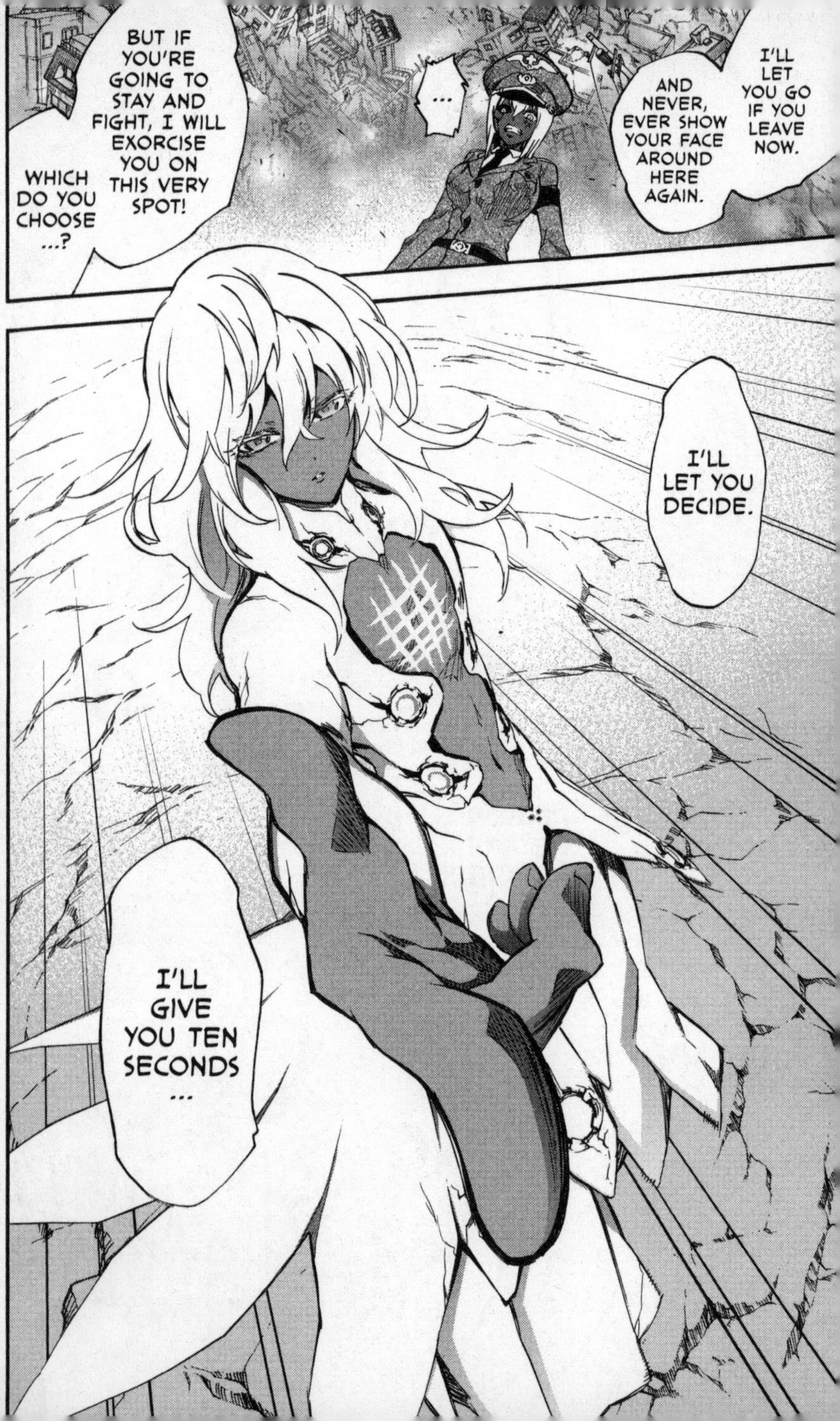
I'LL LET YOU GO IF YOU LEAVE NOW.
AND NEVER, EVER SHOW YOUR FACE AROUND HERE AGAIN.
...
BUT IF YOU'RE GOING TO STAY AND FIGHT, I WILL EXORCISE YOU ON THIS VERY SPOT!
WHICH DO YOU CHOOSE ...?
I'LL LET YOU DECIDE.
I'LL GIVE YOU TEN SECONDS ...

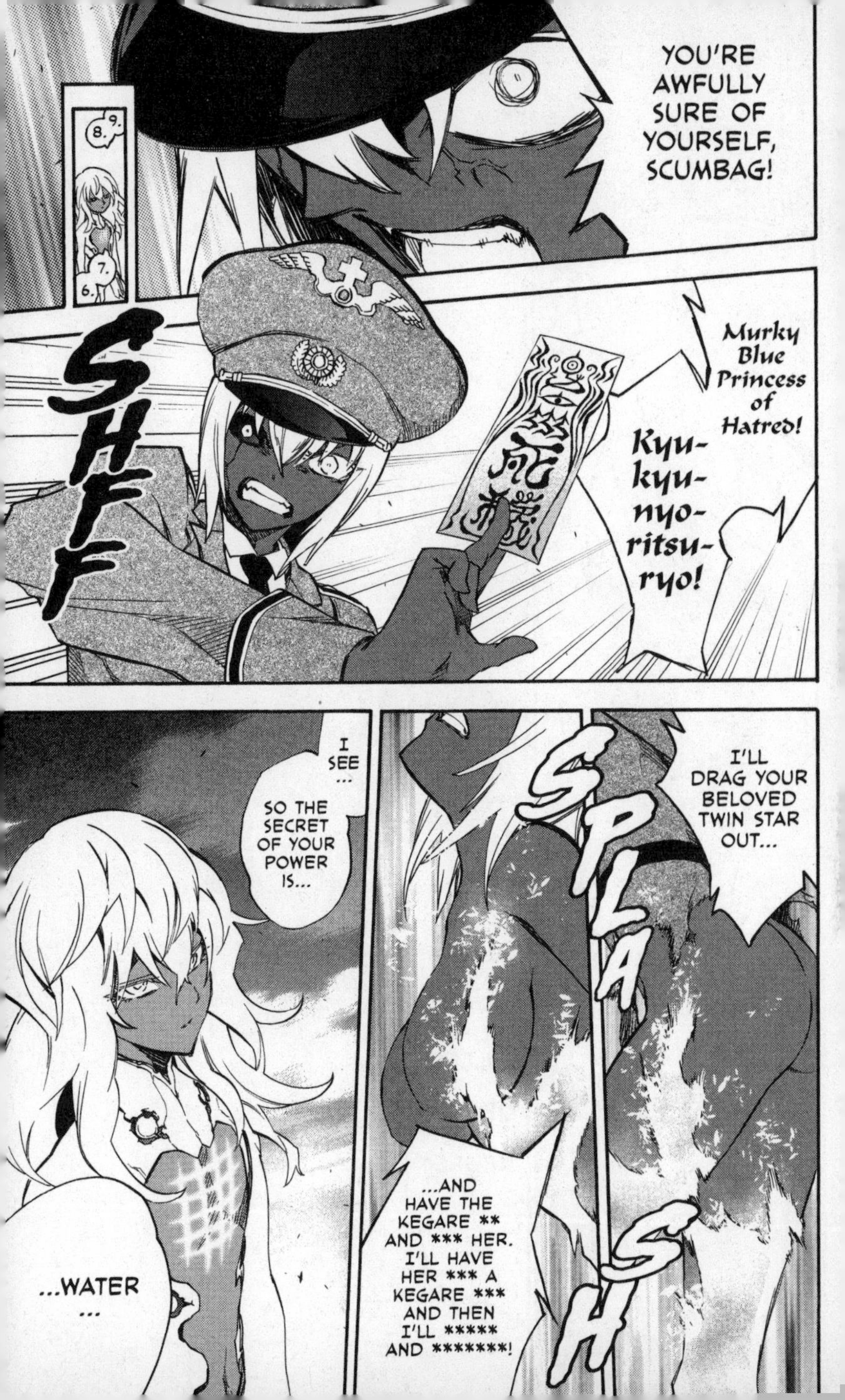
YOU'RE AWFULLY SURE OF YOURSELF, SCUMBAG!
9.
8.
7.
6.
Murky Blue Princess of Hatred!
Kyu-kyu-nyo-ritsu-ryo!
SHFF
I'LL DRAG YOUR BELOVED TWIN STAR OUT...
SPLASH
...AND HAVE THE KEGARE ** AND *** HER. I'LL HAVE HER *** A KEGARE *** AND THEN I'LL ***** AND *******!
I SEE...
SO THE SECRET OF YOUR POWER IS...
...WATER...

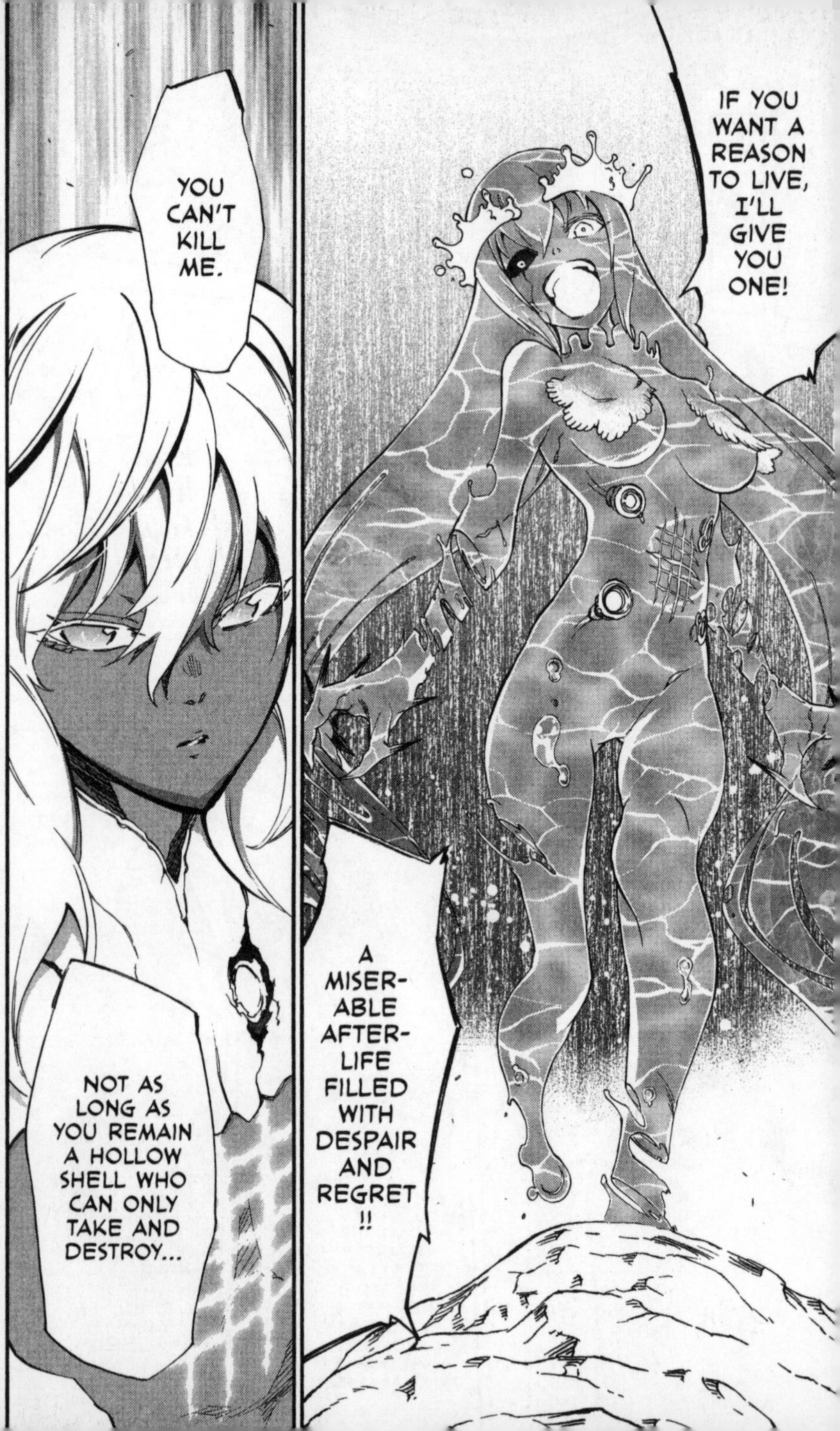
IF YOU WANT A REASON TO LIVE, I'LL GIVE YOU ONE!
A MISERABLE AFTER-LIFE FILLED WITH DESPAIR AND REGRET!!
YOU CAN'T KILL ME.
NOT AS LONG AS YOU REMAIN A HOLLOW SHELL WHO CAN ONLY TAKE AND DESTROY...

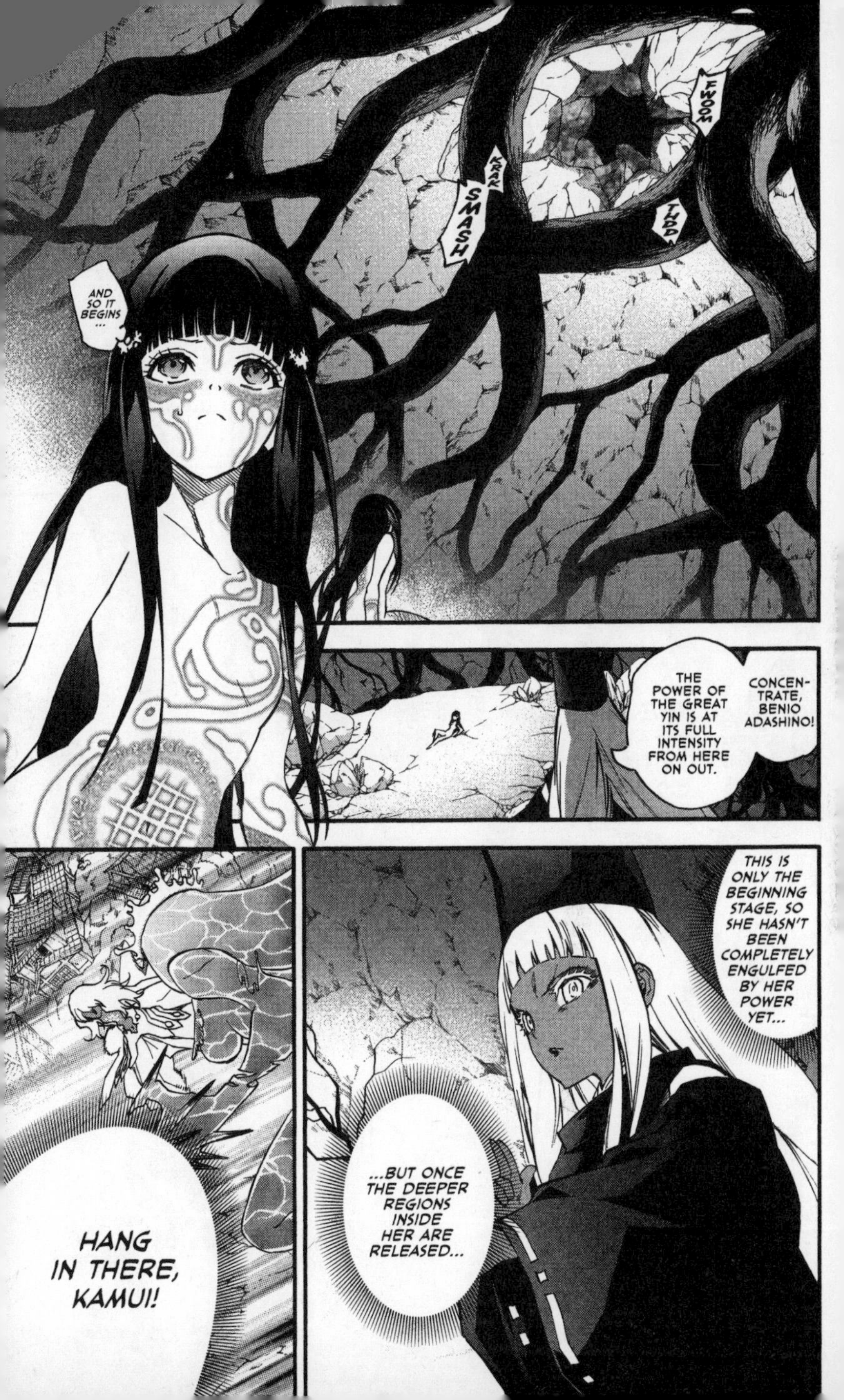
FWOOM
THDD
KRAK
SMASH
AND SO IT BEGINS...
CONCEN-TRATE, BENIO ADASHINO!
THE POWER OF THE GREAT YIN IS AT ITS FULL INTENSITY FROM HERE ON OUT.
THIS IS ONLY THE BEGINNING STAGE, SO SHE HASN'T BEEN COMPLETELY ENGULFED BY HER POWER YET...
...BUT ONCE THE DEEPER REGIONS INSIDE HER ARE RELEASED...
HANG IN THERE, KAMUI!

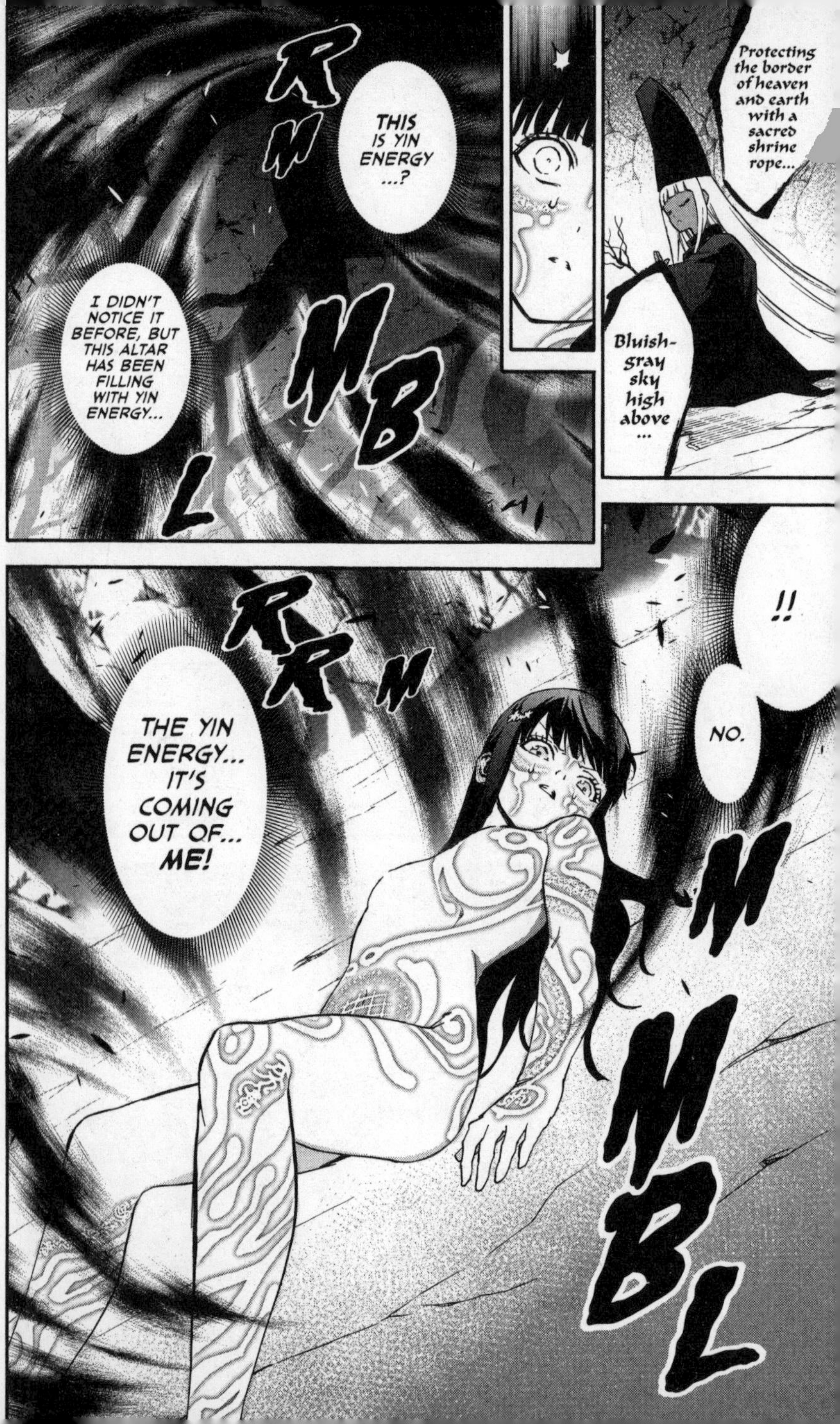

Protecting the border of heaven and earth with a sacred shrine rope...
Bluish-gray sky high above...
THIS IS YIN ENERGY ...?
RM
MBL
I DIDN'T NOTICE IT BEFORE, BUT THIS ALTAR HAS BEEN FILLING WITH YIN ENERGY...
!!
NO.
RRM
THE YIN ENERGY... IT'S COMING OUT OF... ME!
MMMBL

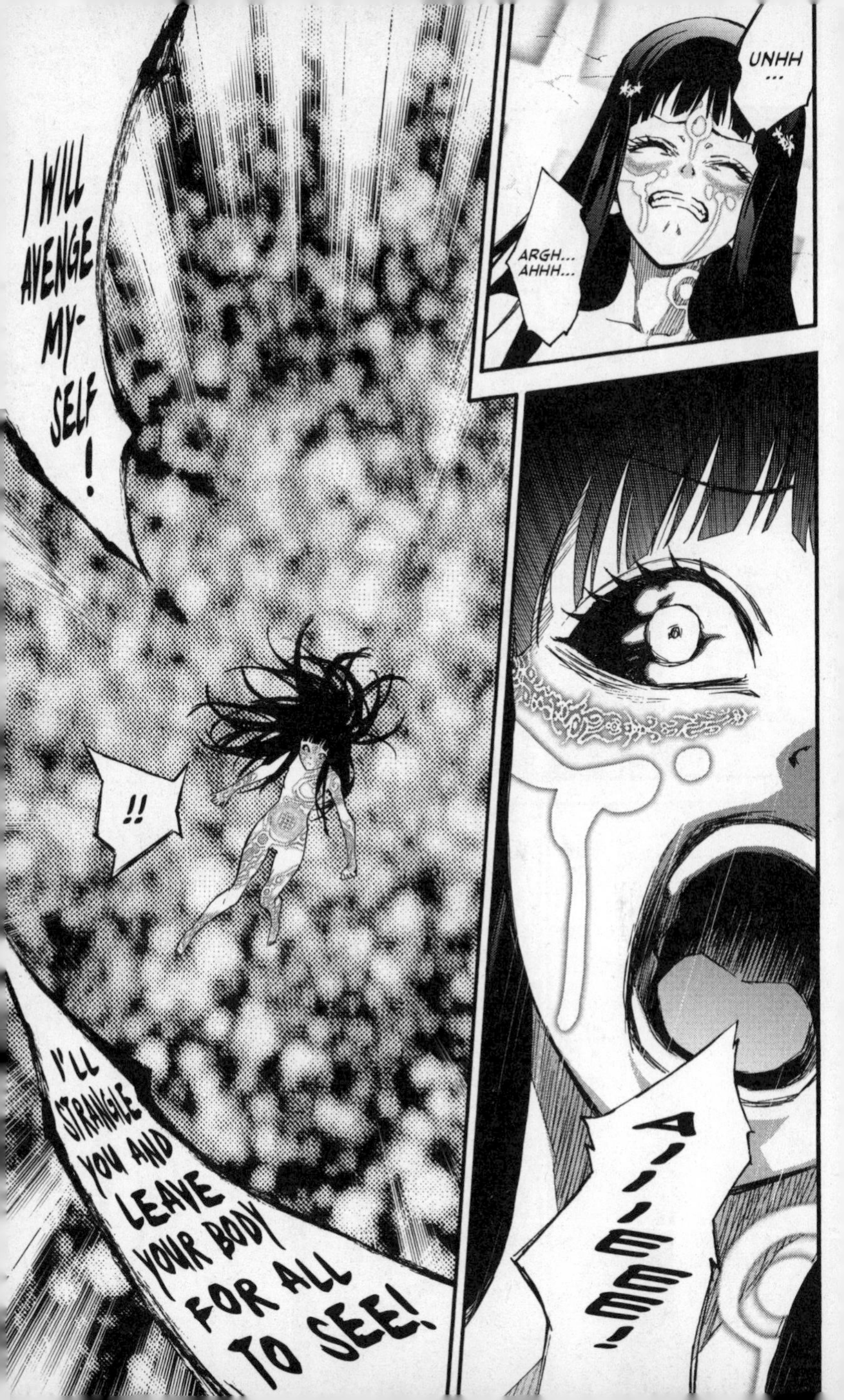
UNHH...
ARGH... AHHH...
AIIEEE!
I WILL AVENGE MYSELF!
!!
I'LL STRANGLE YOU AND LEAVE YOUR BODY FOR ALL TO SEE!

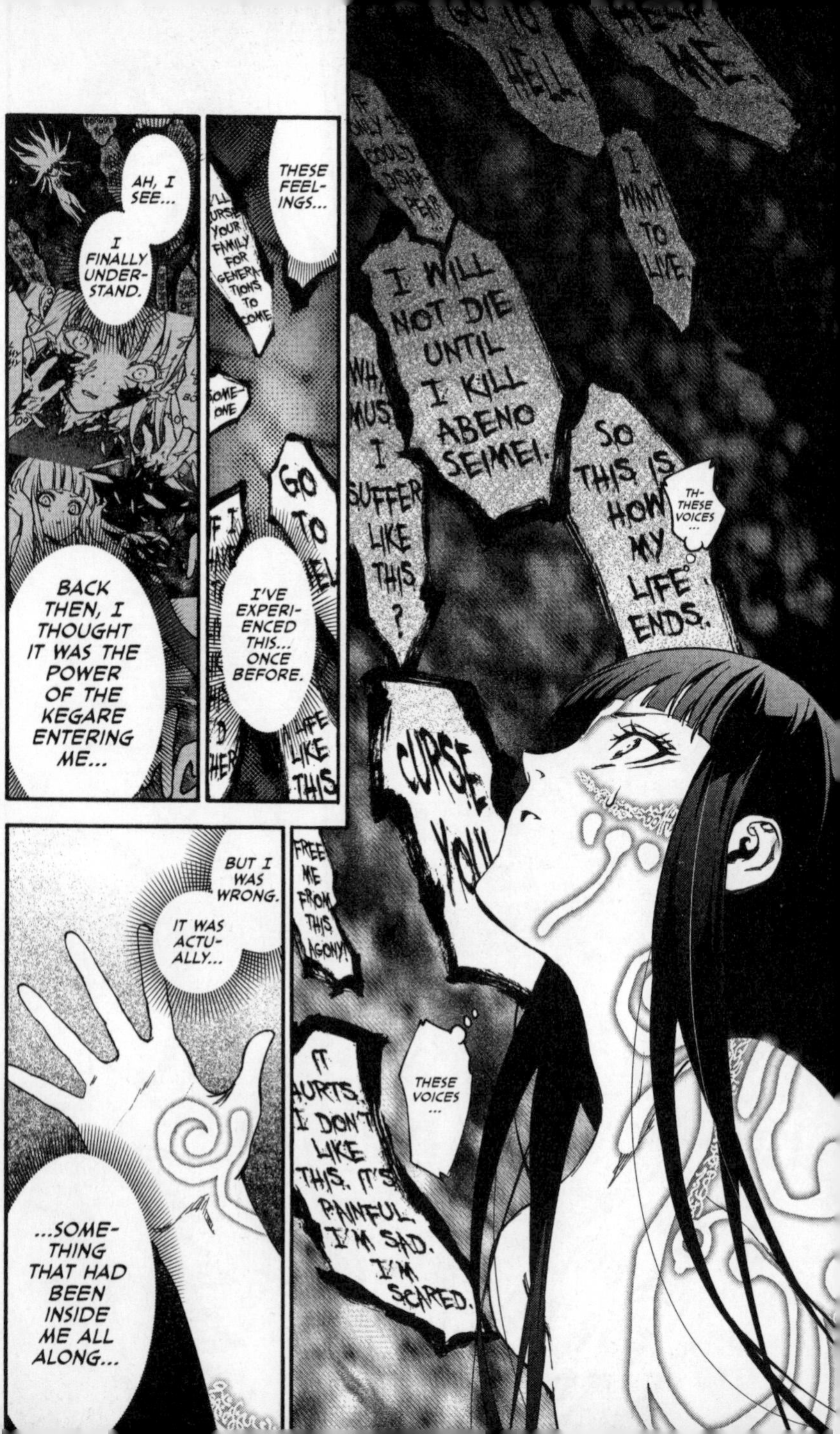

GO TO HELL
IF ONLY I COULD DISAPPEAR
I WANT TO LIVE
I WILL NOT DIE UNTIL I KILL ABENO SEIMEI.
SO THIS IS HOW MY LIFE ENDS.
TH-THESE VOICES...
WHY MUST I SUFFER LIKE THIS?
CURSE YOU!
FREE ME FROM THIS AGONY!
THESE VOICES...
IT HURTS. I DON'T LIKE THIS. IT'S PAINFUL. I'M SAD. I'M SCARED.
THESE FEELINGS...
I'LL CURSE YOUR FAMILY FOR GENERATIONS TO COME
SOMEONE
GO TO
I'VE EXPERIENCED THIS... ONCE BEFORE.
LIFE LIKE THIS
AH, I SEE...
I FINALLY UNDERSTAND.
BACK THEN, I THOUGHT IT WAS THE POWER OF THE KEGARE ENTERING ME...
BUT I WAS WRONG.
IT WAS ACTUALLY...
...SOMETHING THAT HAD BEEN INSIDE ME ALL ALONG...

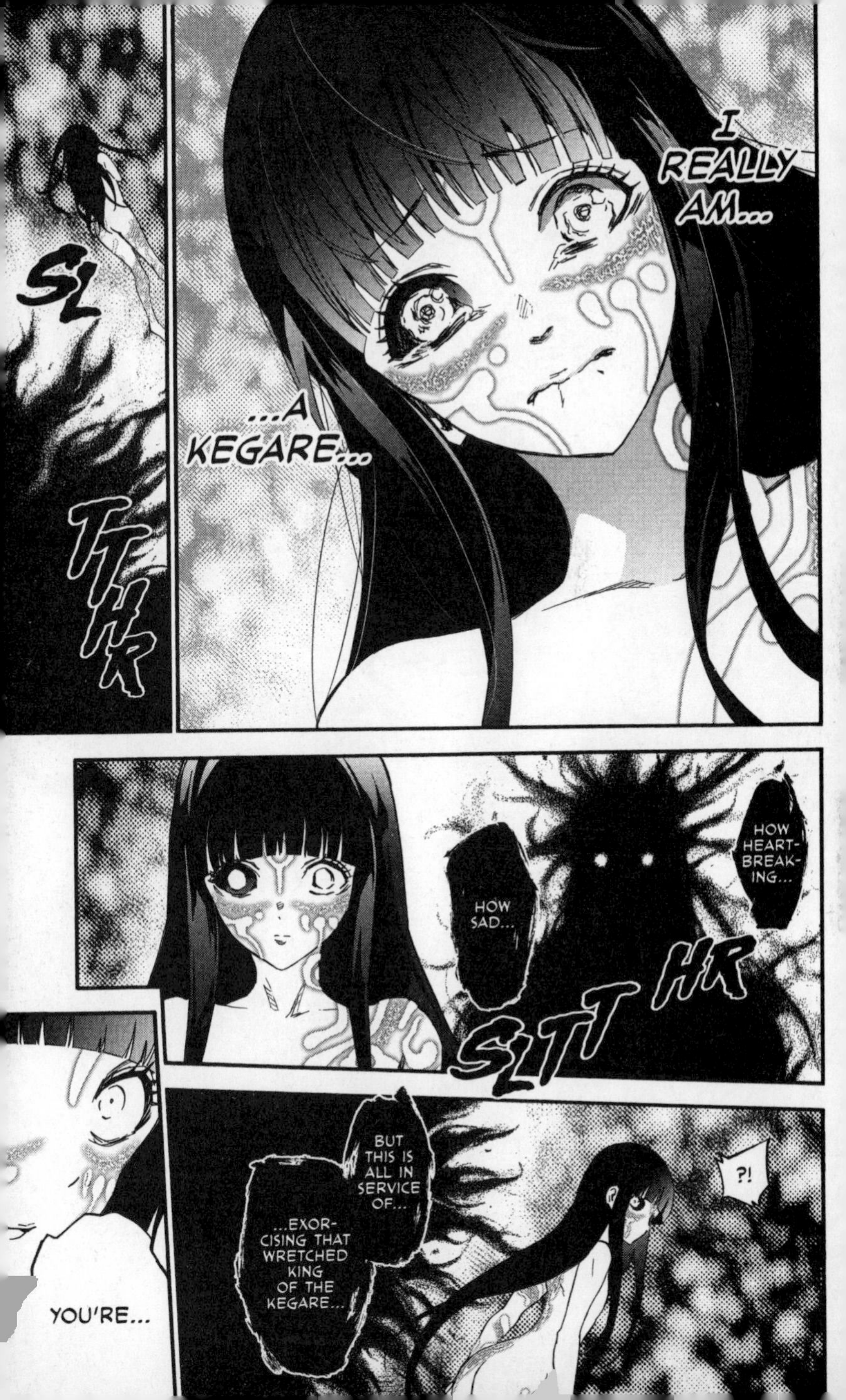
I REALLY AM...
...A KEGARE...
SL
TTHR
HOW HEART-BREAK-ING...
HOW SAD...
HR
SLTT
?!
BUT THIS IS ALL IN SERVICE OF...
...EXORCISING THAT WRETCHED KING OF THE KEGARE...
YOU'RE...

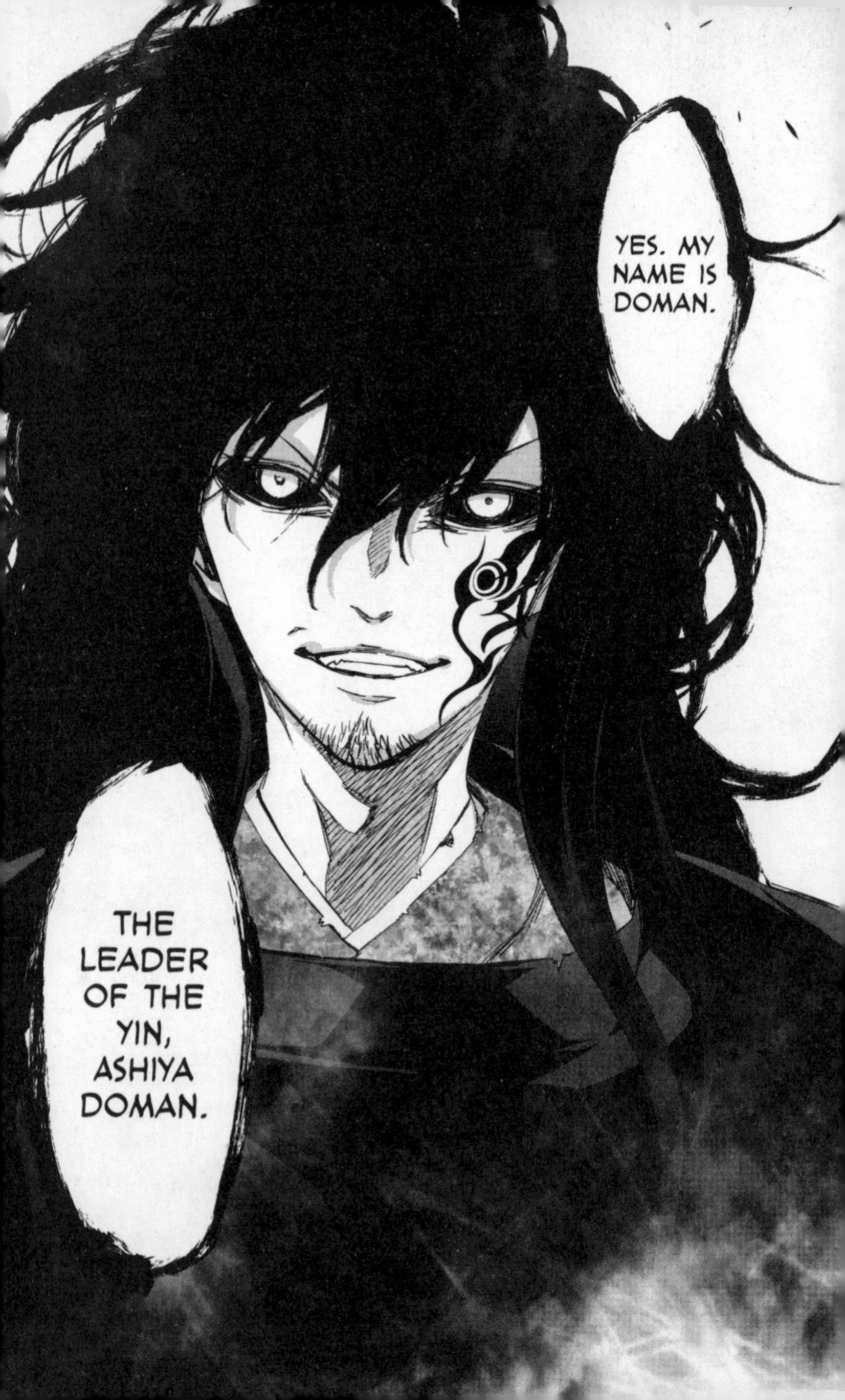
YES. MY NAME IS DOMAN.
THE LEADER OF THE YIN, ASHIYA DOMAN.

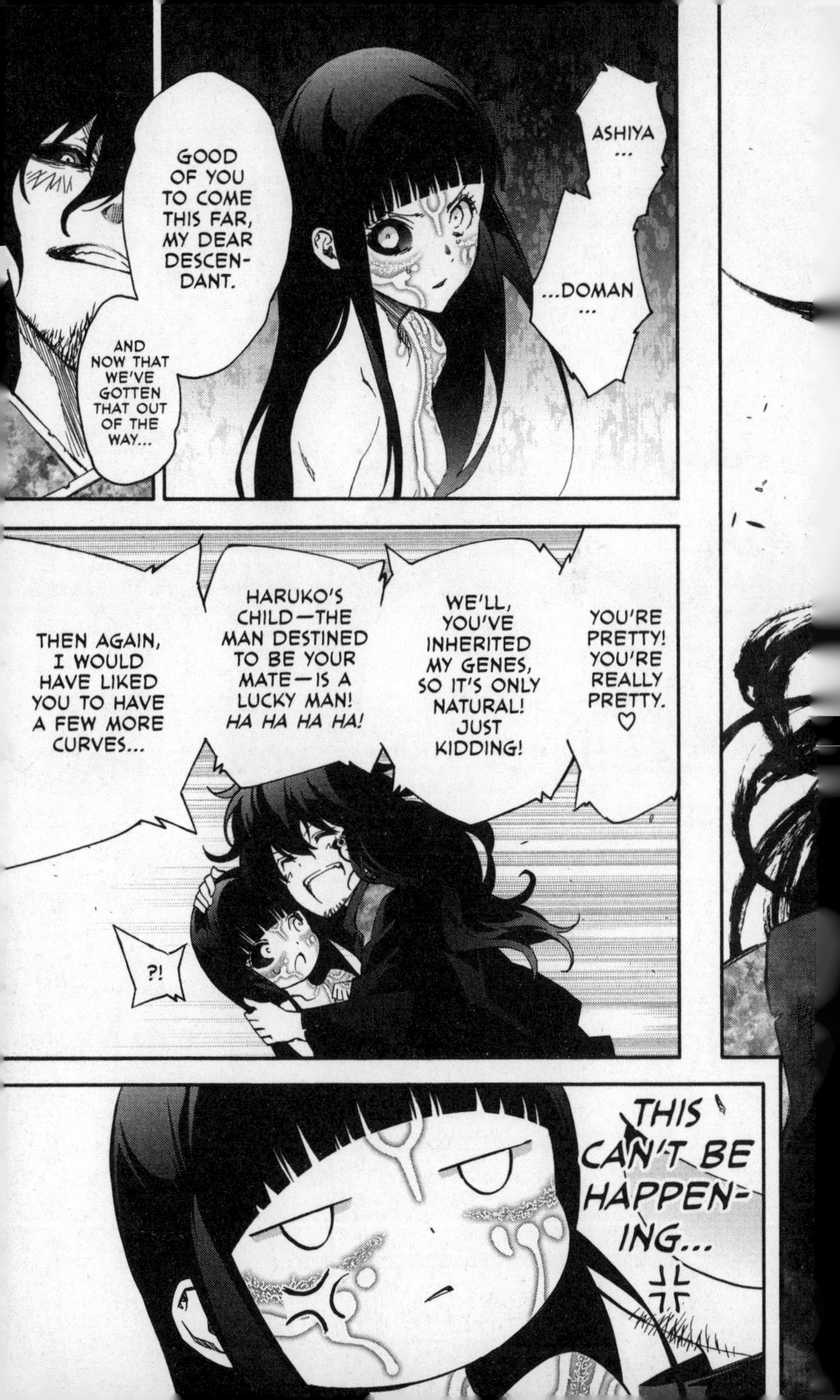
ASHIYA ... ...DOMAN ...
GOOD OF YOU TO COME THIS FAR, MY DEAR DESCENDANT.
AND NOW THAT WE'VE GOTTEN THAT OUT OF THE WAY...
YOU'RE PRETTY! YOU'RE REALLY PRETTY. ♡
WE'LL, YOU'VE INHERITED MY GENES, SO IT'S ONLY NATURAL! JUST KIDDING!
HARUKO'S CHILD—THE MAN DESTINED TO BE YOUR MATE—IS A LUCKY MAN! *HA HA HA HA!*
THEN AGAIN, I WOULD HAVE LIKED YOU TO HAVE A FEW MORE CURVES...
?!
THIS CAN'T BE HAPPENING...

QQnyoritsuryo!

Question Corner

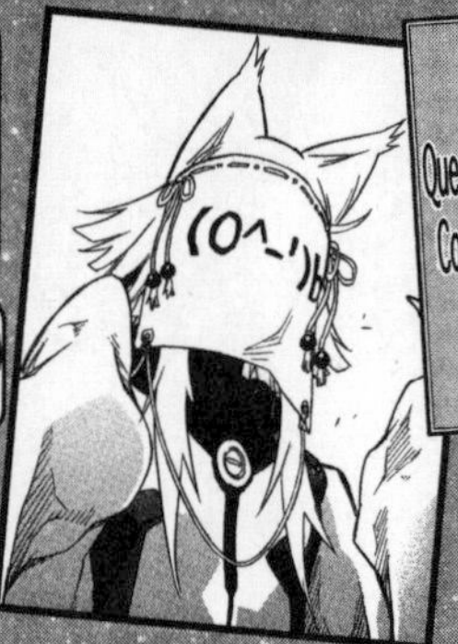

Q How many types of emoticons does Tatara use to express his emotions?
(From Popcorn Kuroshio)

A There are probably more than a hundred. In addition to the emoticons, he also uses traffic signals.

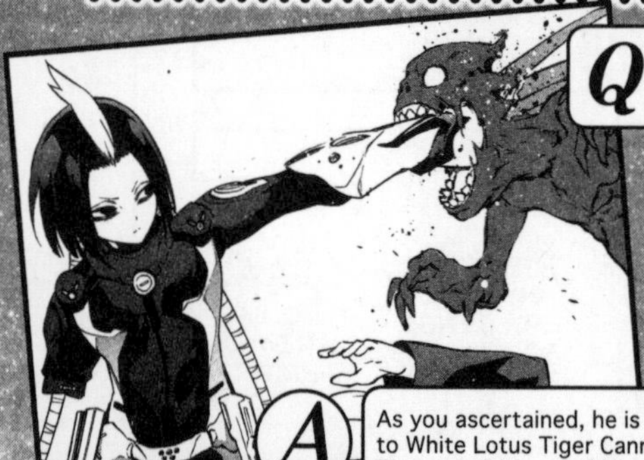

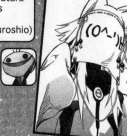

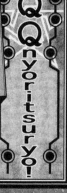

Q Seigen has been using White Lotus Tiger Cannon Arm even after Mayura inherited White Tiger, hasn't he? How can that be? Is he using a different yet similar spell to White Lotus Tiger Cannon Arm? Please explain it to me.
(From Gekka)

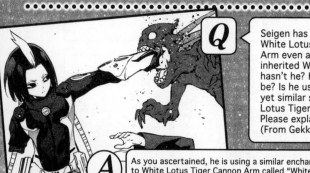

A As you ascertained, he is using a similar enchanment to White Lotus Tiger Cannon Arm called "White Hazy Tiger Jaw." It's one-fifth as powerful as White Lotus Tiger Cannon Arm. The Black Forged Gauntlet that Yuzuru and Jinya are using is about half as powerful as White Hazy Tiger Jaw.

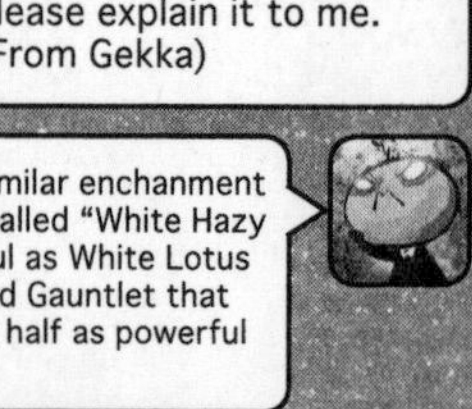
WE HAVE TO FINISH THIS BEFORE THE SALE ENDS AT THE SUPER-MARKET.
WHAT WOULD YOU LIKE FOR DINNER, HYOGA?

Request **R** My nickname is Saki. Would it be possible for Benio's mom's birthday to be May 18? (That's my birthday.)
(From Tayuneko)

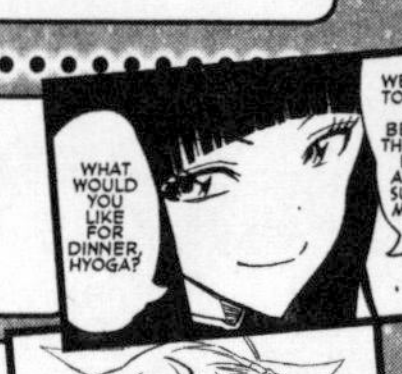

Request **R** Would it be possible for Gabura's birthday to be December 20? Gabura is my favorite *Twin Star Exorcists* character... (><)
(From Sister (Temporarily))

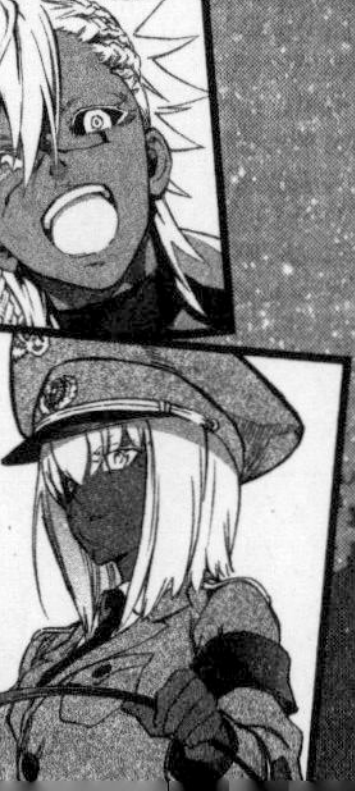
ENNND

Request **R** I know this is out of the blue, but would it be possible for Kaguya's birthday to be December 21? Thank you very much.
(From Ivy Momo-tan)

A All requests granted. Their birthdays will be as you wish.

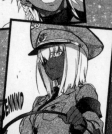

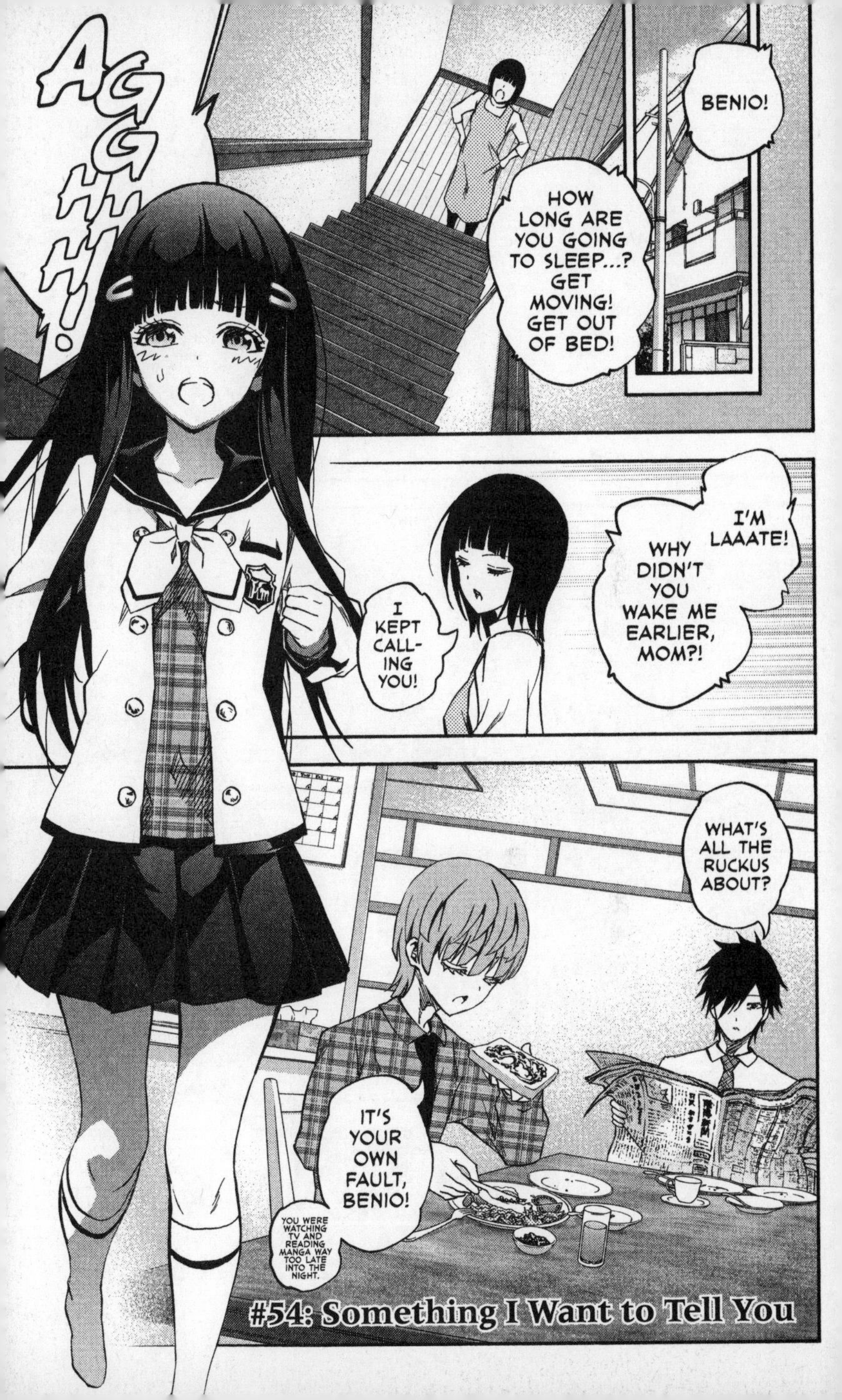
BENIO!
HOW LONG ARE YOU GOING TO SLEEP...? GET MOVING! GET OUT OF BED!
I'M LAAATE!
WHY DIDN'T YOU WAKE ME EARLIER, MOM?!
I KEPT CALL-ING YOU!
WHAT'S ALL THE RUCKUS ABOUT?
IT'S YOUR OWN FAULT, BENIO!
YOU WERE WATCHING TV AND READING MANGA WAY TOO LATE INTO THE NIGHT.
#54: Something I Want to Tell You
AGGHHH!

#54: Something I Want to Tell You

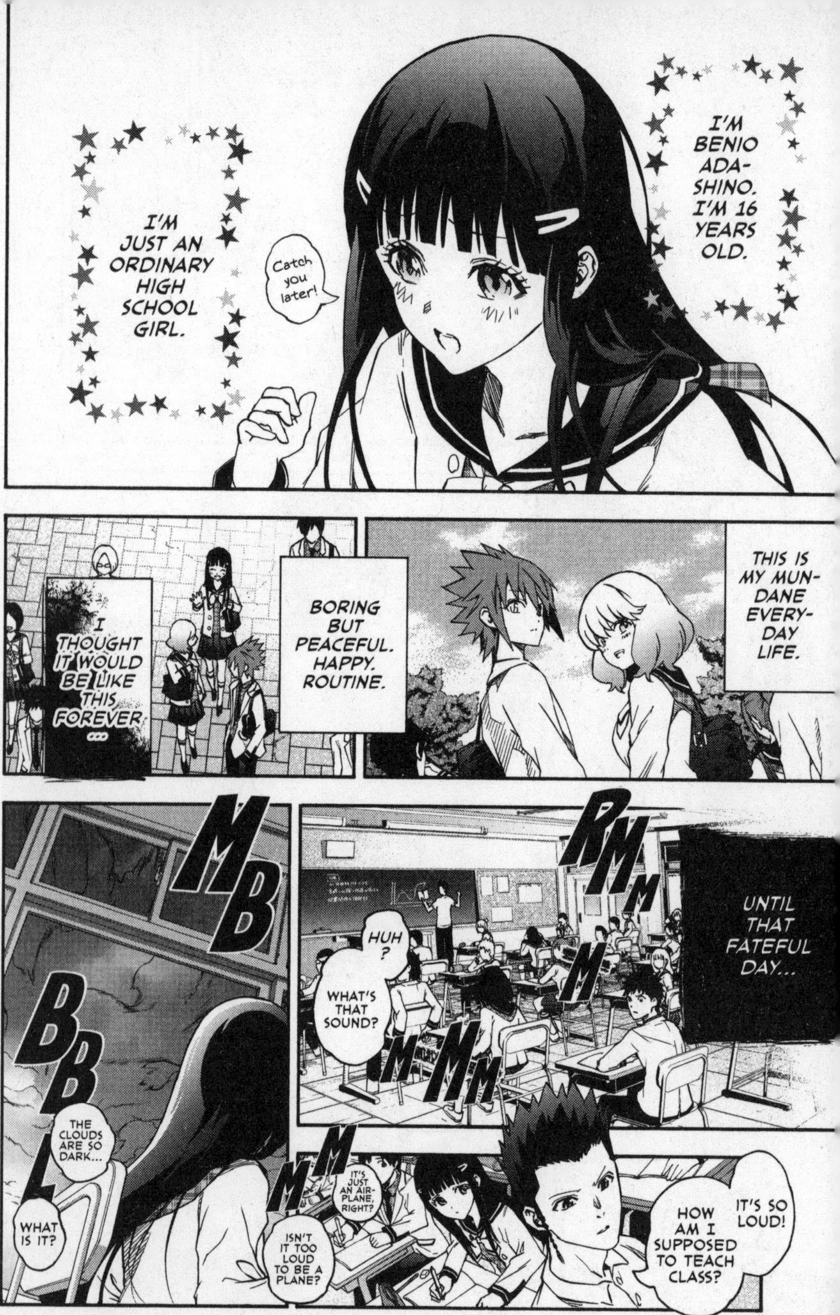
I'M BENIO ADA-SHINO. I'M 16 YEARS OLD.
I'M JUST AN ORDINARY HIGH SCHOOL GIRL.
Catch you later!
THIS IS MY MUN-DANE EVERY-DAY LIFE.
BORING BUT PEACEFUL. HAPPY. ROUTINE.
I THOUGHT IT WOULD BE LIKE THIS FOREVER...
UNTIL THAT FATEFUL DAY...
RMMMM
HUH?
WHAT'S THAT SOUND?
MMM
IT'S SO LOUD!
HOW AM I SUPPOSED TO TEACH CLASS?
IT'S JUST AN AIR-PLANE, RIGHT?
ISN'T IT TOO LOUD TO BE A PLANE?
MM
MB
BBL
THE CLOUDS ARE SO DARK...
WHAT IS IT?

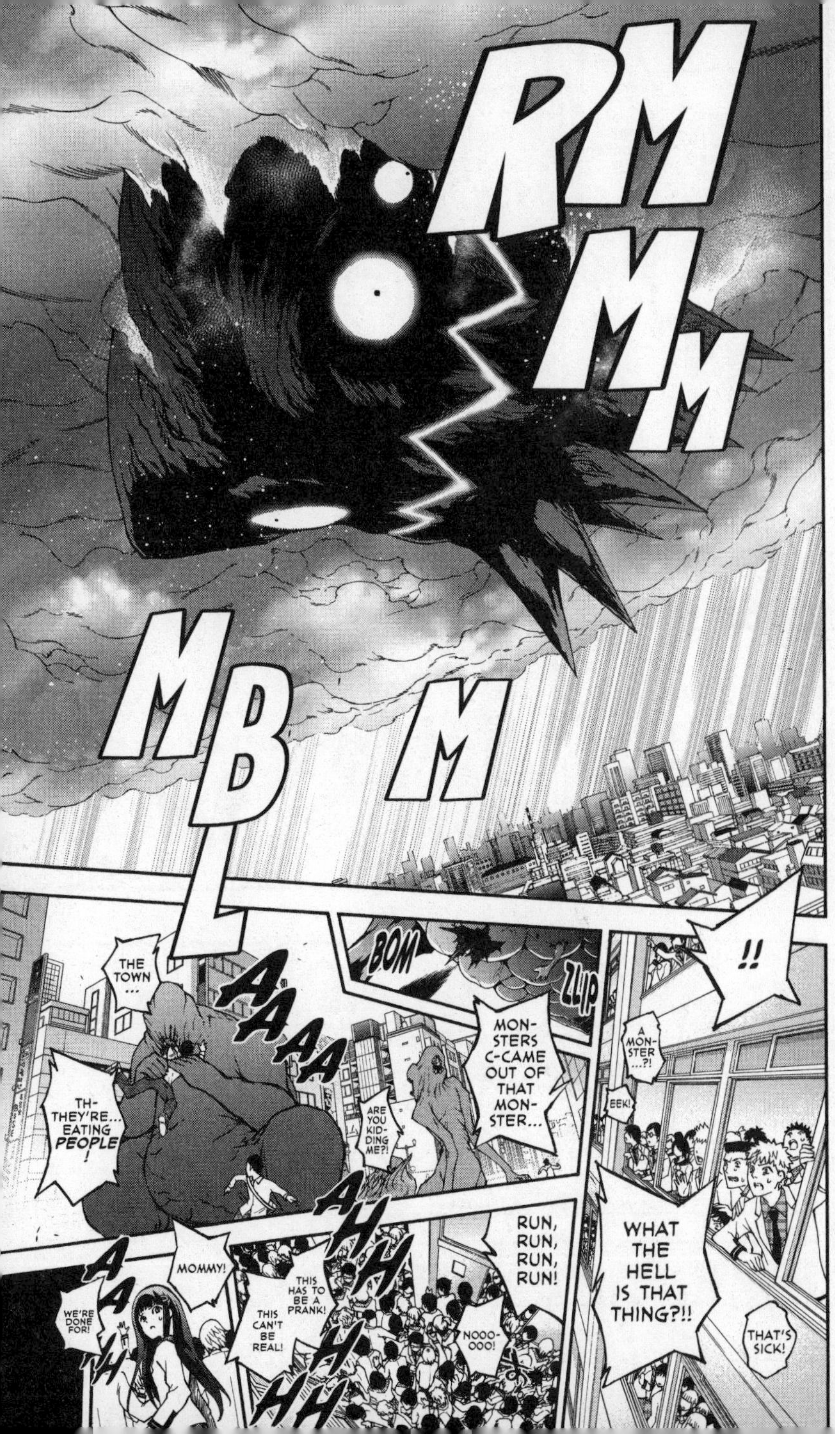
RM
MMM
MBM
L
!!
A MONSTER...?!
EEK!
WHAT THE HELL IS THAT THING?!!
THAT'S SICK!
BOM
ZLIP
MONSTERS C-CAME OUT OF THAT MONSTER...
THE TOWN...
AAAAA
TH-THEY'RE... EATING PEOPLE!
ARE YOU KIDDING ME?!
RUN, RUN, RUN, RUN!
AHHHHHH
NOOO-OOO!
THIS HAS TO BE A PRANK!
THIS CAN'T BE REAL!
MOMMY!
AAAHH
WE'RE DONE FOR!

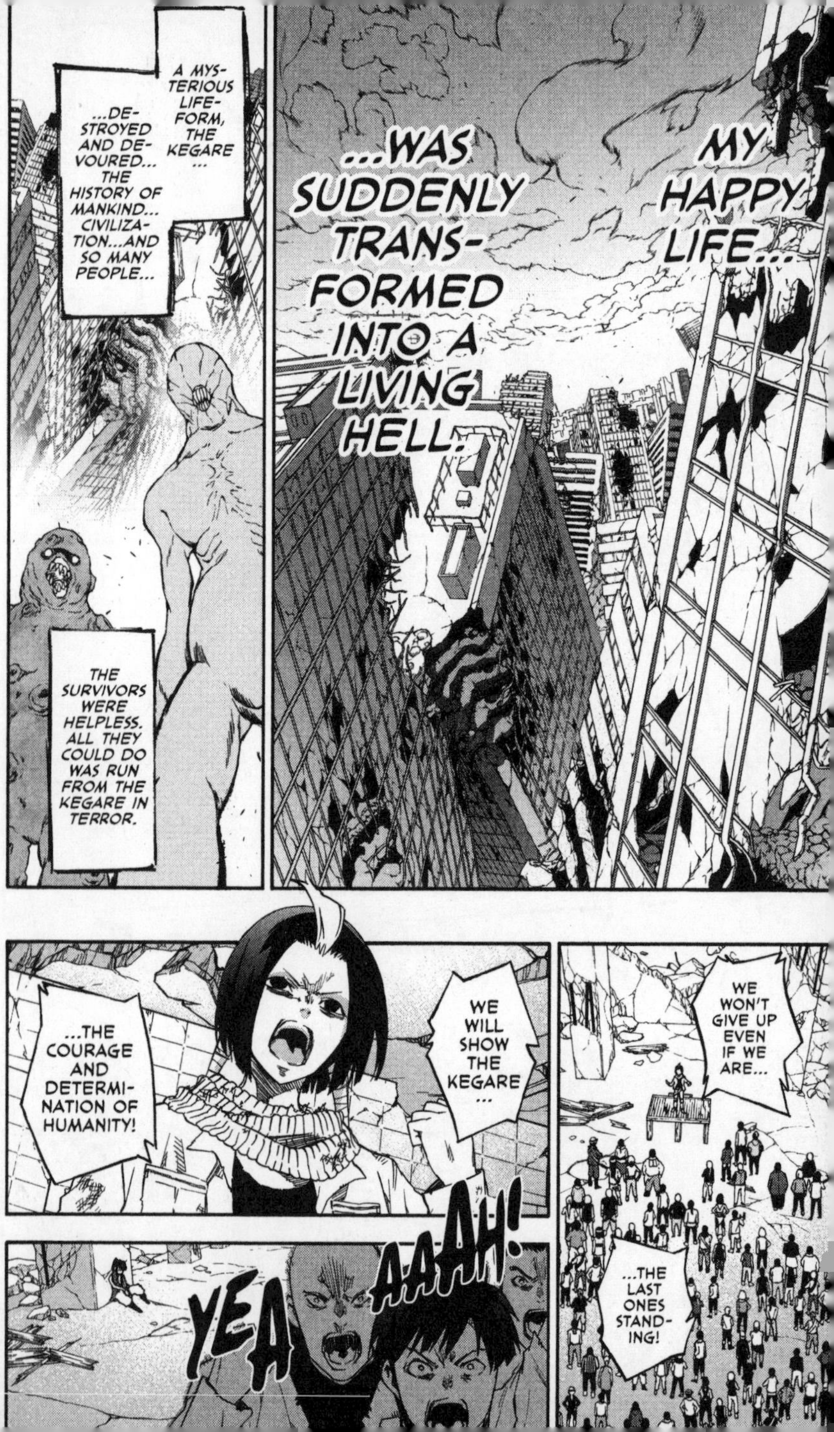
MY HAPPY LIFE...
...WAS SUDDENLY TRANSFORMED INTO A LIVING HELL.
A MYSTERIOUS LIFE-FORM, THE KEGARE...
...DESTROYED AND DEVOURED... THE HISTORY OF MANKIND... CIVILIZATION...AND SO MANY PEOPLE...
THE SURVIVORS WERE HELPLESS. ALL THEY COULD DO WAS RUN FROM THE KEGARE IN TERROR.
WE WON'T GIVE UP EVEN IF WE ARE...
...THE LAST ONES STANDING!
WE WILL SHOW THE KEGARE...
...THE COURAGE AND DETERMINATION OF HUMANITY!
YEAAAAH!

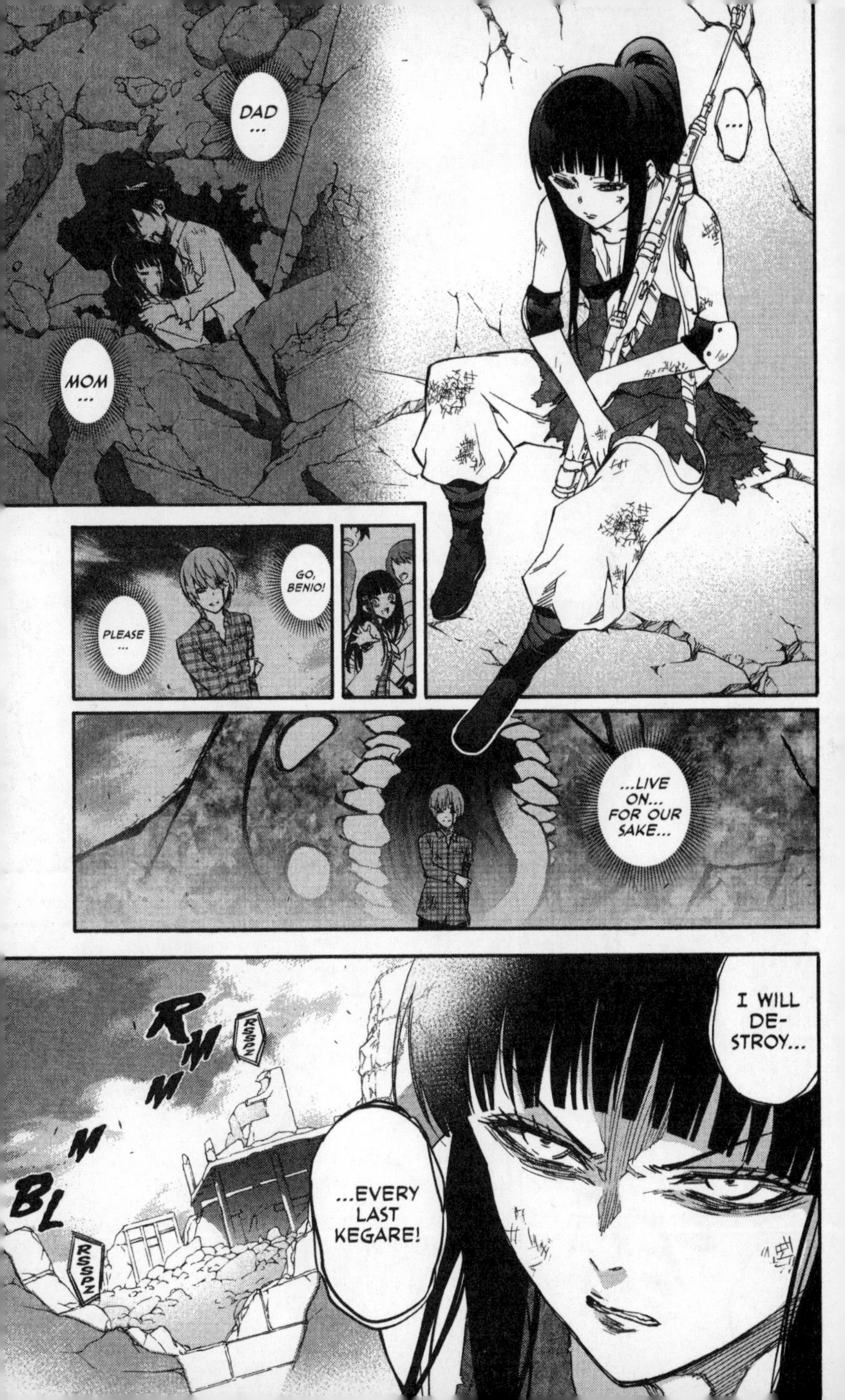
...
DAD ...
MOM ...
GO, BENIO!
PLEASE ...
...LIVE ON... FOR OUR SAKE...
I WILL DE-STROY...
...EVERY LAST KEGARE!
RSSPZ
RMMM
BLMM
RSSPZ

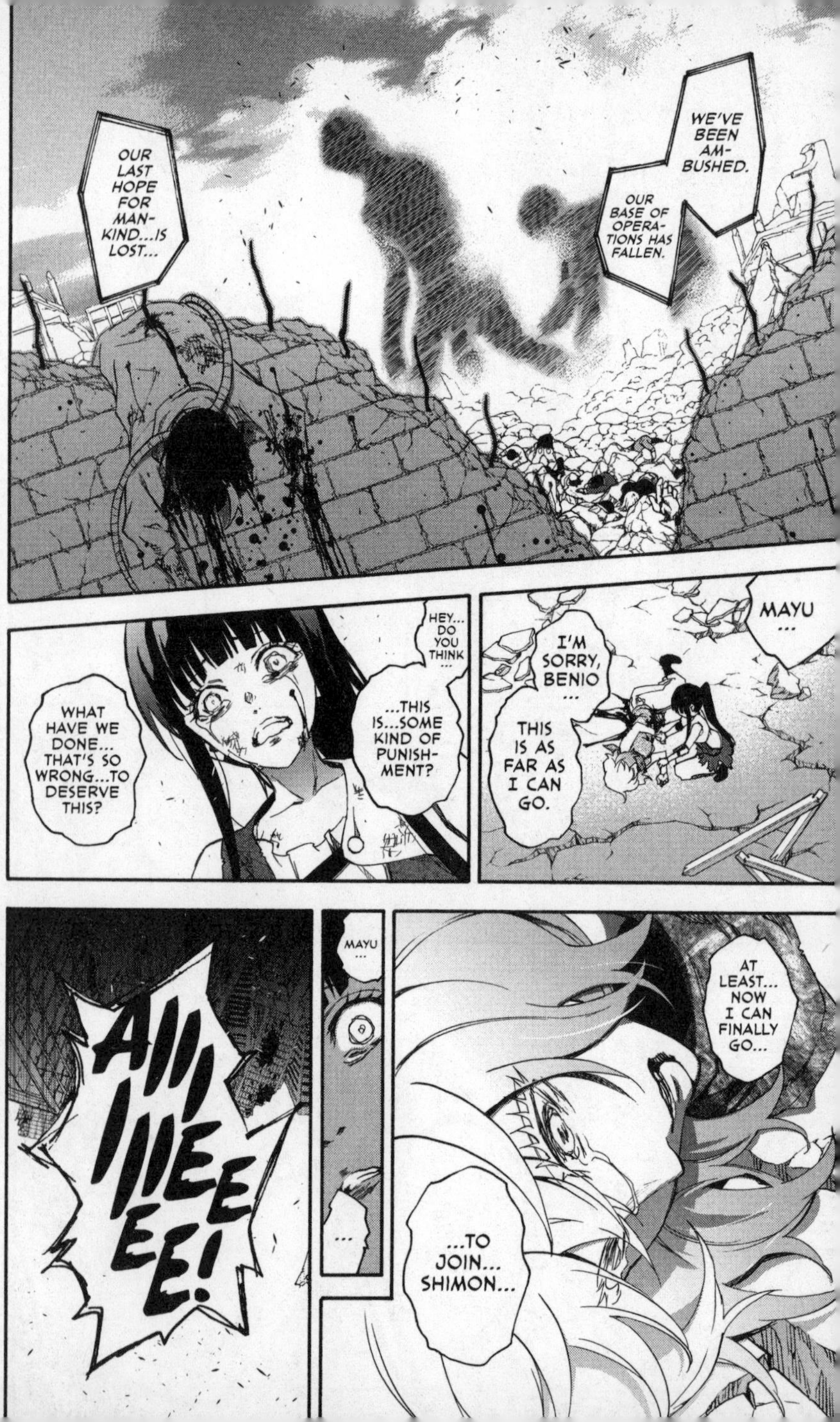
WE'VE BEEN AM-BUSHED.
OUR BASE OF OPERA-TIONS HAS FALLEN.
OUR LAST HOPE FOR MAN-KIND...IS LOST...
MAYU ...
I'M SORRY, BENIO ...
THIS IS AS FAR AS I CAN GO.
HEY... DO YOU THINK ...
...THIS IS...SOME KIND OF PUNISH-MENT?
WHAT HAVE WE DONE... THAT'S SO WRONG...TO DESERVE THIS?
AT LEAST... NOW I CAN FINALLY GO...
...TO JOIN... SHIMON...
MAYU ...
...
AIIIIIEEEEEEE!

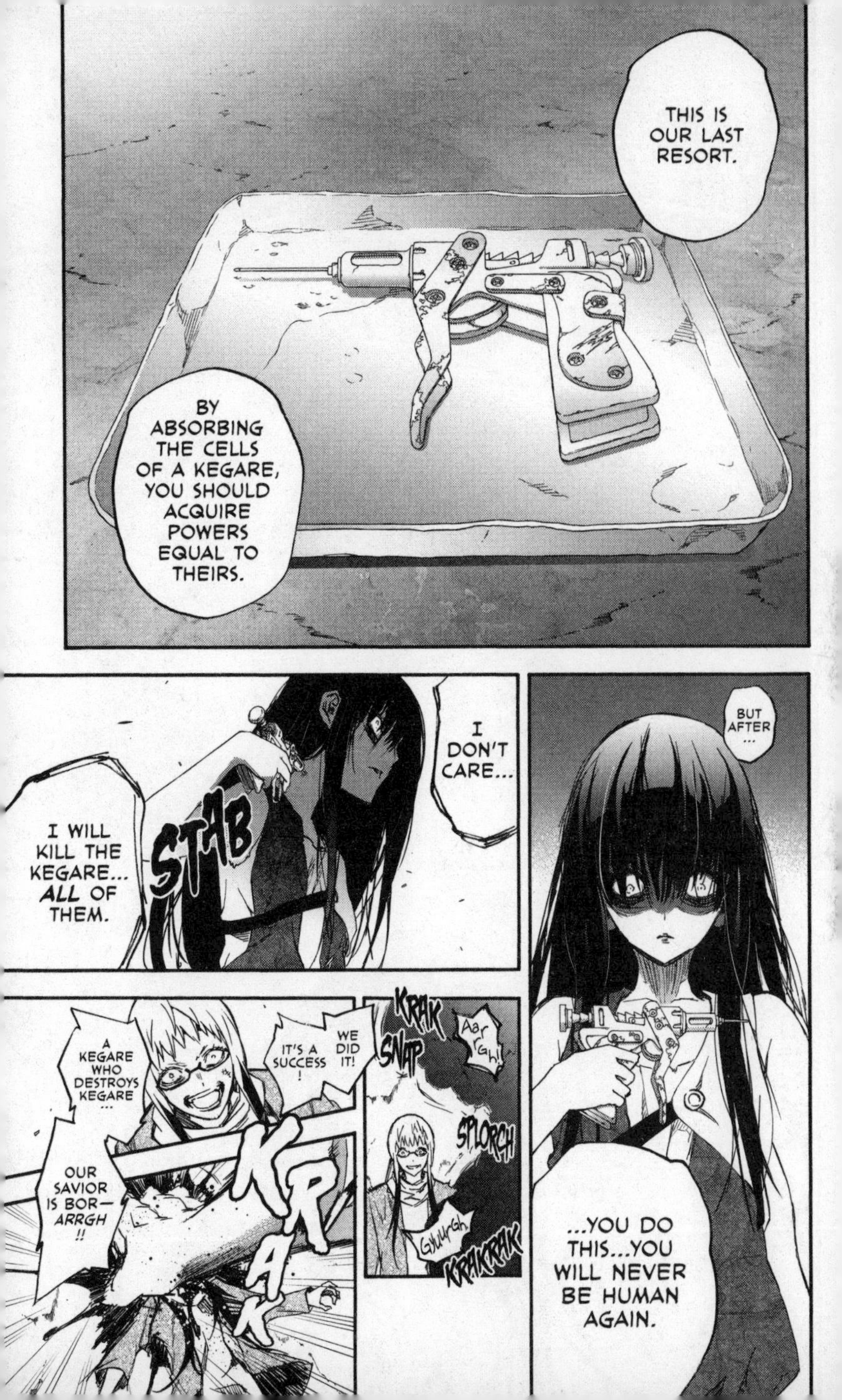
THIS IS OUR LAST RESORT.
BY ABSORBING THE CELLS OF A KEGARE, YOU SHOULD ACQUIRE POWERS EQUAL TO THEIRS.
BUT AFTER...
...YOU DO THIS...YOU WILL NEVER BE HUMAN AGAIN.
I DON'T CARE...
STAB
I WILL KILL THE KEGARE... *ALL* OF THEM.
KRAK
Aargh!
SNAP
SPLORCH
Gyuurgh
KRAKRAK
WE DID IT!
IT'S A SUCCESS!
A KEGARE WHO DESTROYS KEGARE...
OUR SAVIOR IS BOR— *ARRGH*!!
KRAK

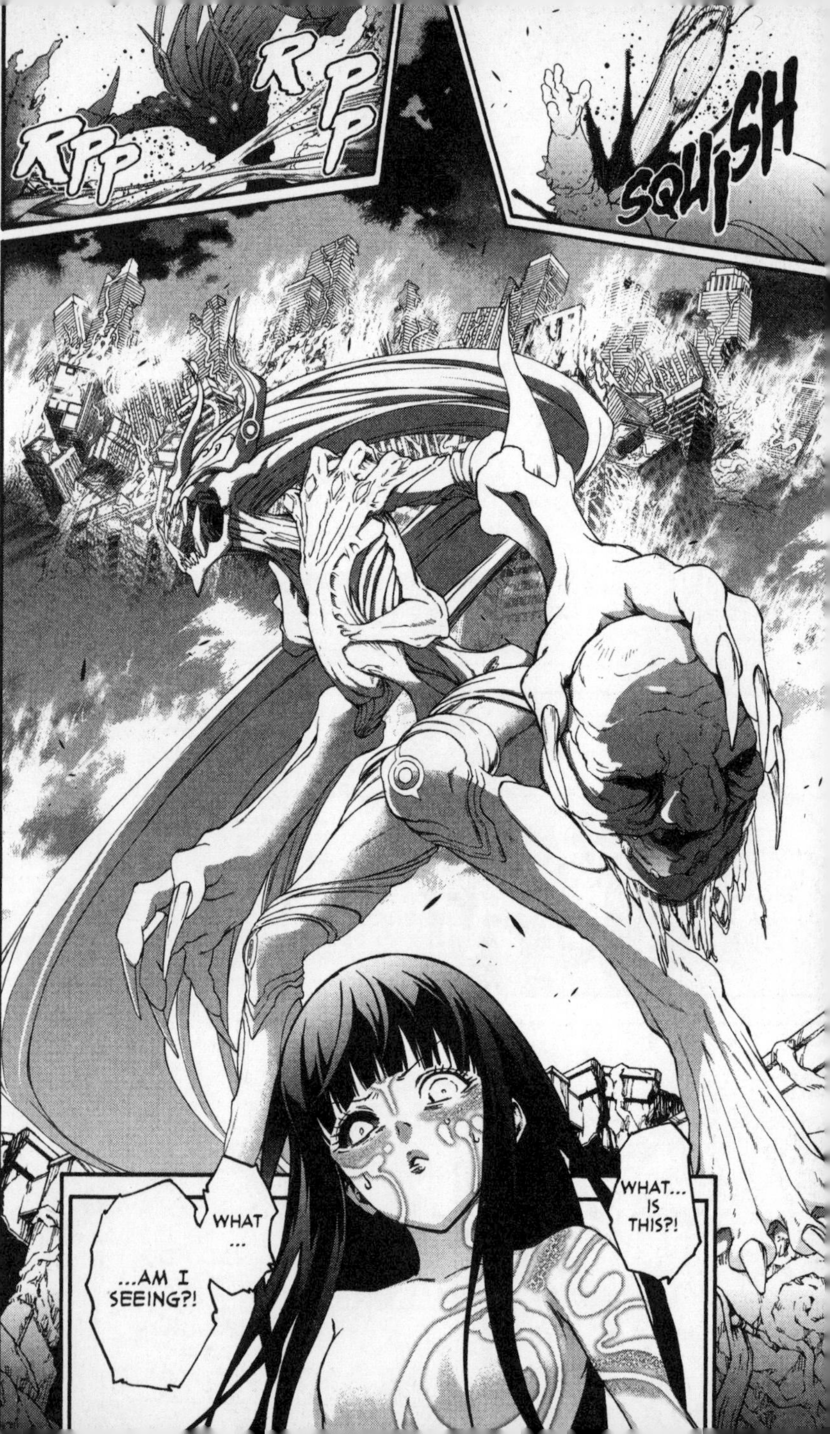
SQUISH
RPP
RPP
WHAT... IS THIS?!
WHAT ...
...AM I SEEING?!

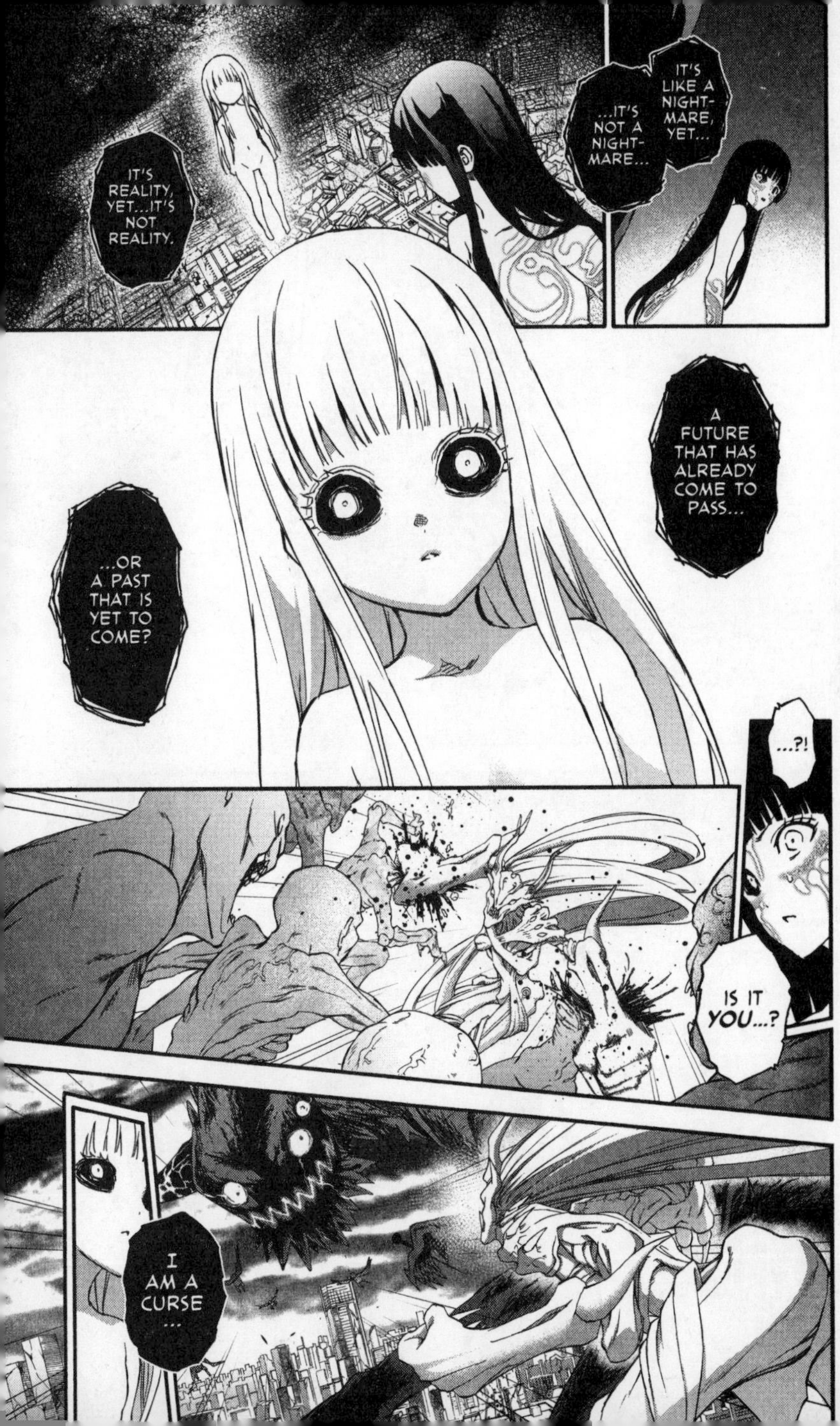
IT'S LIKE A NIGHT-MARE, YET...
...IT'S NOT A NIGHT-MARE...
IT'S REALITY, YET...IT'S NOT REALITY.
A FUTURE THAT HAS ALREADY COME TO PASS...
...OR A PAST THAT IS YET TO COME?
...?!
IS IT *YOU*...?
I AM A CURSE ...

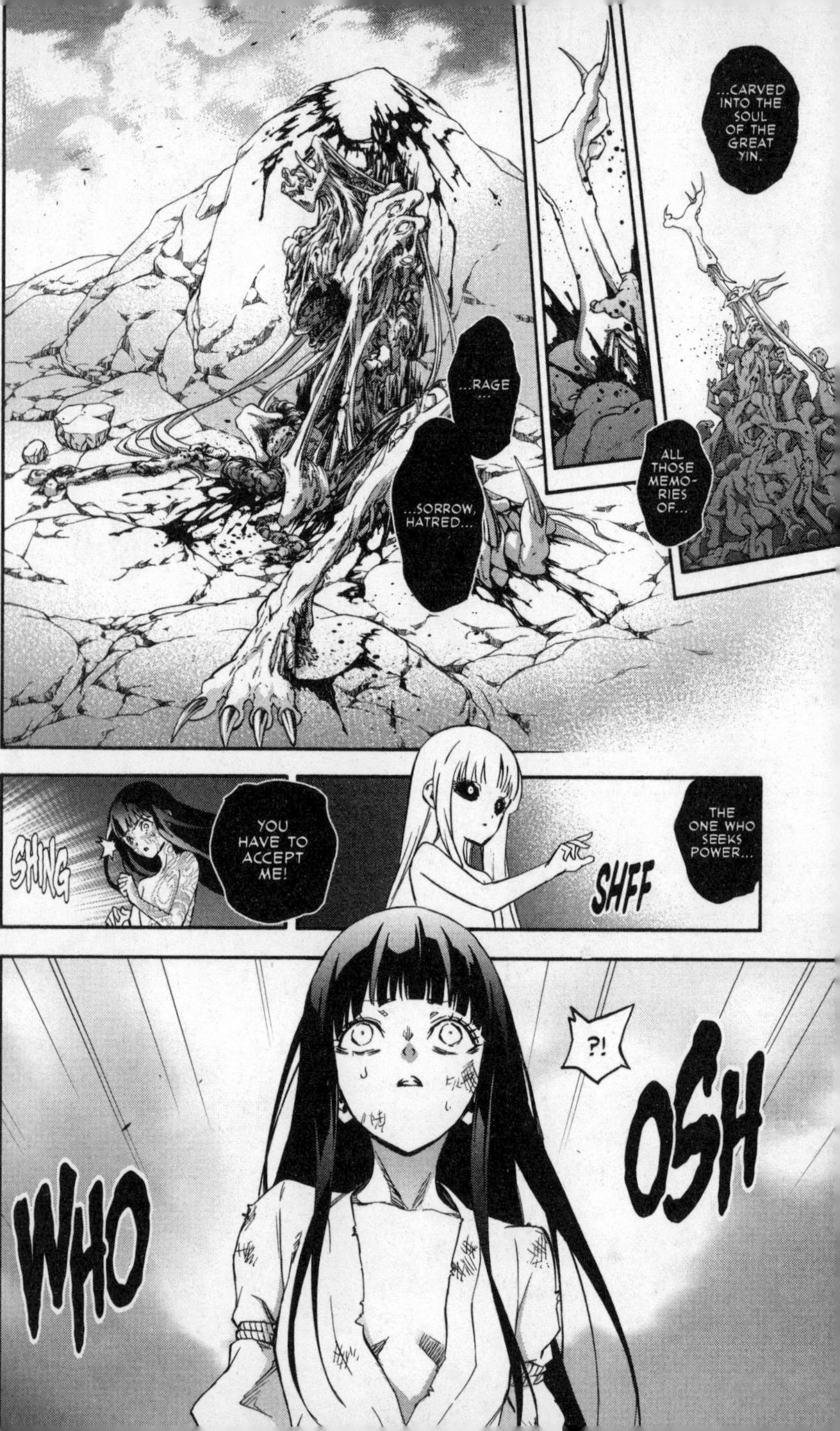
ALL THOSE MEMORIES OF...
...RAGE...
...SORROW, HATRED...
...CARVED INTO THE SOUL OF THE GREAT YIN.
THE ONE WHO SEEKS POWER...
SHFF
YOU HAVE TO ACCEPT ME!
SHING
?!
WHO
OSH

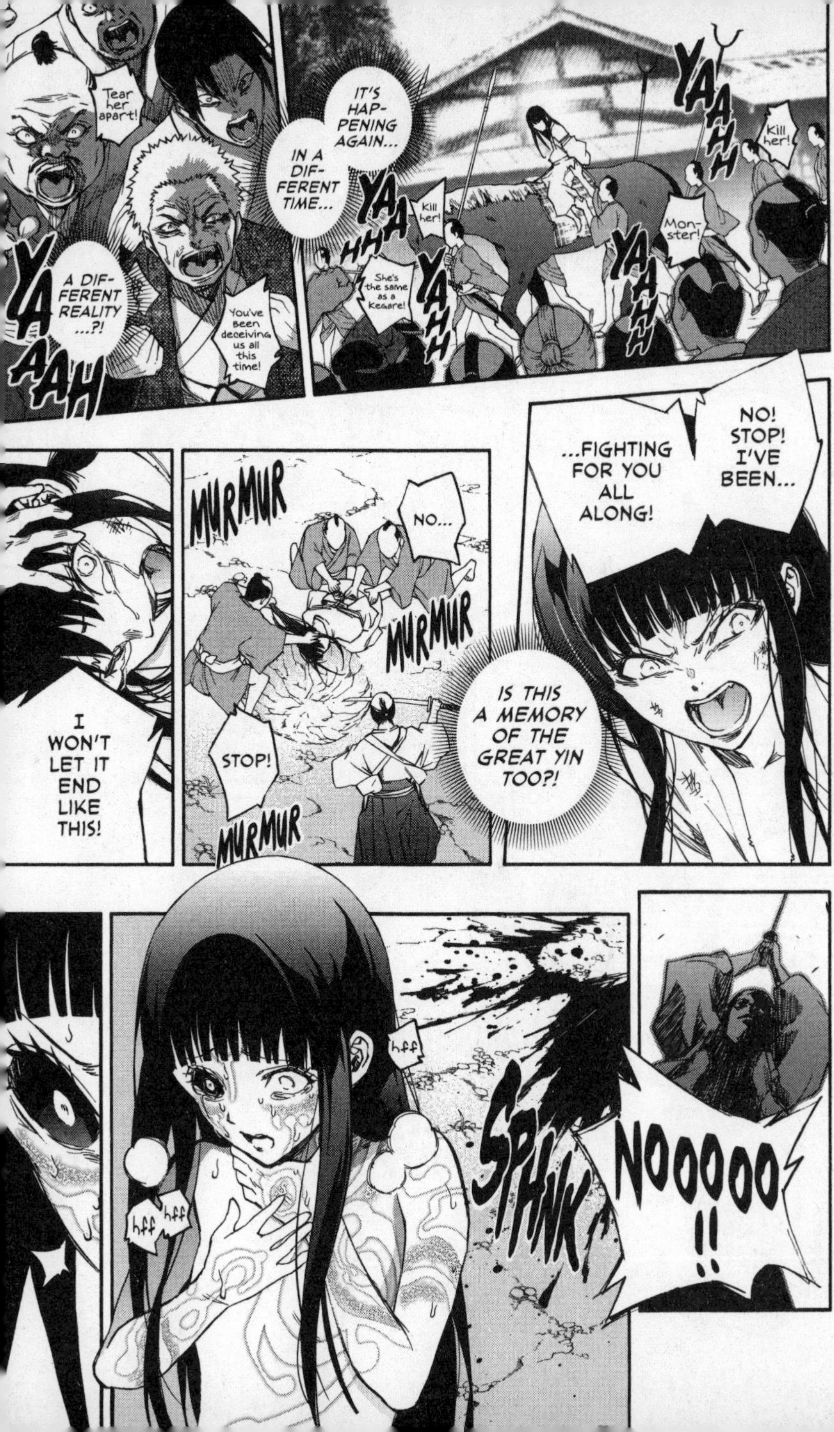
YAAHH
Kill her!
Monster!
YAAHH
Kill her!
YAAHH
YAAHH
She's the same as a Kegare!
IT'S HAPPENING AGAIN...
IN A DIFFERENT TIME...
Tear her apart!
A DIFFERENT REALITY...?!
You've been deceiving us all this time!
YAAAAH
NO! STOP! I'VE BEEN...
...FIGHTING FOR YOU ALL ALONG!
IS THIS A MEMORY OF THE GREAT YIN TOO?!
MURMUR
NO...
MURMUR
STOP!
MURMUR
I WON'T LET IT END LIKE THIS!
NOOOOO!!
SPHNK
hff
hff hff

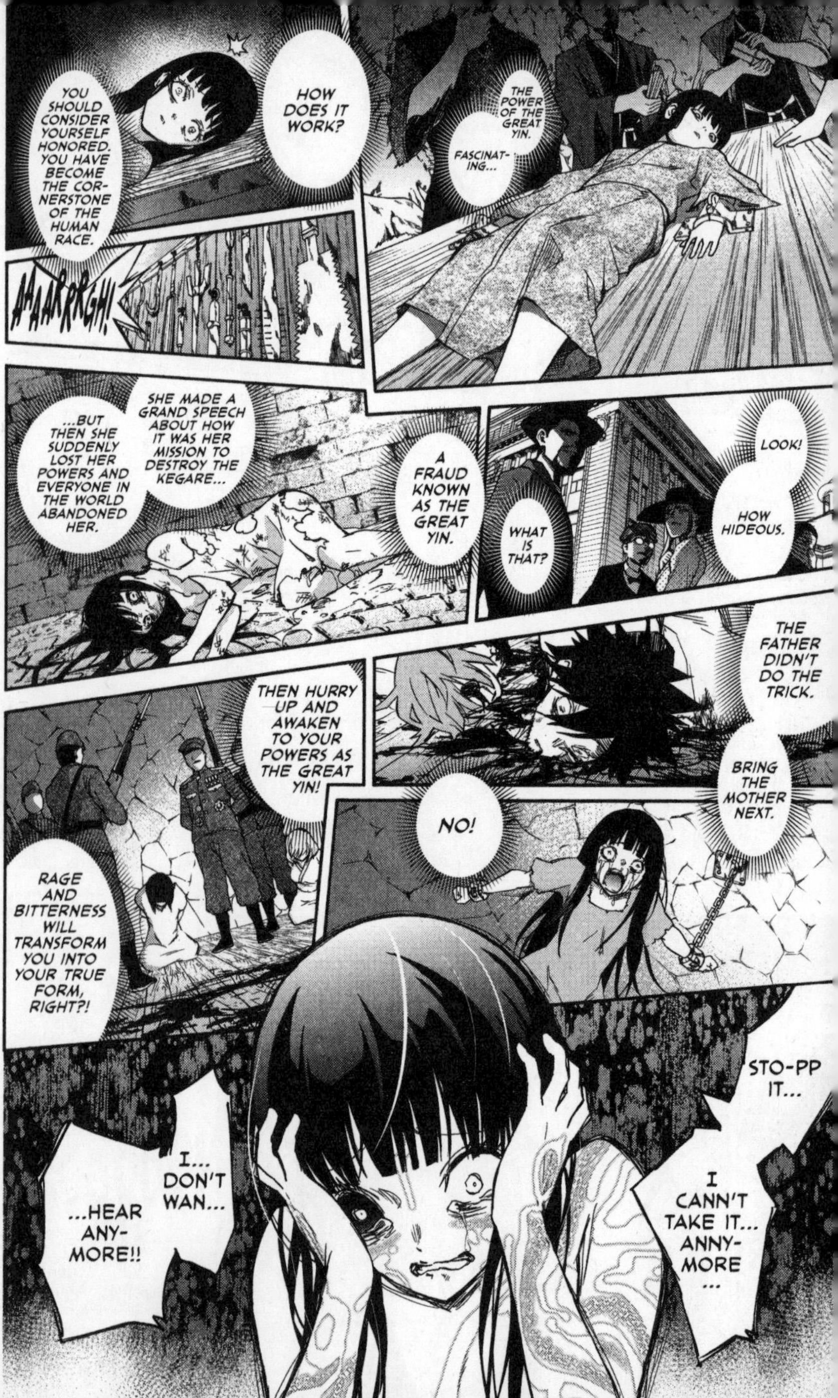
THE POWER OF THE GREAT YIN.
FASCINATING...
HOW DOES IT WORK?
YOU SHOULD CONSIDER YOURSELF HONORED. YOU HAVE BECOME THE CORNERSTONE OF THE HUMAN RACE.
AAAARRRGH!
LOOK!
HOW HIDEOUS.
WHAT IS THAT?
A FRAUD KNOWN AS THE GREAT YIN.
SHE MADE A GRAND SPEECH ABOUT HOW IT WAS HER MISSION TO DESTROY THE KEGARE...
...BUT THEN SHE SUDDENLY LOST HER POWERS AND EVERYONE IN THE WORLD ABANDONED HER.
THE FATHER DIDN'T DO THE TRICK.
BRING THE MOTHER NEXT.
NO!
THEN HURRY UP AND AWAKEN TO YOUR POWERS AS THE GREAT YIN!
RAGE AND BITTERNESS WILL TRANSFORM YOU INTO YOUR TRUE FORM, RIGHT?!
STO-PP IT...
I CANN'T TAKE IT... ANNY-MORE...
I... DON'T WAN...
...HEAR ANYMORE!!

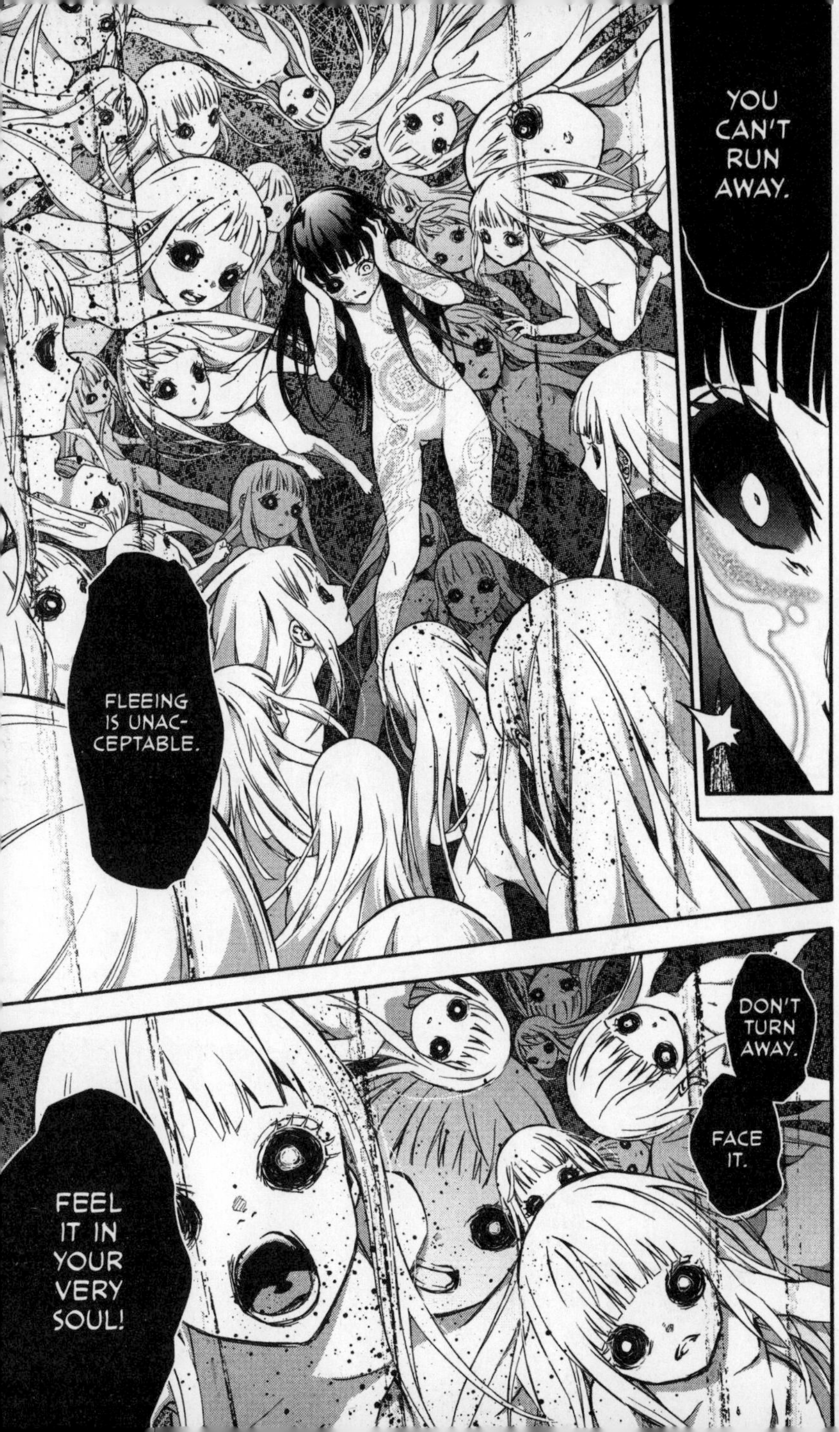
YOU CAN'T RUN AWAY.
FLEEING IS UNACCEPTABLE.
DON'T TURN AWAY.
FACE IT.
FEEL IT IN YOUR VERY SOUL!

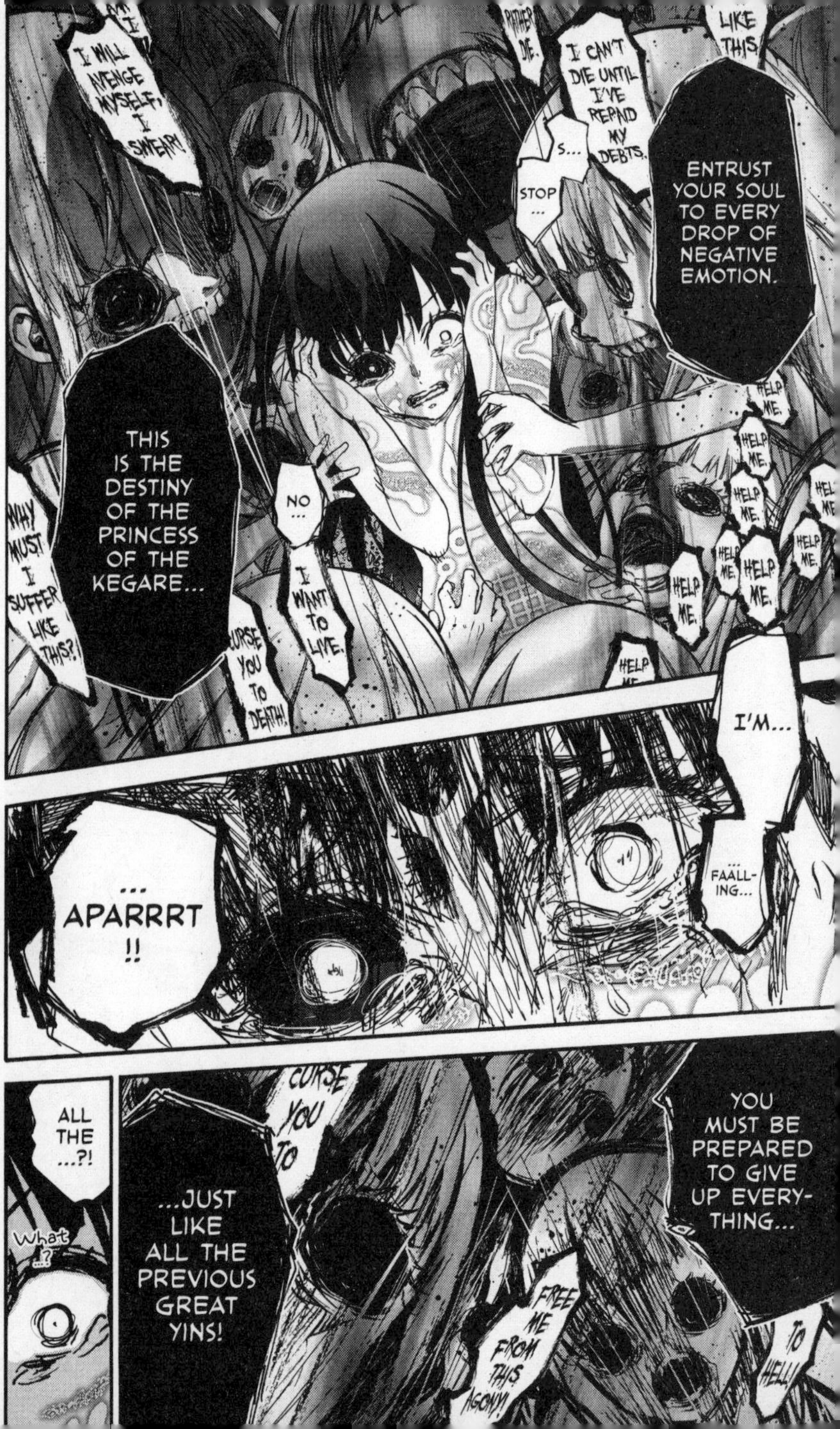
LIKE THIS.
ENTRUST YOUR SOUL TO EVERY DROP OF NEGATIVE EMOTION.
I CAN'T DIE UNTIL I'VE REPAID MY DEBTS.
RATHER DIE.
S... STOP...
I
I WILL AVENGE MYSELF, I SWEAR!
HELP ME.
HELP ME.
HELP ME.
HELP ME.
HELP ME.
HELP ME.
HELP ME.
HELP ME.
HELP
NO...
I WANT TO LIVE.
CURSE YOU TO DEATH!
THIS IS THE DESTINY OF THE PRINCESS OF THE KEGARE...
WHY MUST I SUFFER LIKE THIS?!
I'M...
...FAALL-ING...
...APARRRT!!
YOU MUST BE PREPARED TO GIVE UP EVERY-THING...
CURSE YOU TO
TO HELL!
FREE ME FROM THIS AGONY!
...JUST LIKE ALL THE PREVIOUS GREAT YINS!
ALL THE ...?!
What ...?

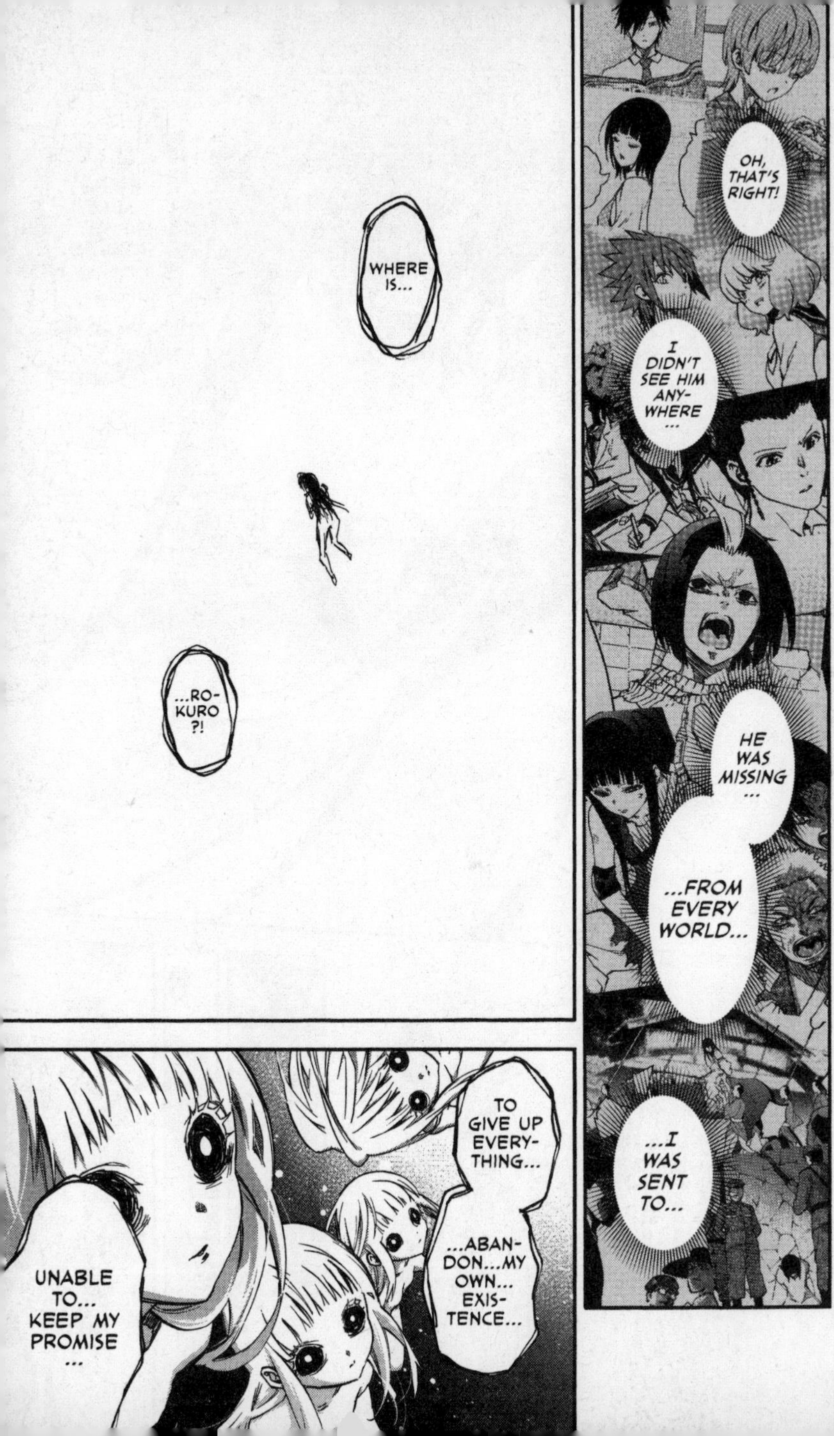
OH, THAT'S RIGHT!
I DIDN'T SEE HIM ANY-WHERE...
HE WAS MISSING...
...FROM EVERY WORLD...
...I WAS SENT TO...
WHERE IS...
...RO-KURO?!
TO GIVE UP EVERY-THING...
...ABAN-DON...MY OWN... EXIS-TENCE...
UNABLE TO... KEEP MY PROMISE...

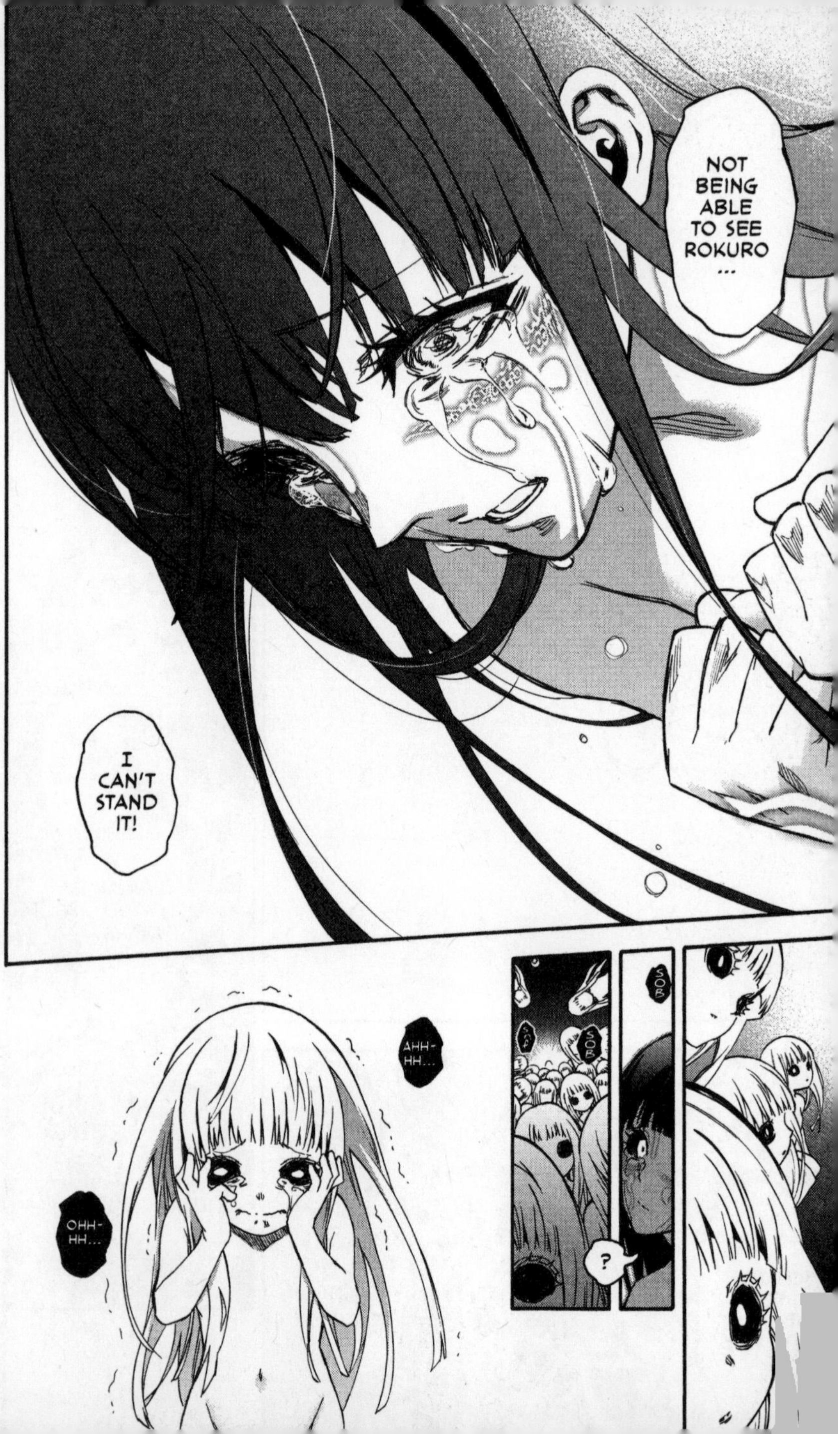
NOT BEING ABLE TO SEE ROKURO ...
I CAN'T STAND IT!
SOB
?
snf
SOB
AHHHH...
OHHHH...

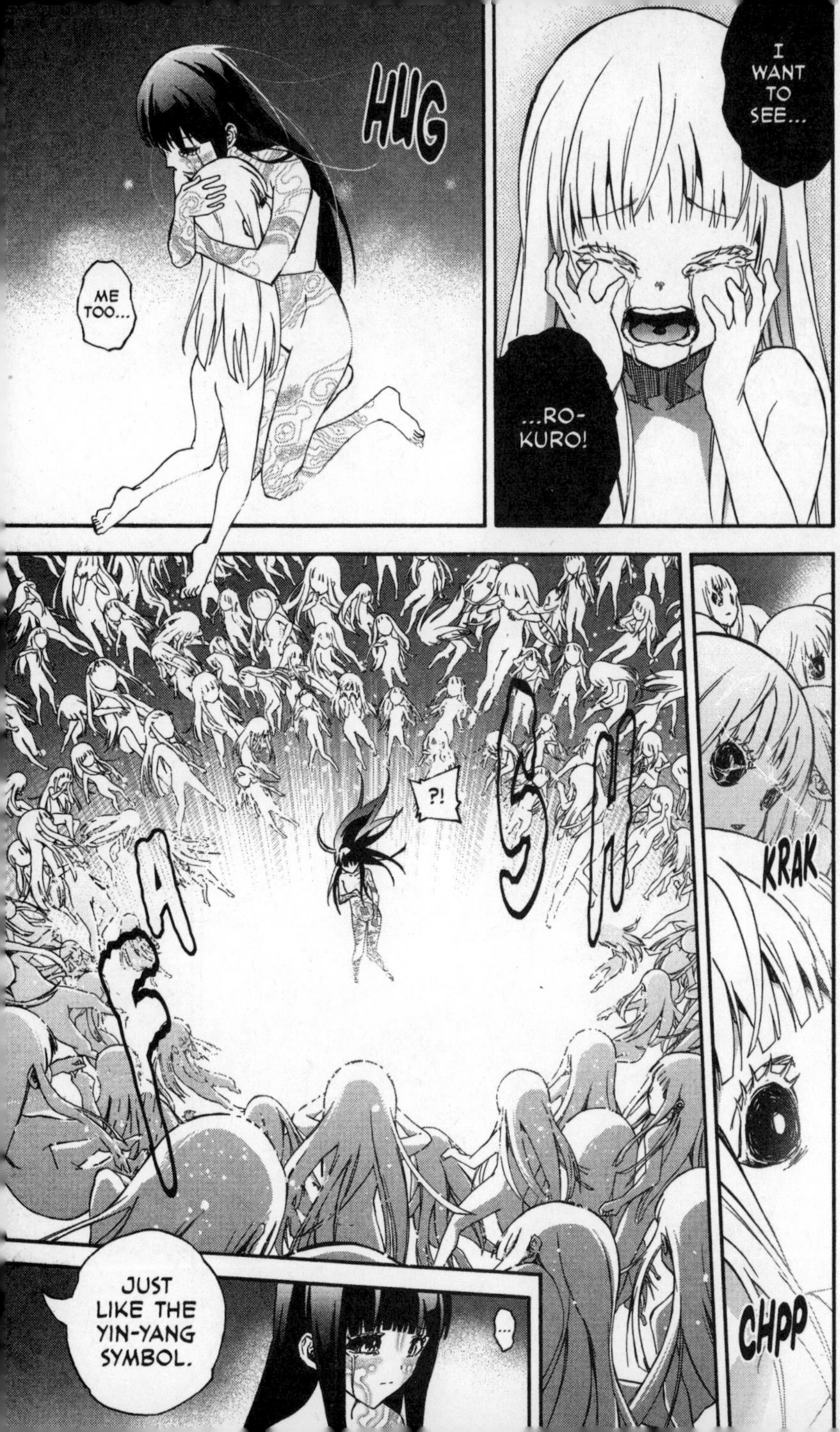
I WANT TO SEE...
...RO-KURO!
HUG
ME TOO...
KRAK
CHPP
?!
...
JUST LIKE THE YIN-YANG SYMBOL.

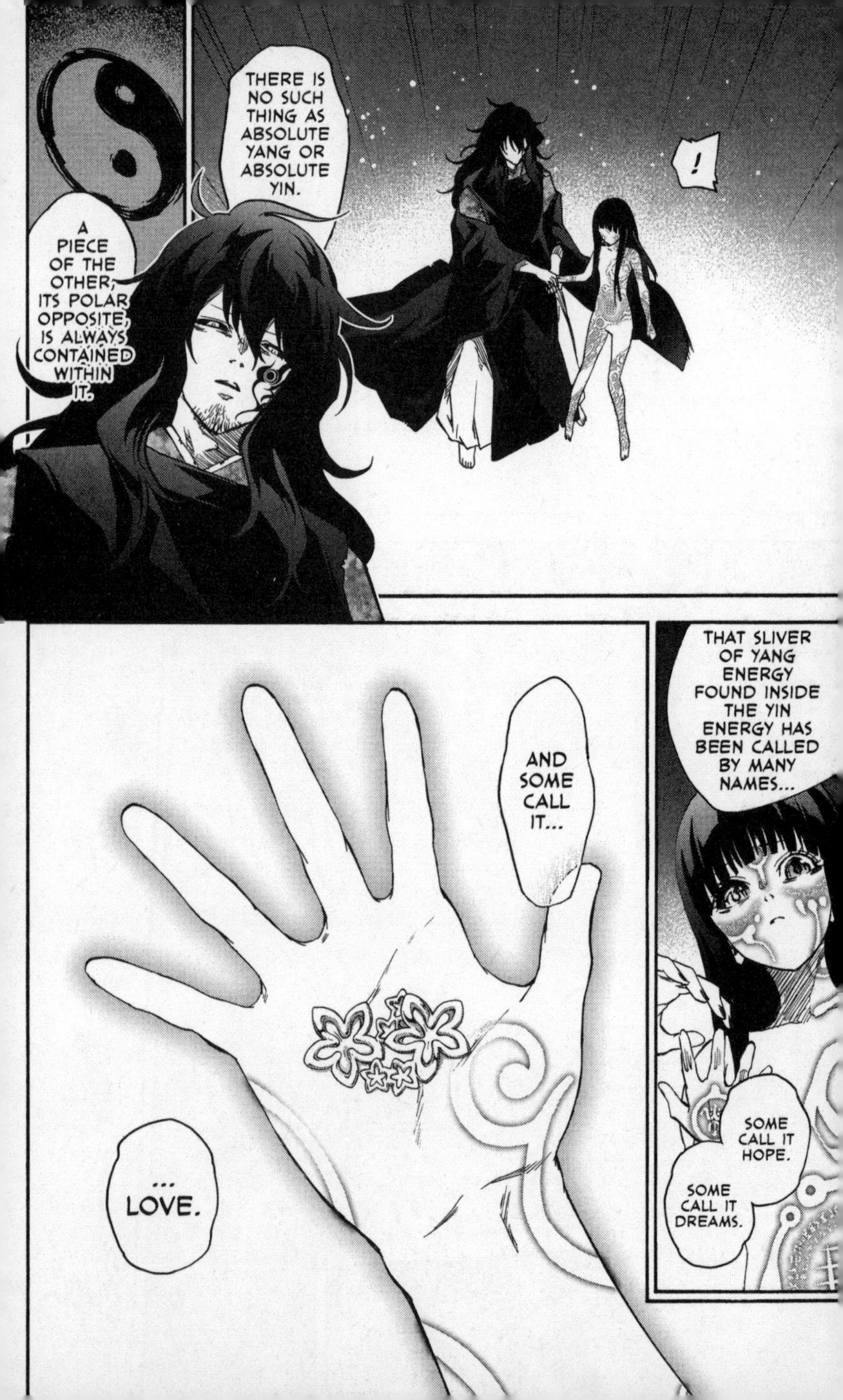
!
THERE IS NO SUCH THING AS ABSOLUTE YANG OR ABSOLUTE YIN.
A PIECE OF THE OTHER, ITS POLAR OPPOSITE, IS ALWAYS CONTAINED WITHIN IT.
THAT SLIVER OF YANG ENERGY FOUND INSIDE THE YIN ENERGY HAS BEEN CALLED BY MANY NAMES...
SOME CALL IT HOPE.
SOME CALL IT DREAMS.
AND SOME CALL IT...
...LOVE.

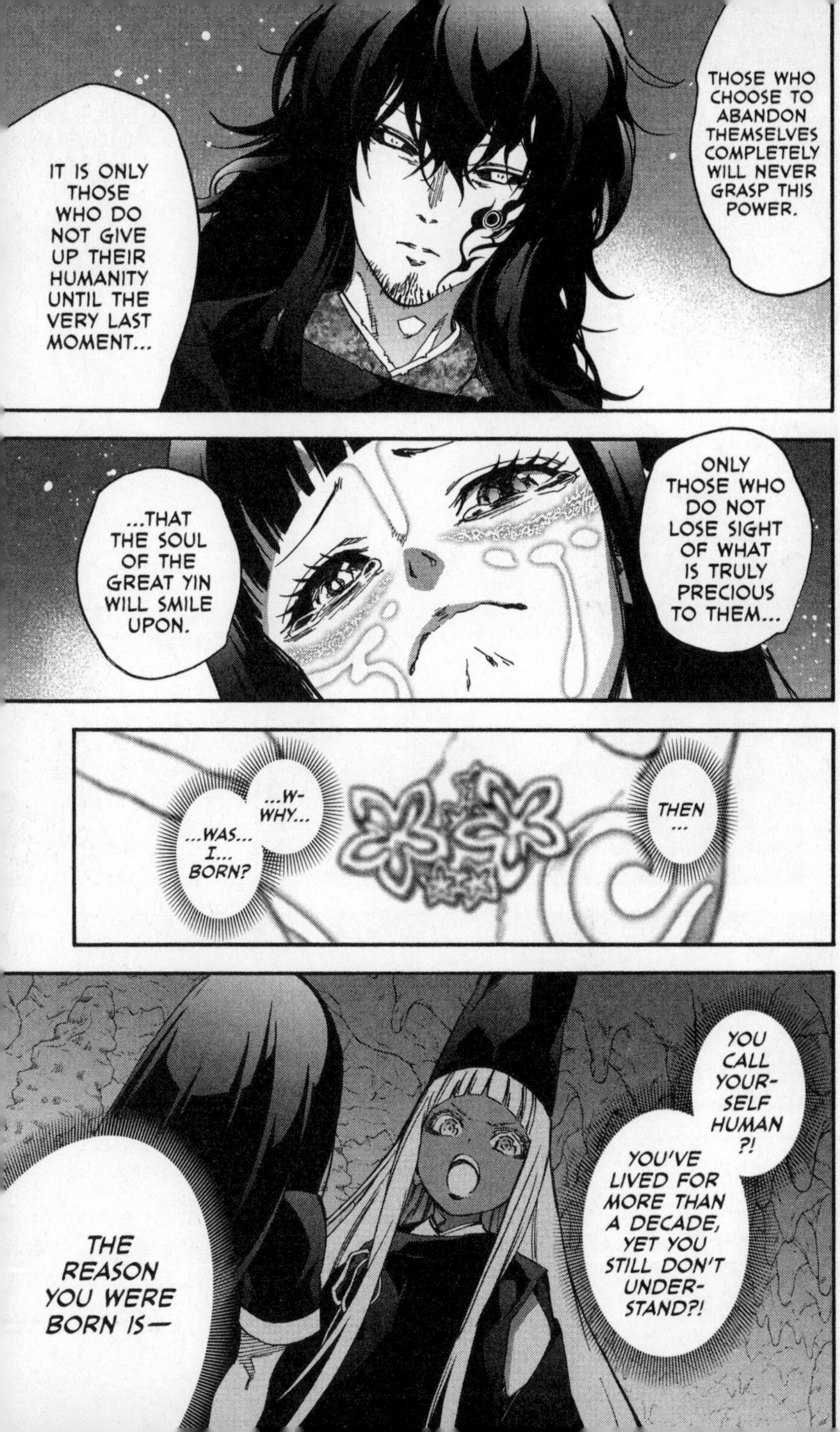
THOSE WHO CHOOSE TO ABANDON THEMSELVES COMPLETELY WILL NEVER GRASP THIS POWER.
IT IS ONLY THOSE WHO DO NOT GIVE UP THEIR HUMANITY UNTIL THE VERY LAST MOMENT...
ONLY THOSE WHO DO NOT LOSE SIGHT OF WHAT IS TRULY PRECIOUS TO THEM...
...THAT THE SOUL OF THE GREAT YIN WILL SMILE UPON.
THEN ...
...W-WHY...
...WAS... I... BORN?
YOU CALL YOUR-SELF HUMAN ?!
YOU'VE LIVED FOR MORE THAN A DECADE, YET YOU STILL DON'T UNDER-STAND?!
THE REASON YOU WERE BORN IS—

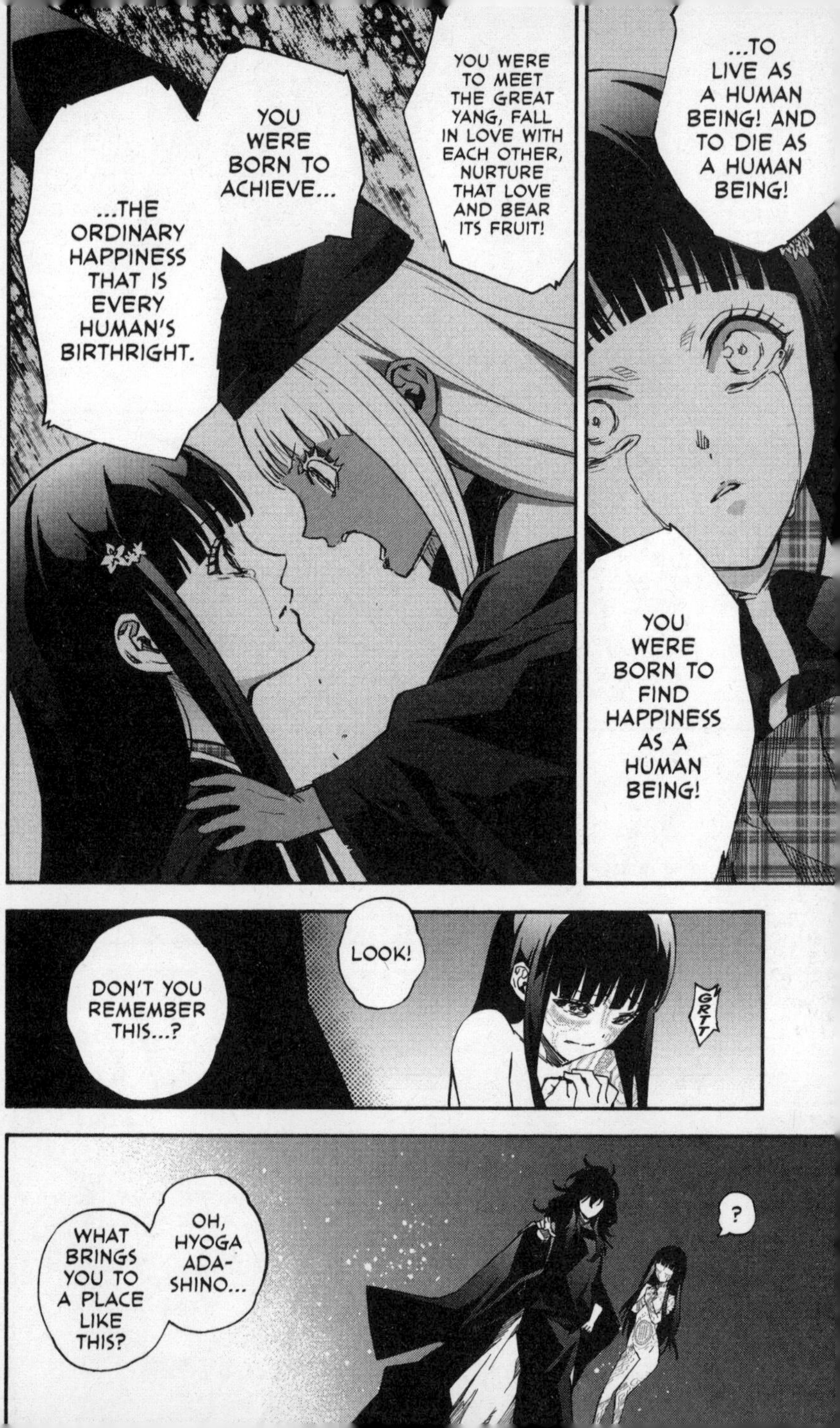
...TO LIVE AS A HUMAN BEING! AND TO DIE AS A HUMAN BEING!
YOU WERE BORN TO FIND HAPPINESS AS A HUMAN BEING!
YOU WERE TO MEET THE GREAT YANG, FALL IN LOVE WITH EACH OTHER, NURTURE THAT LOVE AND BEAR ITS FRUIT!
YOU WERE BORN TO ACHIEVE...
...THE ORDINARY HAPPINESS THAT IS EVERY HUMAN'S BIRTHRIGHT.
GRTT
LOOK!
DON'T YOU REMEMBER THIS...?
?
OH, HYOGA ADA-SHINO...
WHAT BRINGS YOU TO A PLACE LIKE THIS?

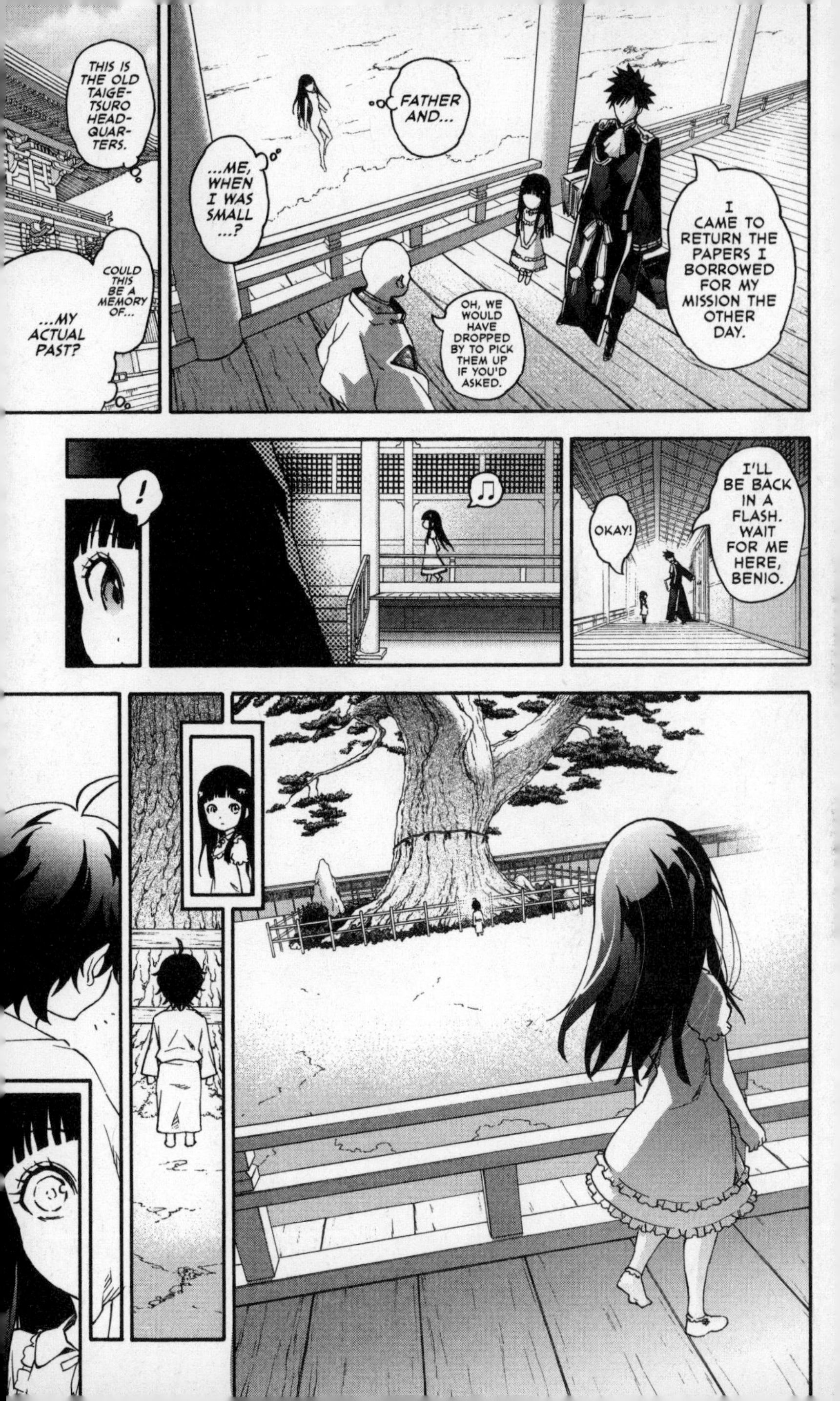
FATHER AND...
...ME, WHEN I WAS SMALL...?
I CAME TO RETURN THE PAPERS I BORROWED FOR MY MISSION THE OTHER DAY.
OH, WE WOULD HAVE DROPPED BY TO PICK THEM UP IF YOU'D ASKED.
THIS IS THE OLD TAIGE-TSURO HEAD-QUAR-TERS.
COULD THIS BE A MEMORY OF...
...MY ACTUAL PAST?
I'LL BE BACK IN A FLASH. WAIT FOR ME HERE, BENIO.
OKAY!
♫
!

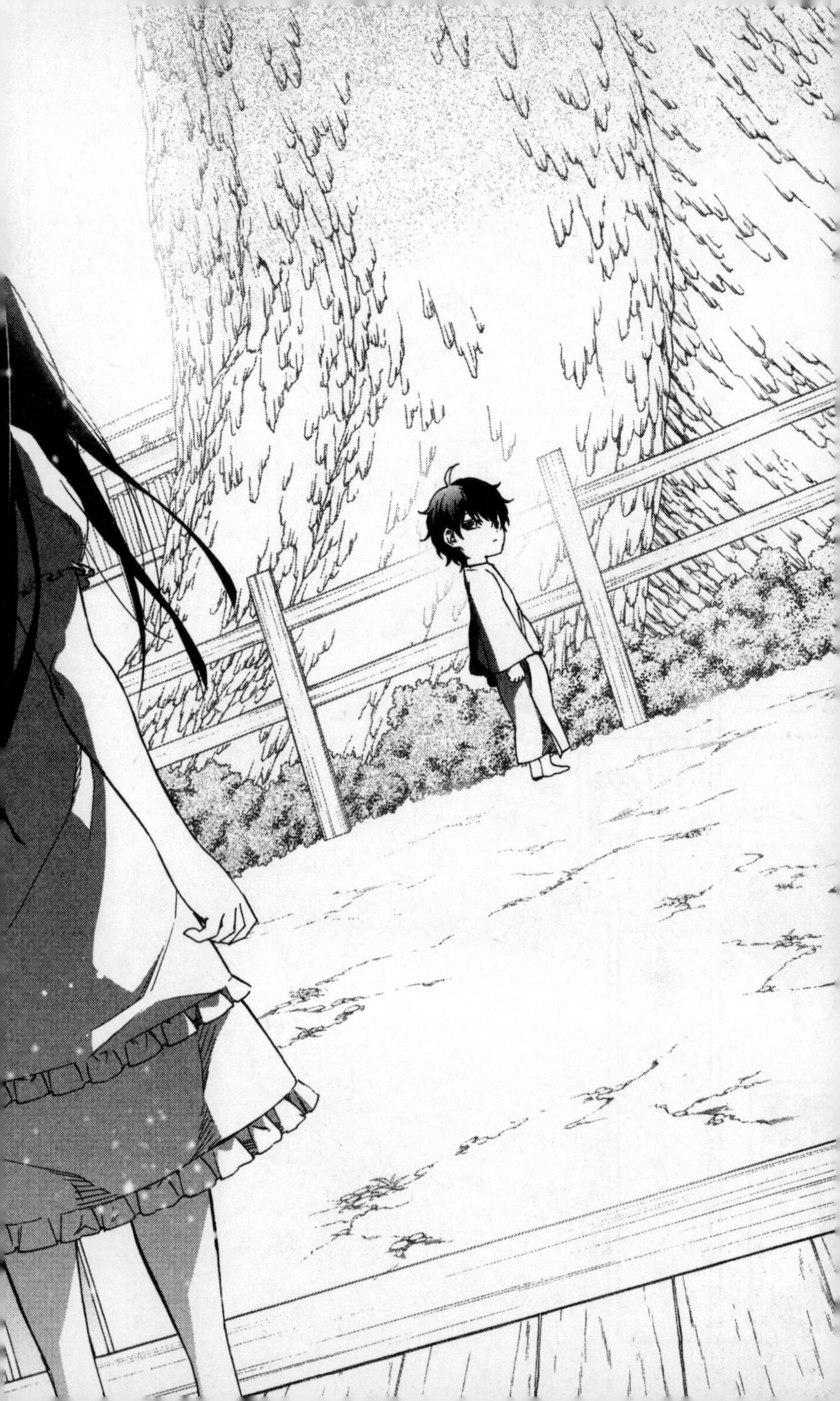

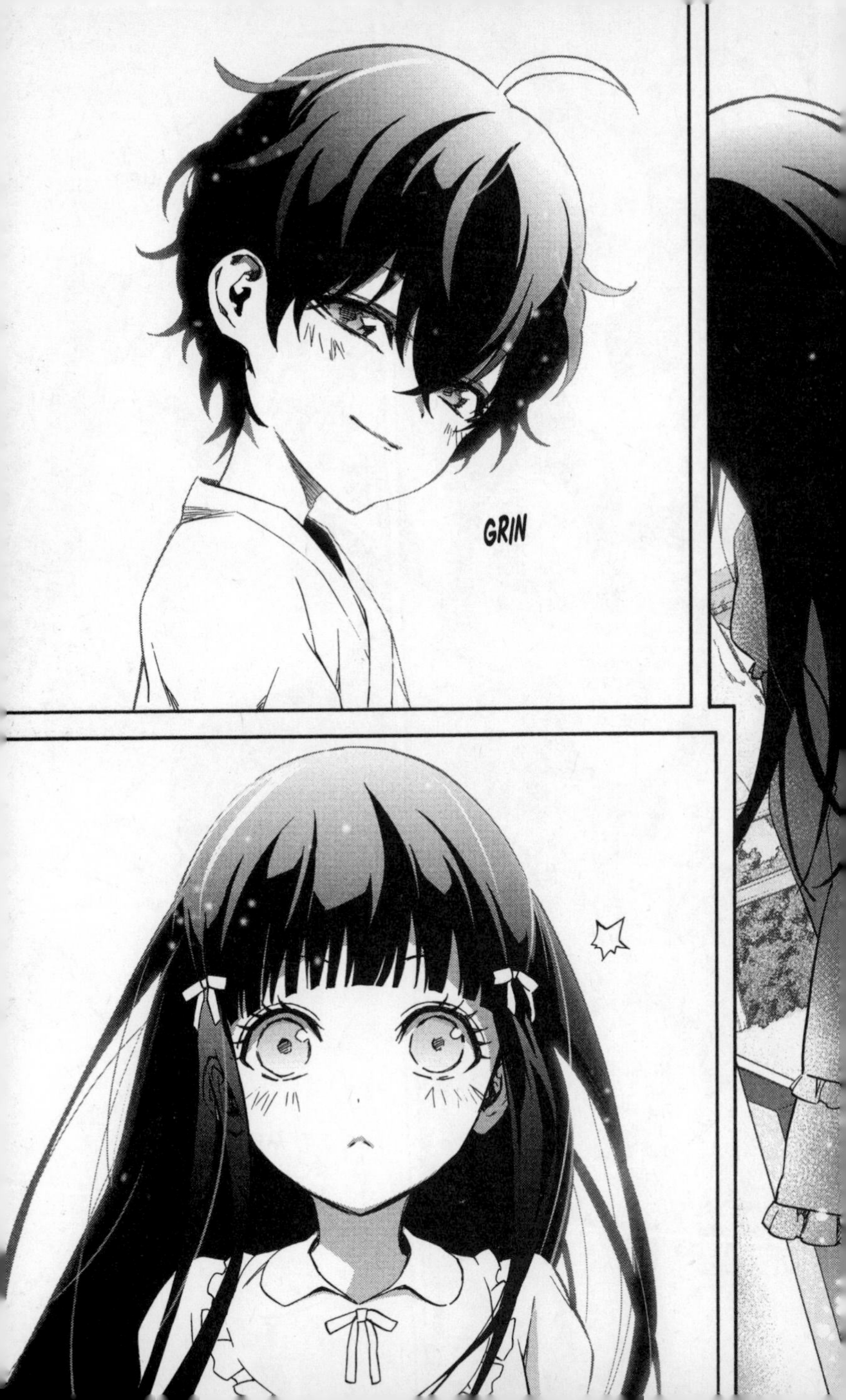
GRIN

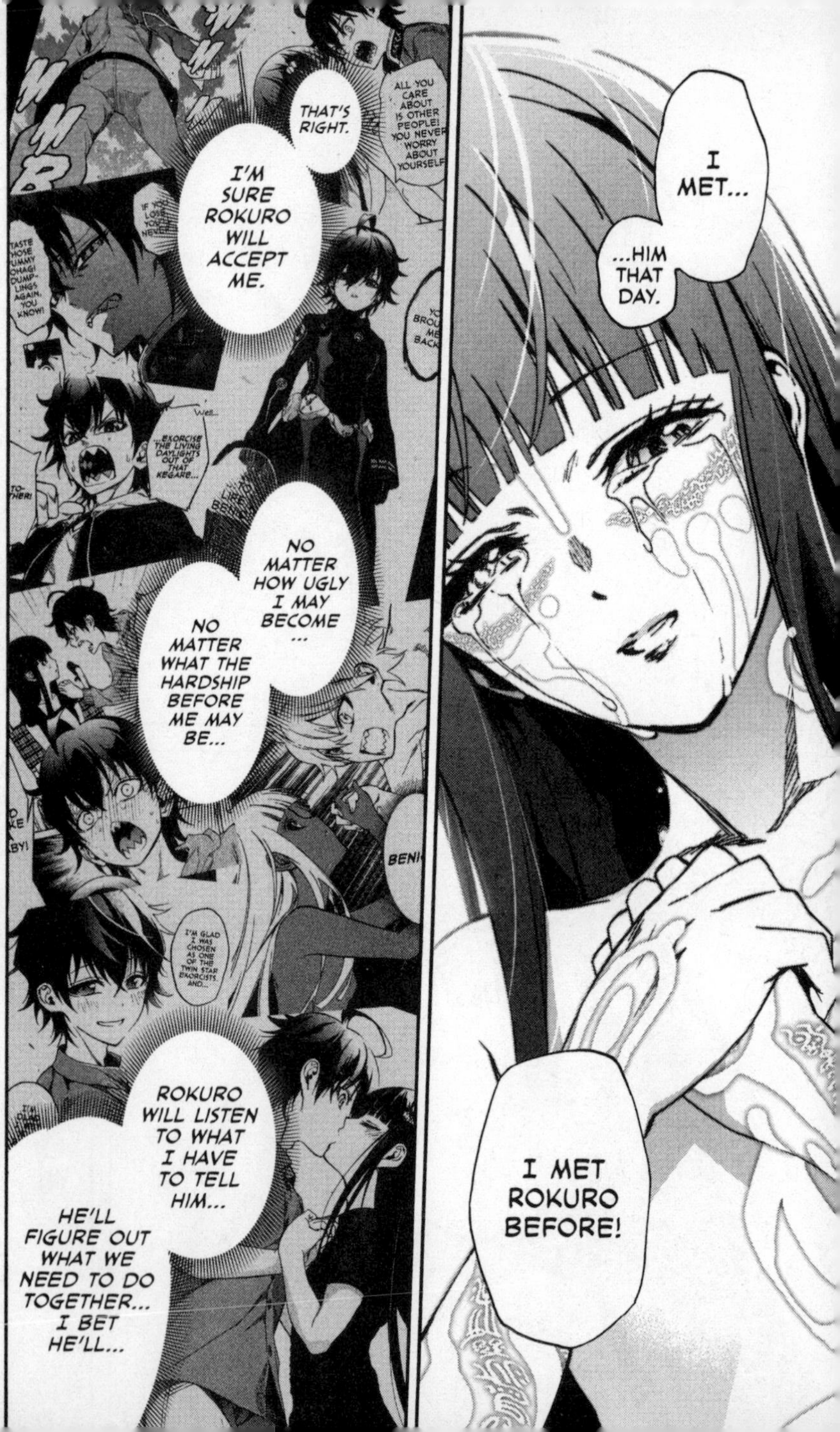
I MET...
...HIM THAT DAY.
I MET ROKURO BEFORE!
ALL YOU CARE ABOUT IS OTHER PEOPLE! YOU NEVER WORRY ABOUT YOURSELF!
THAT'S RIGHT.
I'M SURE ROKURO WILL ACCEPT ME.
Well...
...EXORCISE THE LIVING DAYLIGHTS OUT OF THAT KEGARE...
NO MATTER HOW UGLY I MAY BECOME...
NO MATTER WHAT THE HARDSHIP BEFORE ME MAY BE...
I'M GLAD I WAS CHOSEN AS ONE OF THE TWIN STAR EXORCISTS. AND...
ROKURO WILL LISTEN TO WHAT I HAVE TO TELL HIM...
HE'LL FIGURE OUT WHAT WE NEED TO DO TOGETHER... I BET HE'LL...

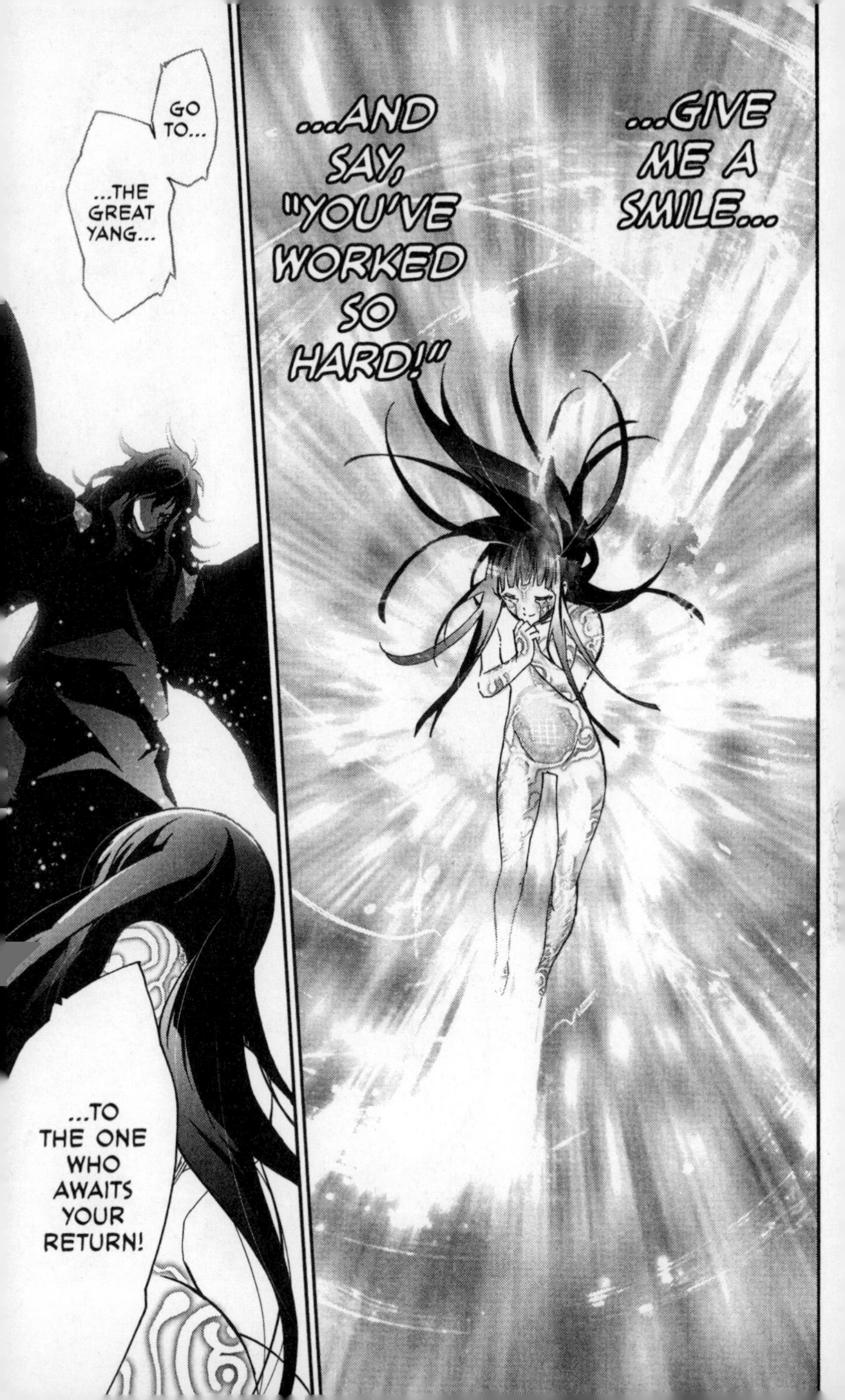
...GIVE ME A SMILE...
...AND SAY, "YOU'VE WORKED SO HARD!"
GO TO...
...THE GREAT YANG...
...TO THE ONE WHO AWAITS YOUR RETURN!

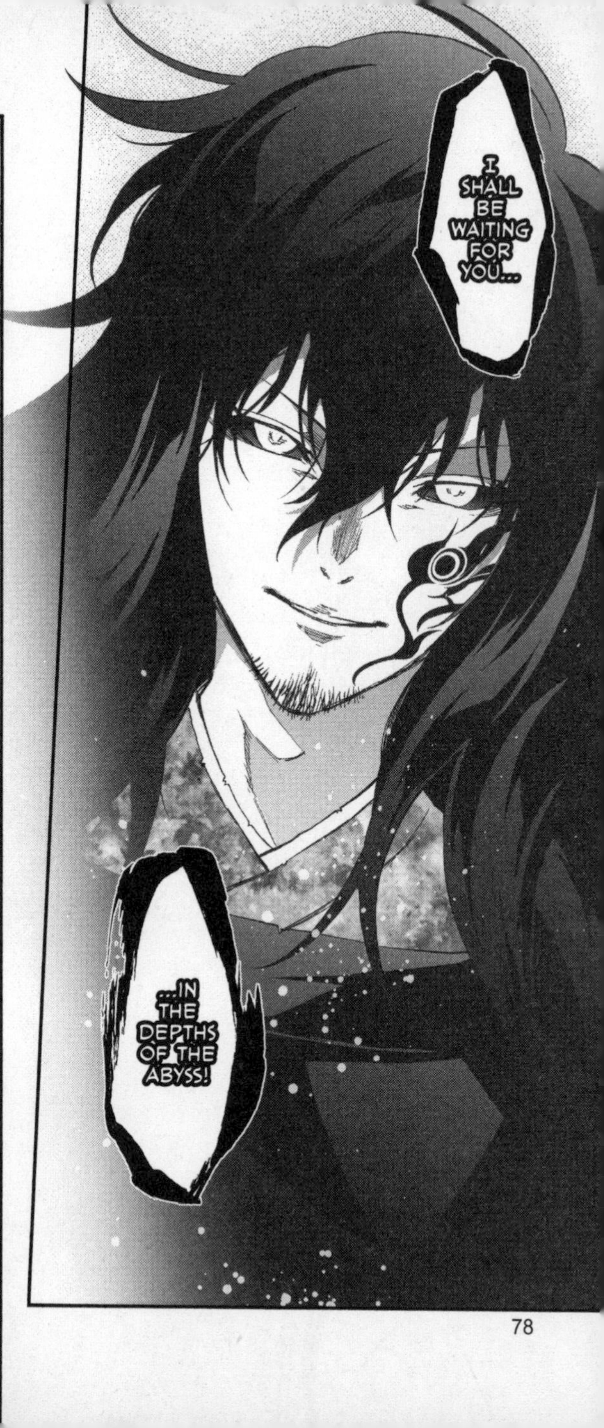
I SHALL BE WAITING FOR YOU...
...IN THE DEPTHS OF THE ABYSS!
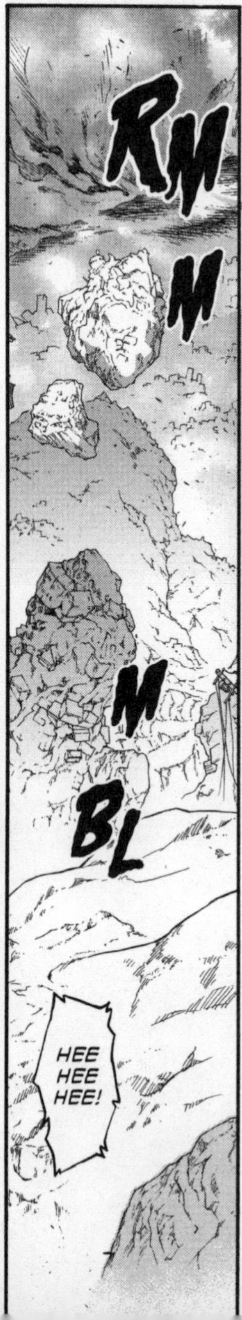
RMMMBL
HEE HEE HEE!

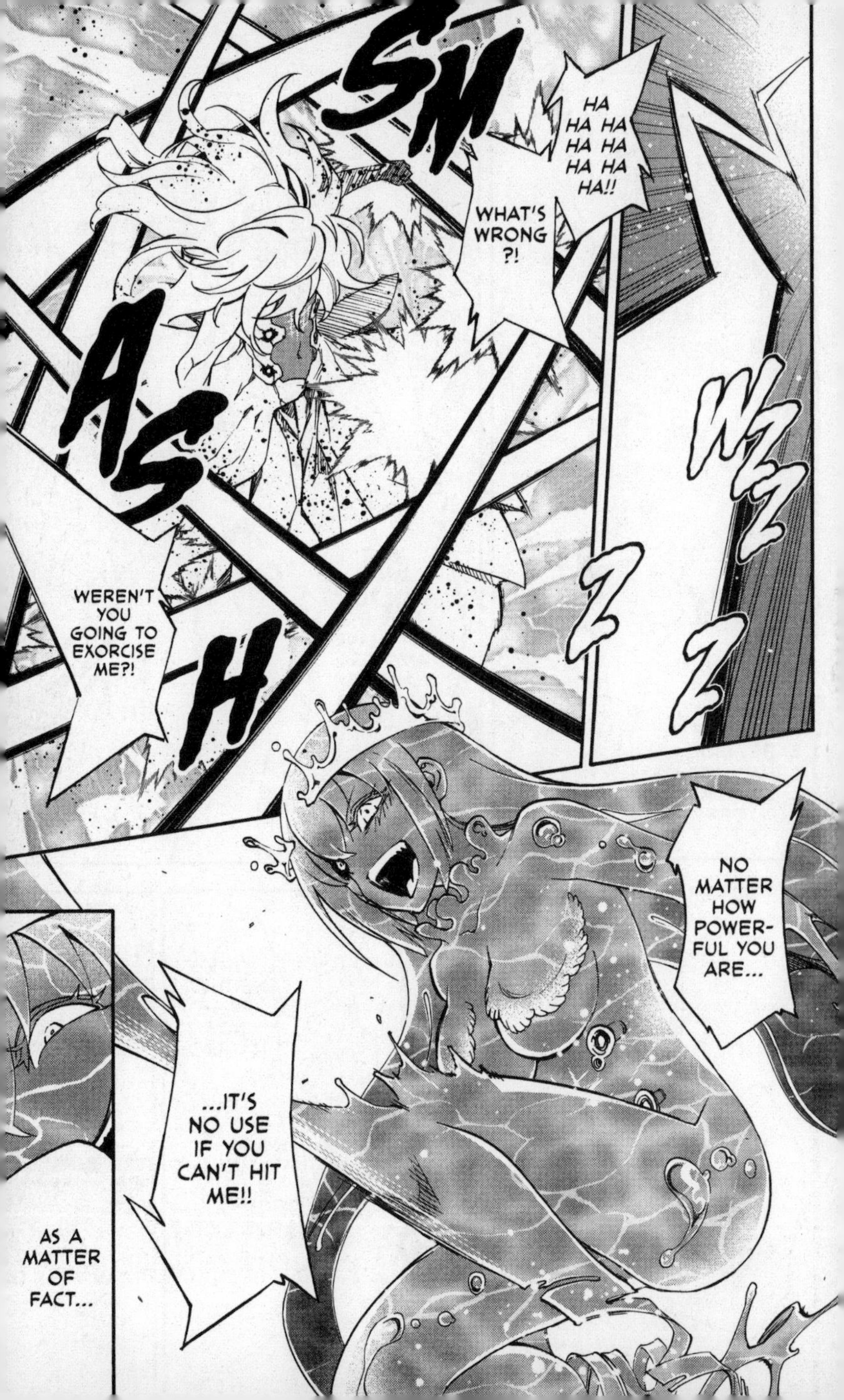
SMASH
HA HA HA HA HA HA HA HA HA!!
WHAT'S WRONG ?!
WEREN'T YOU GOING TO EXORCISE ME?!
WZZZZ
NO MATTER HOW POWER-FUL YOU ARE...
...IT'S NO USE IF YOU CAN'T HIT ME!!
AS A MATTER OF FACT...

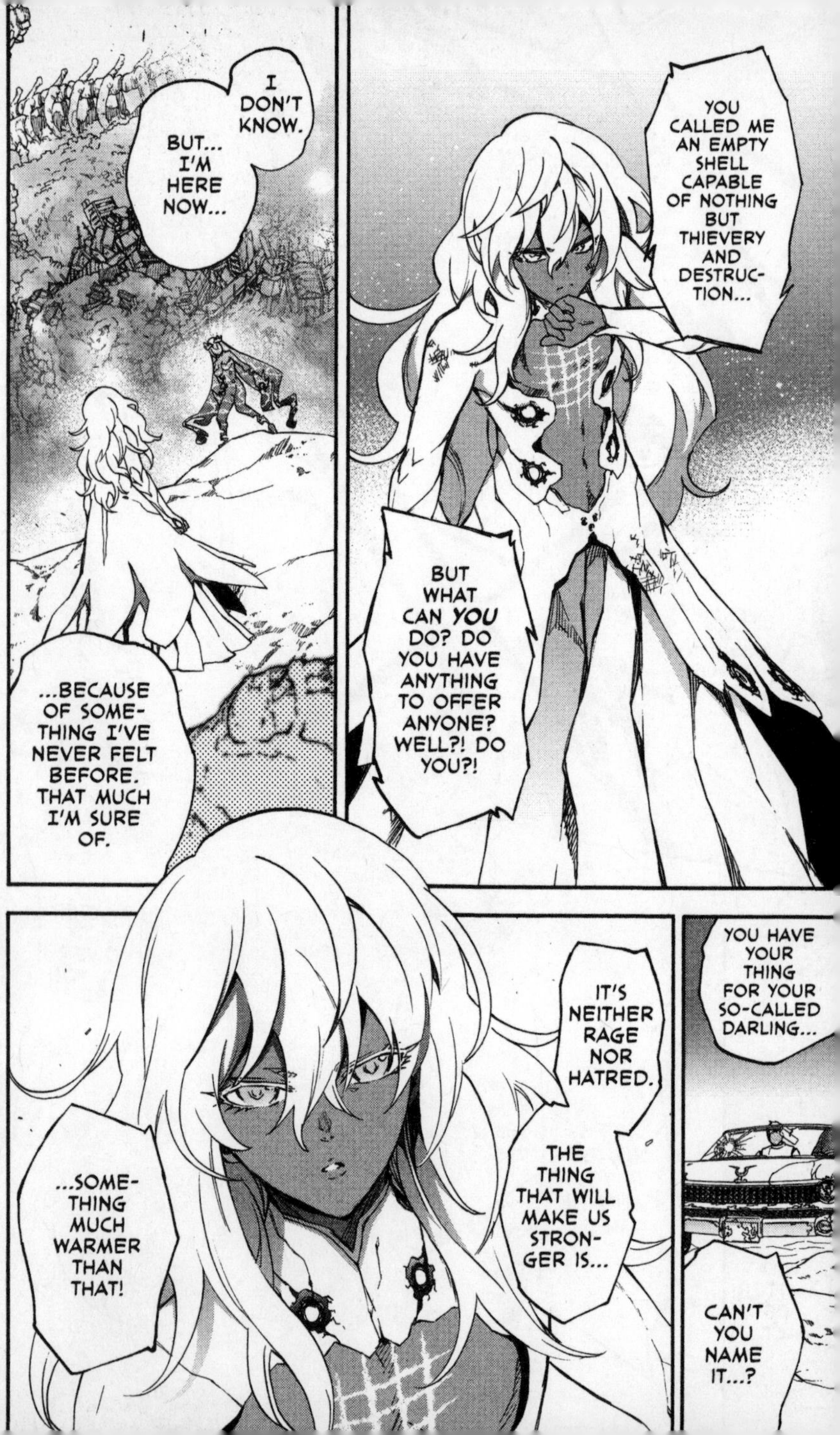
YOU CALLED ME AN EMPTY SHELL CAPABLE OF NOTHING BUT THIEVERY AND DESTRUCTION...
BUT WHAT CAN *YOU* DO? DO YOU HAVE ANYTHING TO OFFER ANYONE? WELL?! DO YOU?!
I DON'T KNOW.
BUT... I'M HERE NOW...
...BECAUSE OF SOMETHING I'VE NEVER FELT BEFORE. THAT MUCH I'M SURE OF.
YOU HAVE YOUR THING FOR YOUR SO-CALLED DARLING...
CAN'T YOU NAME IT...?
IT'S NEITHER RAGE NOR HATRED.
THE THING THAT WILL MAKE US STRONGER IS...
...SOMETHING MUCH WARMER THAN THAT!

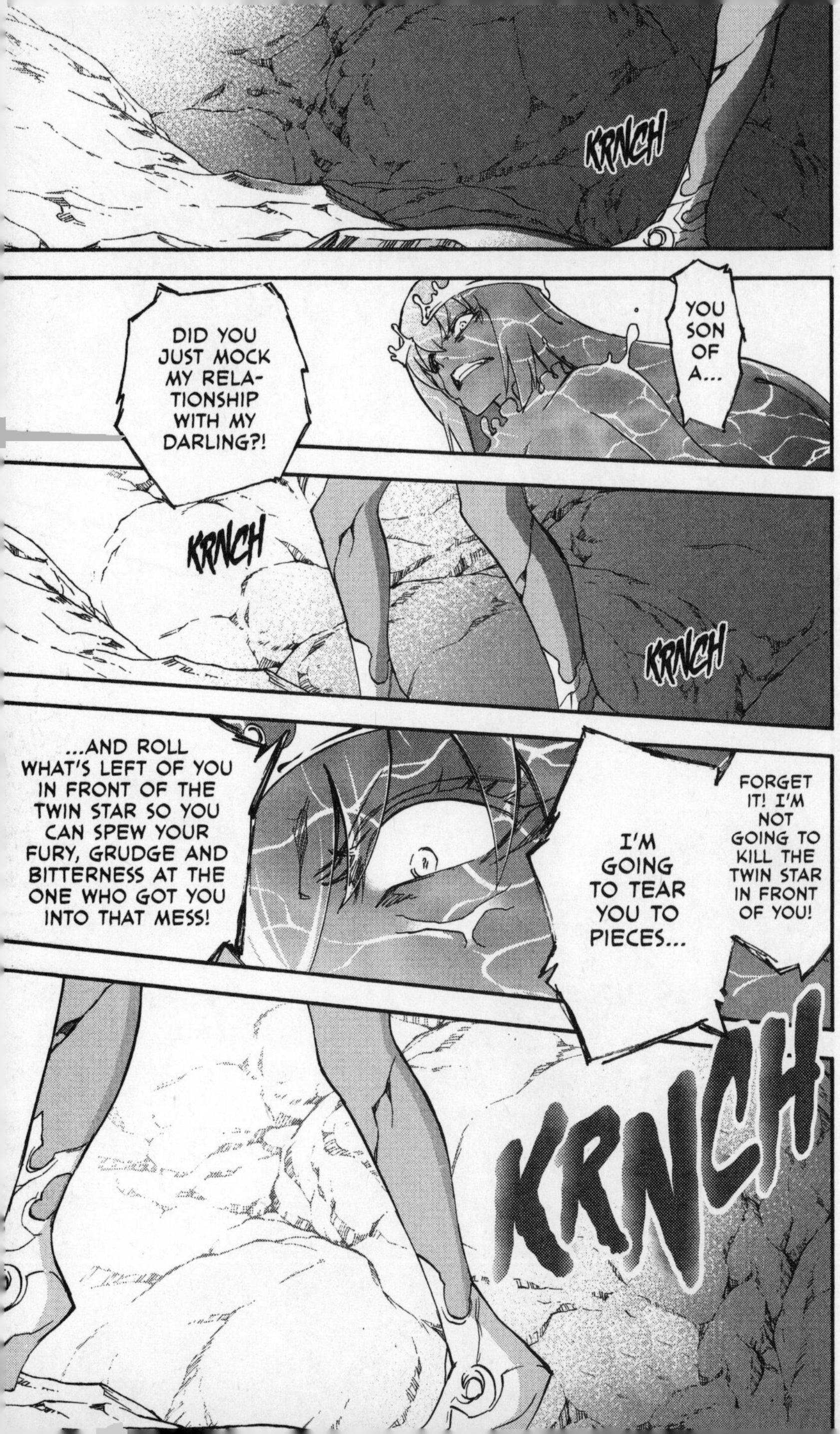
KRNCH
YOU SON OF A...
DID YOU JUST MOCK MY RELA-TIONSHIP WITH MY DARLING?!
KRNCH
KRNCH
FORGET IT! I'M NOT GOING TO KILL THE TWIN STAR IN FRONT OF YOU!
I'M GOING TO TEAR YOU TO PIECES...
...AND ROLL WHAT'S LEFT OF YOU IN FRONT OF THE TWIN STAR SO YOU CAN SPEW YOUR FURY, GRUDGE AND BITTERNESS AT THE ONE WHO GOT YOU INTO THAT MESS!
KRNCH

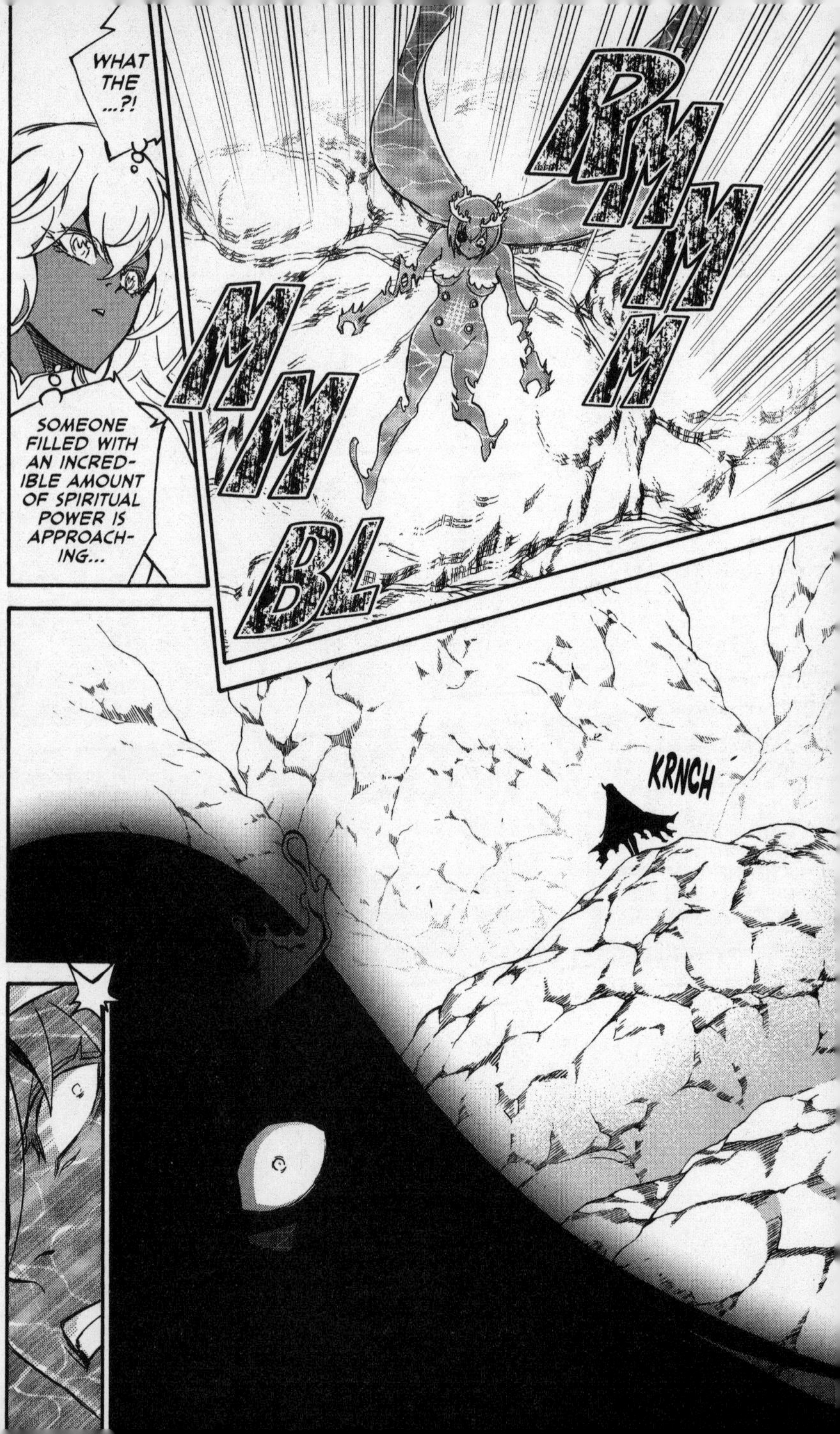
RMMMM
MMBL
WHAT THE ...?!
SOMEONE FILLED WITH AN INCREDIBLE AMOUNT OF SPIRITUAL POWER IS APPROACHING...
KRNCH

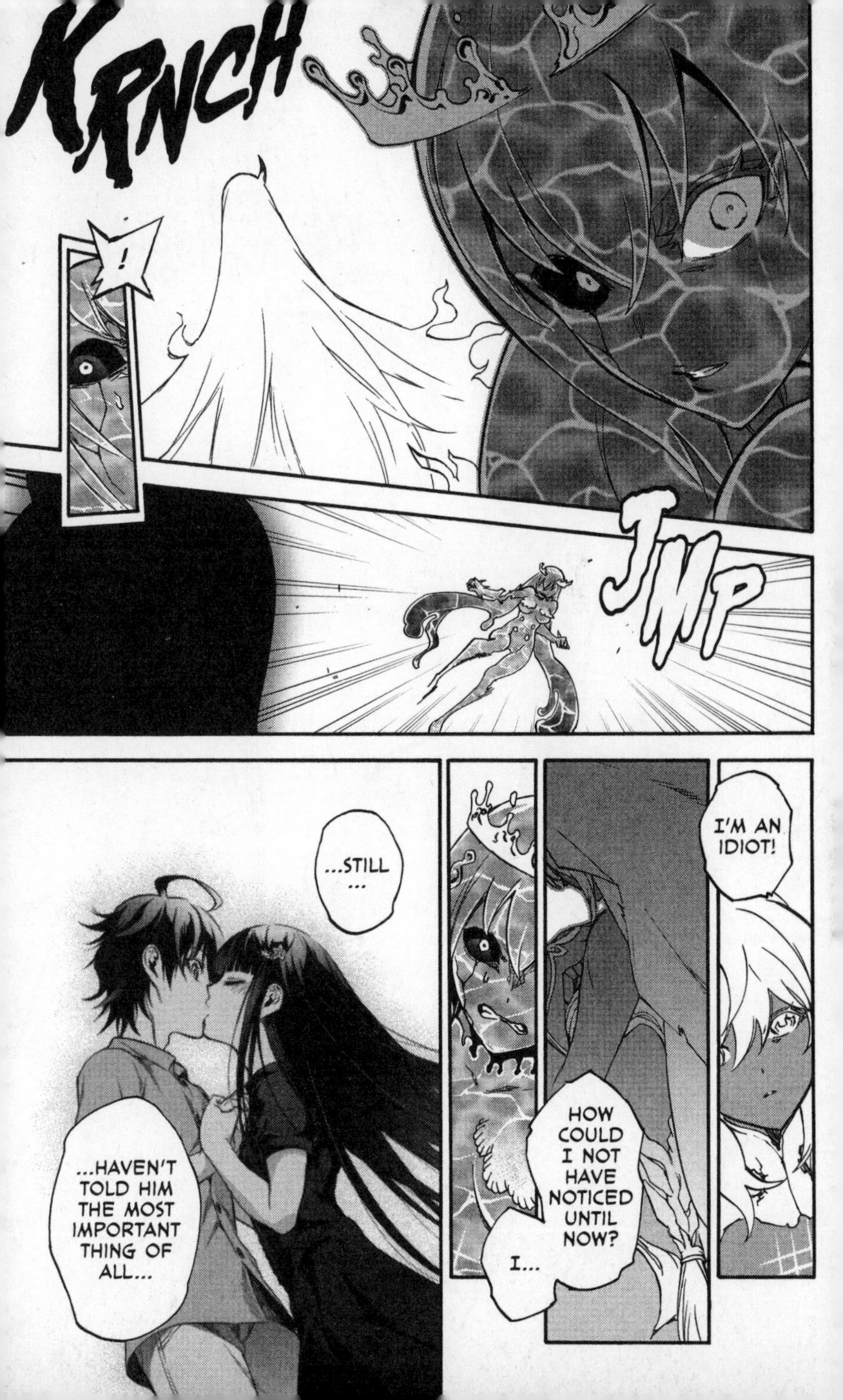
KRNCH
!
JMP
I'M AN IDIOT!
HOW COULD I NOT HAVE NOTICED UNTIL NOW?
I...
...STILL...
...HAVEN'T TOLD HIM THE MOST IMPORTANT THING OF ALL...

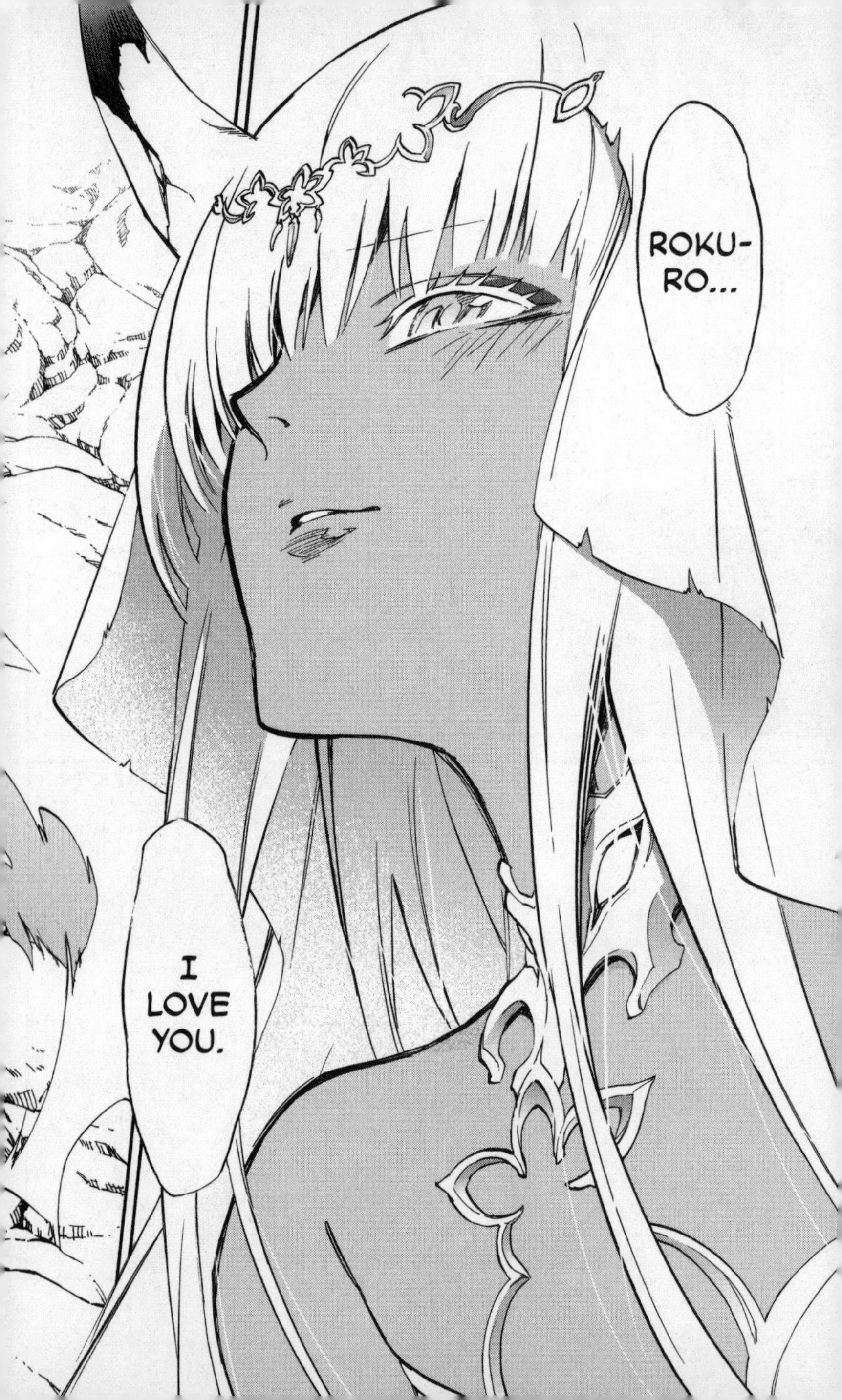
ROKU-RO...
I LOVE YOU.

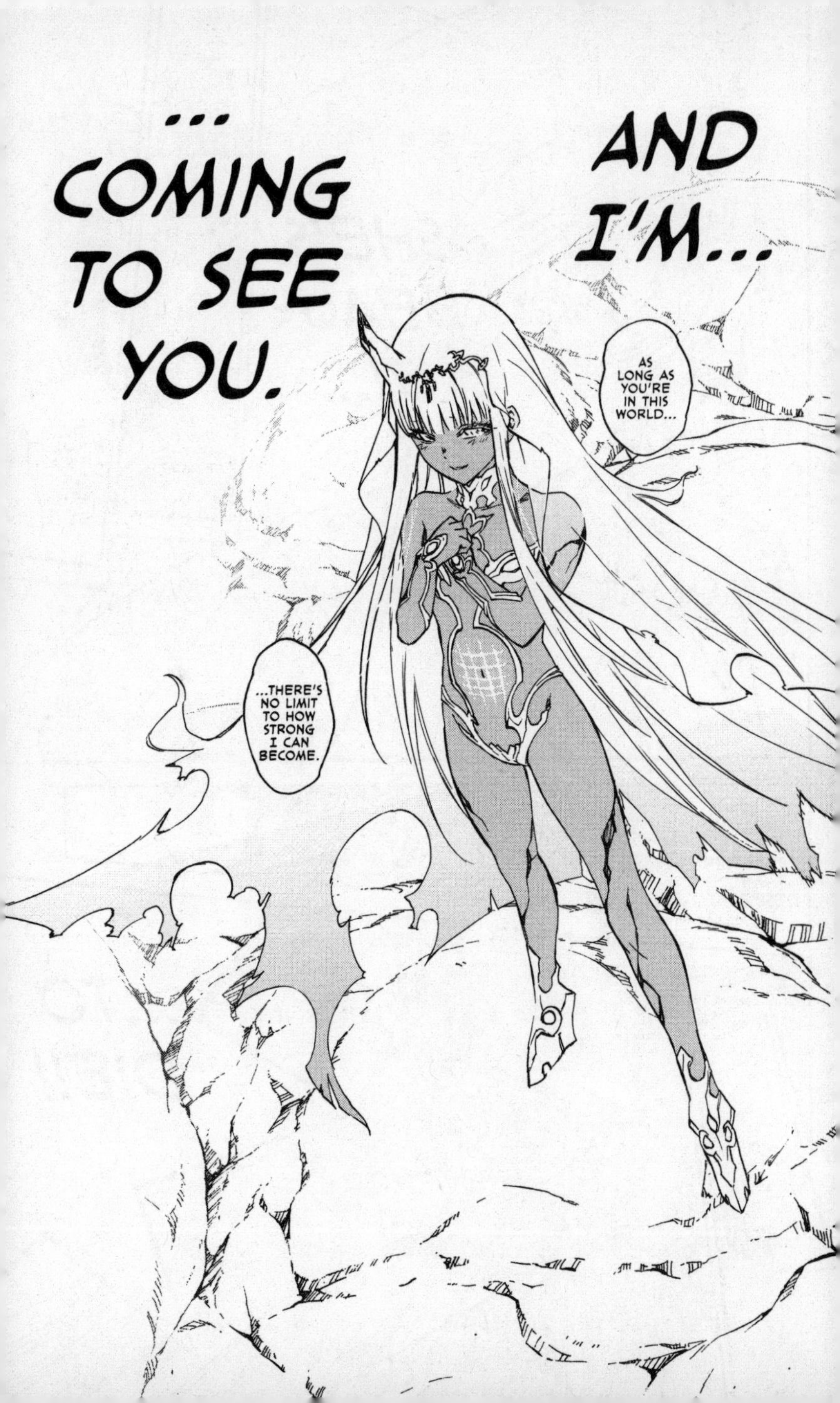
AND I'M...
...COMING TO SEE YOU.
AS LONG AS YOU'RE IN THIS WORLD...
...THERE'S NO LIMIT TO HOW STRONG I CAN BECOME.

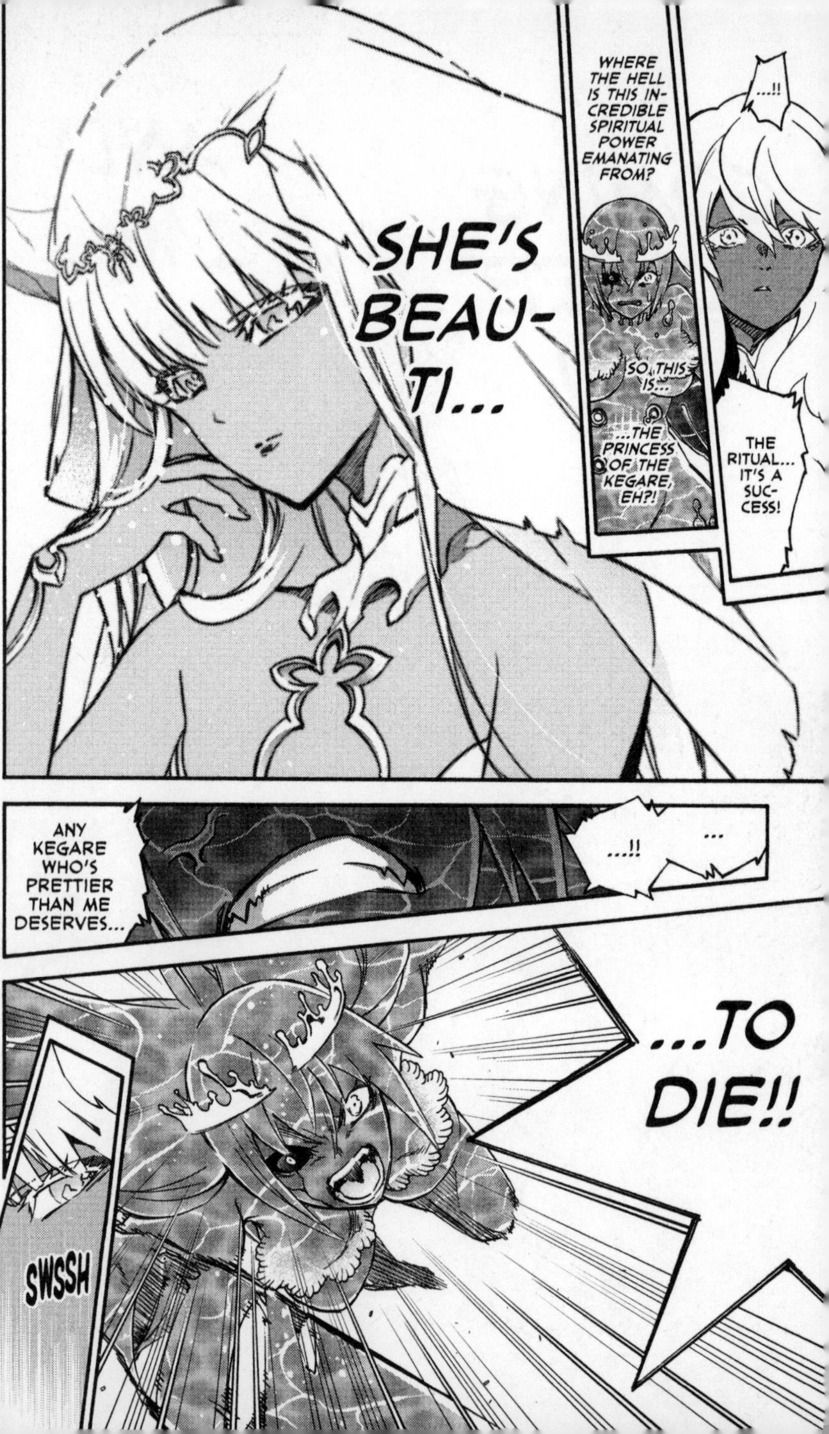
...!!
THE RITUAL... IT'S A SUCCESS!
WHERE THE HELL IS THIS INCREDIBLE SPIRITUAL POWER EMANATING FROM?
SO THIS IS...
...THE PRINCESS OF THE KEGARE, EH?!
SHE'S BEAU-TI...
...
...!!
ANY KEGARE WHO'S PRETTIER THAN ME DESERVES...
...TO DIE!!
SWSSH

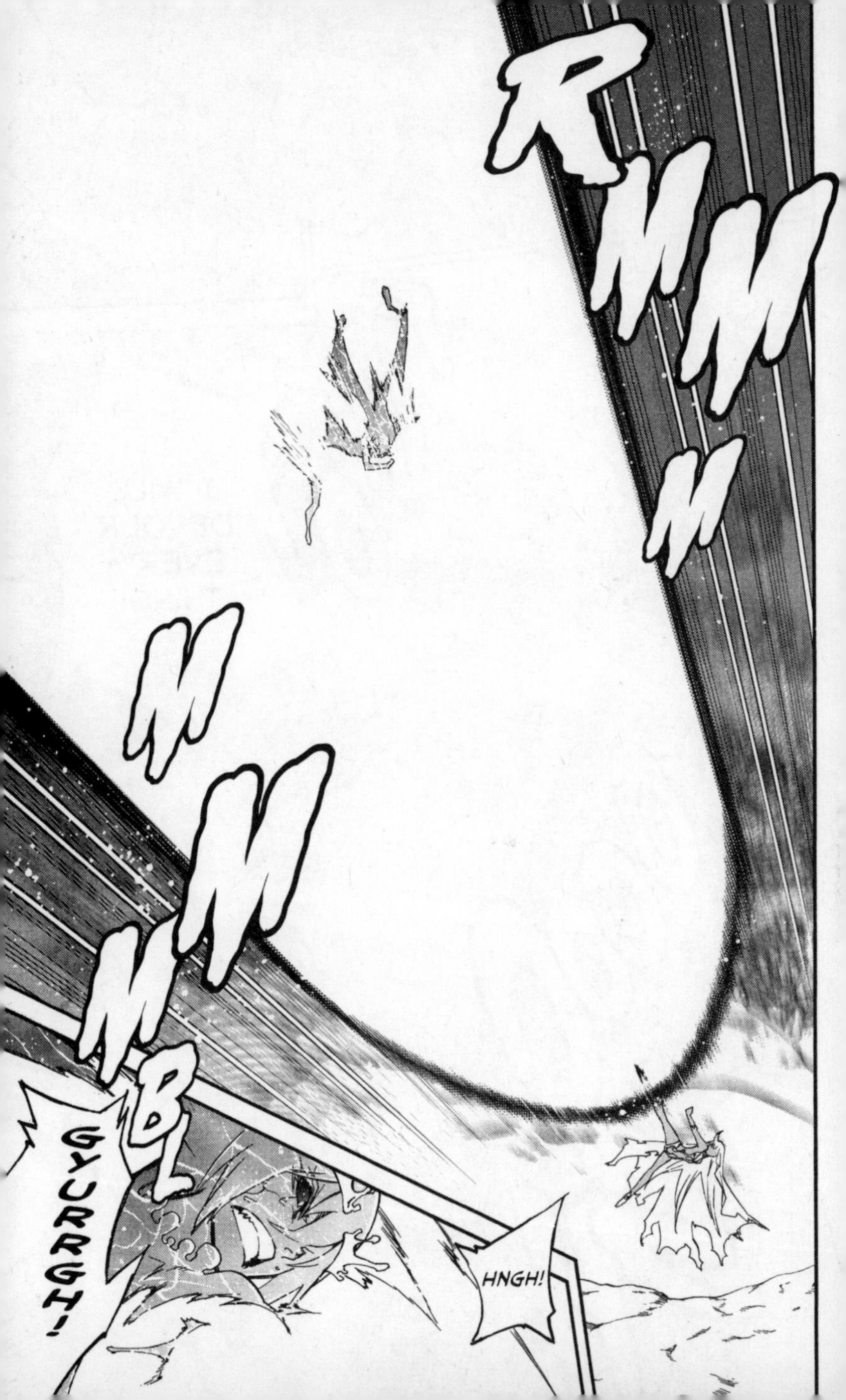
RMMM
MMMB
HNGH!
GYURRGH!

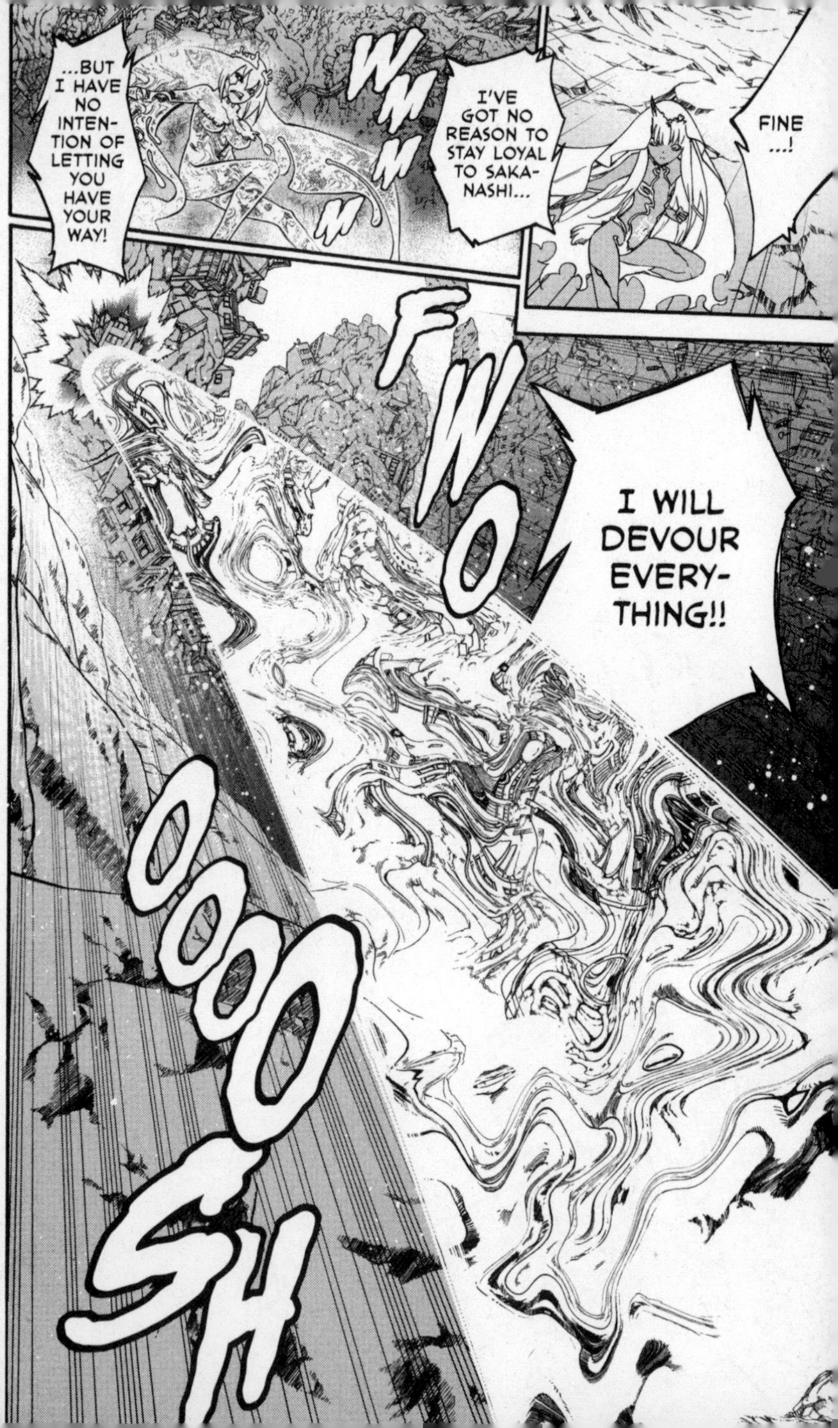
FINE ...!
I'VE GOT NO REASON TO STAY LOYAL TO SAKA-NASHI...
WMMM
...BUT I HAVE NO INTEN-TION OF LETTING YOU HAVE YOUR WAY!
I WILL DEVOUR EVERY-THING!!
FWOOOOOSH

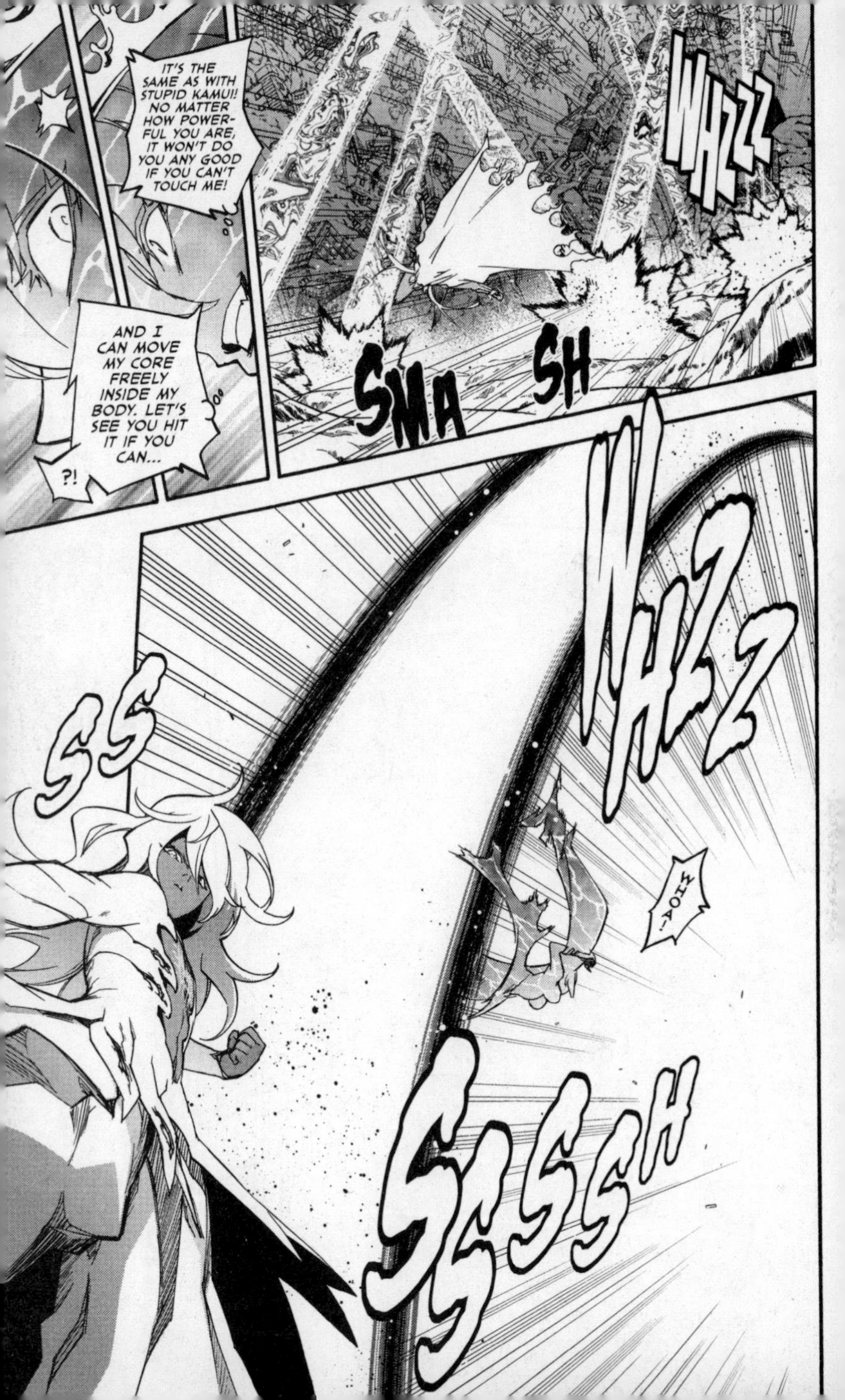
WHZZZ
SMASH
IT'S THE SAME AS WITH STUPID KAMUI! NO MATTER HOW POWERFUL YOU ARE, IT WON'T DO YOU ANY GOOD IF YOU CAN'T TOUCH ME!
AND I CAN MOVE MY CORE FREELY INSIDE MY BODY. LET'S SEE YOU HIT IT IF YOU CAN...
?!
WHZZ
WHOA...!
SS
SSSSH

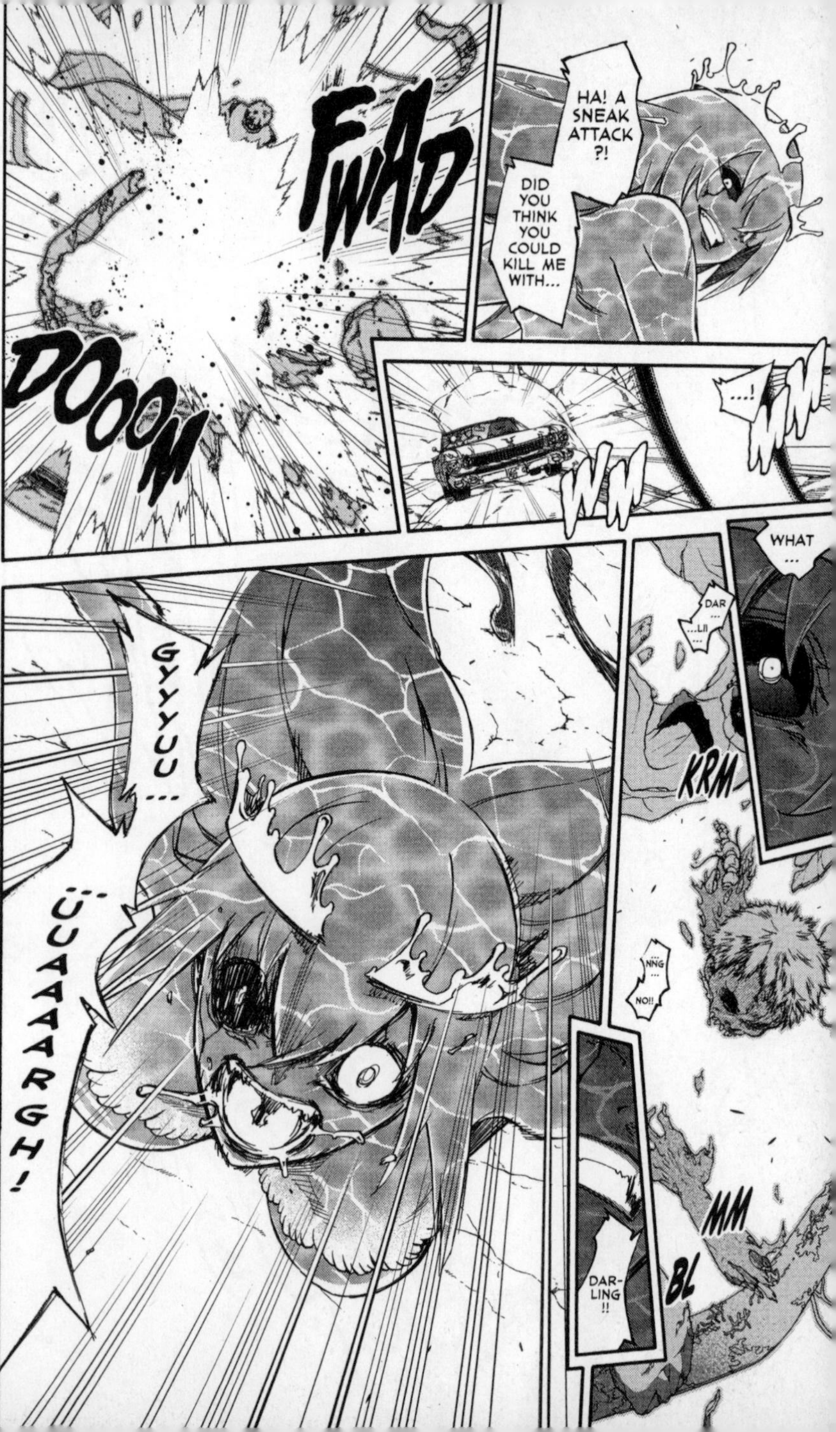

HA! A SNEAK ATTACK ?!
DID YOU THINK YOU COULD KILL ME WITH...
...!
WN WN
WN
FWAD
DOOOM
WHAT ...
DAR ... ...LII ...
KRM
... NNG ...
NO!!
DAR-LING !!
BL
MM
GYYYUU...
...ÜUAAAARGH!

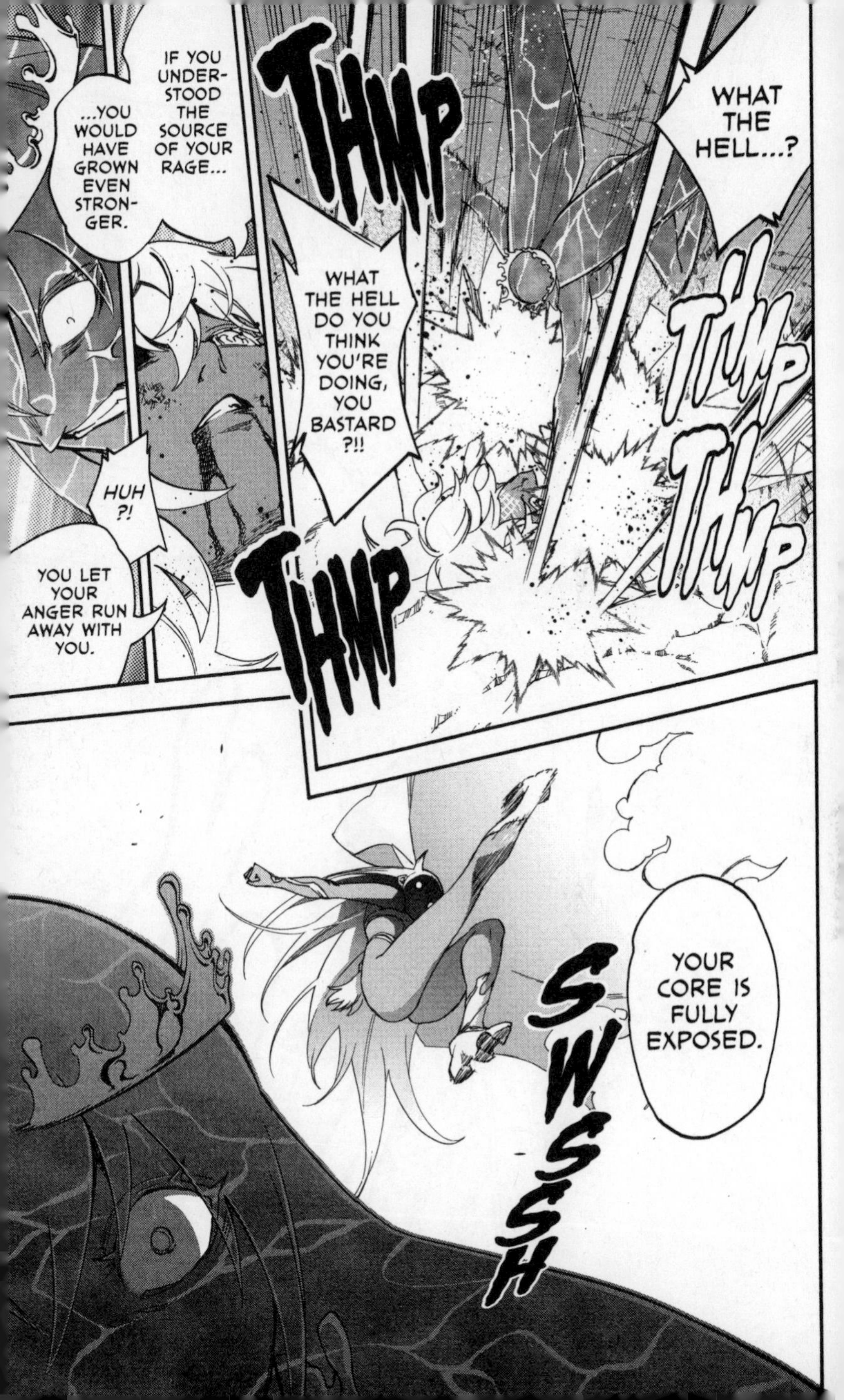
WHAT THE HELL...?
THMP THMP THMP
THMP
WHAT THE HELL DO YOU THINK YOU'RE DOING, YOU BASTARD?!!
THMP
IF YOU UNDERSTOOD THE SOURCE OF YOUR RAGE...
...YOU WOULD HAVE GROWN EVEN STRONGER.
HUH?!
YOU LET YOUR ANGER RUN AWAY WITH YOU.
YOUR CORE IS FULLY EXPOSED.
SWSSH

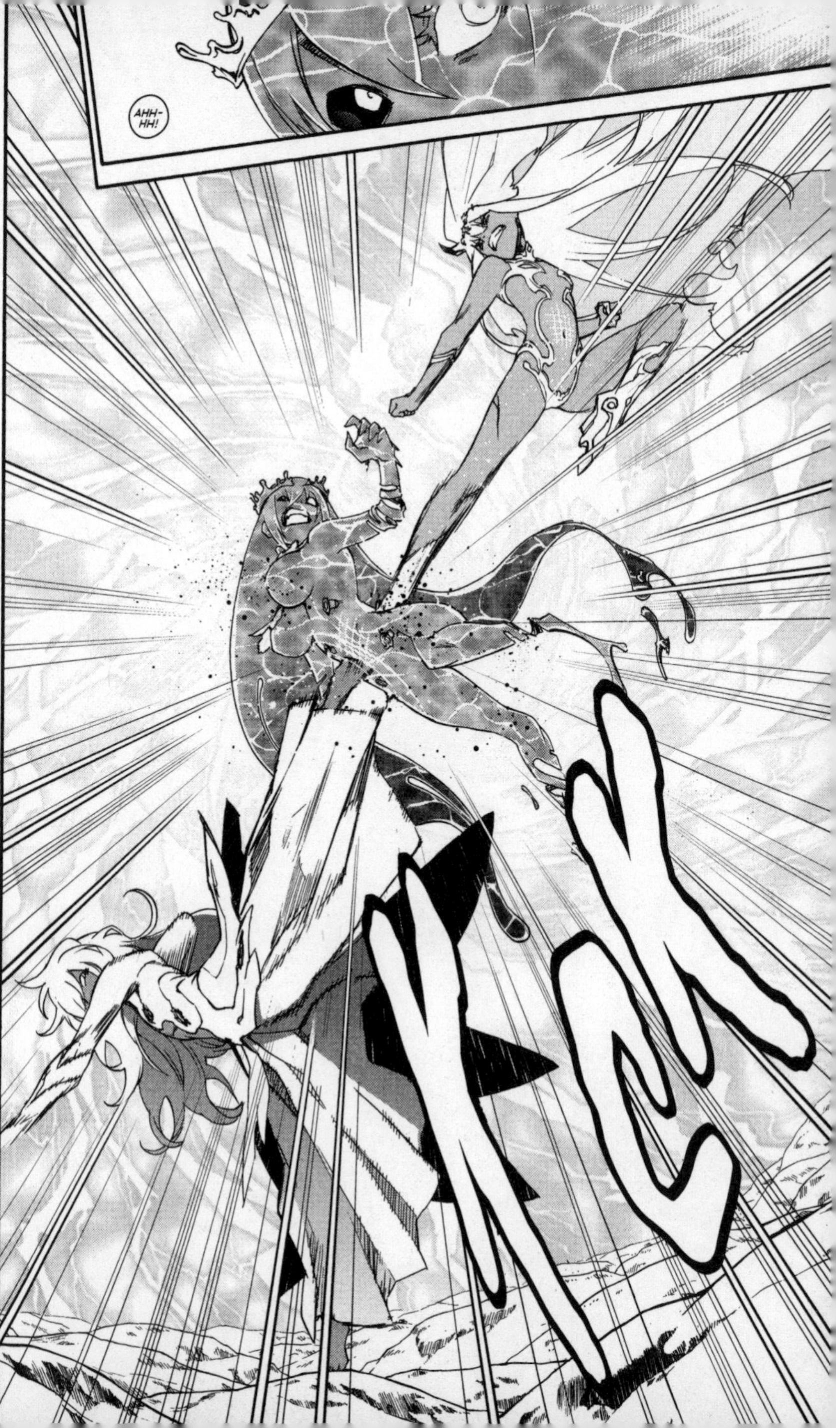
AHH-HH!

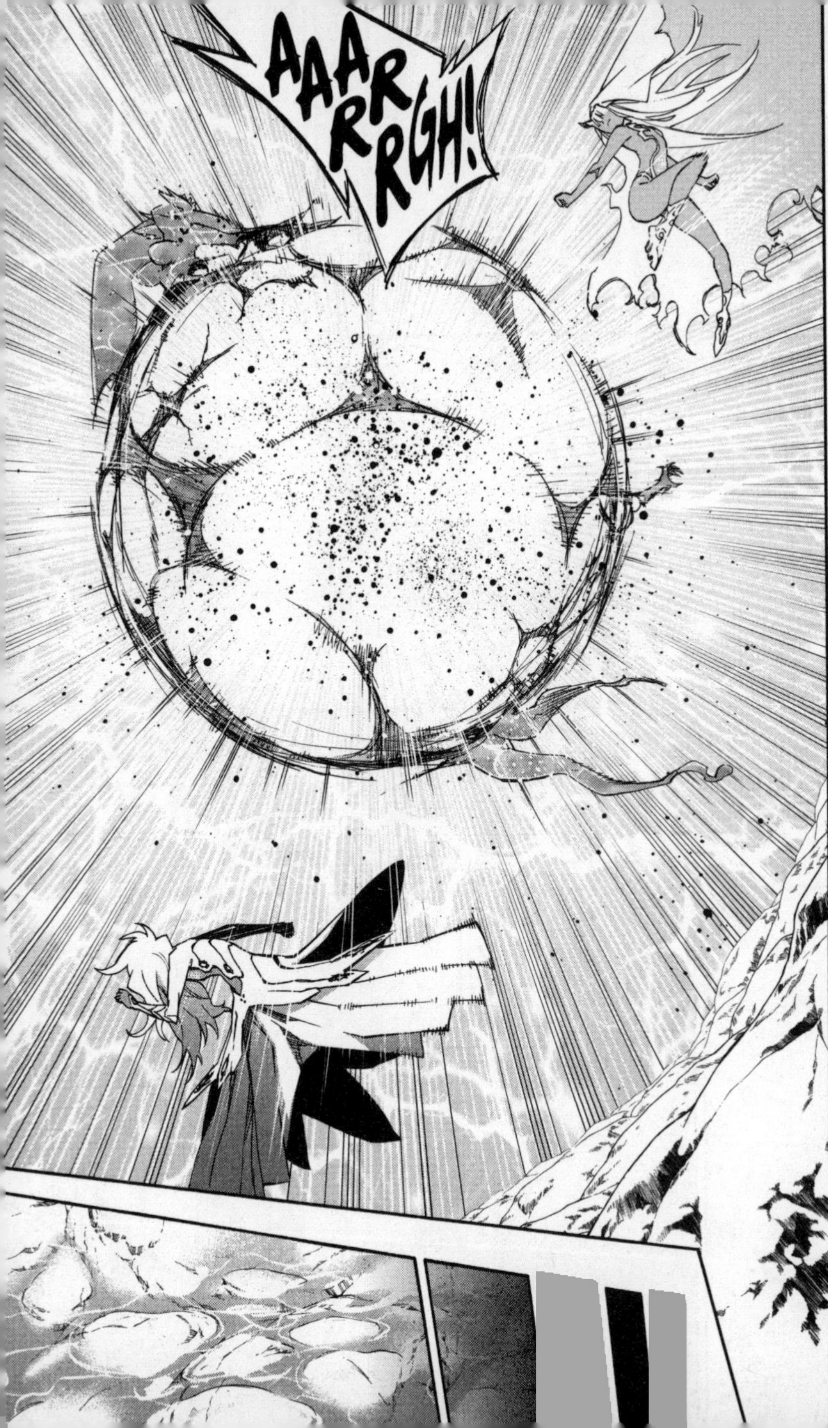
AAARRRGH!

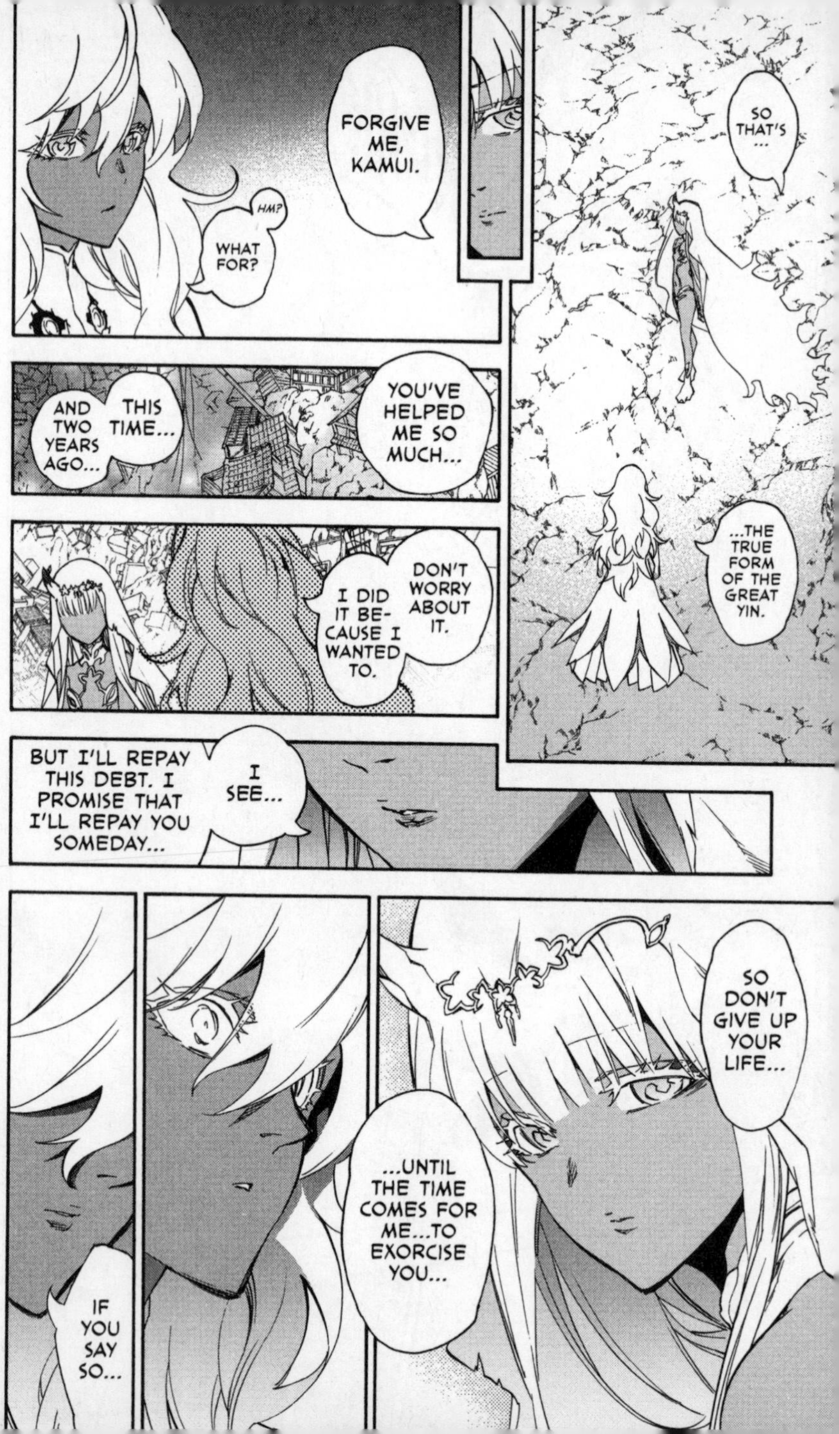
SO THAT'S ...
...THE TRUE FORM OF THE GREAT YIN.
FORGIVE ME, KAMUI.
HM?
WHAT FOR?
YOU'VE HELPED ME SO MUCH...
THIS TIME...
AND TWO YEARS AGO...
DON'T WORRY ABOUT IT.
I DID IT BE-CAUSE I WANTED TO.
I SEE...
BUT I'LL REPAY THIS DEBT. I PROMISE THAT I'LL REPAY YOU SOMEDAY...
SO DON'T GIVE UP YOUR LIFE...
...UNTIL THE TIME COMES FOR ME...TO EXORCISE YOU...
IF YOU SAY SO...

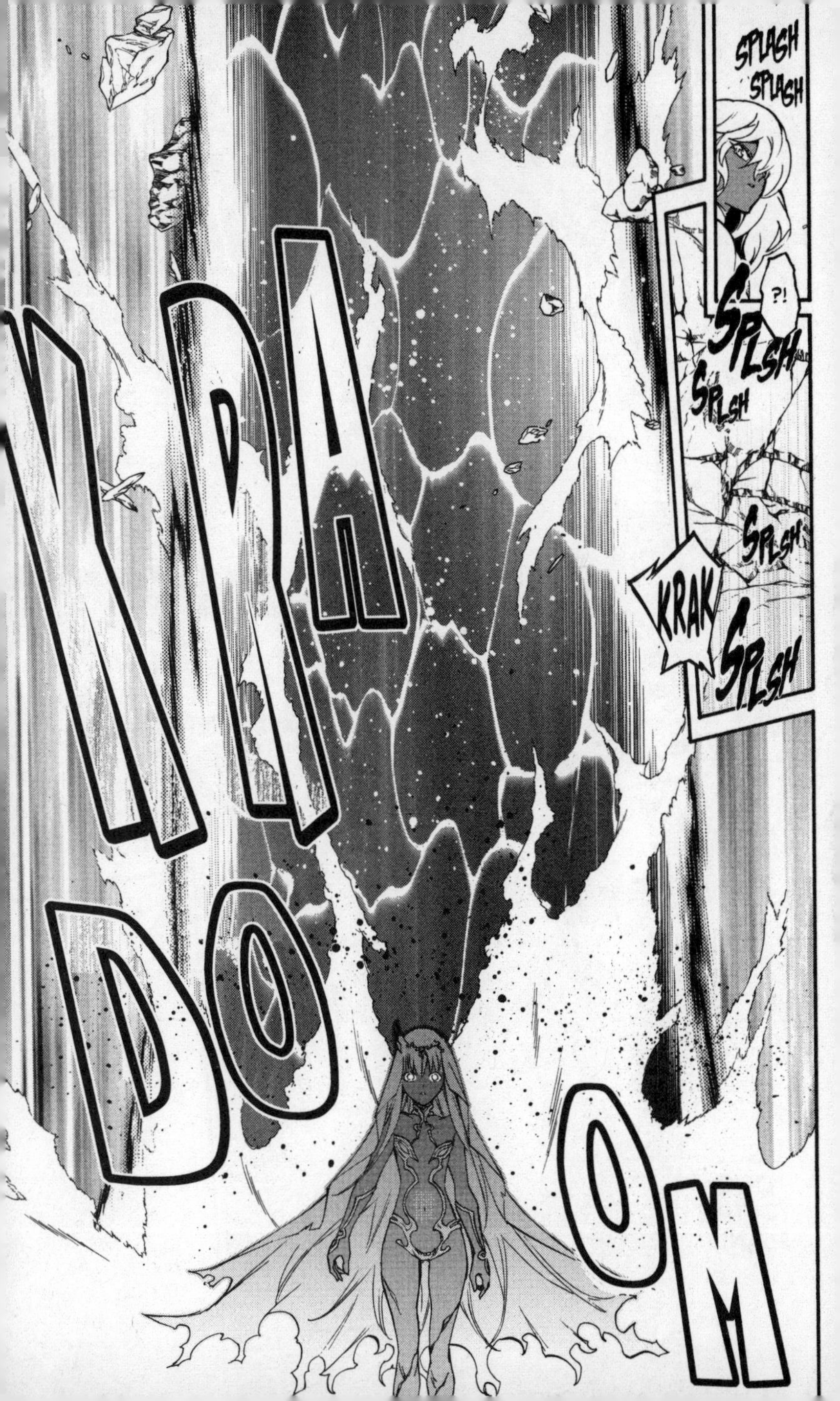
SPLASH
SPLASH
?!
SPLSH
SPLSH
SPLSH
KRAK
SPLSH
KRADOOM

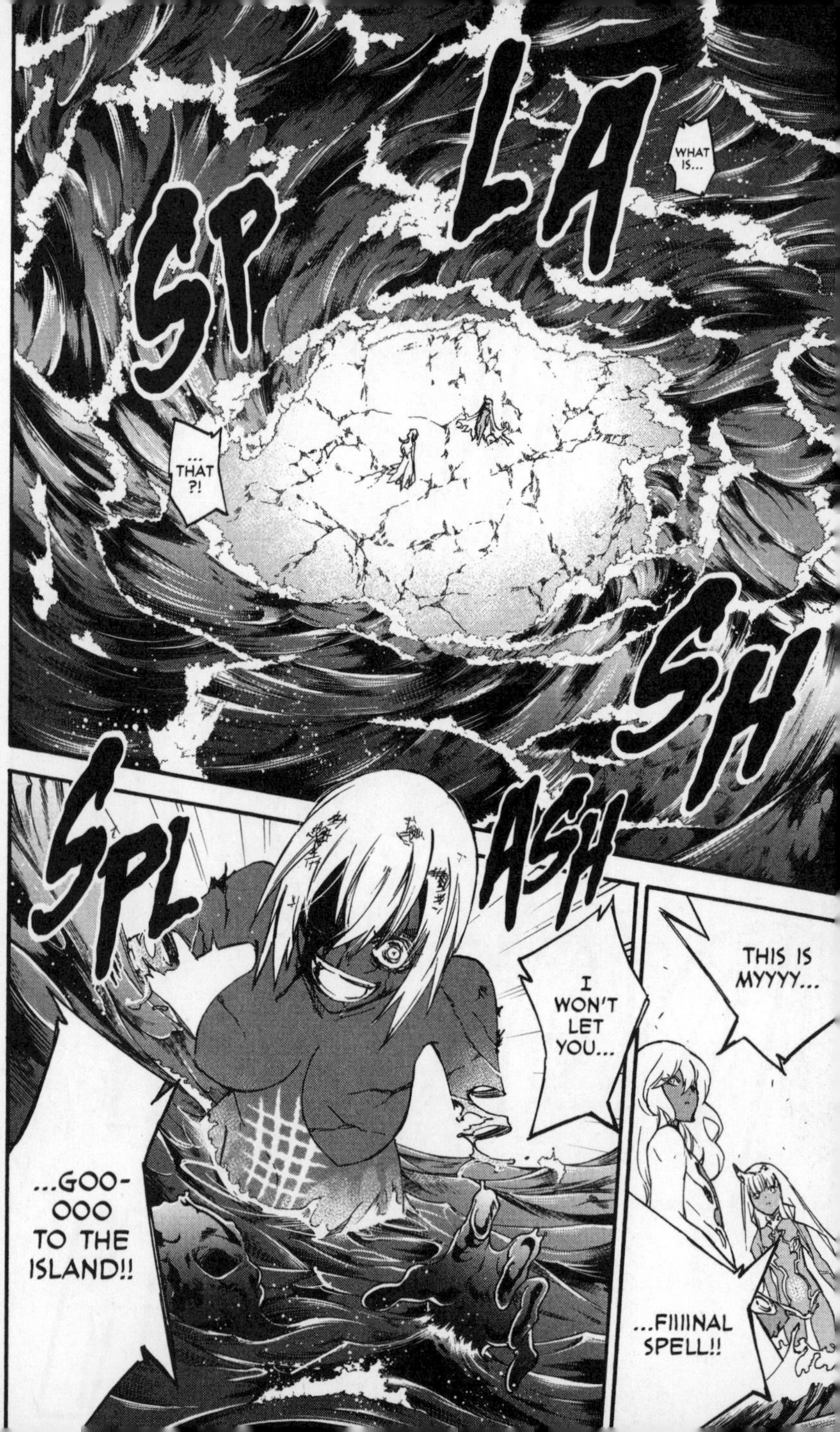
WHAT IS...
SP LA SH
...THAT?!
THIS IS MYYYY...
...FIIIINAL SPELL!!
I WON'T LET YOU...
...GOO-OOO TO THE ISLAND!!
SPL ASH

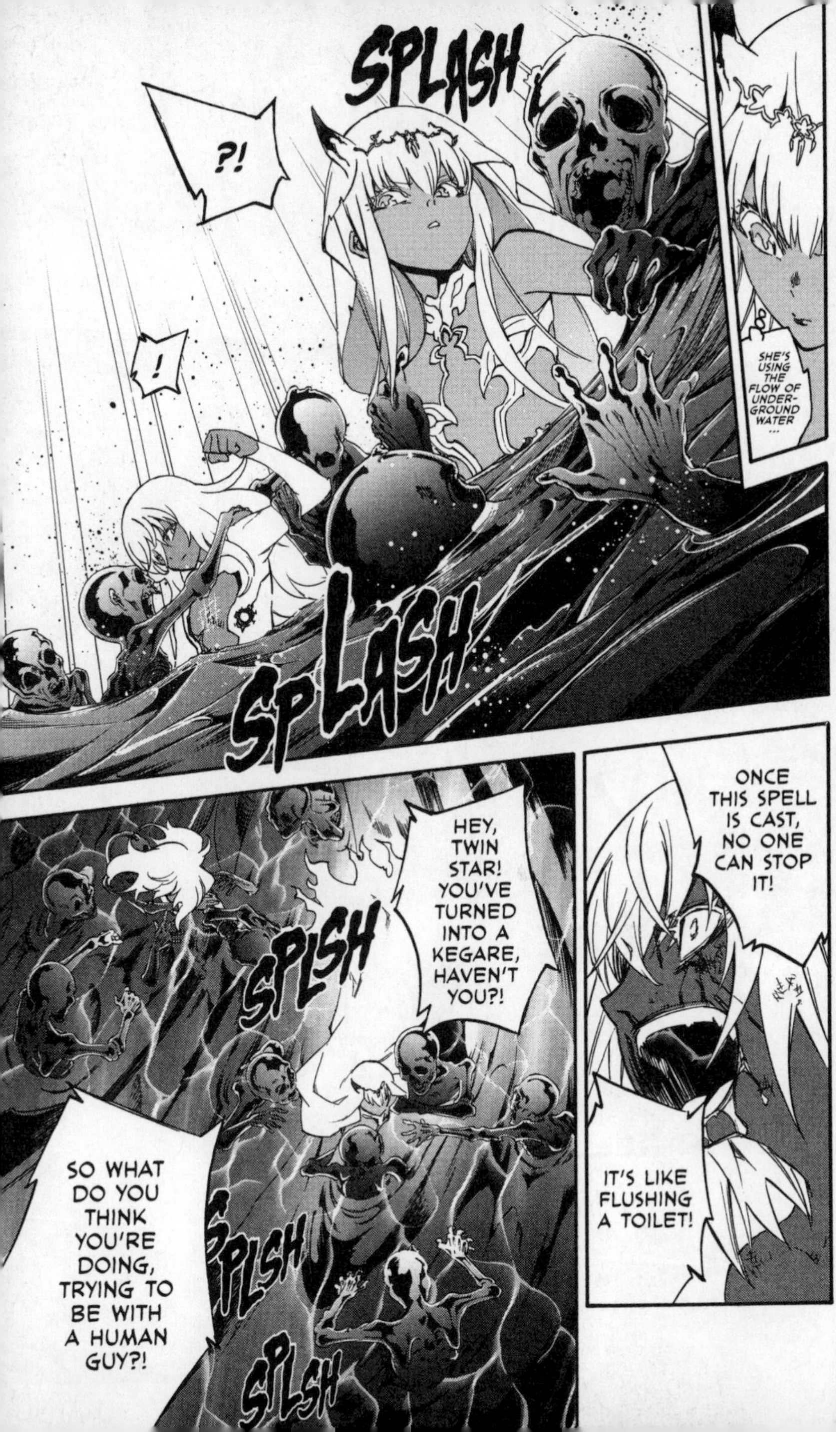
SHE'S USING THE FLOW OF UNDER-GROUND WATER...
SPLASH
?!
!
SPLASH
ONCE THIS SPELL IS CAST, NO ONE CAN STOP IT!
IT'S LIKE FLUSHING A TOILET!
HEY, TWIN STAR! YOU'VE TURNED INTO A KEGARE, HAVEN'T YOU?!
SPLSH
SO WHAT DO YOU THINK YOU'RE DOING, TRYING TO BE WITH A HUMAN GUY?!
SPLSH
SPLSH

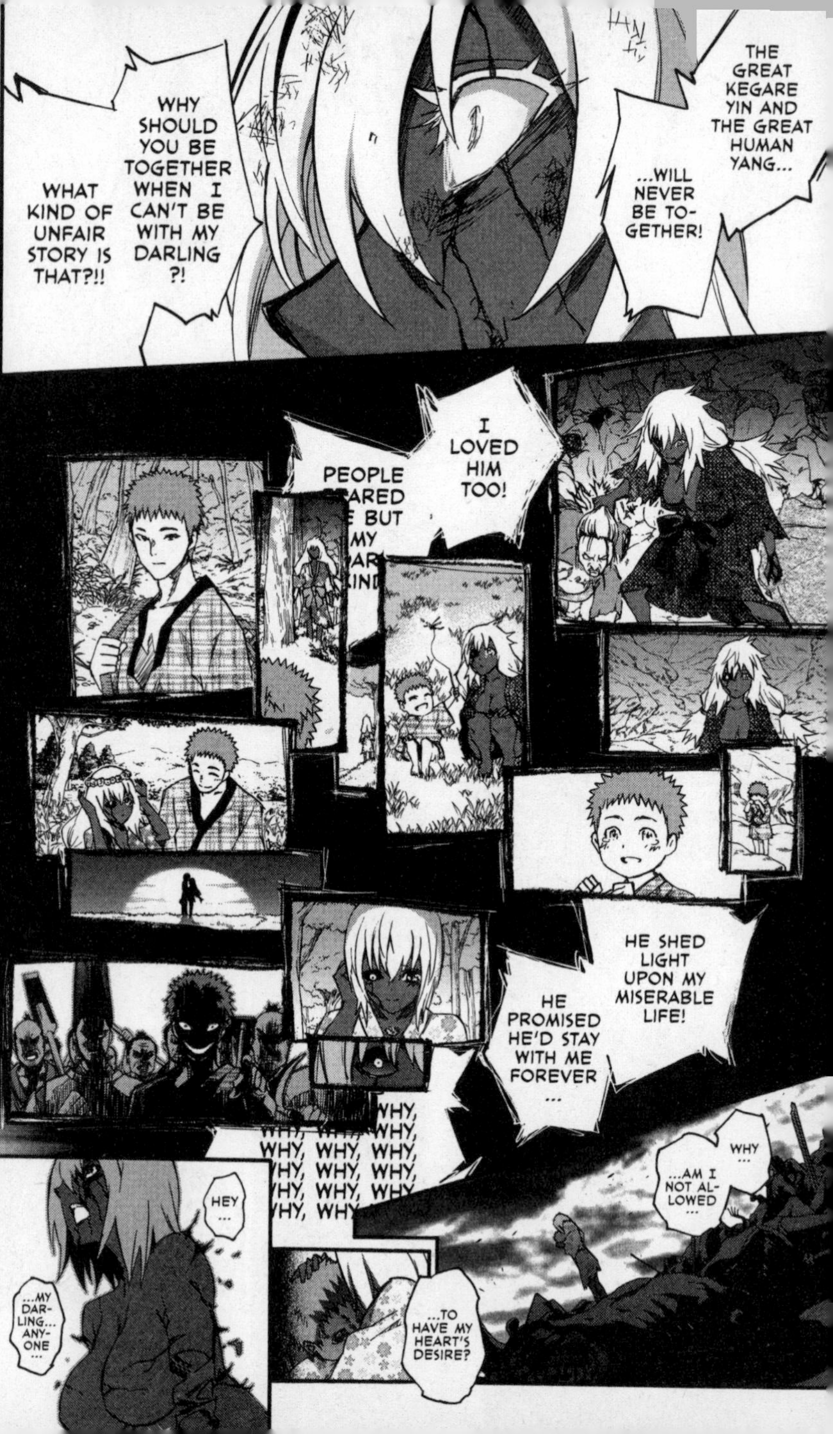
THE GREAT KEGARE YIN AND THE GREAT HUMAN YANG...
...WILL NEVER BE TO-GETHER!
WHY SHOULD YOU BE TOGETHER WHEN I CAN'T BE WITH MY DARLING ?!
WHAT KIND OF UNFAIR STORY IS THAT?!!
I LOVED HIM TOO!
PEOPLE ...ARED ... BUT ... MY ...AR... KIND
HE SHED LIGHT UPON MY MISERABLE LIFE!
HE PROMISED HE'D STAY WITH ME FOREVER ...
WHY, WHY, WHY, WHY, WHY, WHY, WHY, WHY, WHY, WHY, WHY, WHY, WHY, WHY
WHY ...
...AM I NOT AL-LOWED ...
...TO HAVE MY HEART'S DESIRE?
HEY ...
...MY DAR-LING... ANY-ONE ...

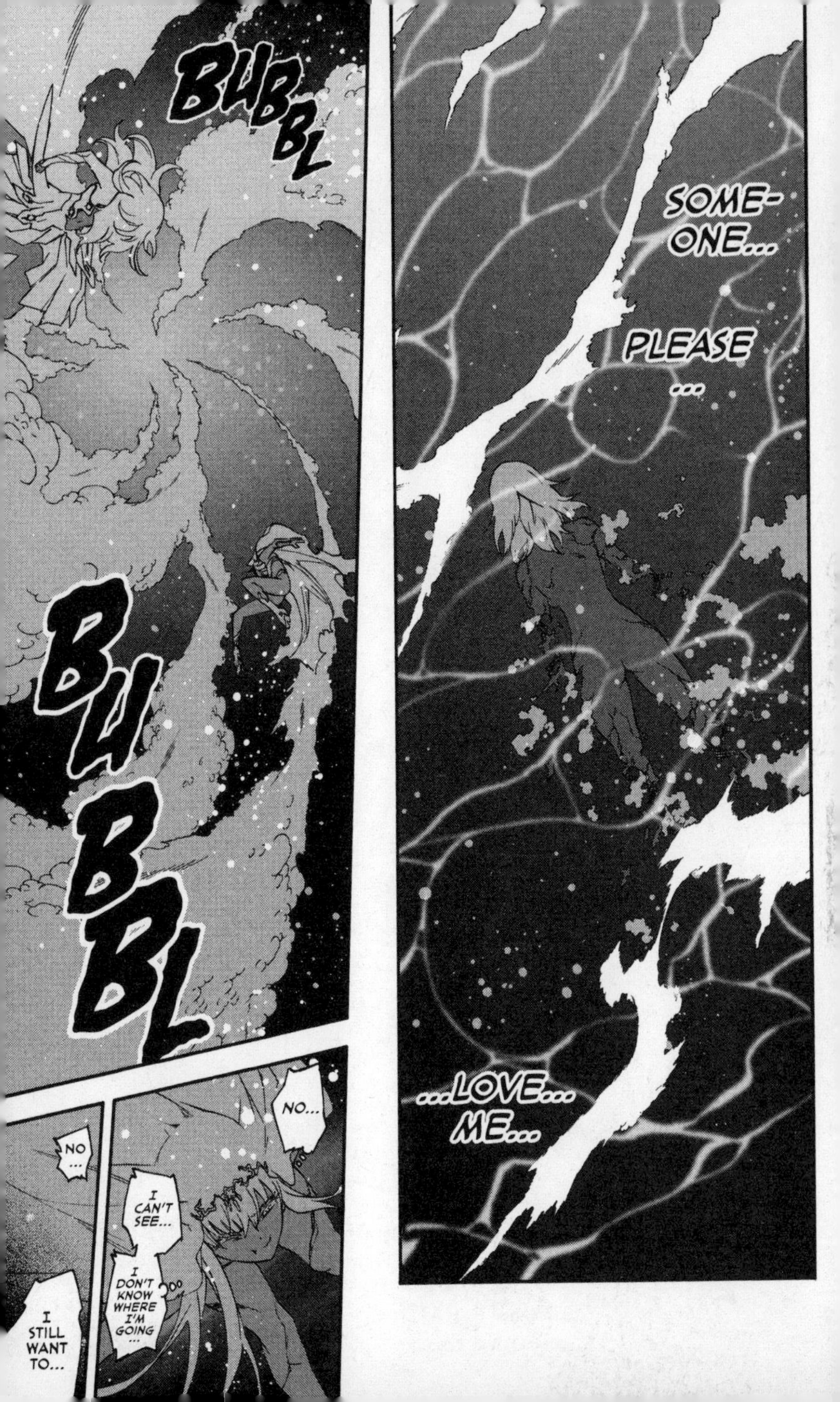
SOME-ONE...
PLEASE ...
...LOVE... ME...
BUBBL
BUBBL
NO...
I CAN'T SEE...
I DON'T KNOW WHERE I'M GOING ...
NO ...
I STILL WANT TO...

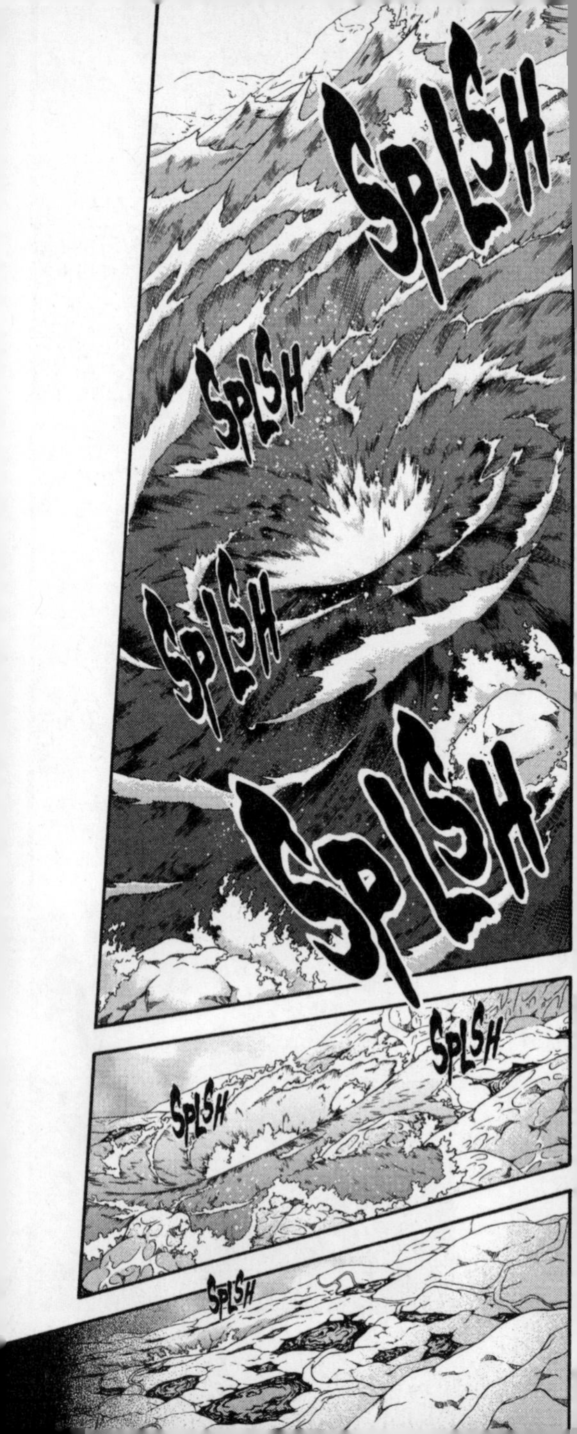
SPLSH
SPLSH
SPLSH
SPLSH
SPLSH
SPLSH
SPLSH

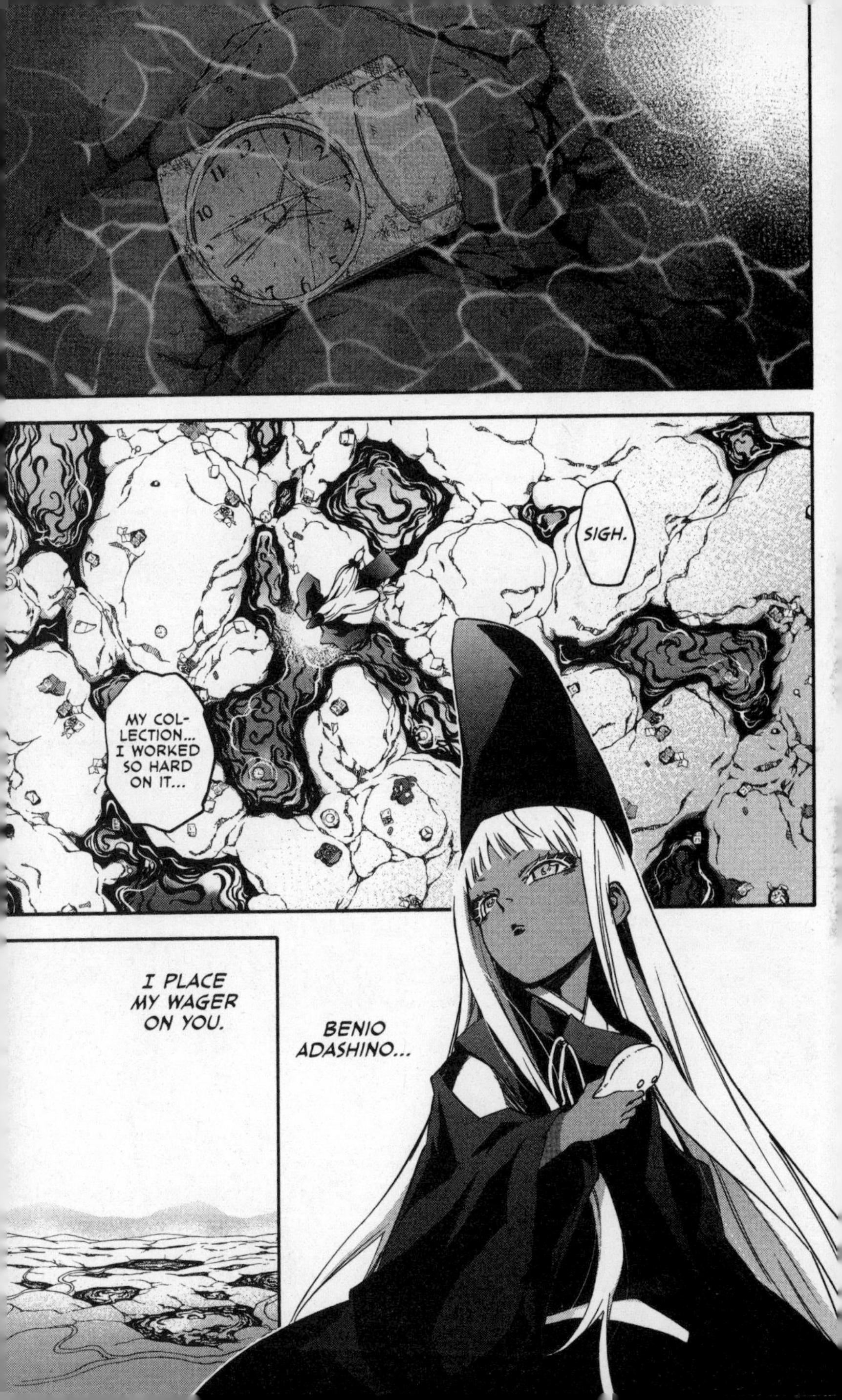
SIGH.
MY COL-LECTION... I WORKED SO HARD ON IT...
BENIO ADASHINO...
I PLACE MY WAGER ON YOU.

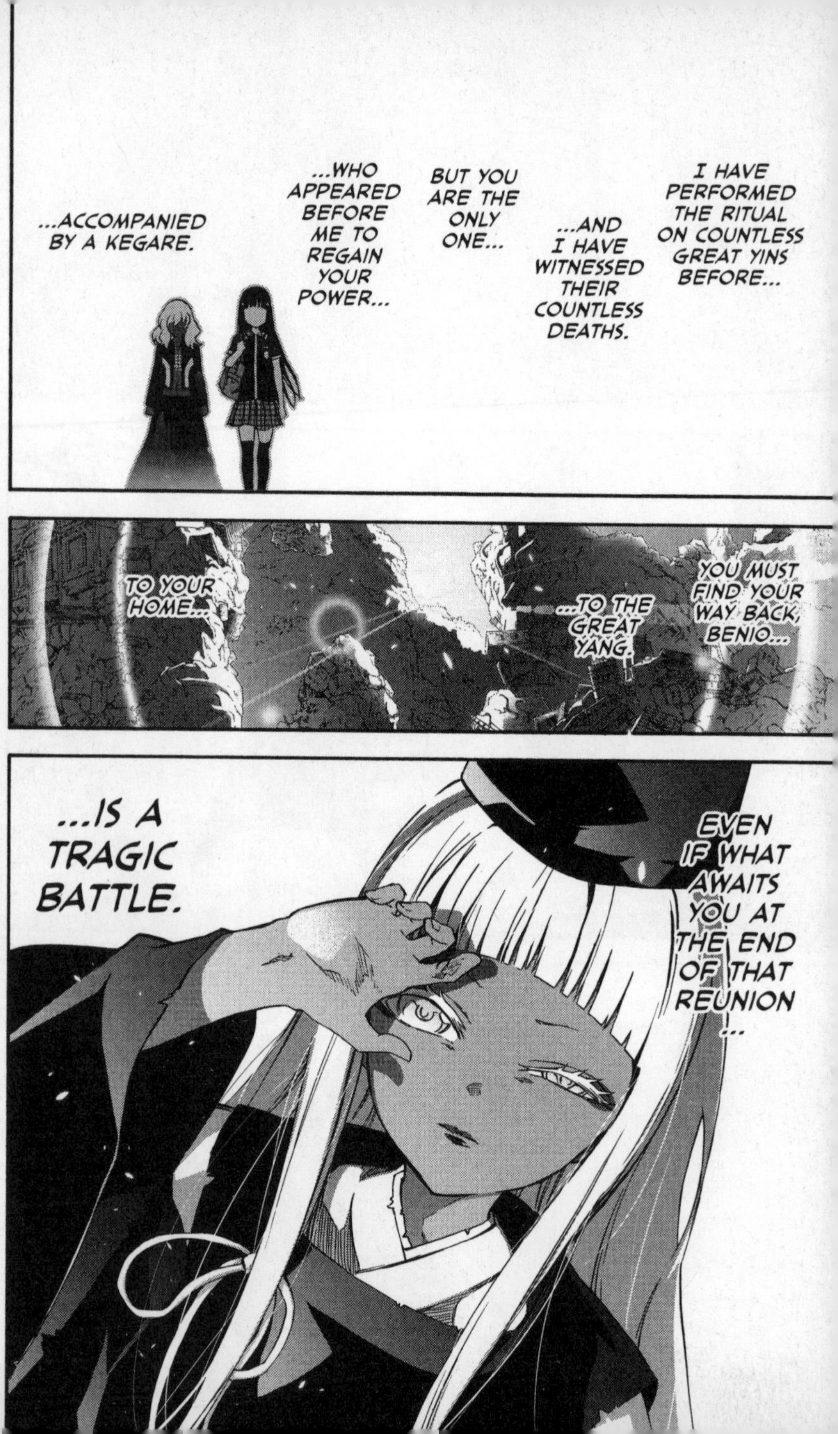
I HAVE PERFORMED THE RITUAL ON COUNTLESS GREAT YINS BEFORE...
...AND I HAVE WITNESSED THEIR COUNTLESS DEATHS.
BUT YOU ARE THE ONLY ONE...
...WHO APPEARED BEFORE ME TO REGAIN YOUR POWER...
...ACCOMPANIED BY A KEGARE.
YOU MUST FIND YOUR WAY BACK, BENIO...
...TO THE GREAT YANG.
TO YOUR HOME...
EVEN IF WHAT AWAITS YOU AT THE END OF THAT REUNION ...
...IS A TRAGIC BATTLE.

PLEASE
PROVE
TO ME
THAT...

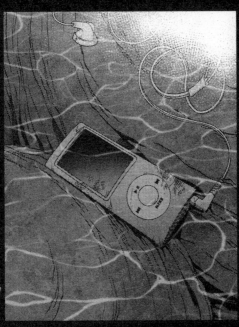

...YOU
HAVE
THE
STRENGTH
TO
PREVAIL.

Twin Star Exorcists
ONMYOJI

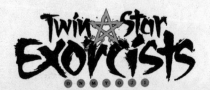

Twin Star Exorcists

ONMYOJI

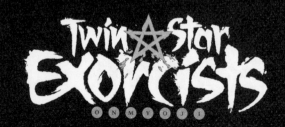

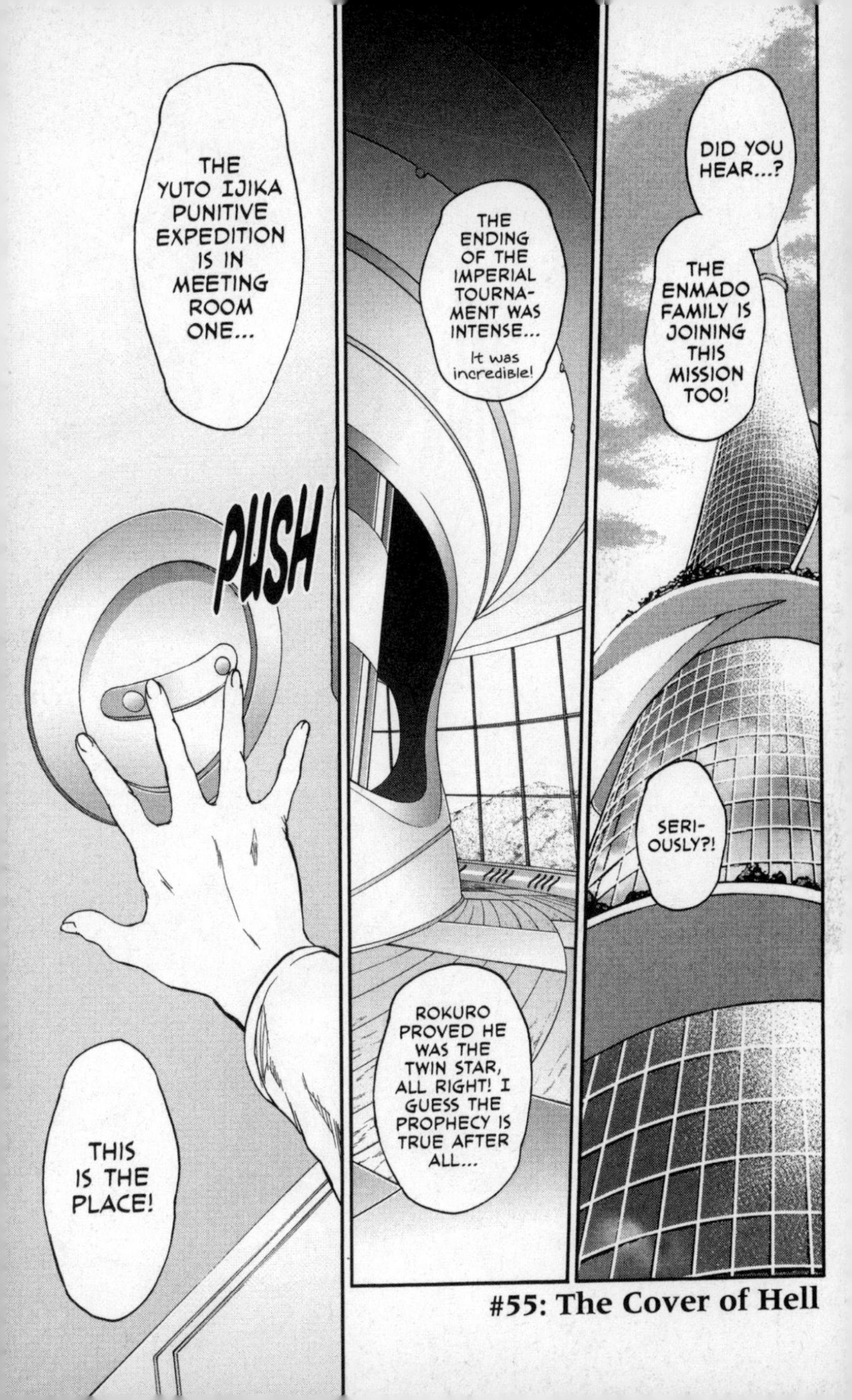
DID YOU HEAR...?
THE ENMADO FAMILY IS JOINING THIS MISSION TOO!
SERI-OUSLY?!
THE ENDING OF THE IMPERIAL TOURNA-MENT WAS INTENSE...
It was incredible!
ROKURO PROVED HE WAS THE TWIN STAR, ALL RIGHT! I GUESS THE PROPHECY IS TRUE AFTER ALL...
THE YUTO IJIKA PUNITIVE EXPEDITION IS IN MEETING ROOM ONE...
PUSH
THIS IS THE PLACE!

#55: The Cover of Hell

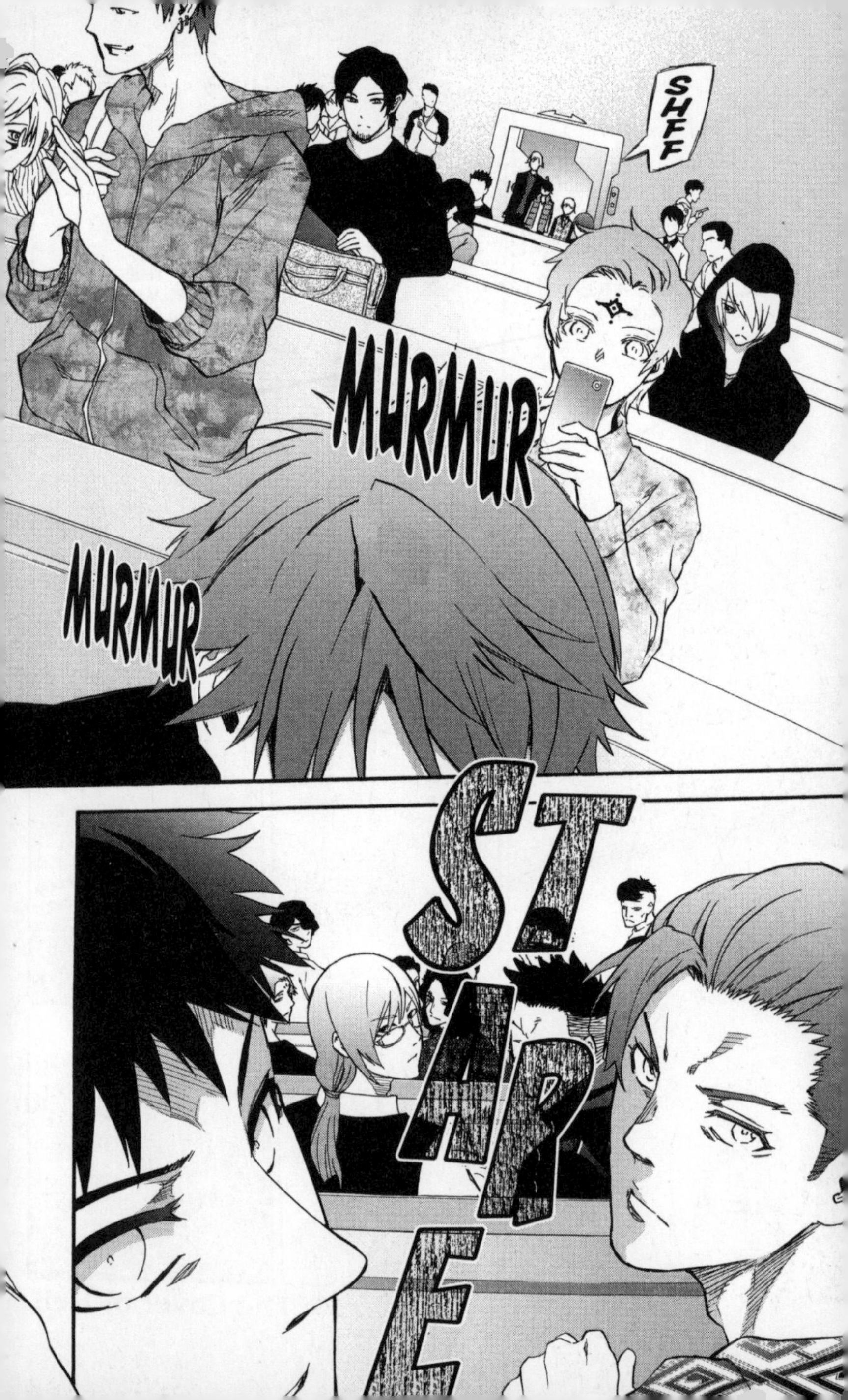
SHFF
MURMUR
MURMUR
STARE

#55: The Cover of Hell

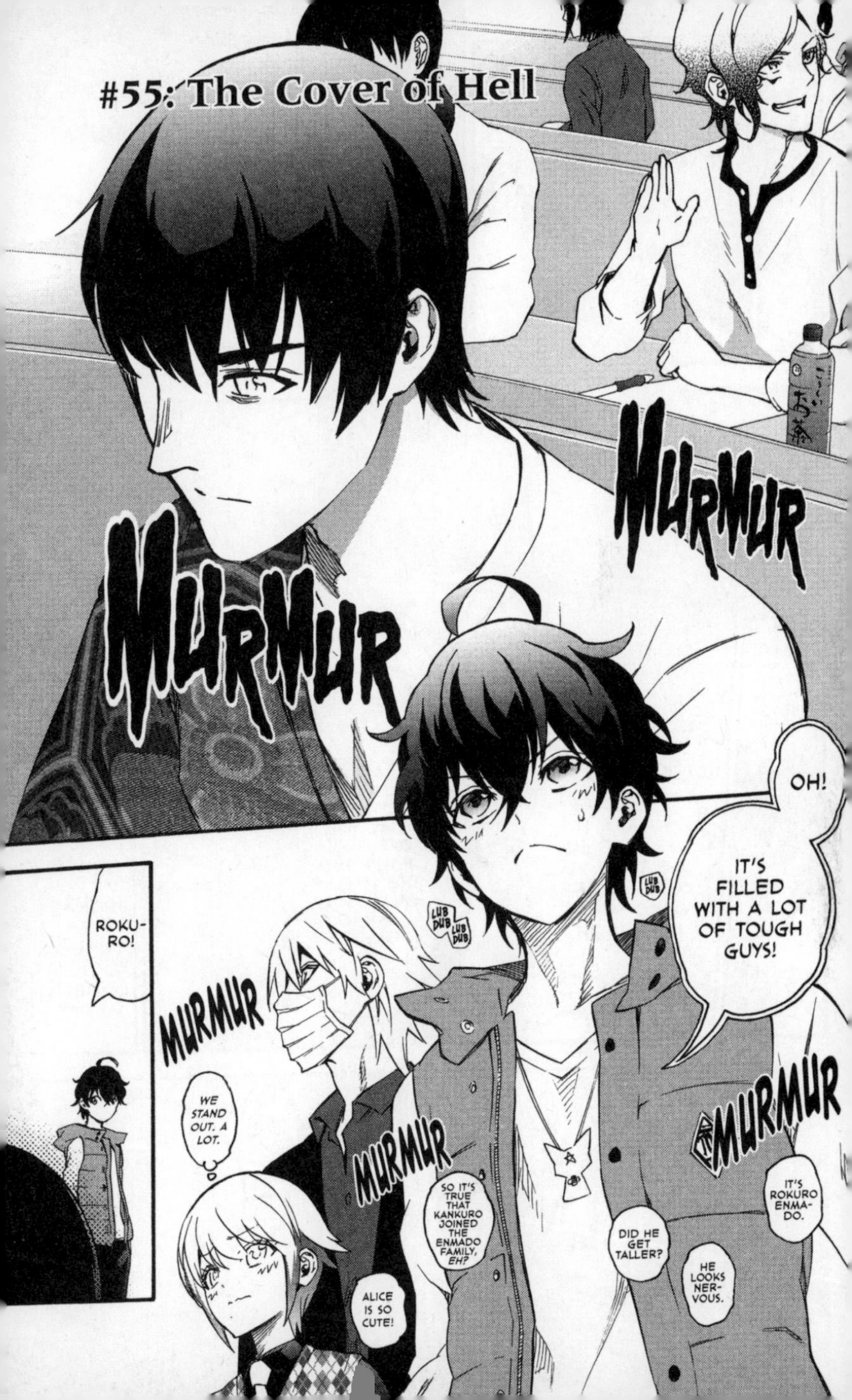
MURMUR
MURMUR
OH!
IT'S FILLED WITH A LOT OF TOUGH GUYS!
LUB DUB
LUB DUB LUB DUB
MURMUR
IT'S ROKURO ENMA-DO.
DID HE GET TALLER?
HE LOOKS NER-VOUS.
SO IT'S TRUE THAT KANKURO JOINED THE ENMADO FAMILY, EH?
MURMUR
WE STAND OUT. A LOT.
MURMUR
ALICE IS SO CUTE!
ROKU-RO!

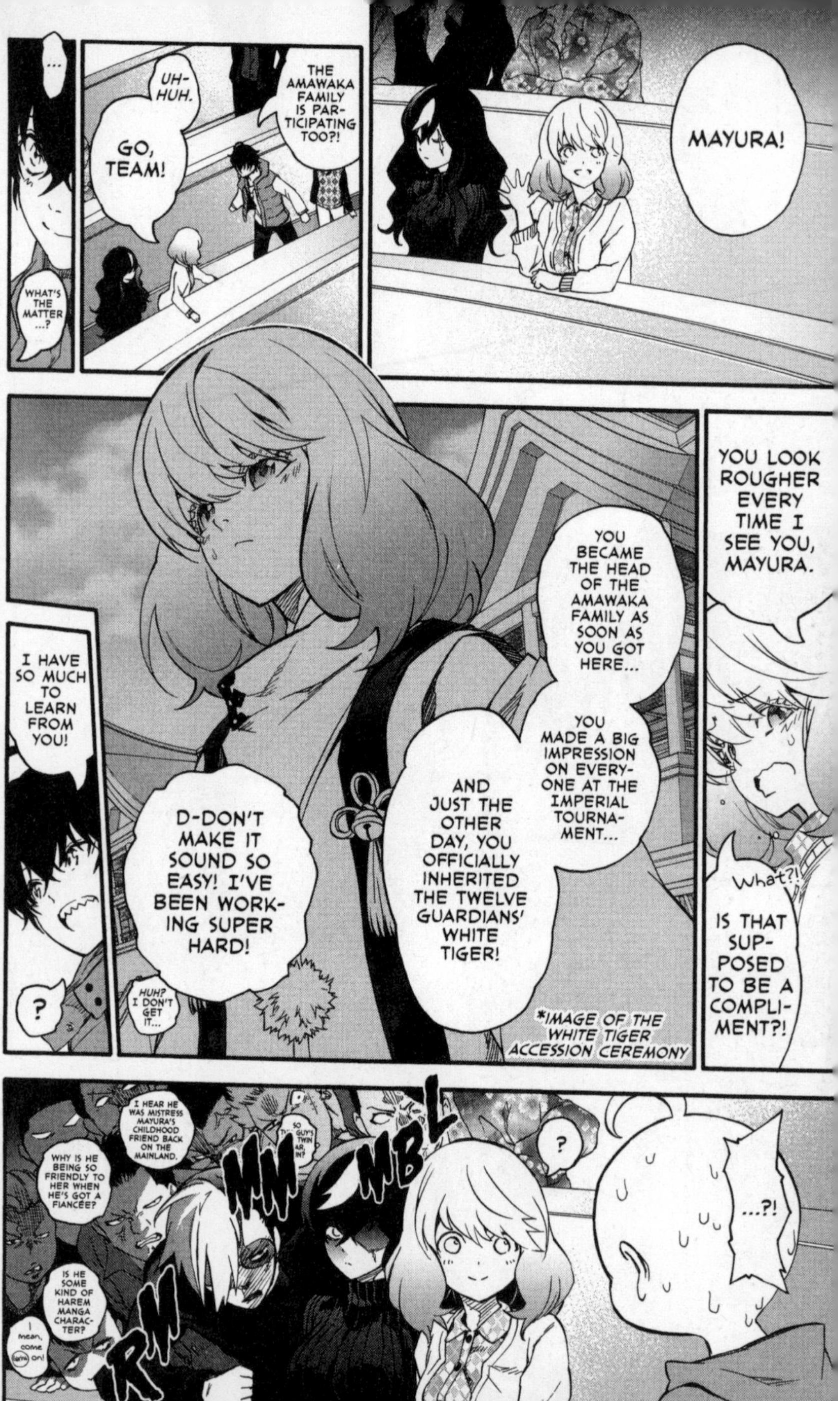
MAYURA!
THE AMAWAKA FAMILY IS PARTICIPATING TOO?!
UH-HUH.
GO, TEAM!
...
WHAT'S THE MATTER...?
YOU LOOK ROUGHER EVERY TIME I SEE YOU, MAYURA.
What?!
IS THAT SUPPOSED TO BE A COMPLIMENT?!
YOU BECAME THE HEAD OF THE AMAWAKA FAMILY AS SOON AS YOU GOT HERE...
YOU MADE A BIG IMPRESSION ON EVERYONE AT THE IMPERIAL TOURNAMENT...
AND JUST THE OTHER DAY, YOU OFFICIALLY INHERITED THE TWELVE GUARDIANS' WHITE TIGER!
*IMAGE OF THE WHITE TIGER ACCESSION CEREMONY
D-DON'T MAKE IT SOUND SO EASY! I'VE BEEN WORKING SUPER HARD!
I HAVE SO MUCH TO LEARN FROM YOU!
HUH? I DON'T GET IT...
?
...?!
?
I HEAR HE WAS MISTRESS MAYURA'S CHILDHOOD FRIEND BACK ON THE MAINLAND.
WHY IS HE BEING SO FRIENDLY TO HER WHEN HE'S GOT A FIANCÉE?
IS HE SOME KIND OF HAREM MANGA CHARACTER?
I mean, come on!
RMMMBL

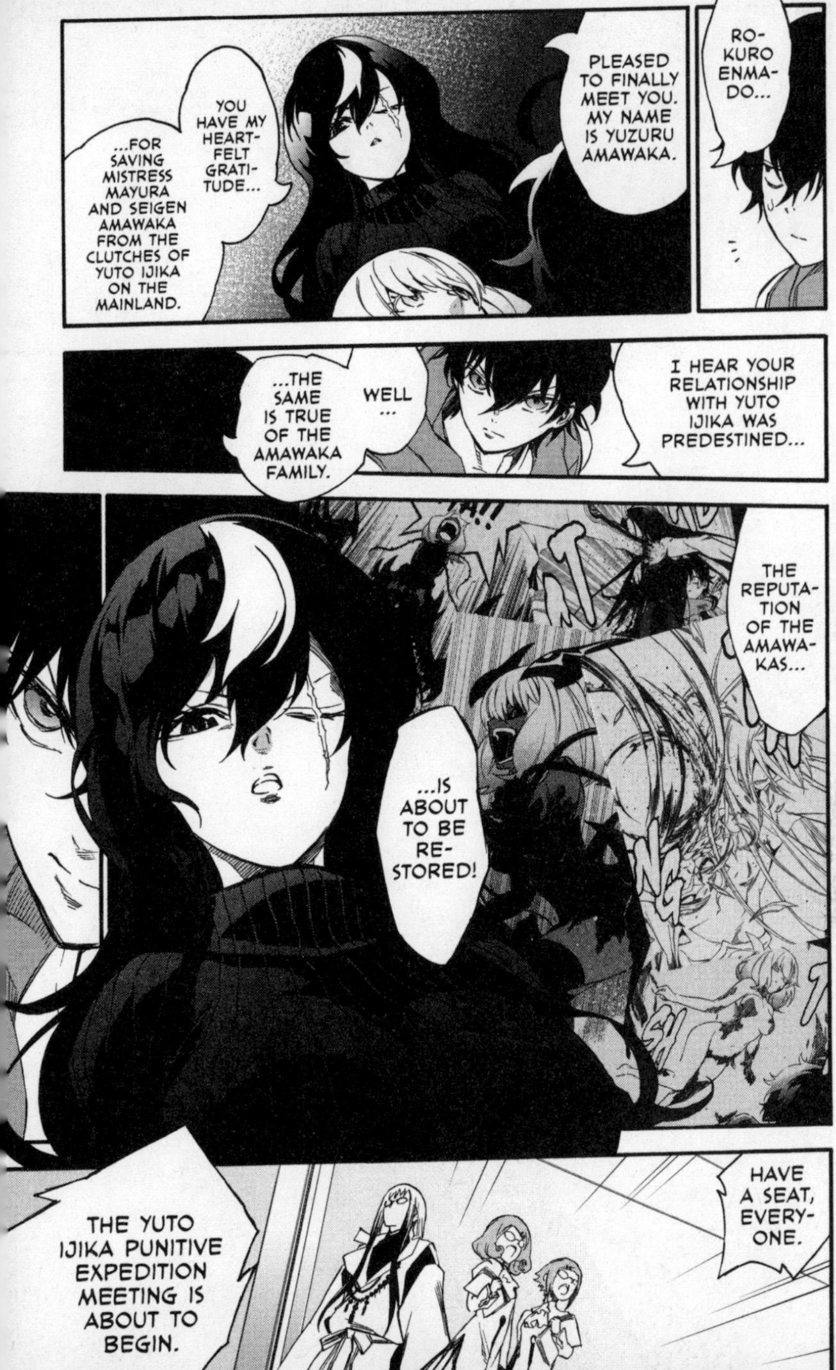
RO-KURO ENMA-DO...
PLEASED TO FINALLY MEET YOU. MY NAME IS YUZURU AMAWAKA.
YOU HAVE MY HEART-FELT GRATI-TUDE...
...FOR SAVING MISTRESS MAYURA AND SEIGEN AMAWAKA FROM THE CLUTCHES OF YUTO IJIKA ON THE MAINLAND.
I HEAR YOUR RELATIONSHIP WITH YUTO IJIKA WAS PREDESTINED...
WELL ...
...THE SAME IS TRUE OF THE AMAWAKA FAMILY.
THE REPUTA-TION OF THE AMAWA-KAS...
...IS ABOUT TO BE RE-STORED!
HAVE A SEAT, EVERY-ONE.
THE YUTO IJIKA PUNITIVE EXPEDITION MEETING IS ABOUT TO BEGIN.

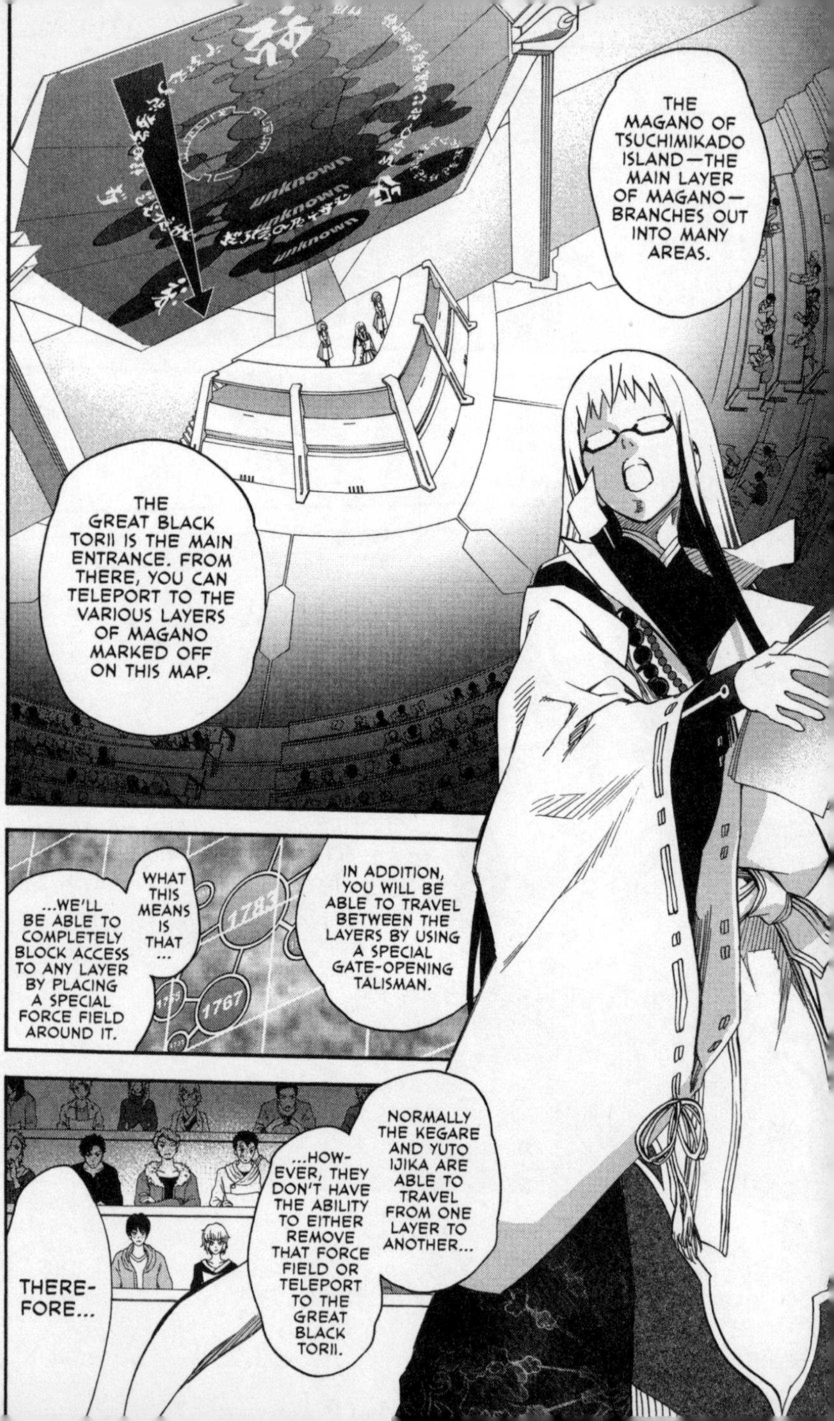
THE MAGANO OF TSUCHIMIKADO ISLAND—THE MAIN LAYER OF MAGANO—BRANCHES OUT INTO MANY AREAS.
THE GREAT BLACK TORII IS THE MAIN ENTRANCE. FROM THERE, YOU CAN TELEPORT TO THE VARIOUS LAYERS OF MAGANO MARKED OFF ON THIS MAP.
IN ADDITION, YOU WILL BE ABLE TO TRAVEL BETWEEN THE LAYERS BY USING A SPECIAL GATE-OPENING TALISMAN.
WHAT THIS MEANS IS THAT...
...WE'LL BE ABLE TO COMPLETELY BLOCK ACCESS TO ANY LAYER BY PLACING A SPECIAL FORCE FIELD AROUND IT.
NORMALLY THE KEGARE AND YUTO IJIKA ARE ABLE TO TRAVEL FROM ONE LAYER TO ANOTHER...
...HOW-EVER, THEY DON'T HAVE THE ABILITY TO EITHER REMOVE THAT FORCE FIELD OR TELEPORT TO THE GREAT BLACK TORII.
THERE-FORE...

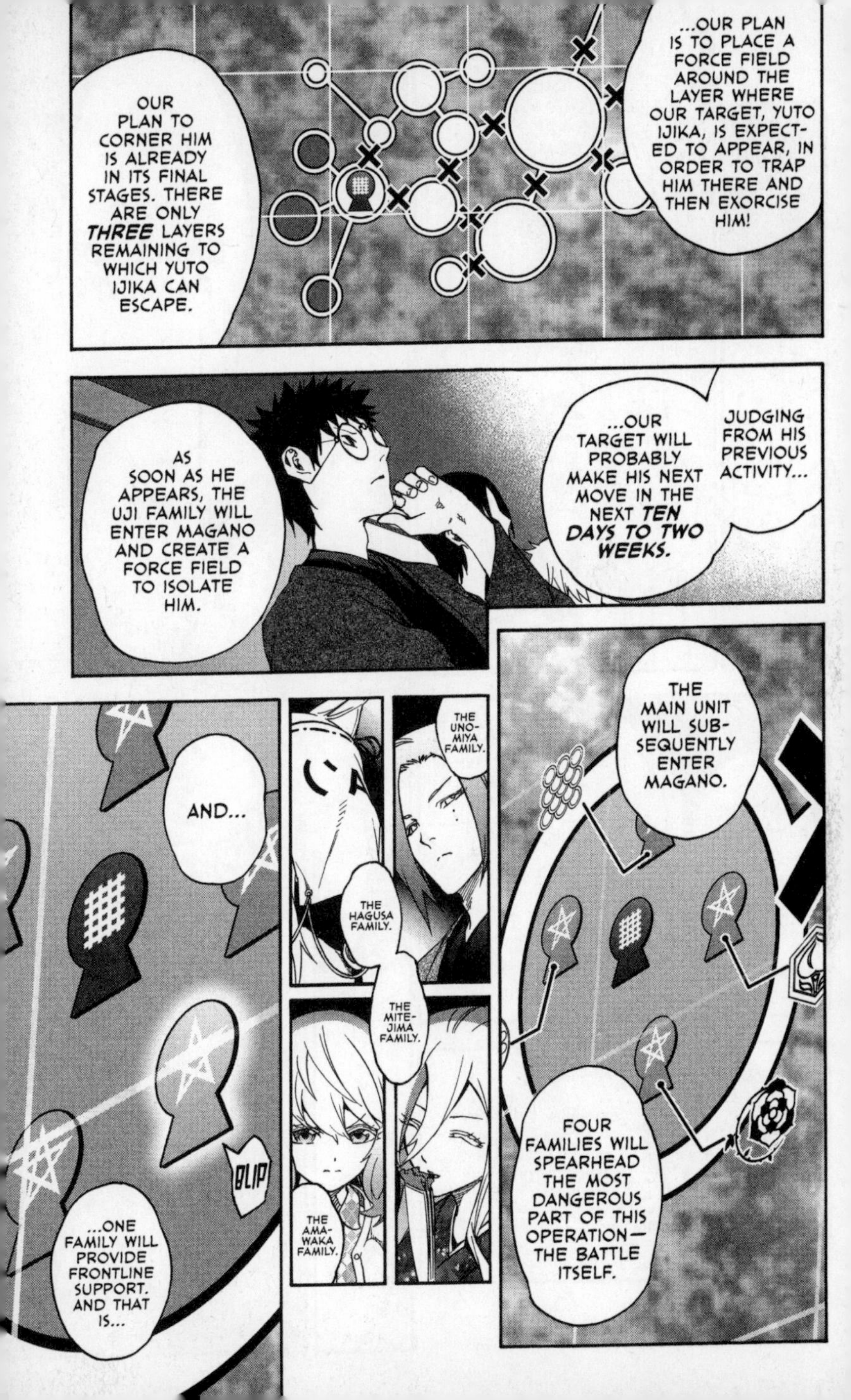
...OUR PLAN IS TO PLACE A FORCE FIELD AROUND THE LAYER WHERE OUR TARGET, YUTO IJIKA, IS EXPECTED TO APPEAR, IN ORDER TO TRAP HIM THERE AND THEN EXORCISE HIM!
OUR PLAN TO CORNER HIM IS ALREADY IN ITS FINAL STAGES. THERE ARE ONLY *THREE* LAYERS REMAINING TO WHICH YUTO IJIKA CAN ESCAPE.
JUDGING FROM HIS PREVIOUS ACTIVITY...
...OUR TARGET WILL PROBABLY MAKE HIS NEXT MOVE IN THE NEXT *TEN DAYS TO TWO WEEKS.*
AS SOON AS HE APPEARS, THE UJI FAMILY WILL ENTER MAGANO AND CREATE A FORCE FIELD TO ISOLATE HIM.
THE MAIN UNIT WILL SUBSEQUENTLY ENTER MAGANO.
FOUR FAMILIES WILL SPEARHEAD THE MOST DANGEROUS PART OF THIS OPERATION—THE BATTLE ITSELF.
THE UNOMIYA FAMILY.
THE HAGUSA FAMILY.
THE MITEJIMA FAMILY.
THE AMAWAKA FAMILY.
AND...
BLIP
...ONE FAMILY WILL PROVIDE FRONTLINE SUPPORT. AND THAT IS...

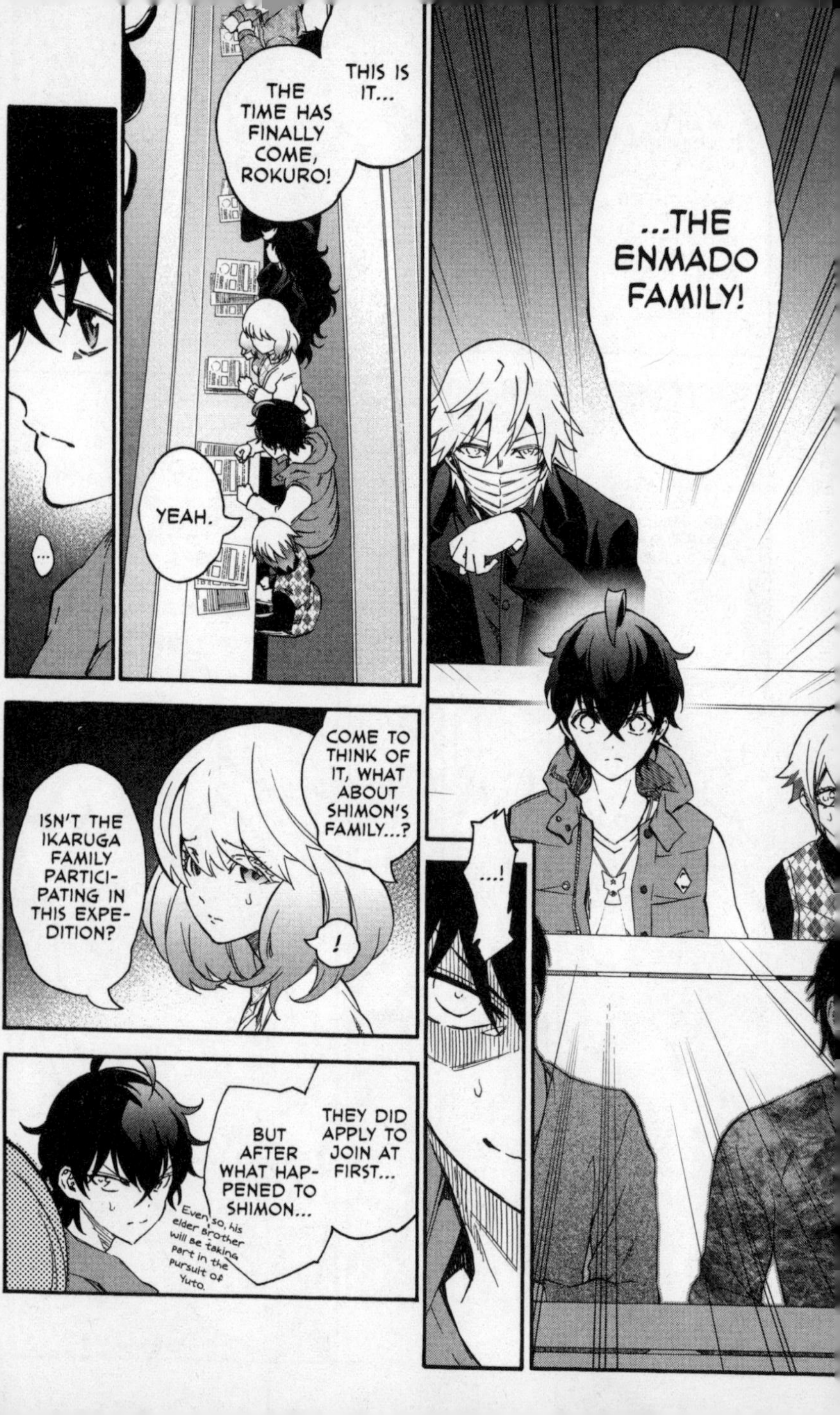
...THE ENMADO FAMILY!
THIS IS IT...
THE TIME HAS FINALLY COME, ROKURO!
YEAH.
...
...!
COME TO THINK OF IT, WHAT ABOUT SHIMON'S FAMILY...?
ISN'T THE IKARUGA FAMILY PARTICIPATING IN THIS EXPEDITION?
!
THEY DID APPLY TO JOIN AT FIRST...
BUT AFTER WHAT HAPPENED TO SHIMON...
Even so, his elder brother will be taking part in the pursuit of Yuto.

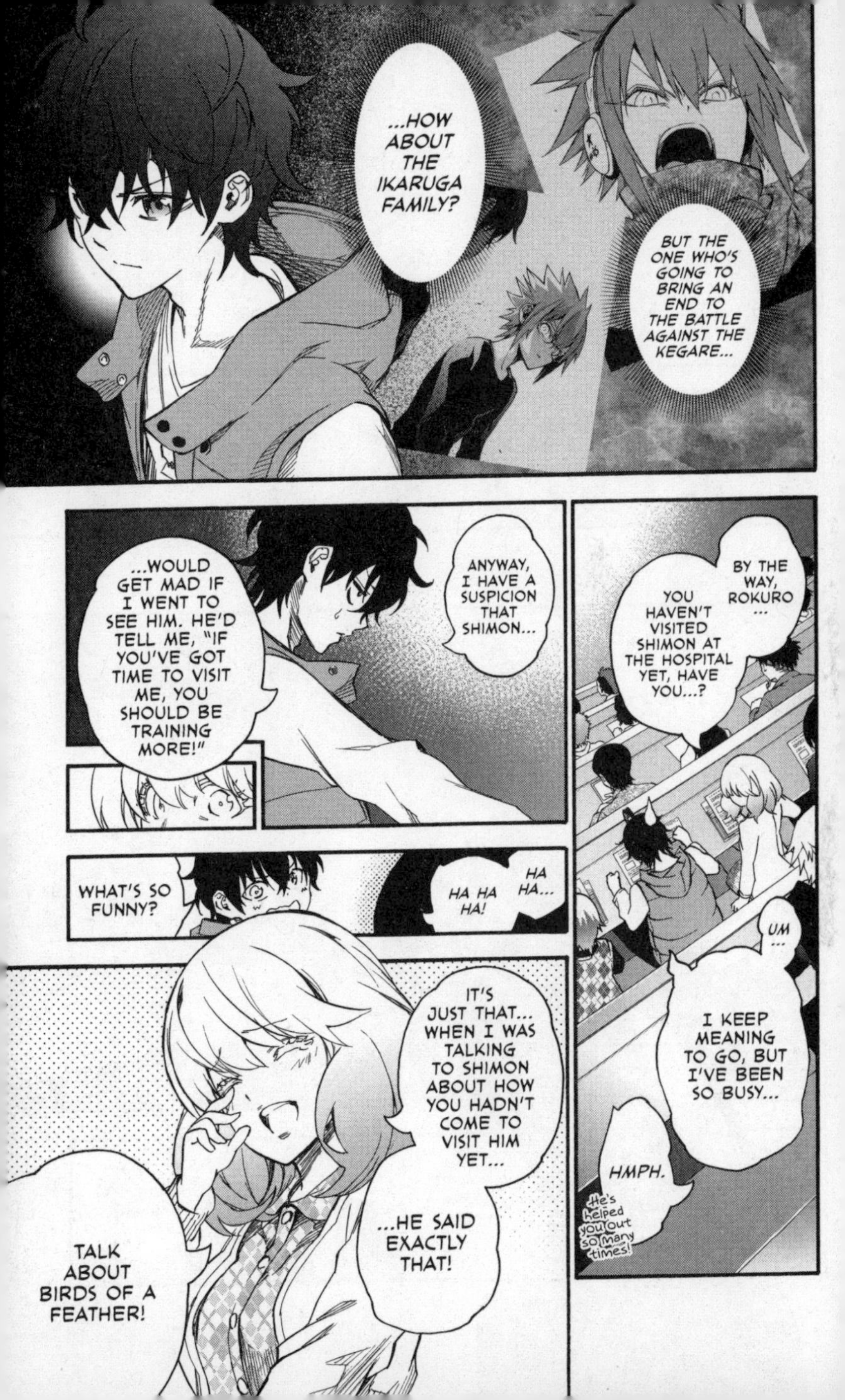
BUT THE ONE WHO'S GOING TO BRING AN END TO THE BATTLE AGAINST THE KEGARE...
...HOW ABOUT THE IKARUGA FAMILY?
BY THE WAY, ROKURO...
YOU HAVEN'T VISITED SHIMON AT THE HOSPITAL YET, HAVE YOU...?
UM...
I KEEP MEANING TO GO, BUT I'VE BEEN SO BUSY...
HMPH.
He's helped you out so many times!
ANYWAY, I HAVE A SUSPICION THAT SHIMON...
...WOULD GET MAD IF I WENT TO SEE HIM. HE'D TELL ME, "IF YOU'VE GOT TIME TO VISIT ME, YOU SHOULD BE TRAINING MORE!"
HA HA...
HA HA HA!
WHAT'S SO FUNNY?
IT'S JUST THAT... WHEN I WAS TALKING TO SHIMON ABOUT HOW YOU HADN'T COME TO VISIT HIM YET...
...HE SAID EXACTLY THAT!
TALK ABOUT BIRDS OF A FEATHER!

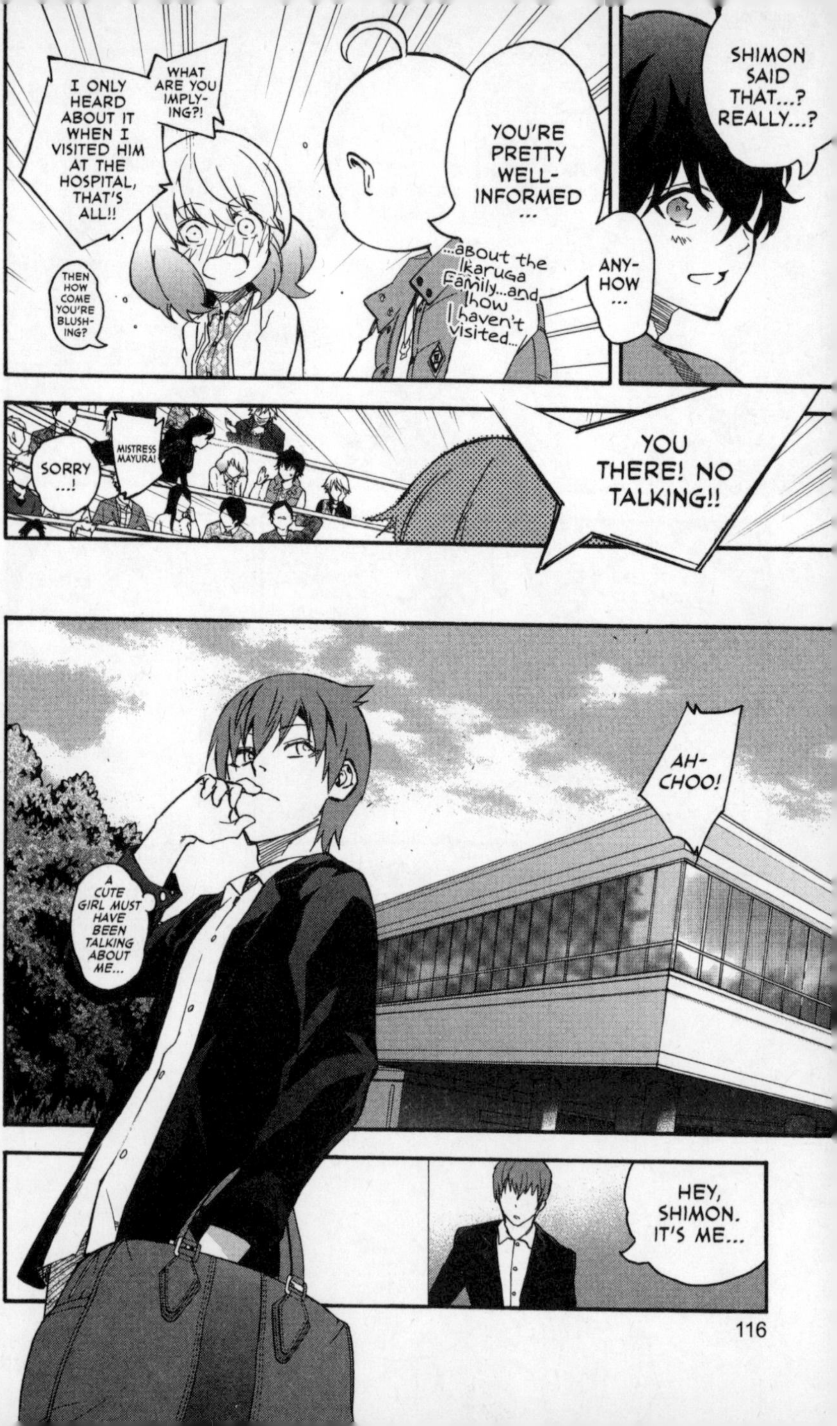
SHIMON SAID THAT...? REALLY...?
ANYHOW...
YOU'RE PRETTY WELL-INFORMED...
...about the Ikaruga Family...and how I haven't visited...
WHAT ARE YOU IMPLYING?!
I ONLY HEARD ABOUT IT WHEN I VISITED HIM AT THE HOSPITAL, THAT'S ALL!!
THEN HOW COME YOU'RE BLUSHING?
YOU THERE! NO TALKING!!
MISTRESS MAYURA!
SORRY...!
AH-CHOO!
A CUTE GIRL MUST HAVE BEEN TALKING ABOUT ME...
HEY, SHIMON. IT'S ME...

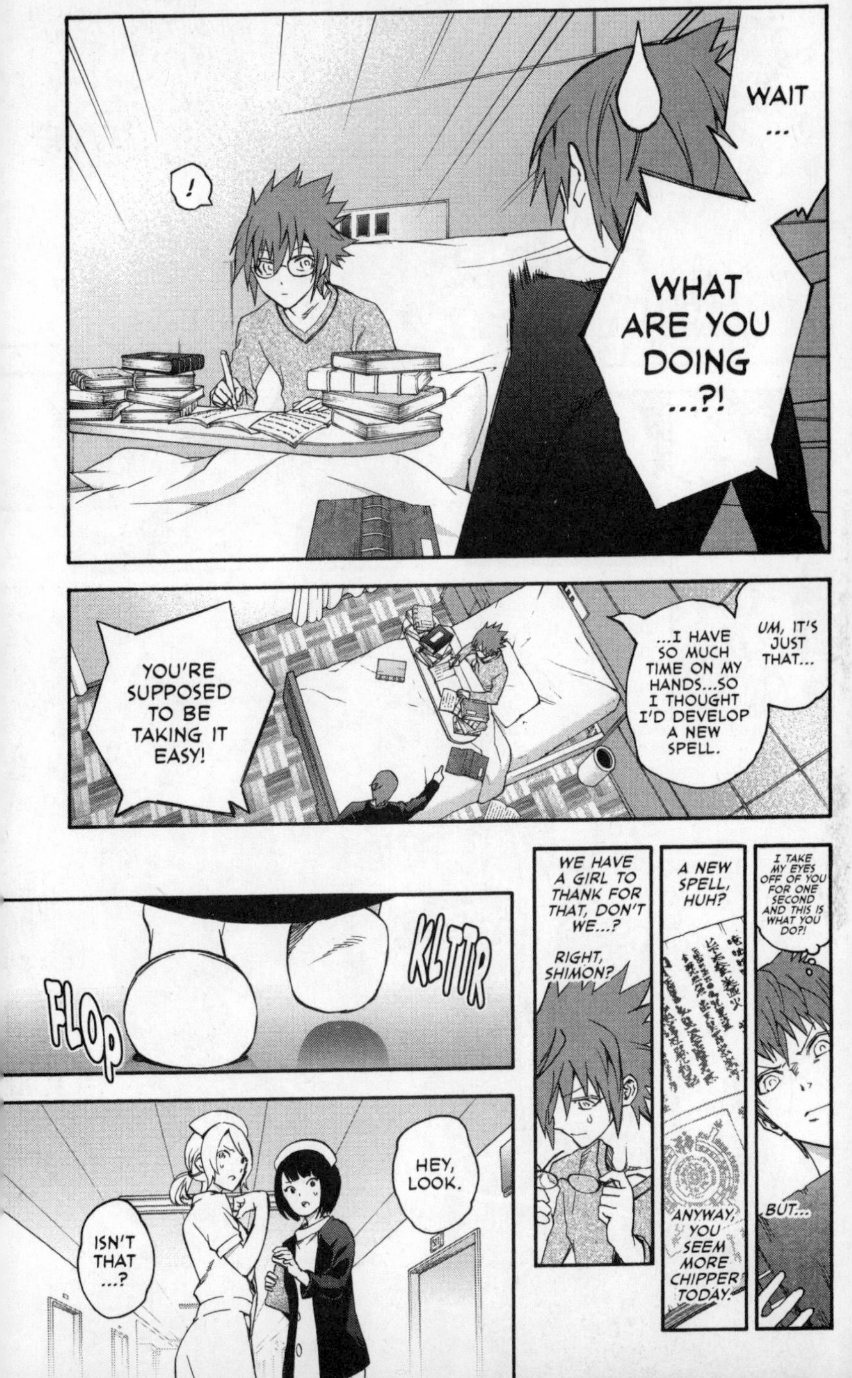
WAIT ...
WHAT ARE YOU DOING ...?!
!
UM, IT'S JUST THAT...
...I HAVE SO MUCH TIME ON MY HANDS...SO I THOUGHT I'D DEVELOP A NEW SPELL.
YOU'RE SUPPOSED TO BE TAKING IT EASY!
I TAKE MY EYES OFF OF YOU FOR ONE SECOND AND THIS IS WHAT YOU DO?!
BUT...
A NEW SPELL, HUH?
ANYWAY, YOU SEEM MORE CHIPPER TODAY.
WE HAVE A GIRL TO THANK FOR THAT, DON'T WE...?
RIGHT, SHIMON?
KLTTR
FLOP
HEY, LOOK.
ISN'T THAT ...?

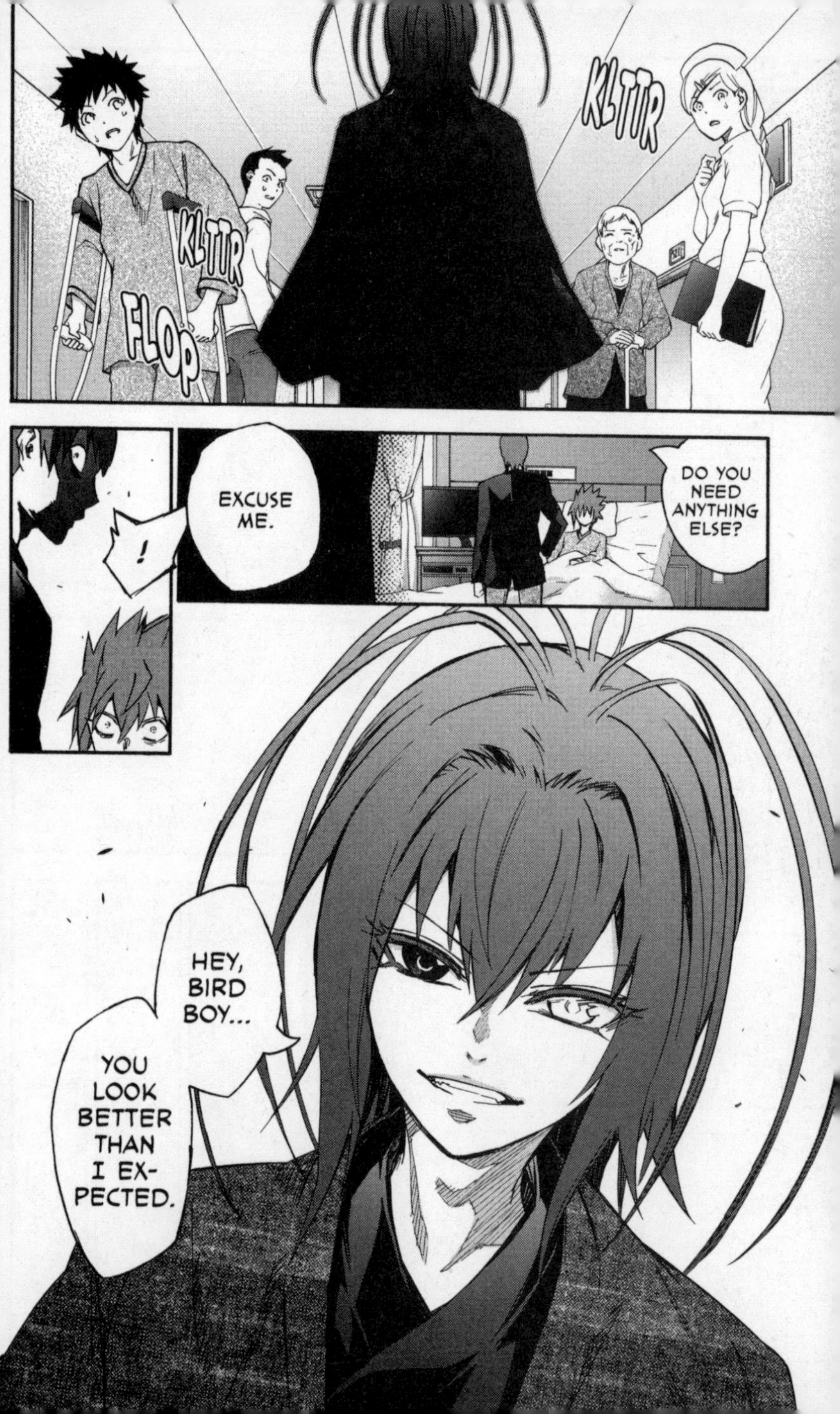
KLTTR
KLTTR
FLOP
DO YOU NEED ANYTHING ELSE?
EXCUSE ME.
!
HEY, BIRD BOY...
YOU LOOK BETTER THAN I EX-PECTED.

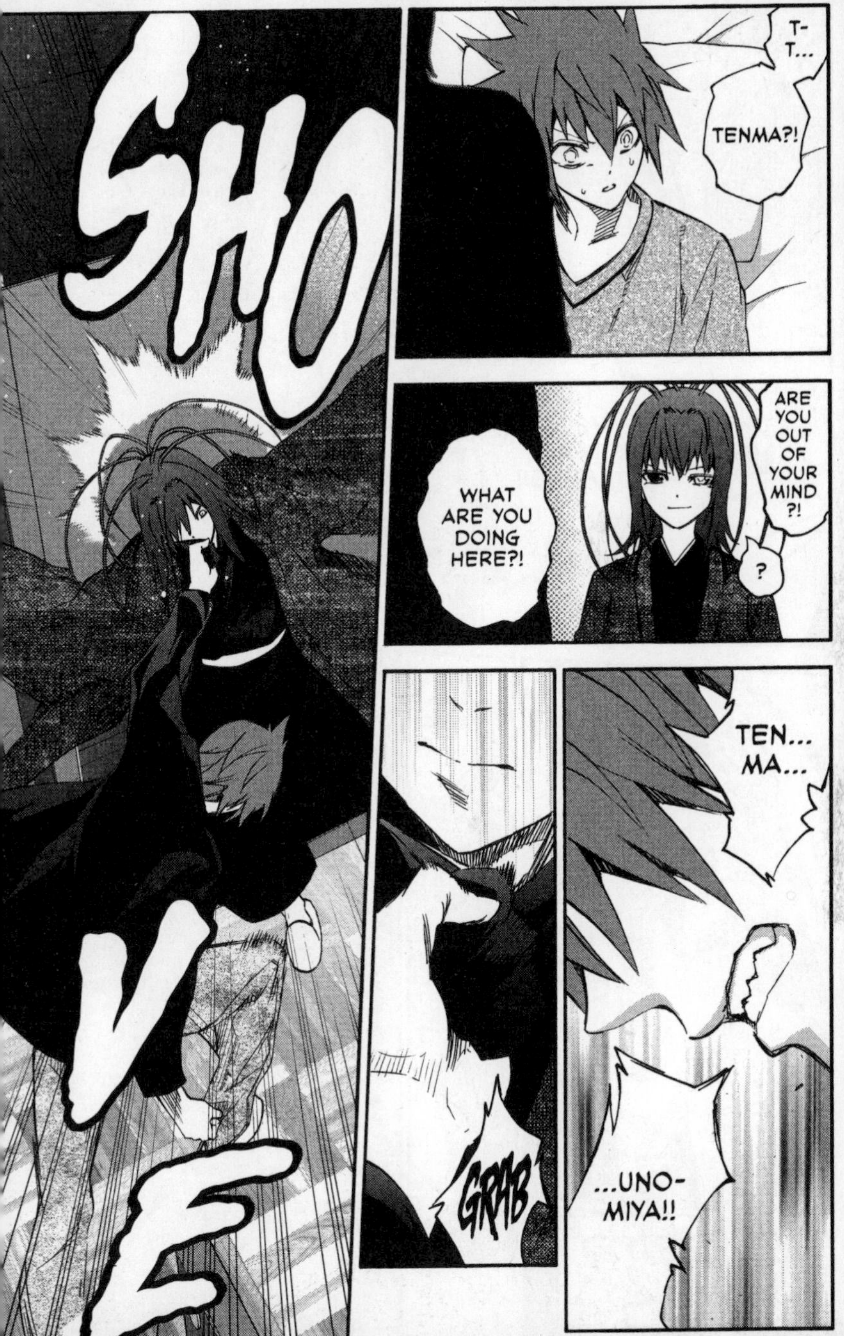
T- T...
TENMA?!
ARE YOU OUT OF YOUR MIND?!
?
WHAT ARE YOU DOING HERE?!
TEN... MA...
...UNO-MIYA!!
GRAB
SHOVE

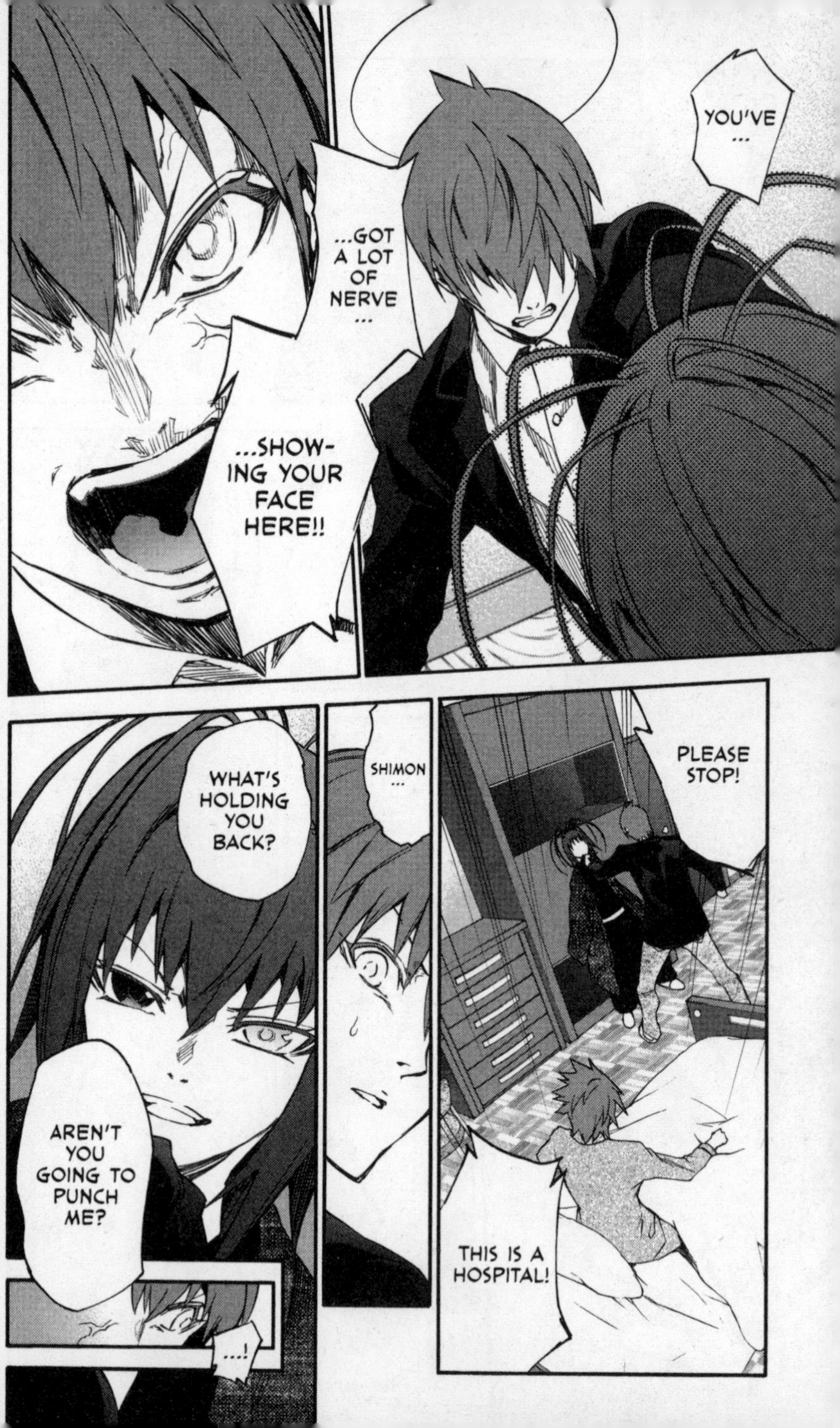
YOU'VE ...
...GOT A LOT OF NERVE ...
...SHOWING YOUR FACE HERE!!
PLEASE STOP!
THIS IS A HOSPITAL!
SHIMON ...
WHAT'S HOLDING YOU BACK?
AREN'T YOU GOING TO PUNCH ME?
...!

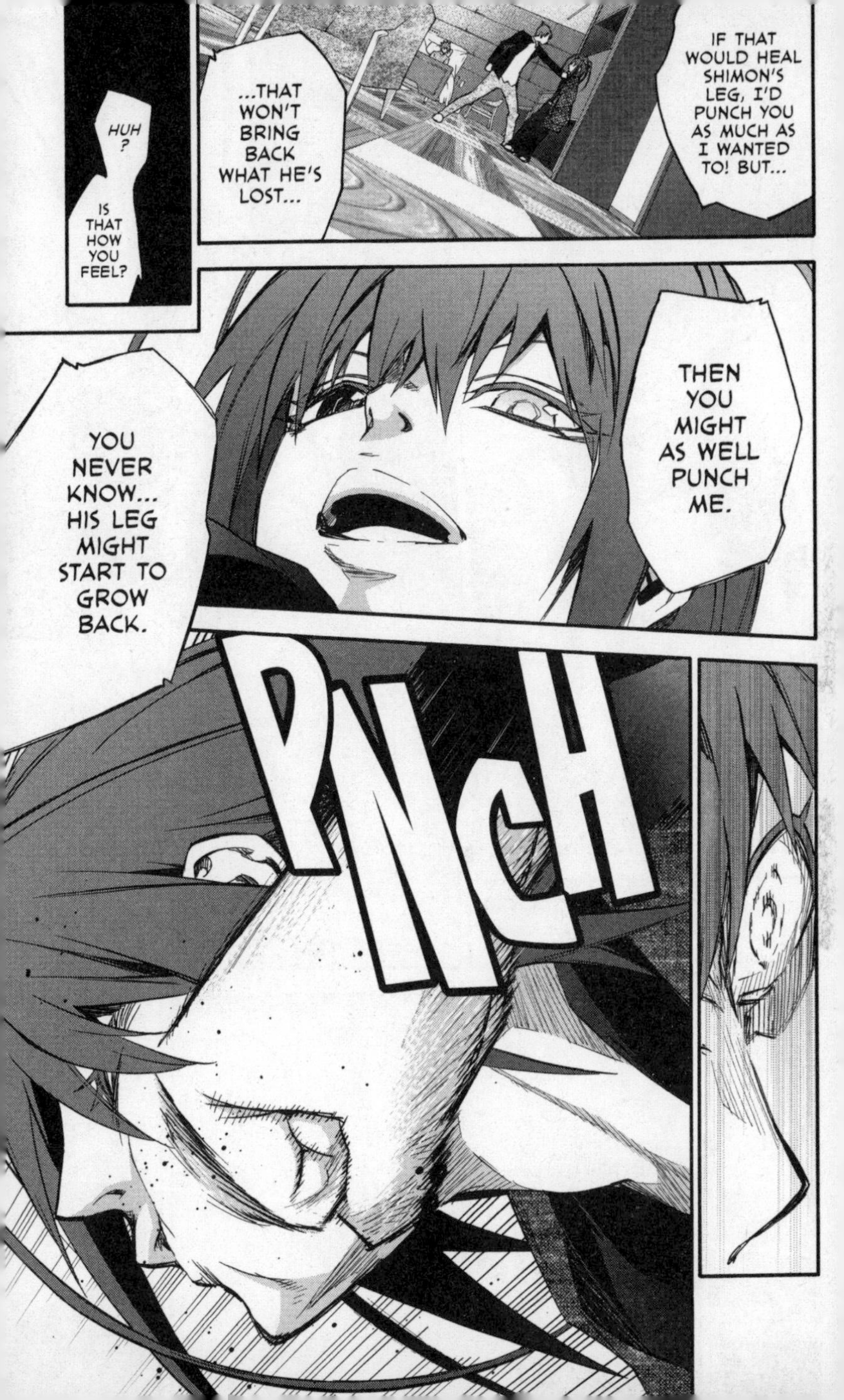
IF THAT WOULD HEAL SHIMON'S LEG, I'D PUNCH YOU AS MUCH AS I WANTED TO! BUT...
...THAT WON'T BRING BACK WHAT HE'S LOST...
HUH?
IS THAT HOW YOU FEEL?
THEN YOU MIGHT AS WELL PUNCH ME.
YOU NEVER KNOW... HIS LEG MIGHT START TO GROW BACK.
PNCH

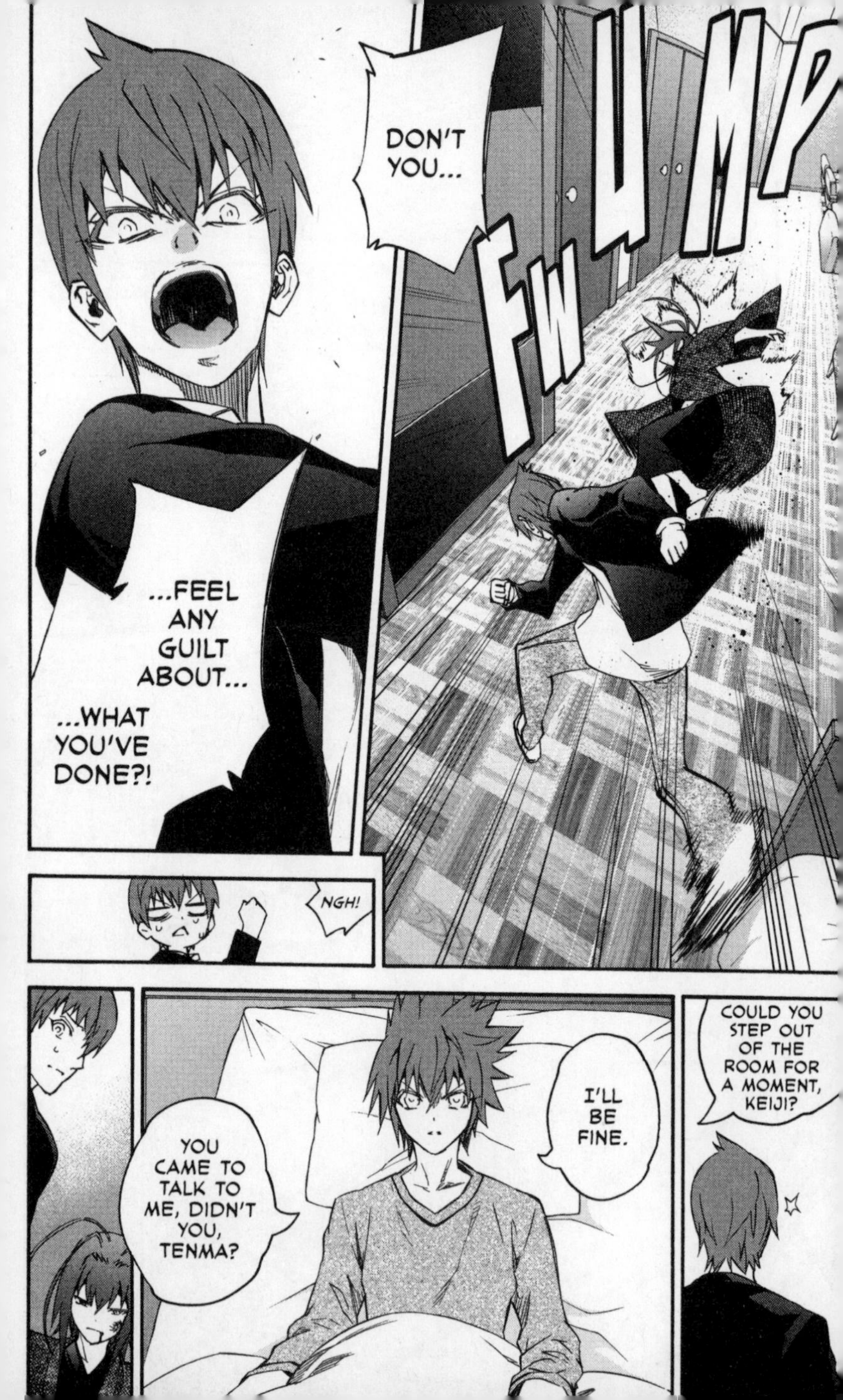
FWUMP
DON'T YOU...
...FEEL ANY GUILT ABOUT...
...WHAT YOU'VE DONE?!
NGH!
COULD YOU STEP OUT OF THE ROOM FOR A MOMENT, KEIJI?
I'LL BE FINE.
YOU CAME TO TALK TO ME, DIDN'T YOU, TENMA?

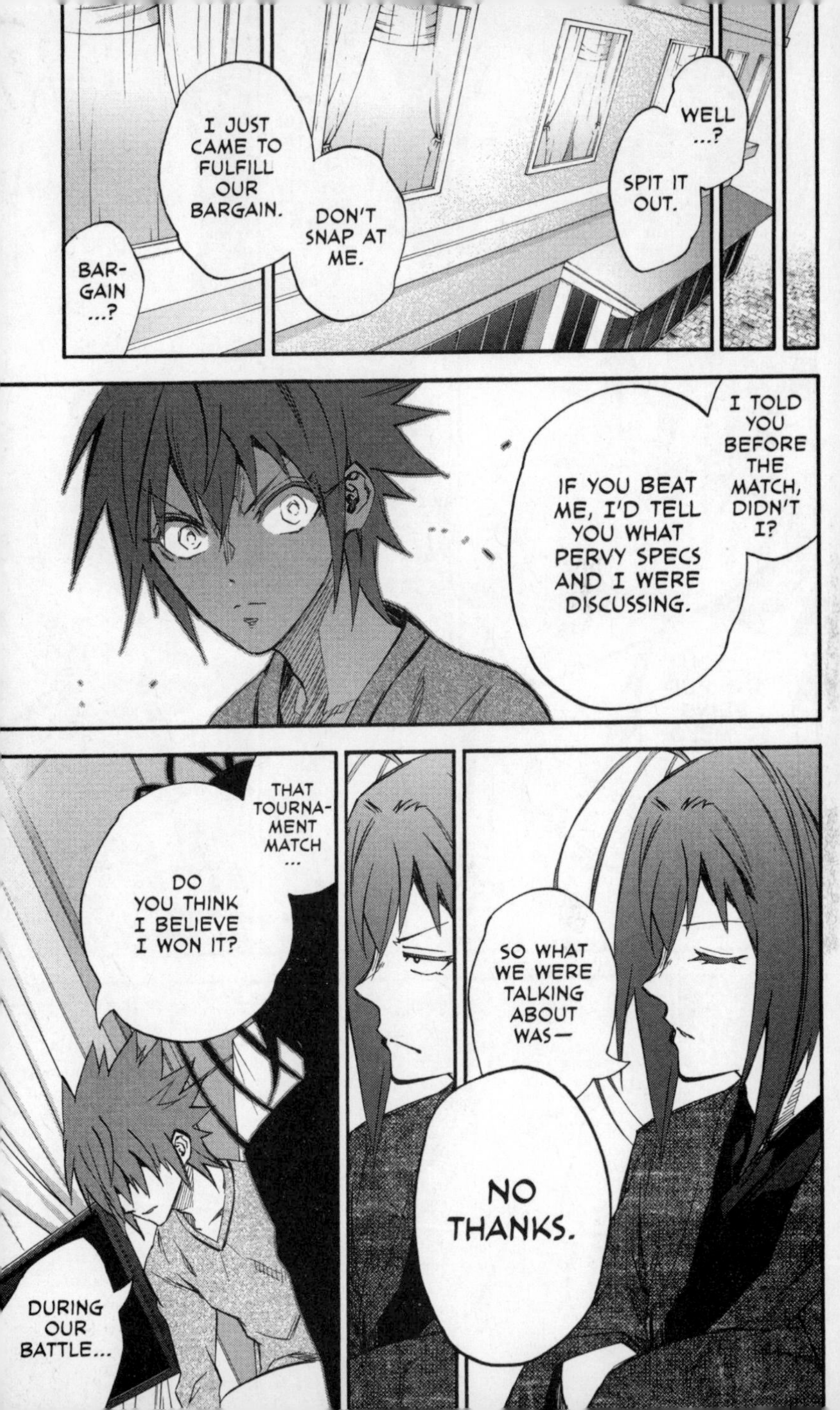
WELL ...?
SPIT IT OUT.
DON'T SNAP AT ME.
I JUST CAME TO FULFILL OUR BARGAIN.
BAR-GAIN ...?
I TOLD YOU BEFORE THE MATCH, DIDN'T I?
IF YOU BEAT ME, I'D TELL YOU WHAT PERVY SPECS AND I WERE DISCUSSING.
SO WHAT WE WERE TALKING ABOUT WAS—
NO THANKS.
THAT TOURNA-MENT MATCH ...
DO YOU THINK I BELIEVE I WON IT?
DURING OUR BATTLE...

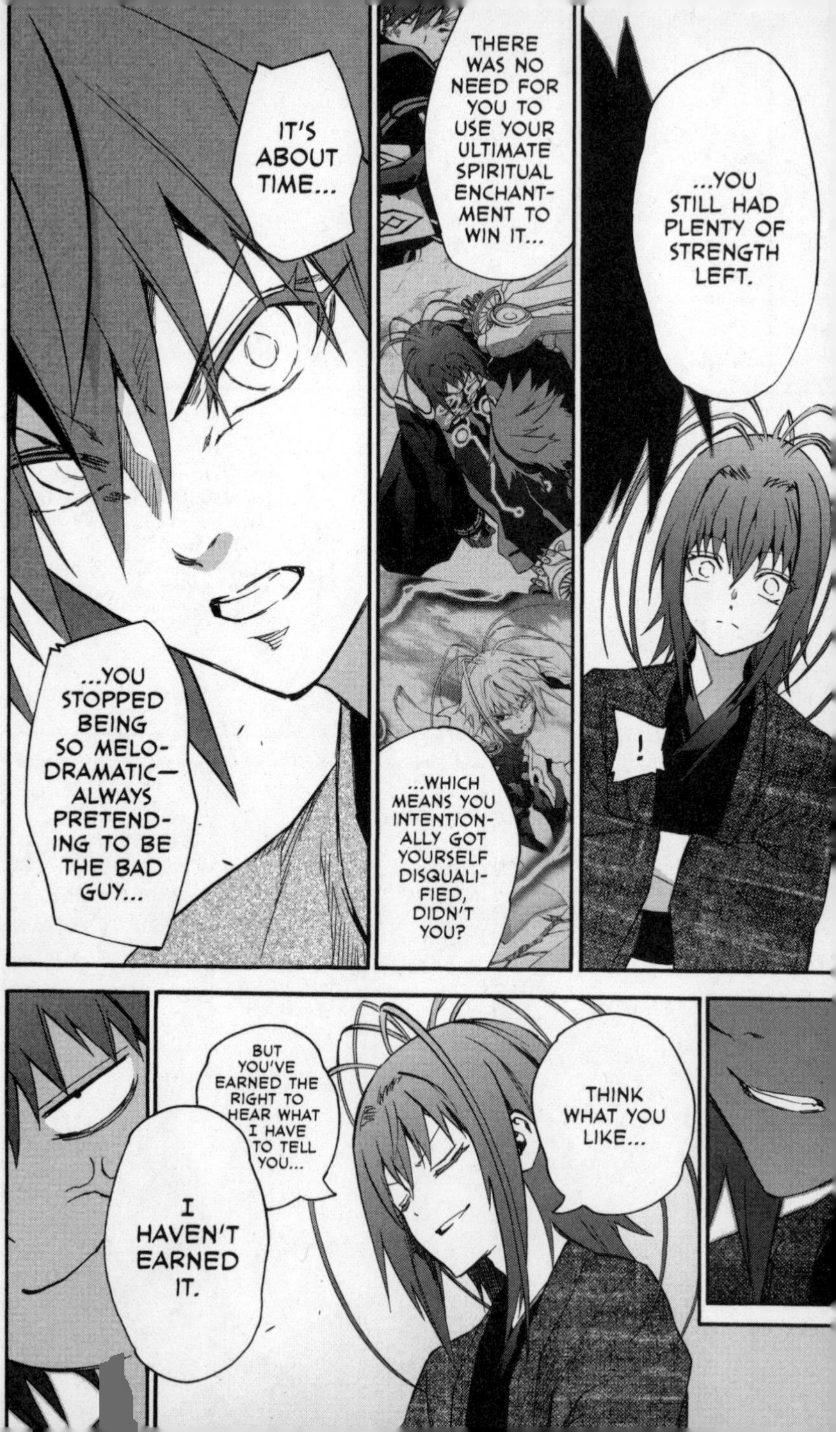
...YOU STILL HAD PLENTY OF STRENGTH LEFT.
!
THERE WAS NO NEED FOR YOU TO USE YOUR ULTIMATE SPIRITUAL ENCHANT-MENT TO WIN IT...
...WHICH MEANS YOU INTENTION-ALLY GOT YOURSELF DISQUALI-FIED, DIDN'T YOU?
IT'S ABOUT TIME...
...YOU STOPPED BEING SO MELO-DRAMATIC—ALWAYS PRETEND-ING TO BE THE BAD GUY...
THINK WHAT YOU LIKE...
BUT YOU'VE EARNED THE RIGHT TO HEAR WHAT I HAVE TO TELL YOU...
I HAVEN'T EARNED IT.

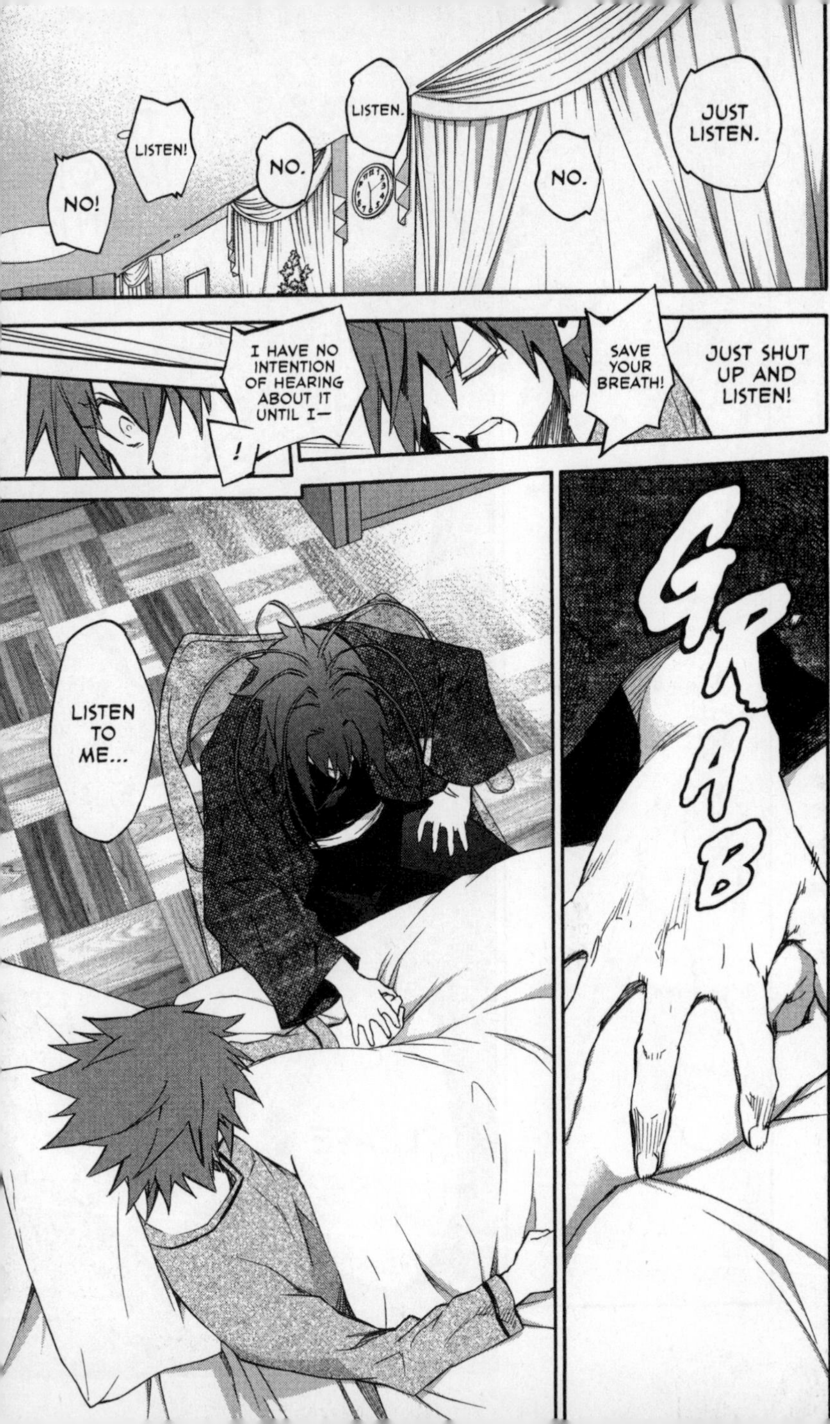
JUST LISTEN.
NO.
LISTEN.
NO.
LISTEN!
NO!
JUST SHUT UP AND LISTEN!
SAVE YOUR BREATH!
I HAVE NO INTENTION OF HEARING ABOUT IT UNTIL I—
!
GRAB
LISTEN TO ME...

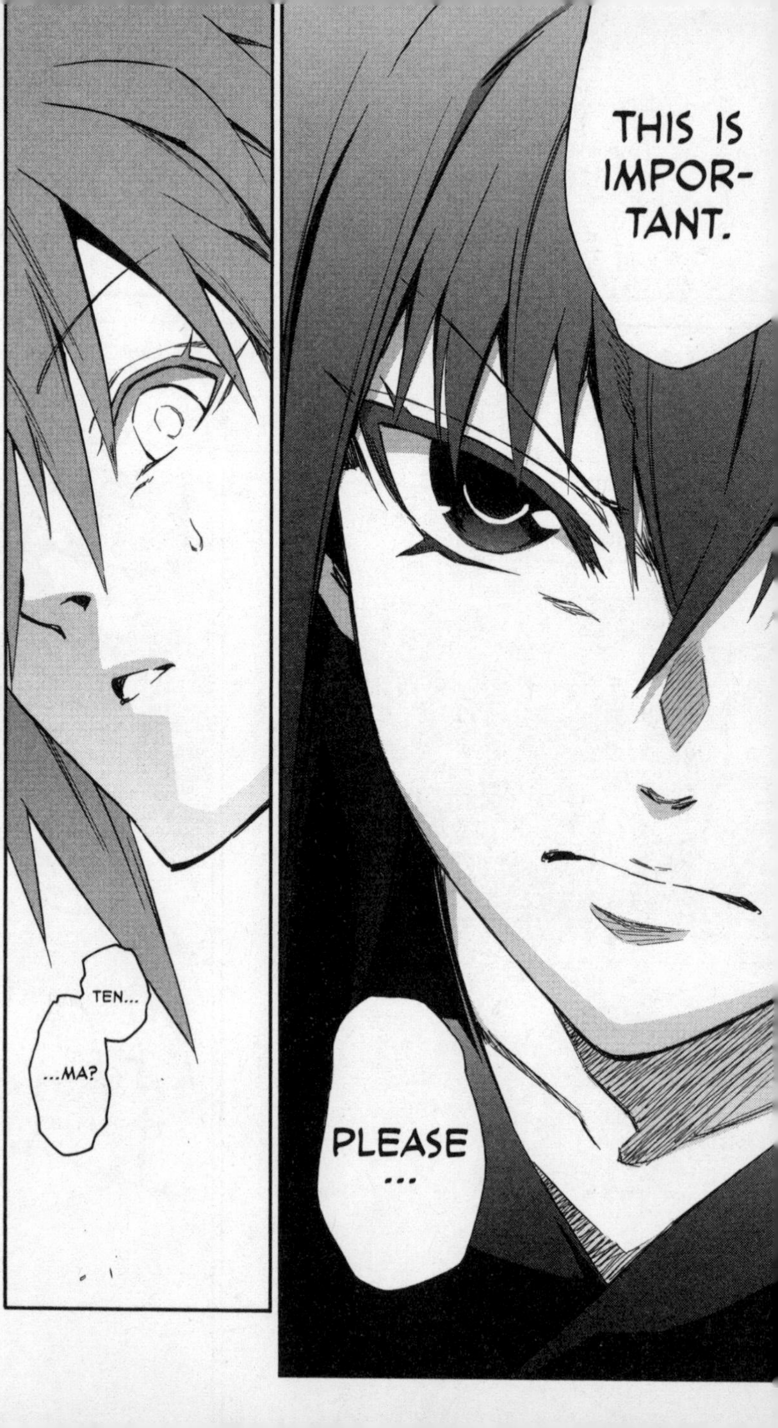
THIS IS IMPOR-TANT.
PLEASE ...
TEN...
...MA?

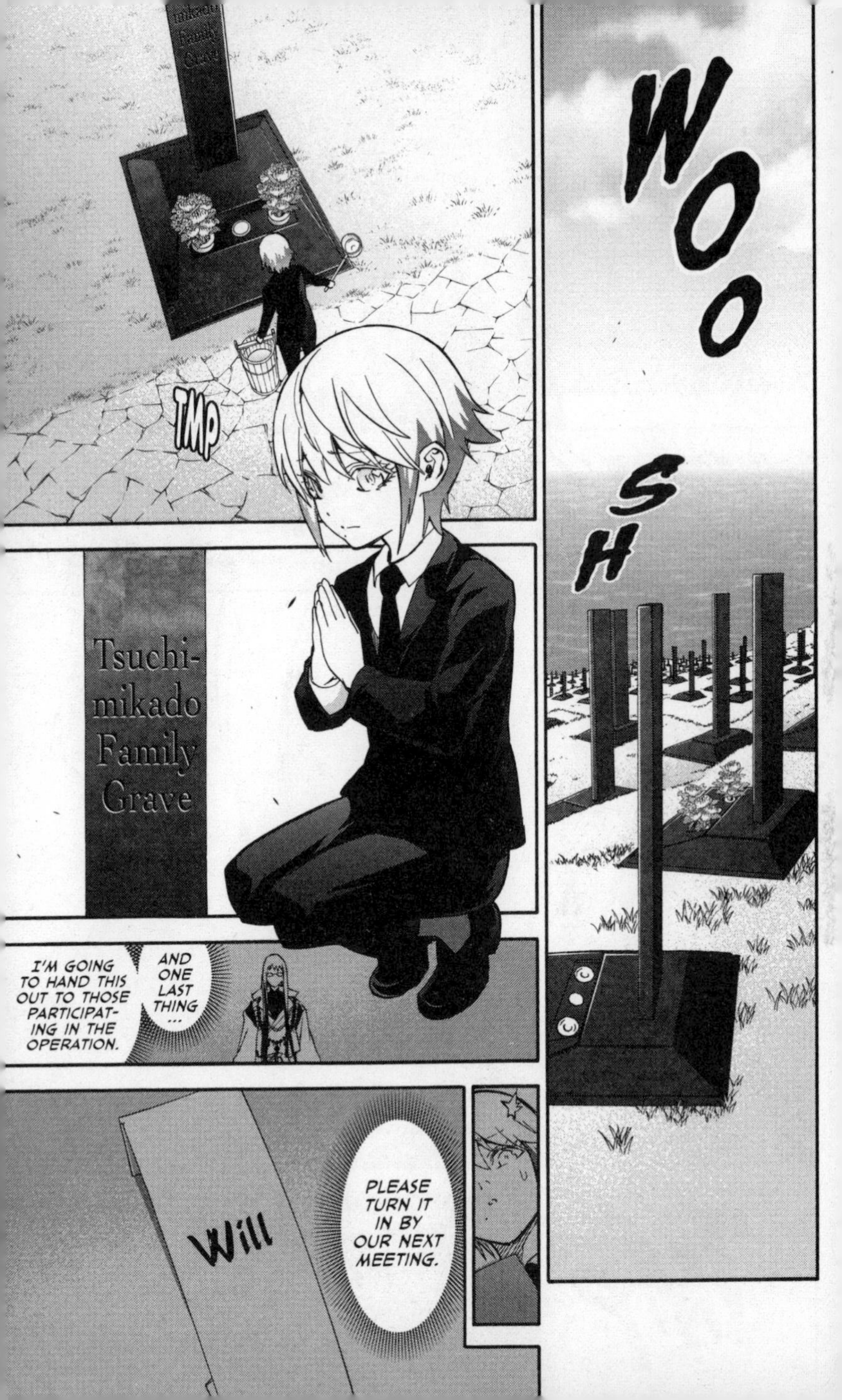

WOOOSH
TMP
Tsuchi-
mikado
Family
Grave
AND ONE LAST THING...
I'M GOING TO HAND THIS OUT TO THOSE PARTICIPATING IN THE OPERATION.
PLEASE TURN IT IN BY OUR NEXT MEETING.
Will

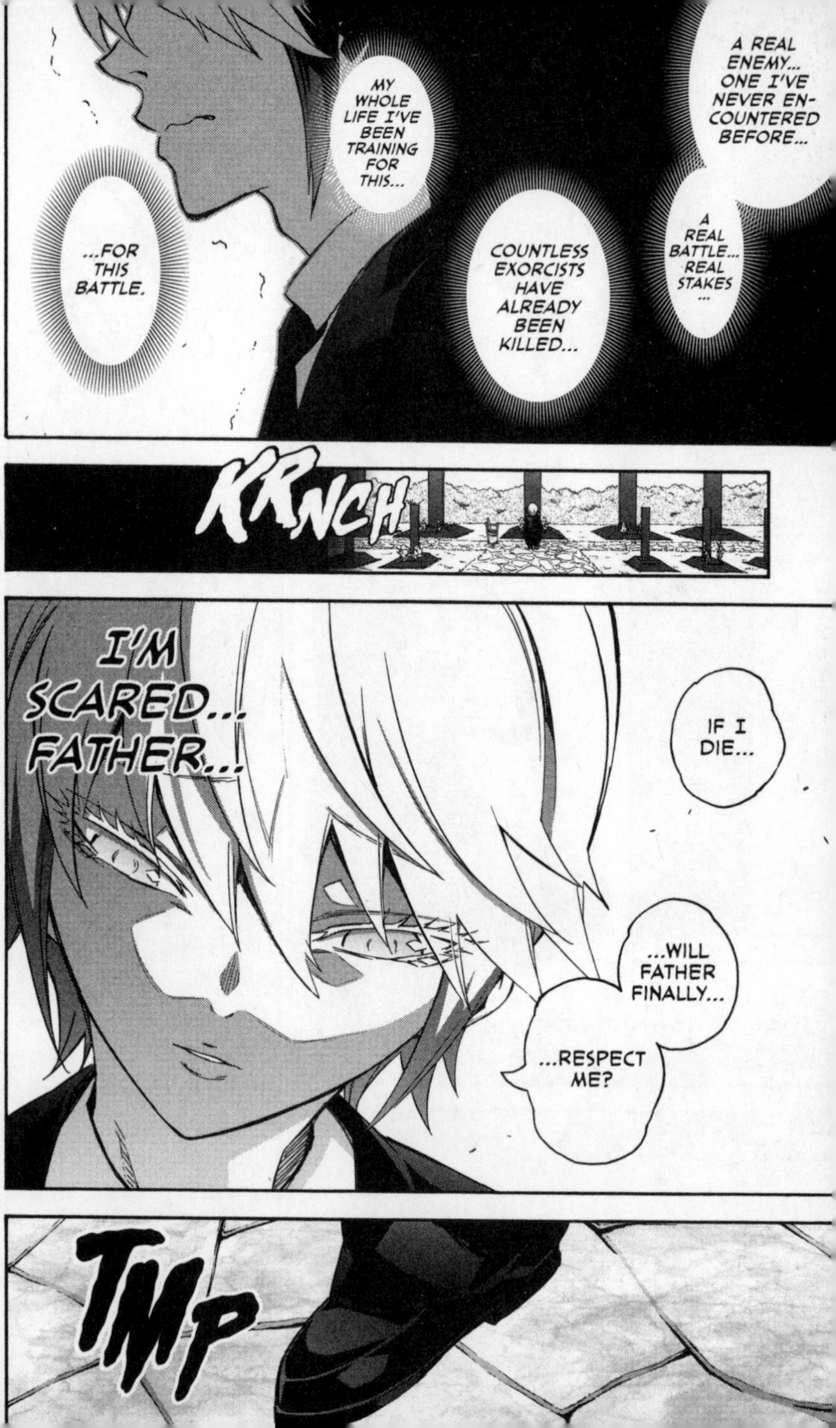
A REAL ENEMY... ONE I'VE NEVER EN-COUNTERED BEFORE...
A REAL BATTLE... REAL STAKES...
COUNTLESS EXORCISTS HAVE ALREADY BEEN KILLED...
MY WHOLE LIFE I'VE BEEN TRAINING FOR THIS...
...FOR THIS BATTLE.
KRNCH
IF I DIE...
...WILL FATHER FINALLY...
...RESPECT ME?
I'M SCARED... FATHER...
TMP

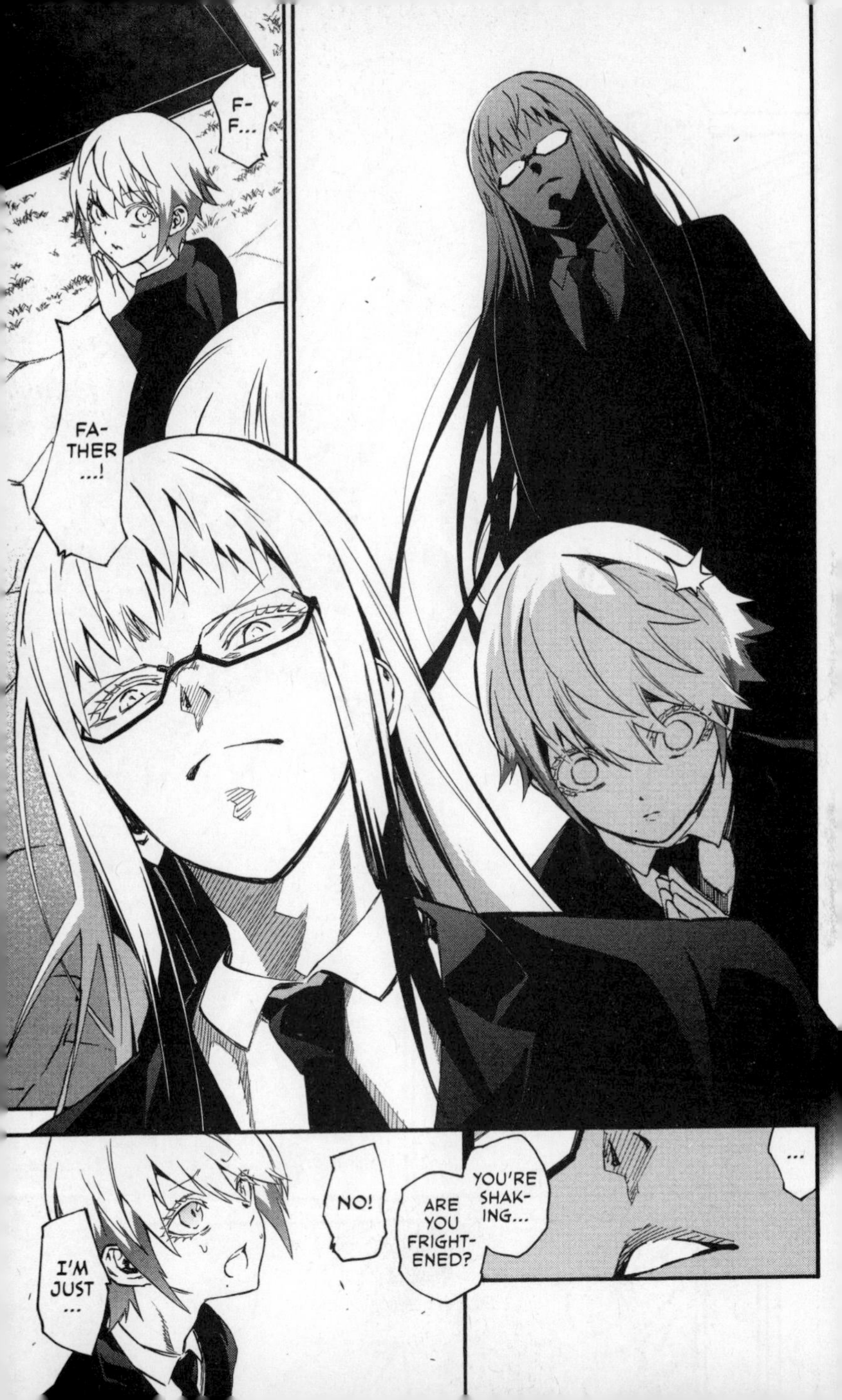
F-
F...
FA-
THER
...!
...
YOU'RE
SHAK-
ING...
ARE
YOU
FRIGHT-
ENED?
NO!
I'M
JUST
...

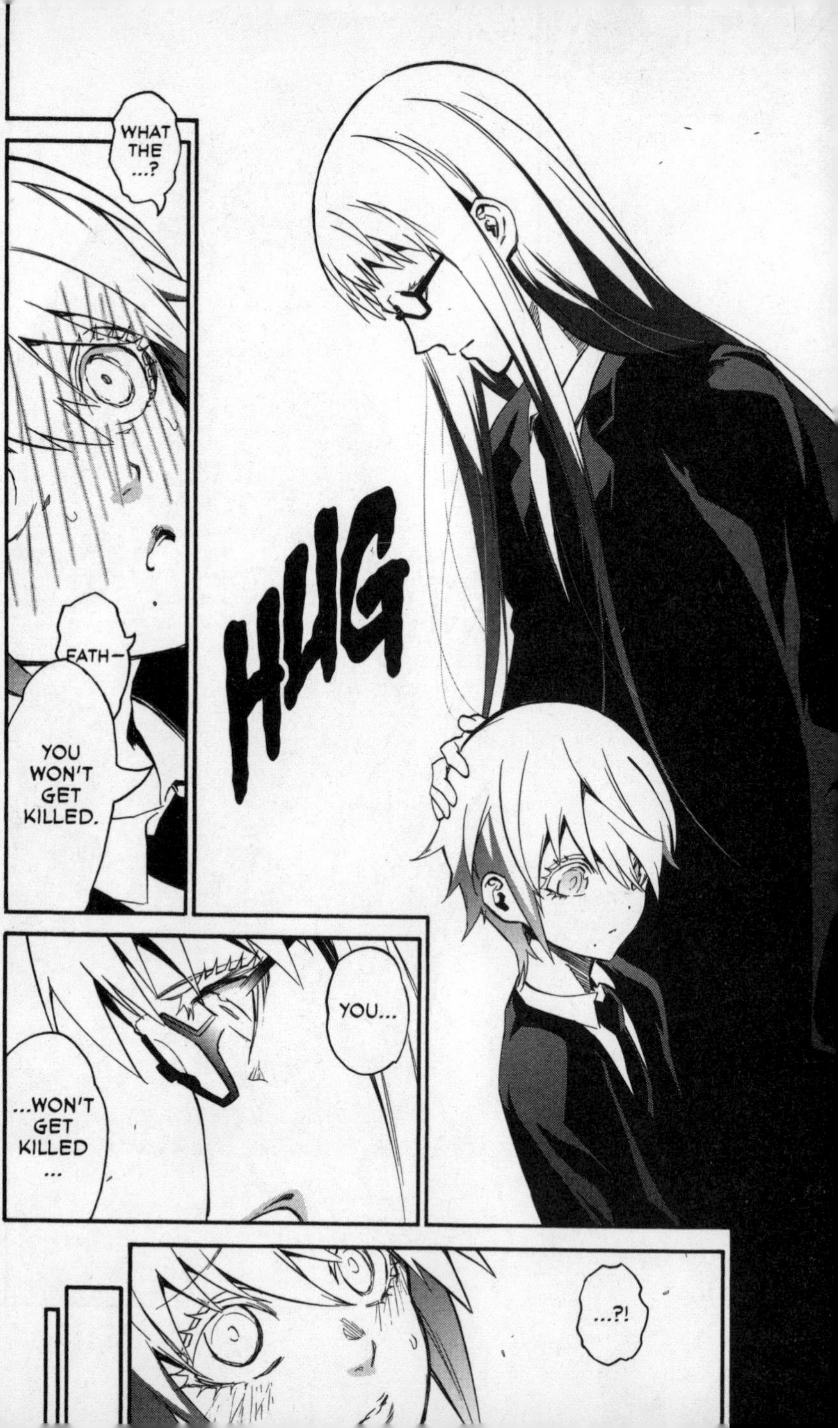
HUG
WHAT THE ...?
FATH—
YOU WON'T GET KILLED.
YOU...
...WON'T GET KILLED ...
...?!

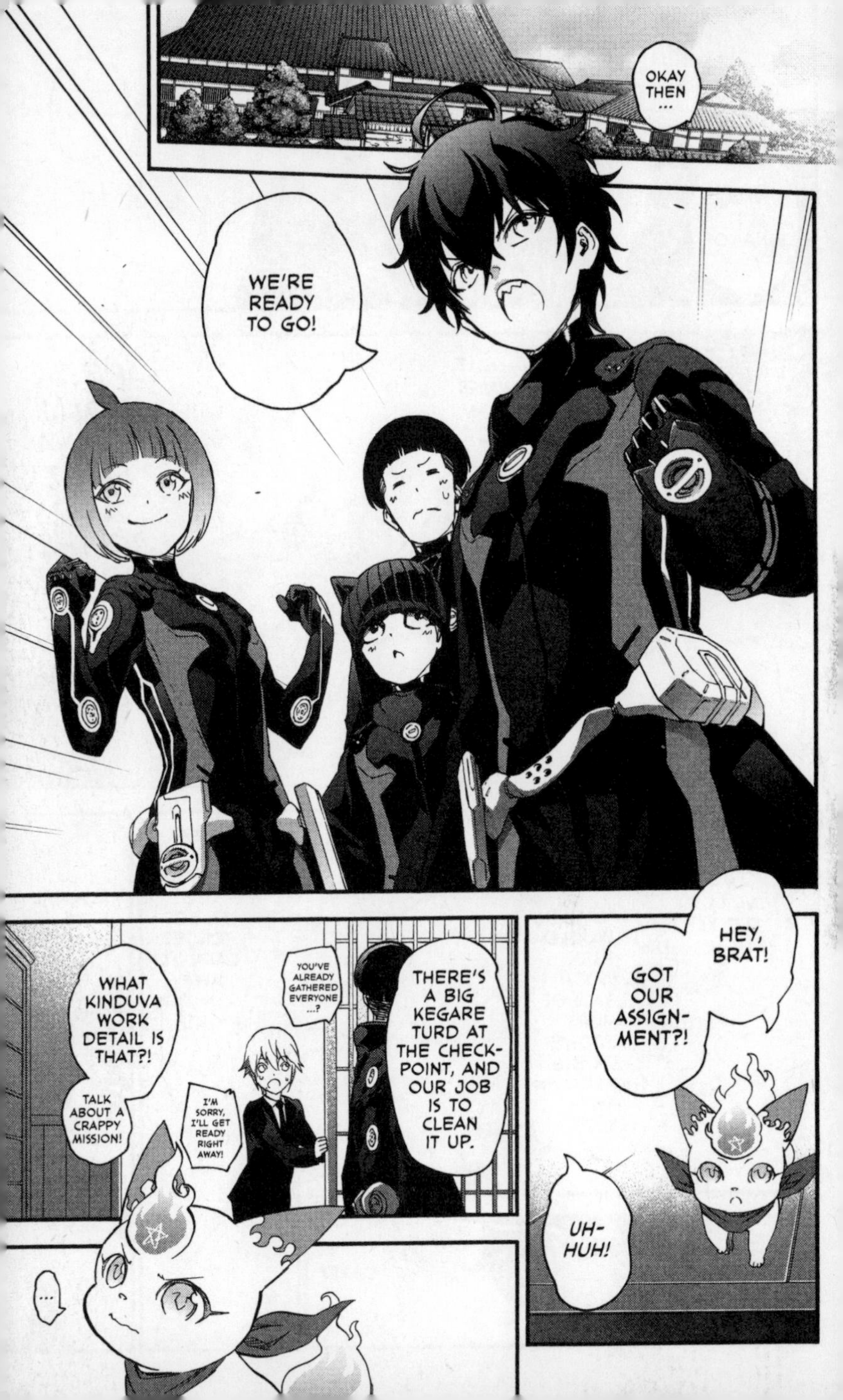
OKAY THEN ...
WE'RE READY TO GO!
HEY, BRAT!
GOT OUR ASSIGNMENT?!
UH-HUH!
THERE'S A BIG KEGARE TURD AT THE CHECKPOINT, AND OUR JOB IS TO CLEAN IT UP.
YOU'VE ALREADY GATHERED EVERYONE ...?
WHAT KINDUVA WORK DETAIL IS THAT?!
I'M SORRY, I'LL GET READY RIGHT AWAY!
TALK ABOUT A CRAPPY MISSION!
...

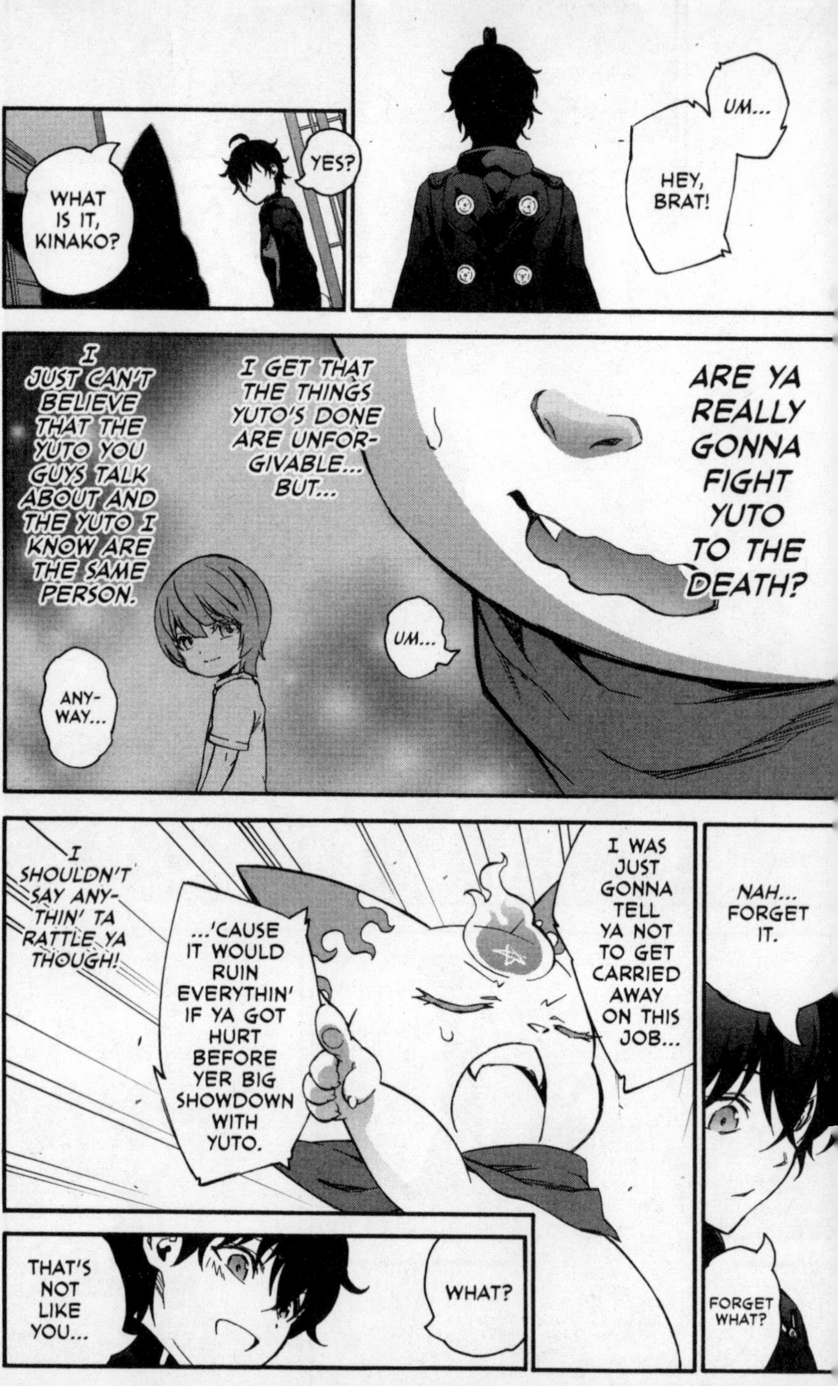
UM...
HEY, BRAT!
YES?
WHAT IS IT, KINAKO?
ARE YA REALLY GONNA FIGHT YUTO TO THE DEATH?
I GET THAT THE THINGS YUTO'S DONE ARE UNFORGIVABLE... BUT...
I JUST CAN'T BELIEVE THAT THE YUTO YOU GUYS TALK ABOUT AND THE YUTO I KNOW ARE THE SAME PERSON.
UM...
ANYWAY...
NAH... FORGET IT.
FORGET WHAT?
I WAS JUST GONNA TELL YA NOT TO GET CARRIED AWAY ON THIS JOB...
...'CAUSE IT WOULD RUIN EVERYTHIN' IF YA GOT HURT BEFORE YER BIG SHOWDOWN WITH YUTO.
I SHOULDN'T SAY ANYTHIN' TA RATTLE YA THOUGH!
WHAT?
THAT'S NOT LIKE YOU...

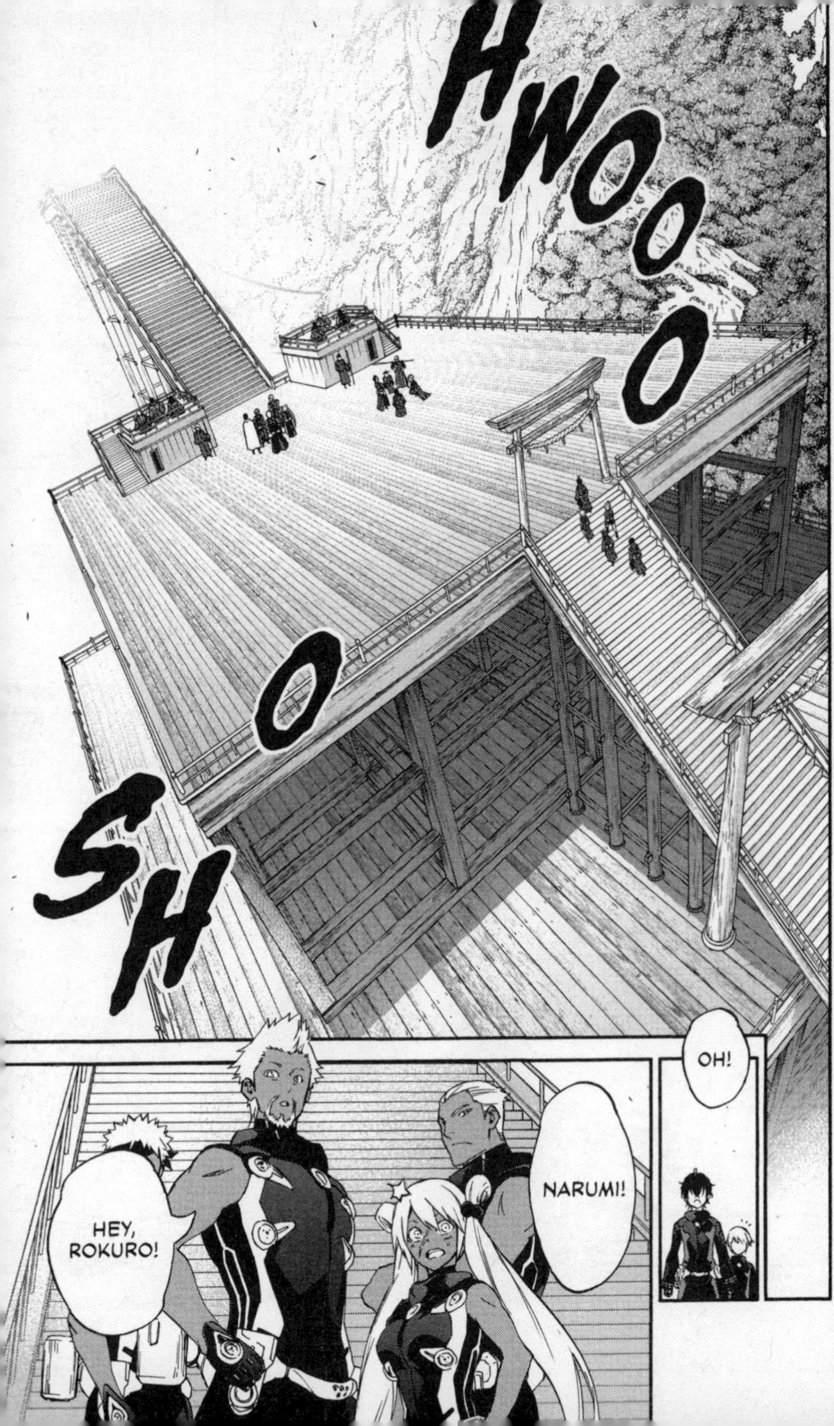
HWOOOOOSH
OH!
NARUMI!
HEY, ROKURO!

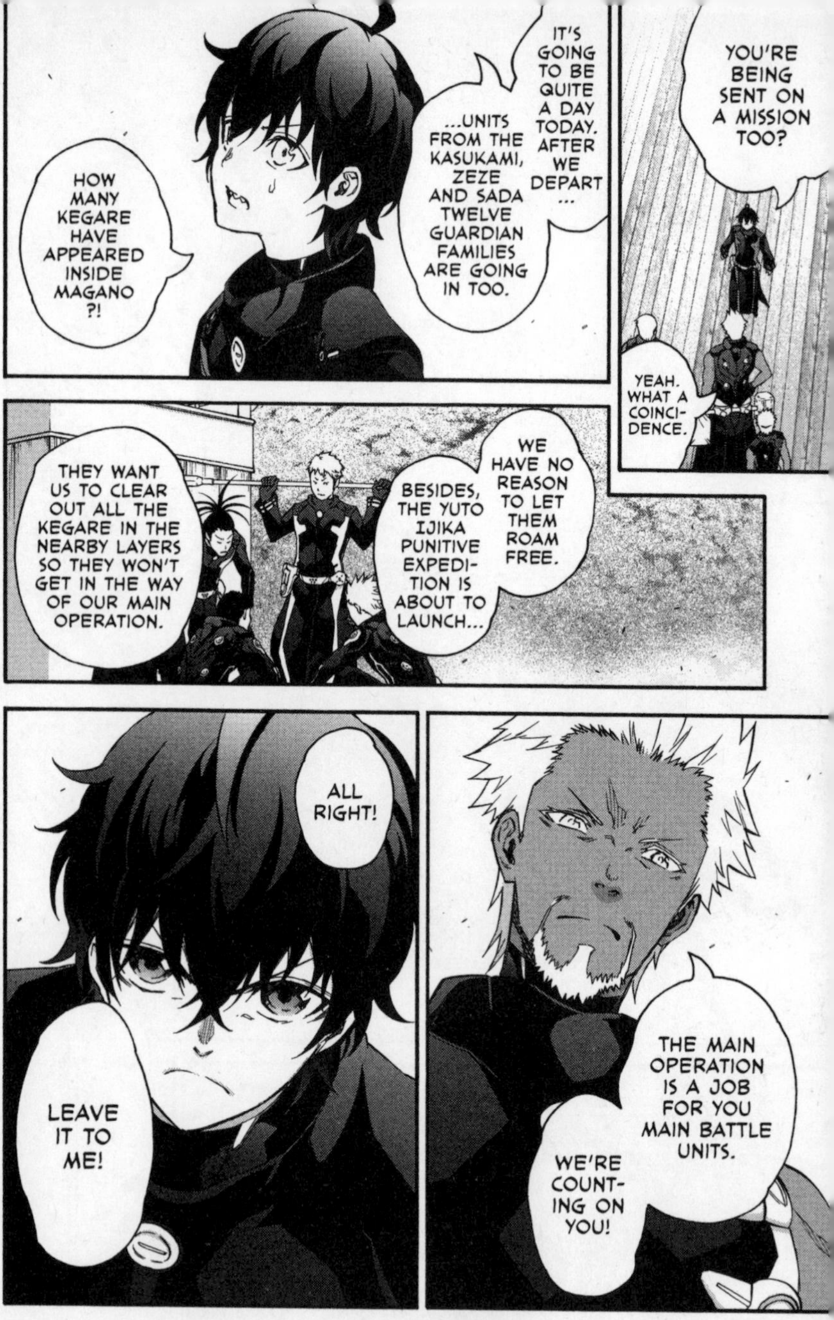
YOU'RE BEING SENT ON A MISSION TOO?
YEAH. WHAT A COINCIDENCE.
IT'S GOING TO BE QUITE A DAY TODAY. AFTER WE DEPART...
...UNITS FROM THE KASUKAMI, ZEZE AND SADA TWELVE GUARDIAN FAMILIES ARE GOING IN TOO.
HOW MANY KEGARE HAVE APPEARED INSIDE MAGANO?!
WE HAVE NO REASON TO LET THEM ROAM FREE.
BESIDES, THE YUTO IJIKA PUNITIVE EXPEDITION IS ABOUT TO LAUNCH...
THEY WANT US TO CLEAR OUT ALL THE KEGARE IN THE NEARBY LAYERS SO THEY WON'T GET IN THE WAY OF OUR MAIN OPERATION.
THE MAIN OPERATION IS A JOB FOR YOU MAIN BATTLE UNITS.
WE'RE COUNTING ON YOU!
ALL RIGHT!
LEAVE IT TO ME!

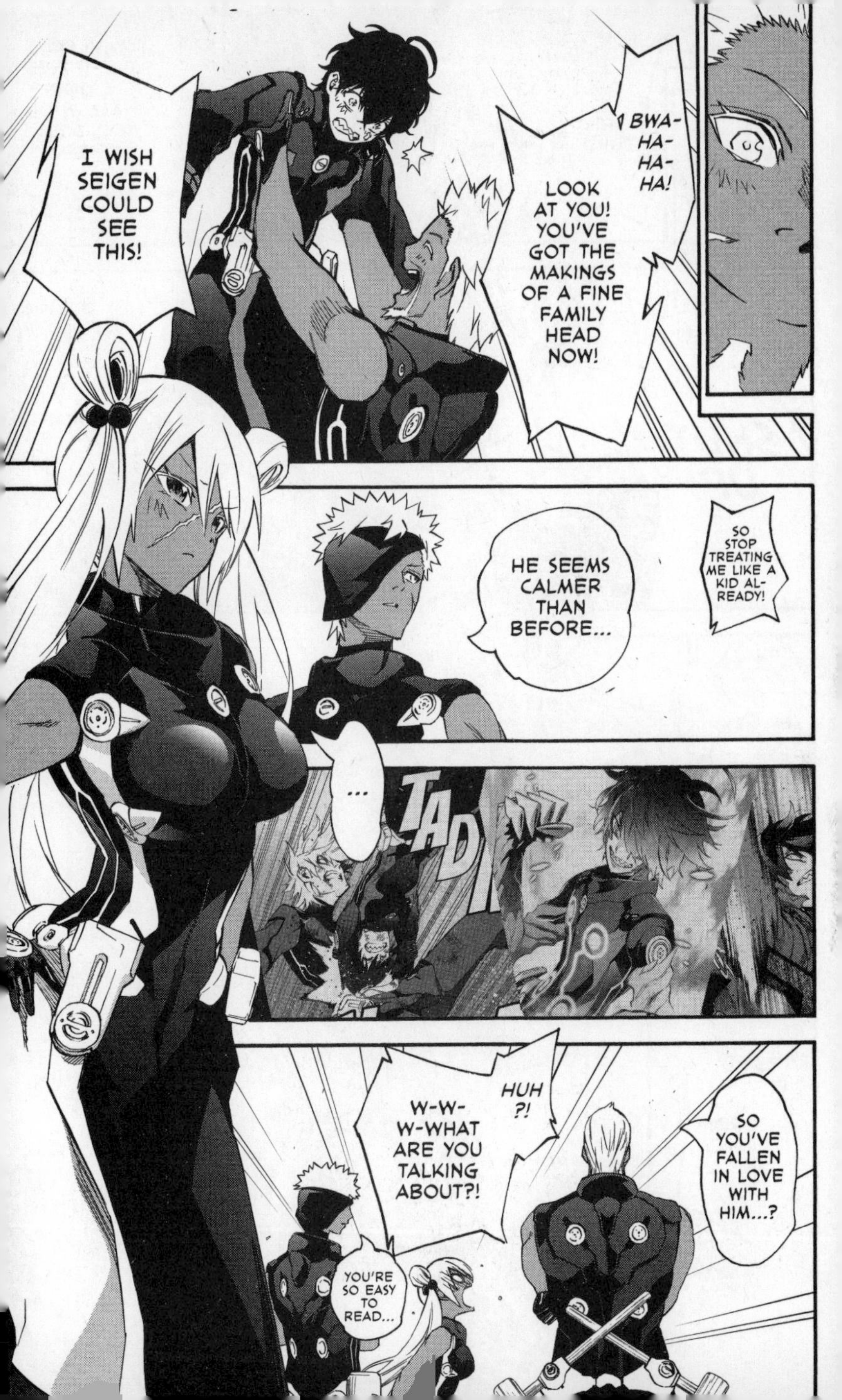
BWA-HA-HA-HA!
LOOK AT YOU! YOU'VE GOT THE MAKINGS OF A FINE FAMILY HEAD NOW!
I WISH SEIGEN COULD SEE THIS!
SO STOP TREATING ME LIKE A KID AL-READY!
HE SEEMS CALMER THAN BEFORE...
...
TAD
SO YOU'VE FALLEN IN LOVE WITH HIM...?
HUH?!
W-W-W-WHAT ARE YOU TALKING ABOUT?!
YOU'RE SO EASY TO READ...

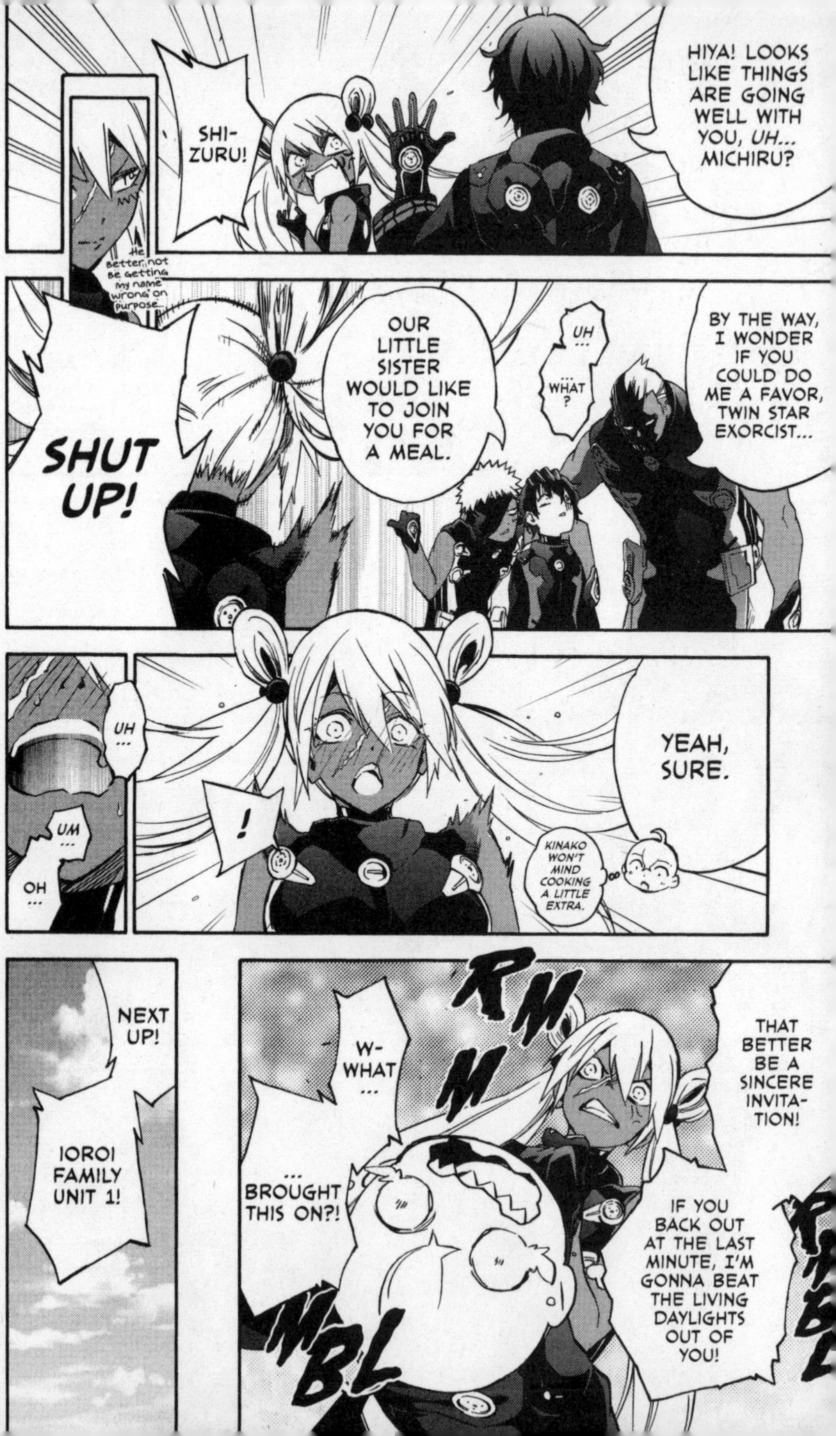
HIYA! LOOKS LIKE THINGS ARE GOING WELL WITH YOU, UH... MICHIRU?
SHI-ZURU!
He better not be getting my name wrong on purpose...
BY THE WAY, I WONDER IF YOU COULD DO ME A FAVOR, TWIN STAR EXORCIST...
UH ...
... WHAT ?
OUR LITTLE SISTER WOULD LIKE TO JOIN YOU FOR A MEAL.
SHUT UP!
YEAH, SURE.
KINAKO WON'T MIND COOKING A LITTLE EXTRA.
!
UH ...
UM ...
OH ...
THAT BETTER BE A SINCERE INVITATION!
IF YOU BACK OUT AT THE LAST MINUTE, I'M GONNA BEAT THE LIVING DAYLIGHTS OUT OF YOU!
RMM
W-WHAT ...
... BROUGHT THIS ON?!
MBL
NEXT UP!
IOROI FAMILY UNIT 1!

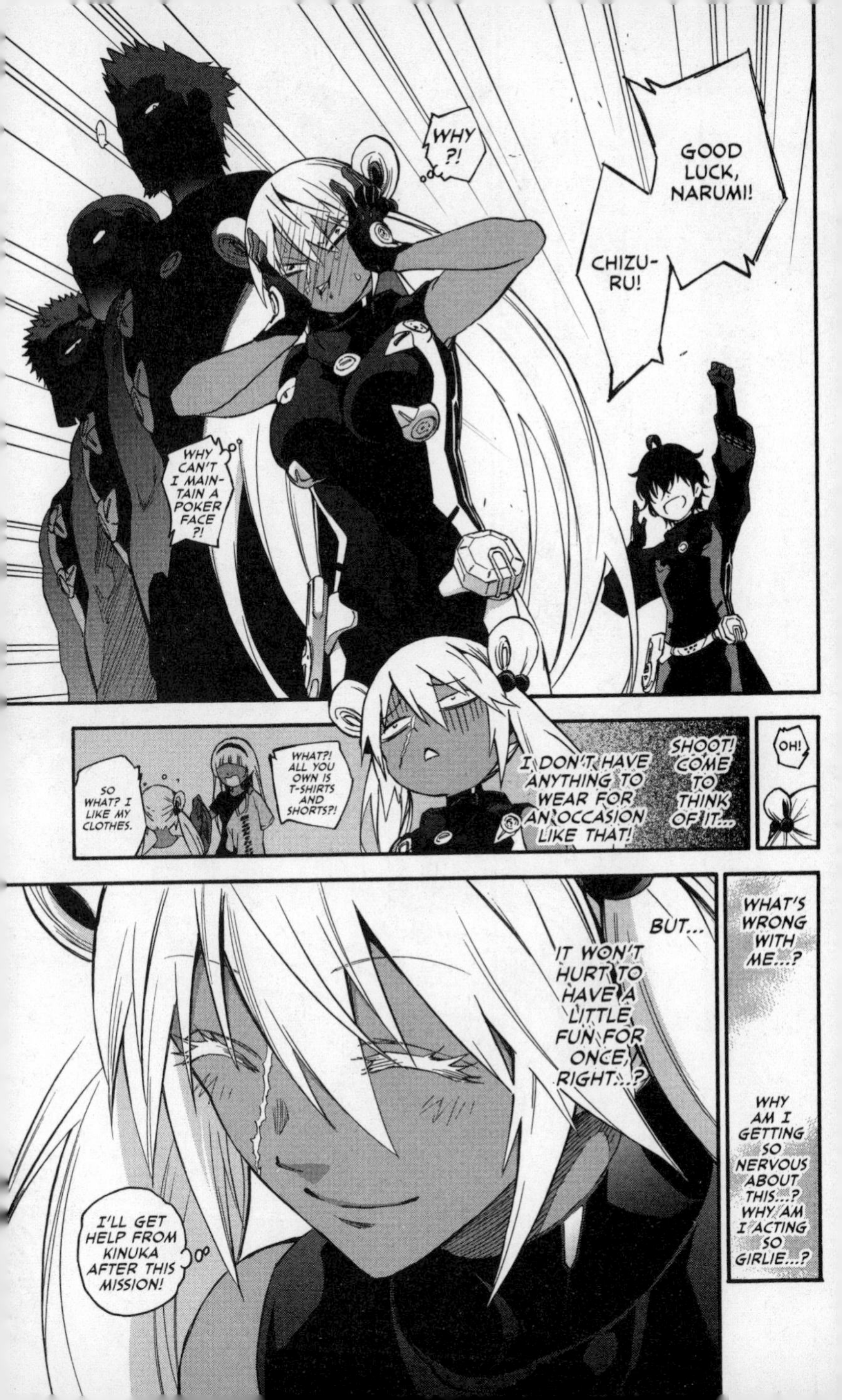
GOOD LUCK, NARUMI!
CHIZU-RU!
WHY ?!
WHY CAN'T I MAIN-TAIN A POKER FACE ?!
OH!
SHOOT! COME TO THINK OF IT...
I DON'T HAVE ANYTHING TO WEAR FOR AN OCCASION LIKE THAT!
WHAT?! ALL YOU OWN IS T-SHIRTS AND SHORTS?!
SO WHAT? I LIKE MY CLOTHES.
WHAT'S WRONG WITH ME...?
WHY AM I GETTING SO NERVOUS ABOUT THIS...? WHY AM I ACTING SO GIRLIE...?
BUT...
IT WON'T HURT TO HAVE A LITTLE FUN FOR ONCE, RIGHT...?
I'LL GET HELP FROM KINUKA AFTER THIS MISSION!

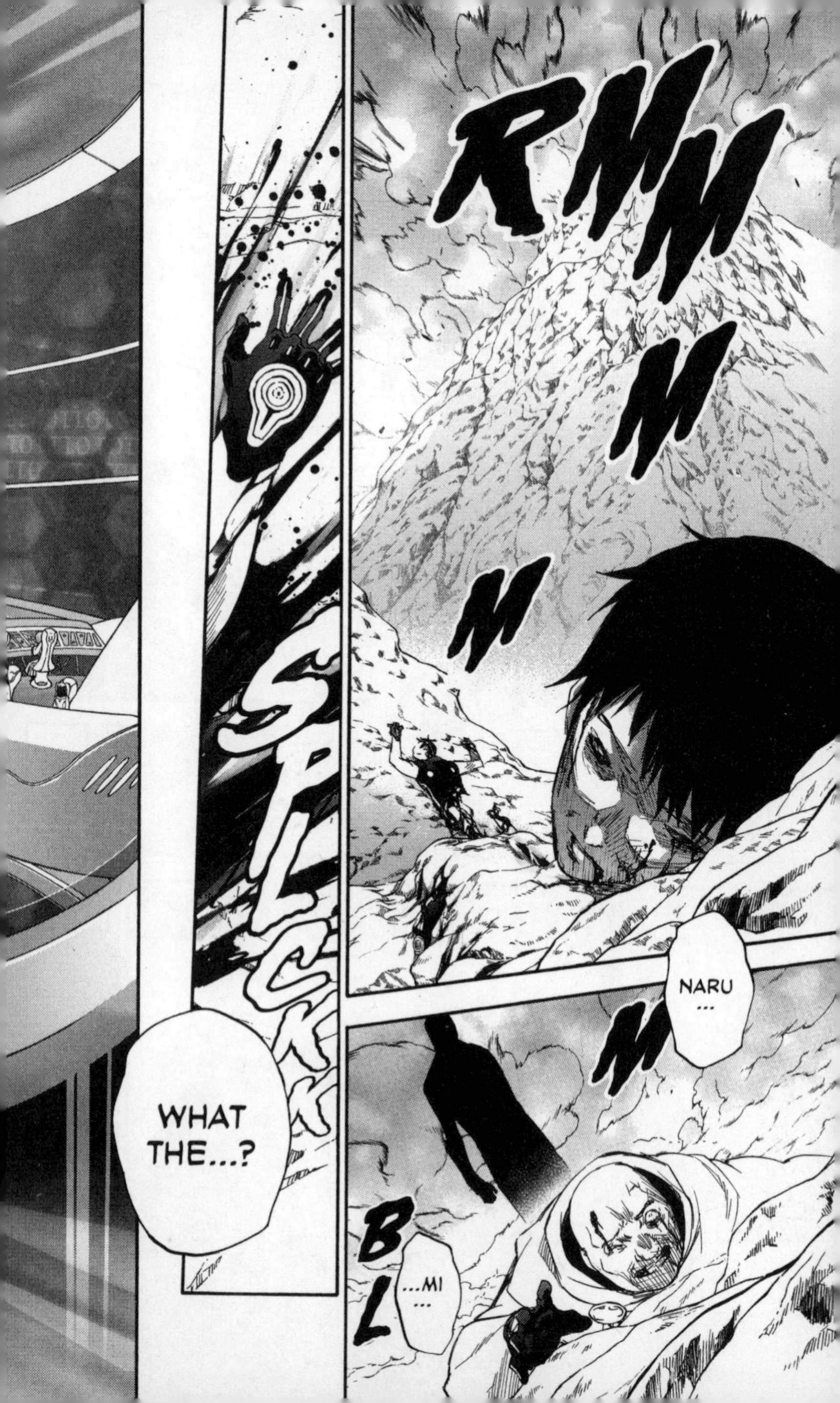
RMMMM
NARU...
M
BL
...MI...
SPLCK
WHAT THE...?

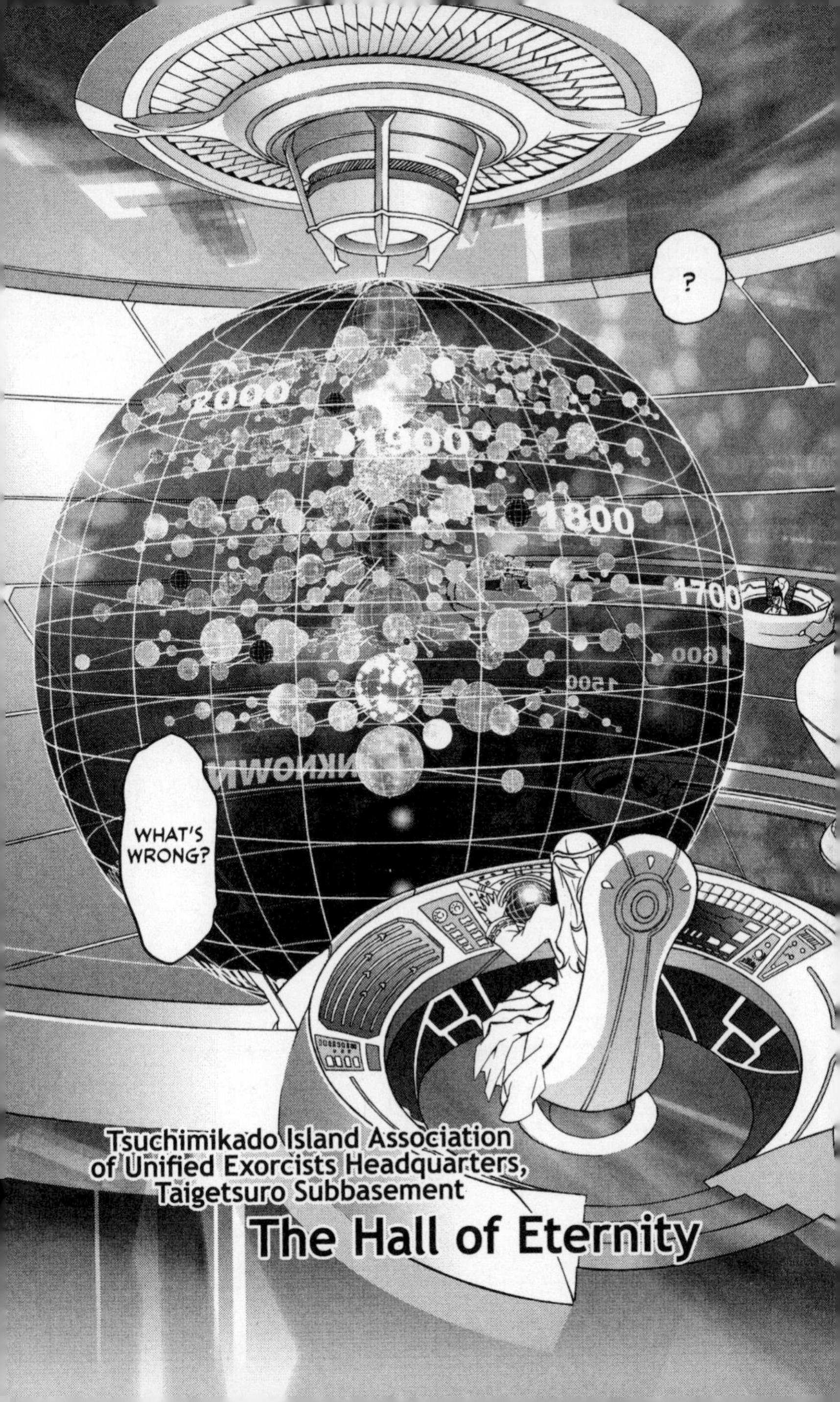
?
2000
1900
1800
1700
WHAT'S WRONG?
Tsuchimikado Island Association of Unified Exorcists Headquarters, Taigetsuro Subbasement
The Hall of Eternity

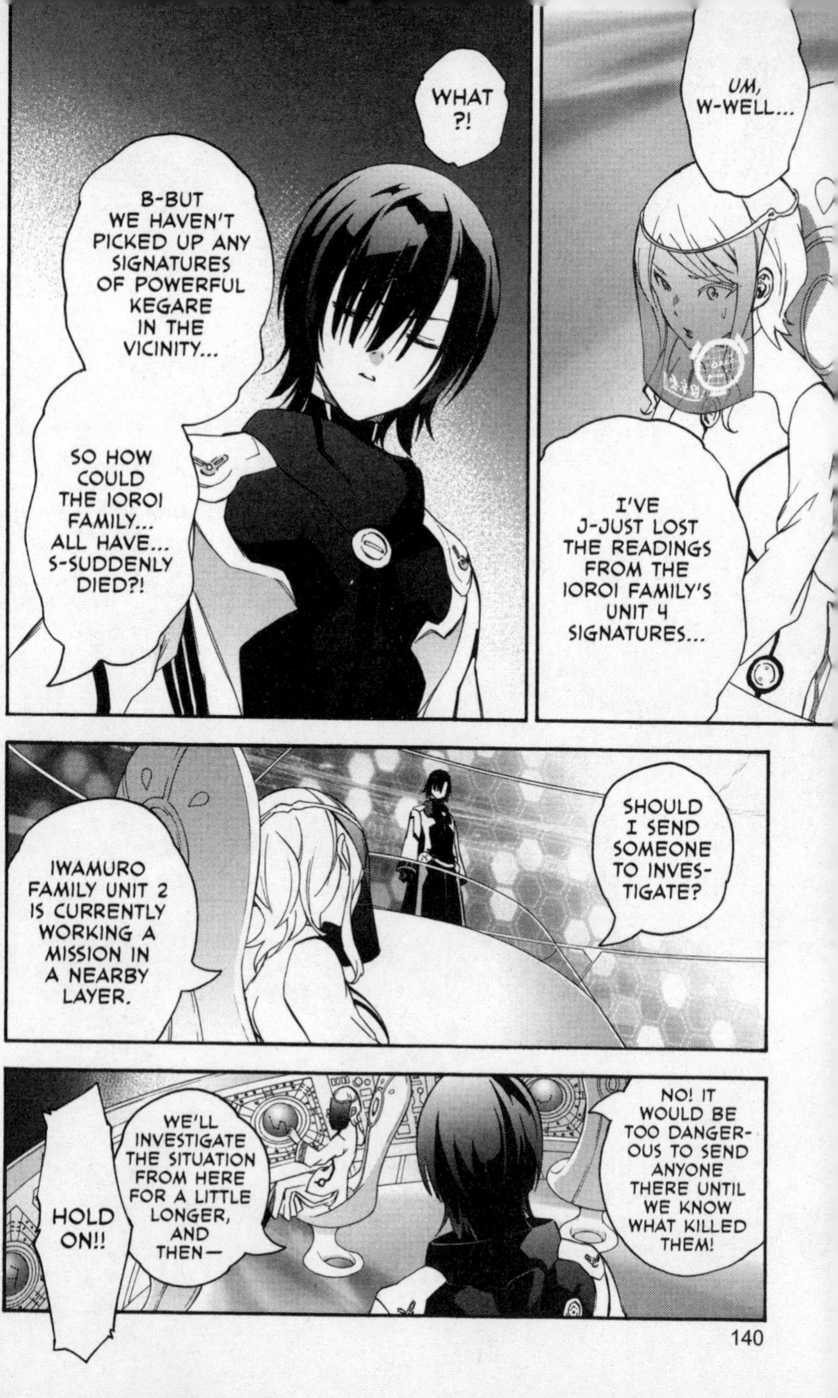
UM, W-WELL...
I'VE J-JUST LOST THE READINGS FROM THE IOROI FAMILY'S UNIT 4 SIGNATURES...
WHAT?!
B-BUT WE HAVEN'T PICKED UP ANY SIGNATURES OF POWERFUL KEGARE IN THE VICINITY...
SO HOW COULD THE IOROI FAMILY... ALL HAVE... S-SUDDENLY DIED?!
SHOULD I SEND SOMEONE TO INVES-TIGATE?
IWAMURO FAMILY UNIT 2 IS CURRENTLY WORKING A MISSION IN A NEARBY LAYER.
NO! IT WOULD BE TOO DANGER-OUS TO SEND ANYONE THERE UNTIL WE KNOW WHAT KILLED THEM!
WE'LL INVESTIGATE THE SITUATION FROM HERE FOR A LITTLE LONGER, AND THEN—
HOLD ON!!

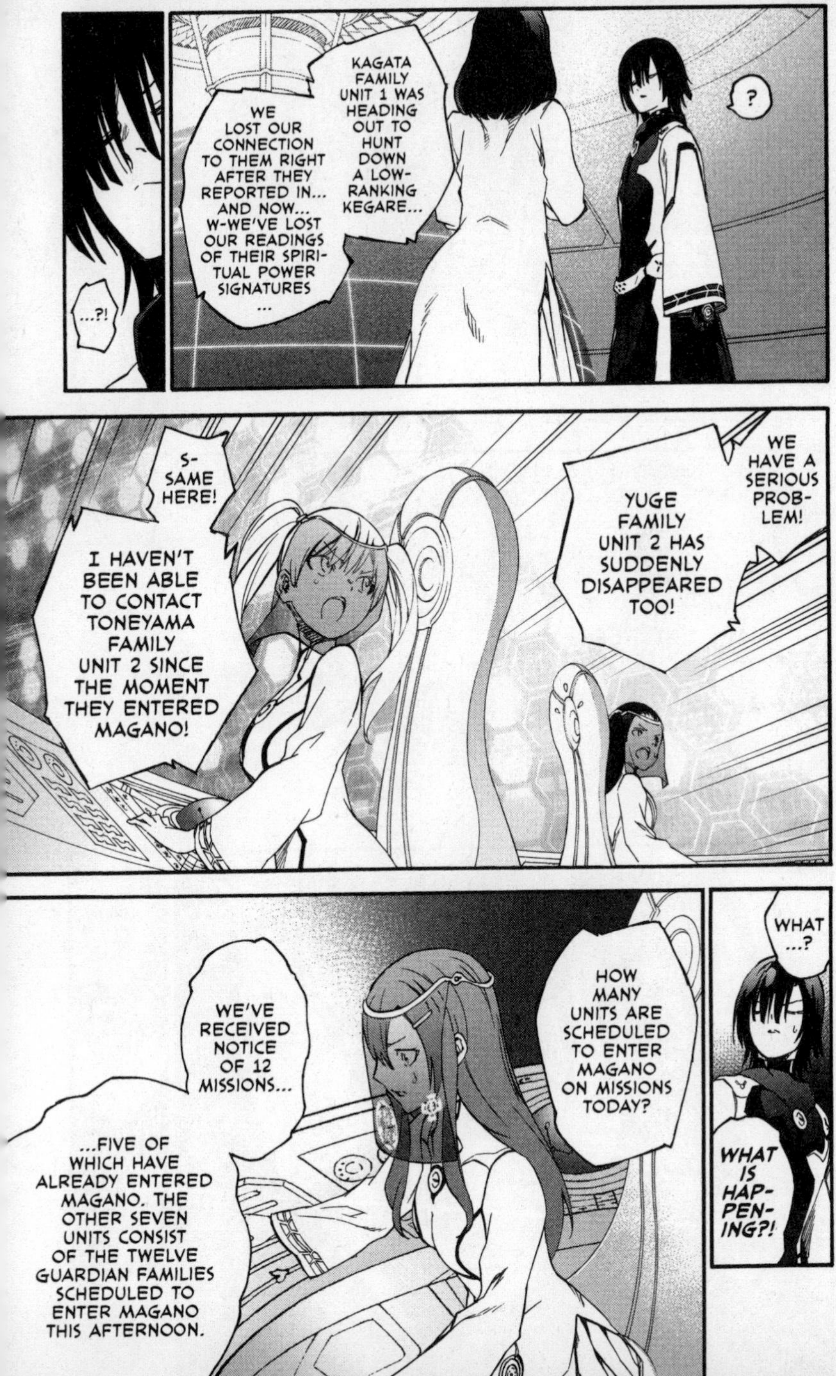
?
KAGATA FAMILY UNIT 1 WAS HEADING OUT TO HUNT DOWN A LOW-RANKING KEGARE...
WE LOST OUR CONNECTION TO THEM RIGHT AFTER THEY REPORTED IN... AND NOW... W-WE'VE LOST OUR READINGS OF THEIR SPIRITUAL POWER SIGNATURES...
...?!
WE HAVE A SERIOUS PROBLEM!
YUGE FAMILY UNIT 2 HAS SUDDENLY DISAPPEARED TOO!
S-SAME HERE!
I HAVEN'T BEEN ABLE TO CONTACT TONEYAMA FAMILY UNIT 2 SINCE THE MOMENT THEY ENTERED MAGANO!
WHAT ...?
WHAT IS HAPPENING?!
HOW MANY UNITS ARE SCHEDULED TO ENTER MAGANO ON MISSIONS TODAY?
WE'VE RECEIVED NOTICE OF 12 MISSIONS...
...FIVE OF WHICH HAVE ALREADY ENTERED MAGANO. THE OTHER SEVEN UNITS CONSIST OF THE TWELVE GUARDIAN FAMILIES SCHEDULED TO ENTER MAGANO THIS AFTERNOON.

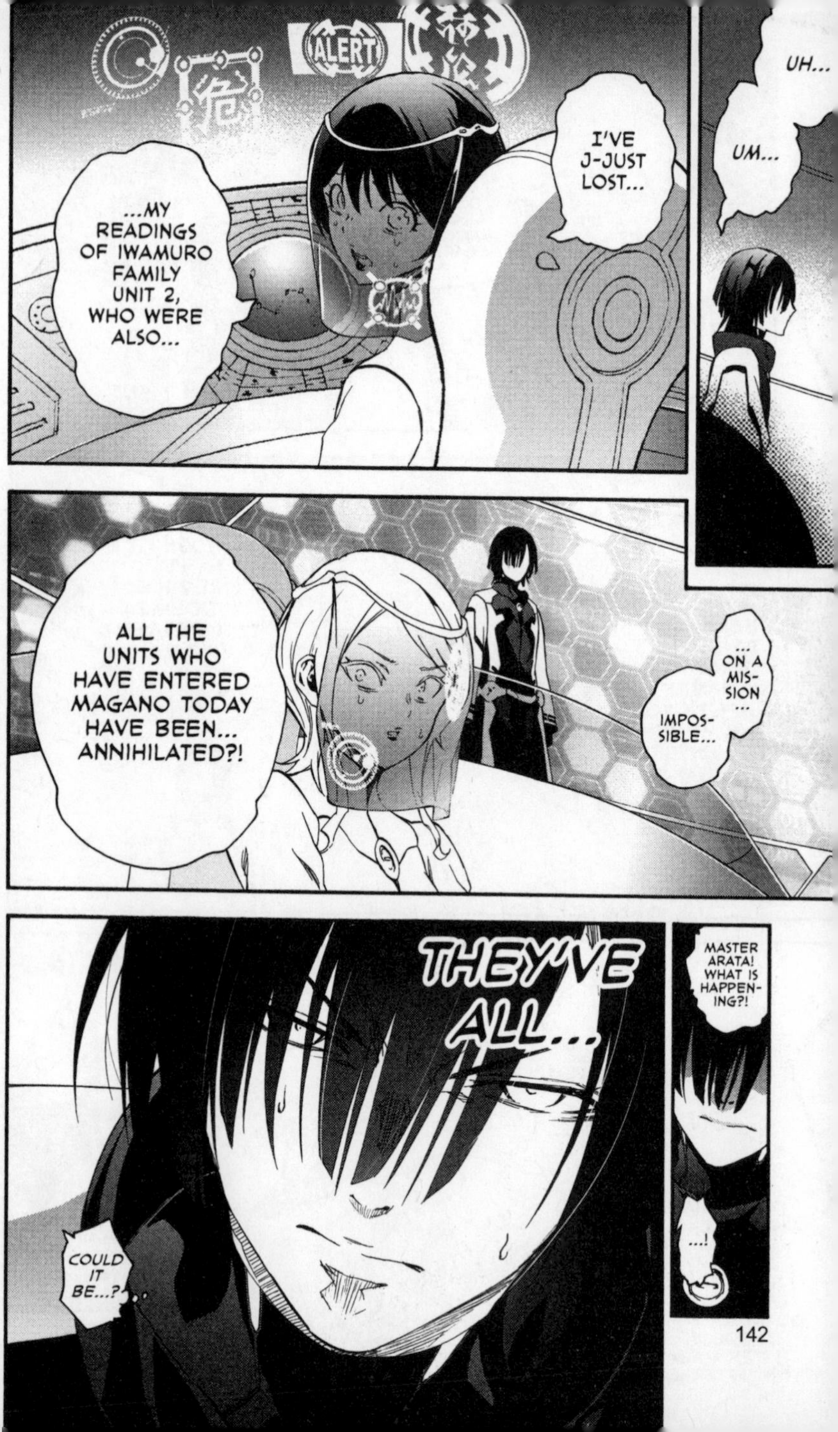
UH...
UM...
I'VE J-JUST LOST...
...MY READINGS OF IWAMURO FAMILY UNIT 2, WHO WERE ALSO...
... ON A MISSION ...
IMPOSSIBLE...
ALL THE UNITS WHO HAVE ENTERED MAGANO TODAY HAVE BEEN... ANNIHILATED?!
MASTER ARATA! WHAT IS HAPPENING?!
...!
THEY'VE ALL...
COULD IT BE...?
ALERT

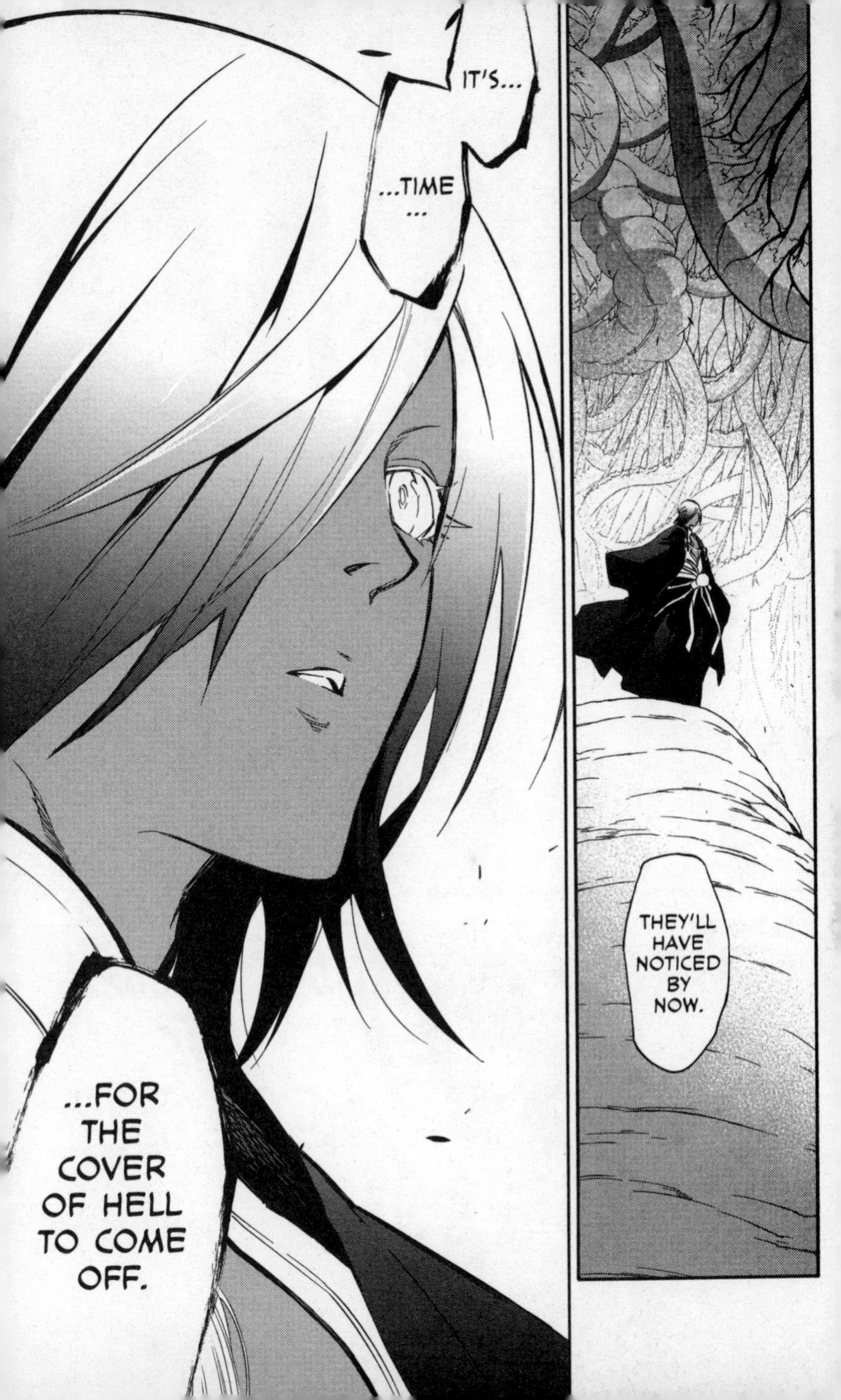
THEY'LL HAVE NOTICED BY NOW.
IT'S...
...TIME ...
...FOR THE COVER OF HELL TO COME OFF.

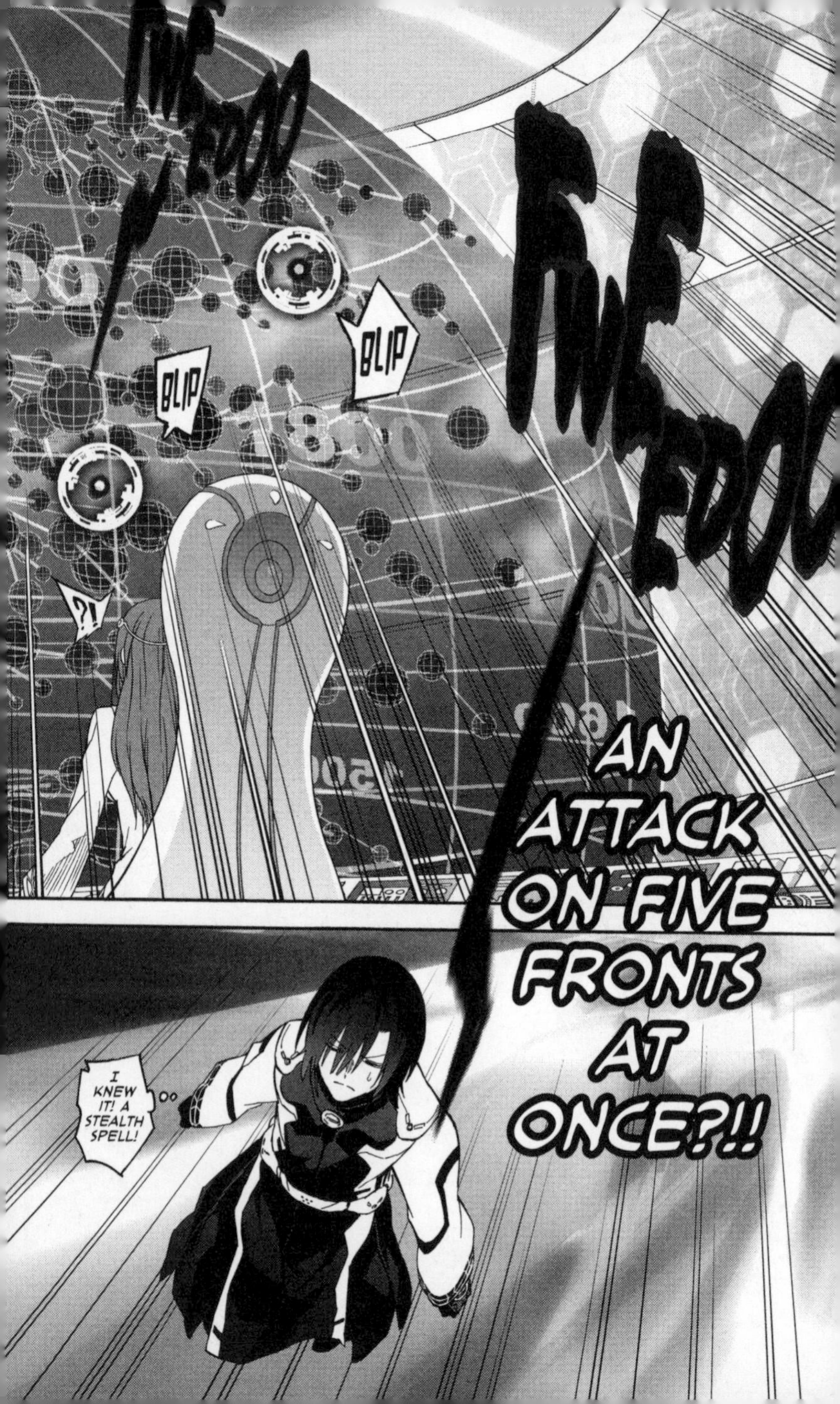
FWEDOO
FWEDOO
BLIP
BLIP
?!
AN ATTACK ON FIVE FRONTS AT ONCE?!!
I KNEW IT! A STEALTH SPELL!

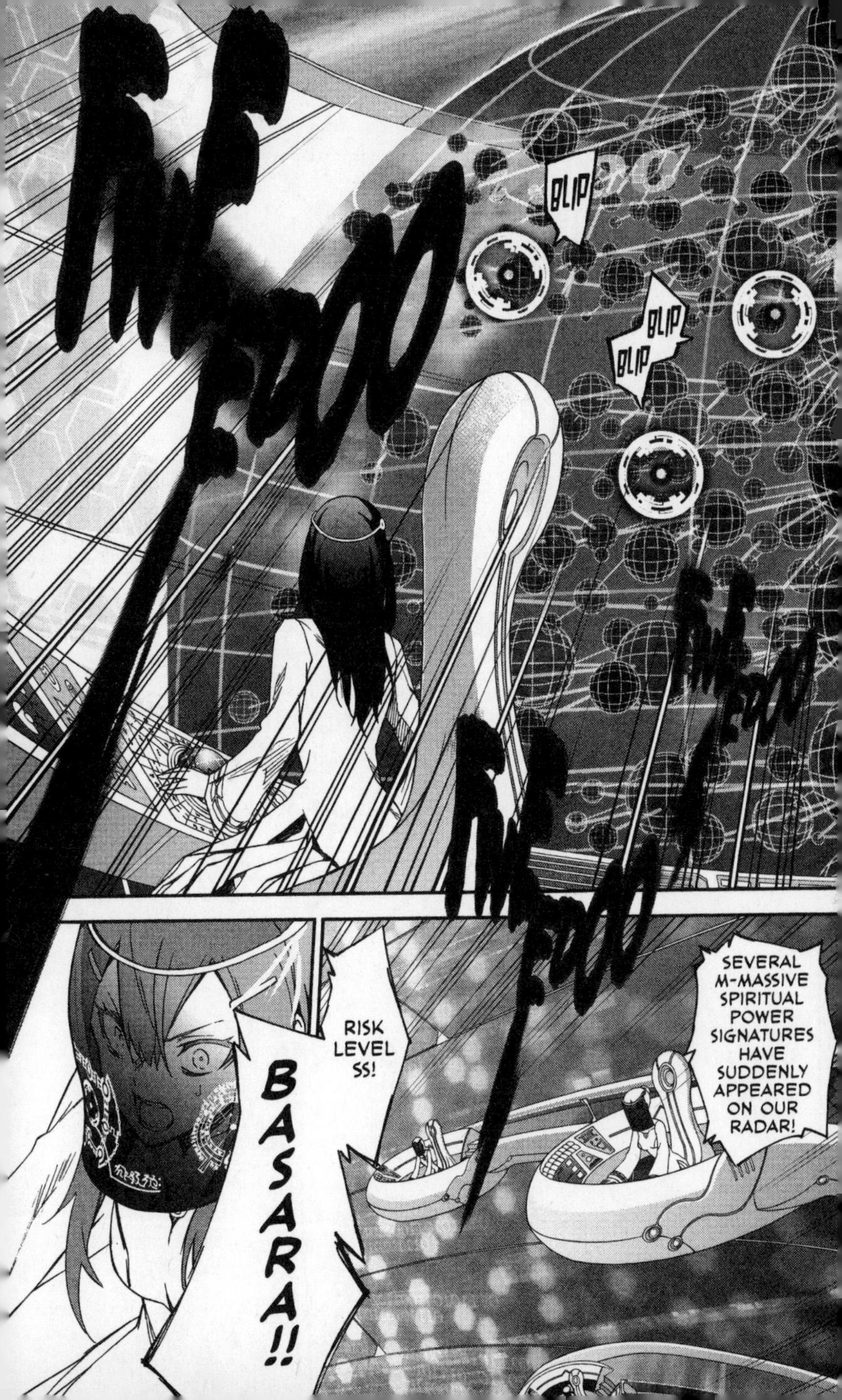
BLIP
BLIP
BLIP
SEVERAL M-MASSIVE SPIRITUAL POWER SIGNATURES HAVE SUDDENLY APPEARED ON OUR RADAR!
RISK LEVEL SS!
BASARA!!

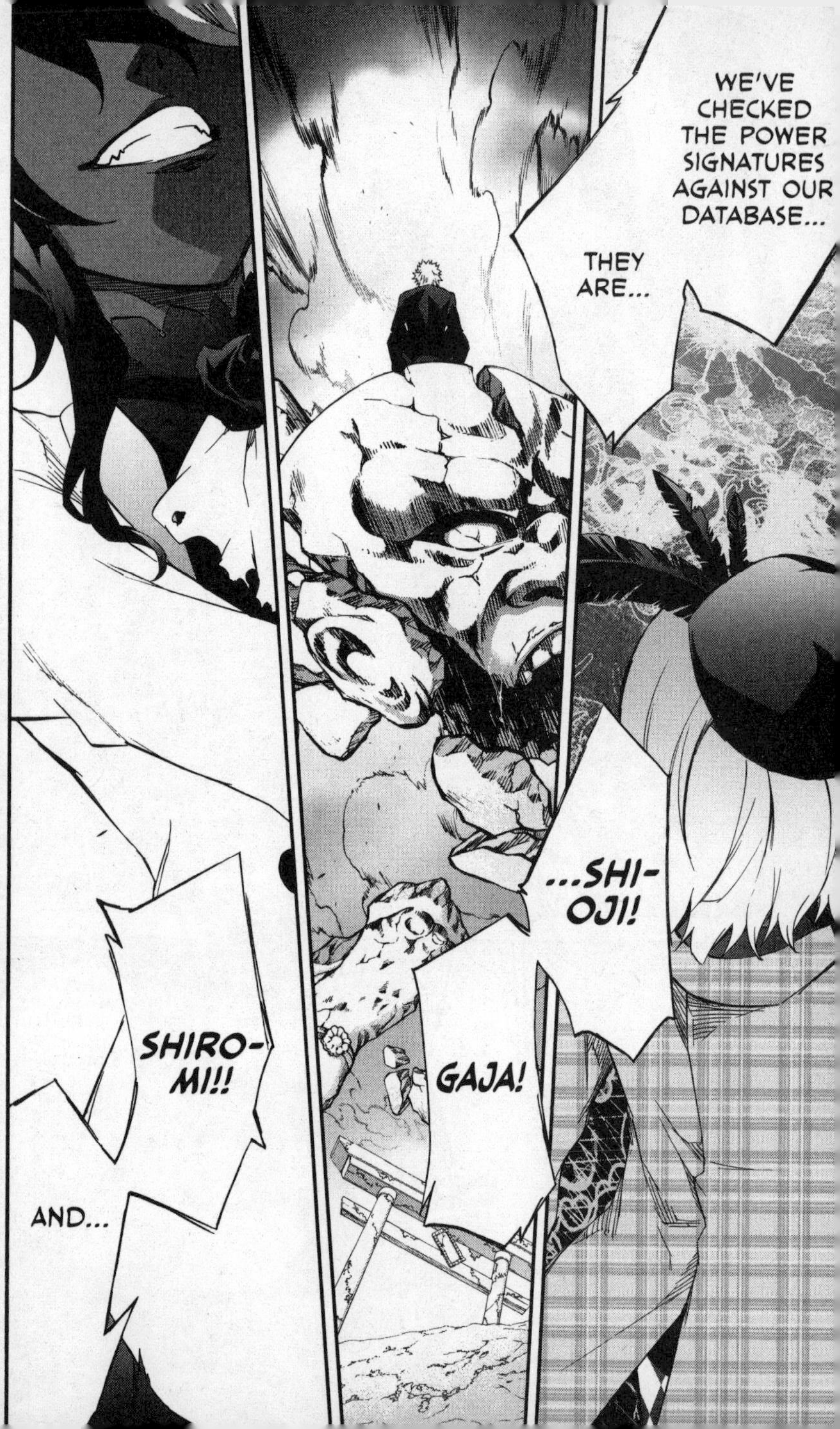
WE'VE CHECKED THE POWER SIGNATURES AGAINST OUR DATABASE...
THEY ARE...
...SHI-OJI!
GAJA!
SHIRO-MI!!
AND...

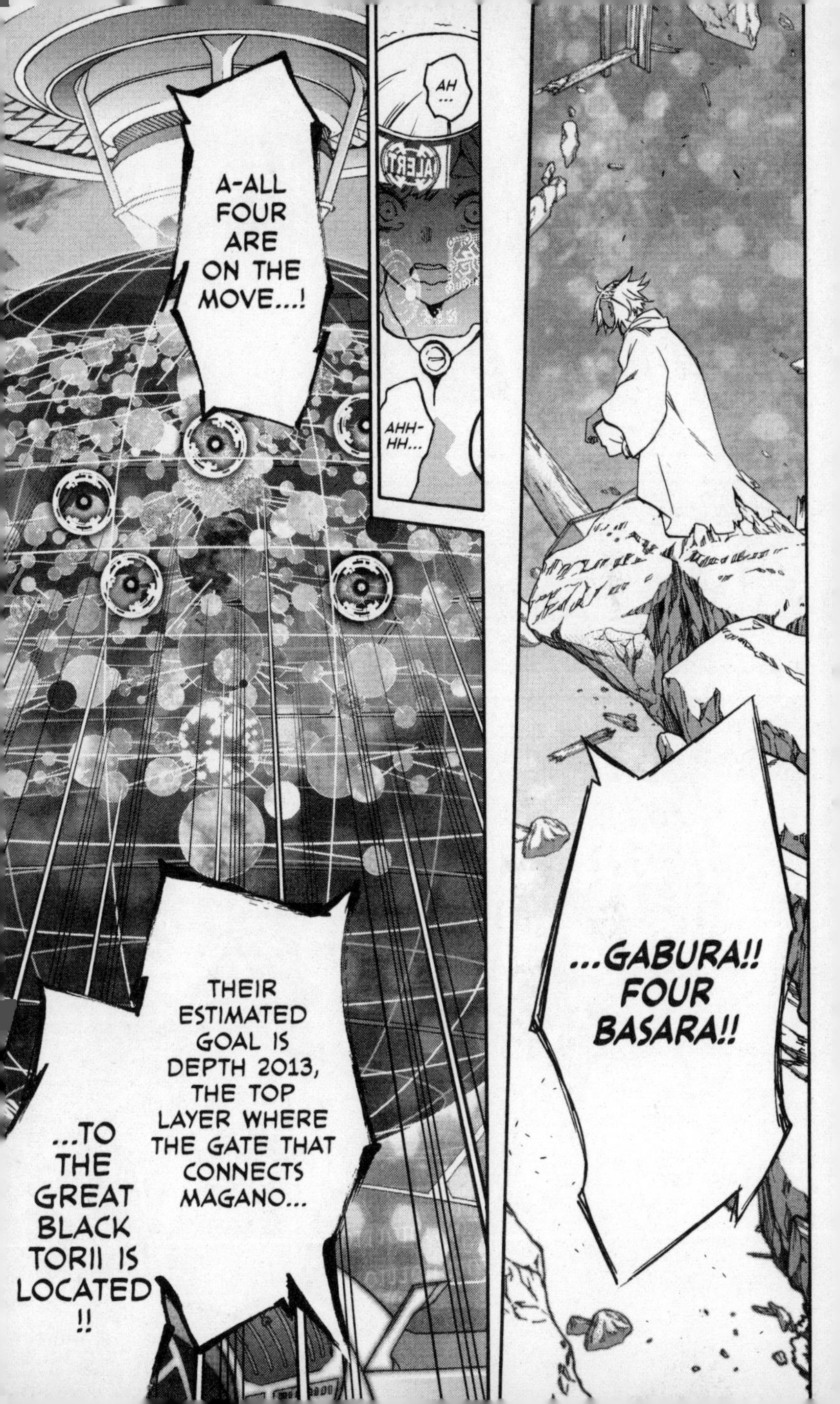

...GABURA!! FOUR BASARA!!
AH ...
AHHHH...
A-ALL FOUR ARE ON THE MOVE...!
THEIR ESTIMATED GOAL IS DEPTH 2013, THE TOP LAYER WHERE THE GATE THAT CONNECTS MAGANO...
...TO THE GREAT BLACK TORII IS LOCATED!!

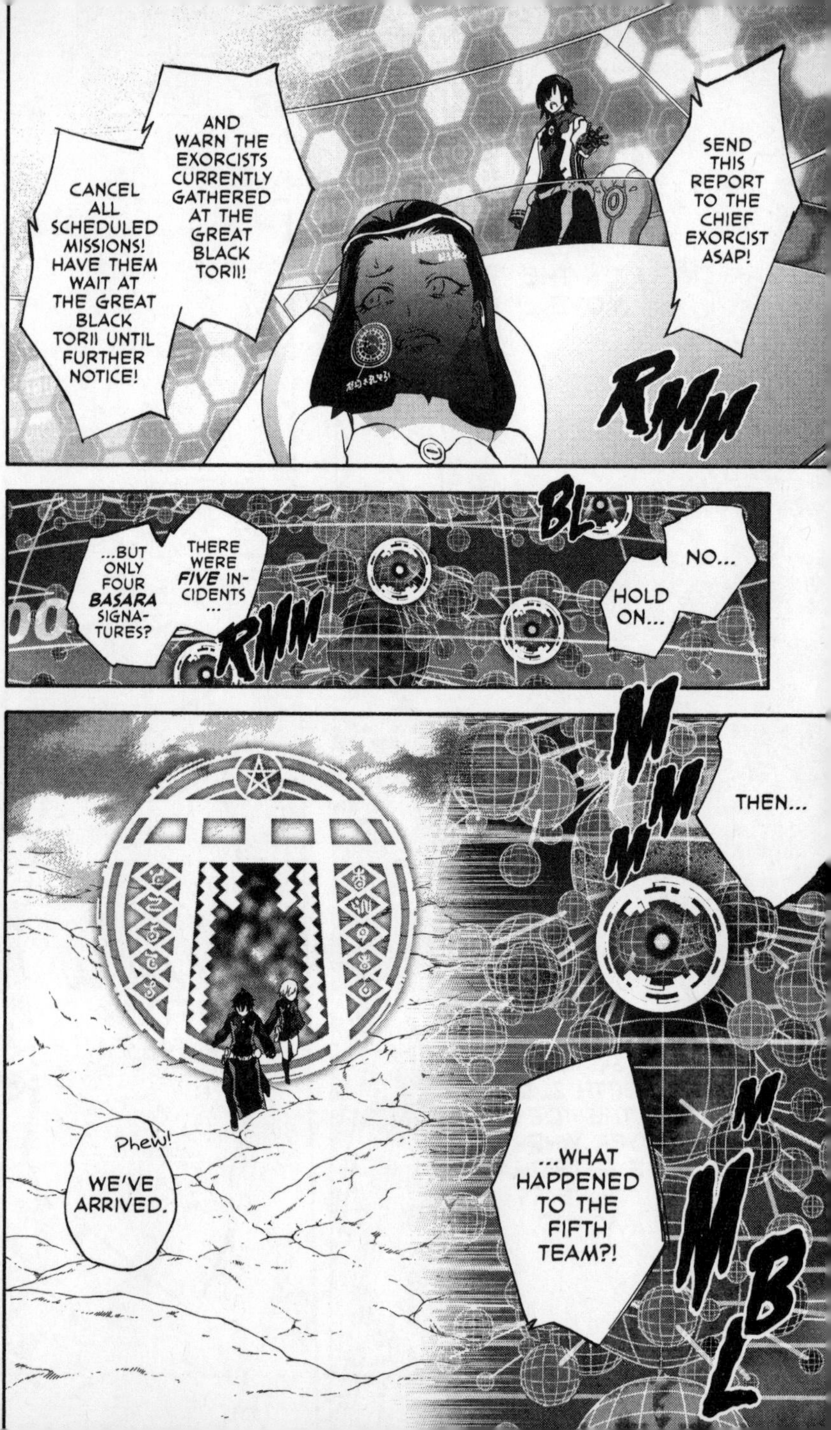
SEND THIS REPORT TO THE CHIEF EXORCIST ASAP!
AND WARN THE EXORCISTS CURRENTLY GATHERED AT THE GREAT BLACK TORII!
CANCEL ALL SCHEDULED MISSIONS! HAVE THEM WAIT AT THE GREAT BLACK TORII UNTIL FURTHER NOTICE!
RMM
BL
NO...
HOLD ON...
THERE WERE *FIVE* IN-CIDENTS...
...BUT ONLY FOUR *BASARA* SIGNA-TURES?
RMM
MMM
THEN...
...WHAT HAPPENED TO THE FIFTH TEAM?!
MMBL
Phew!
WE'VE ARRIVED.

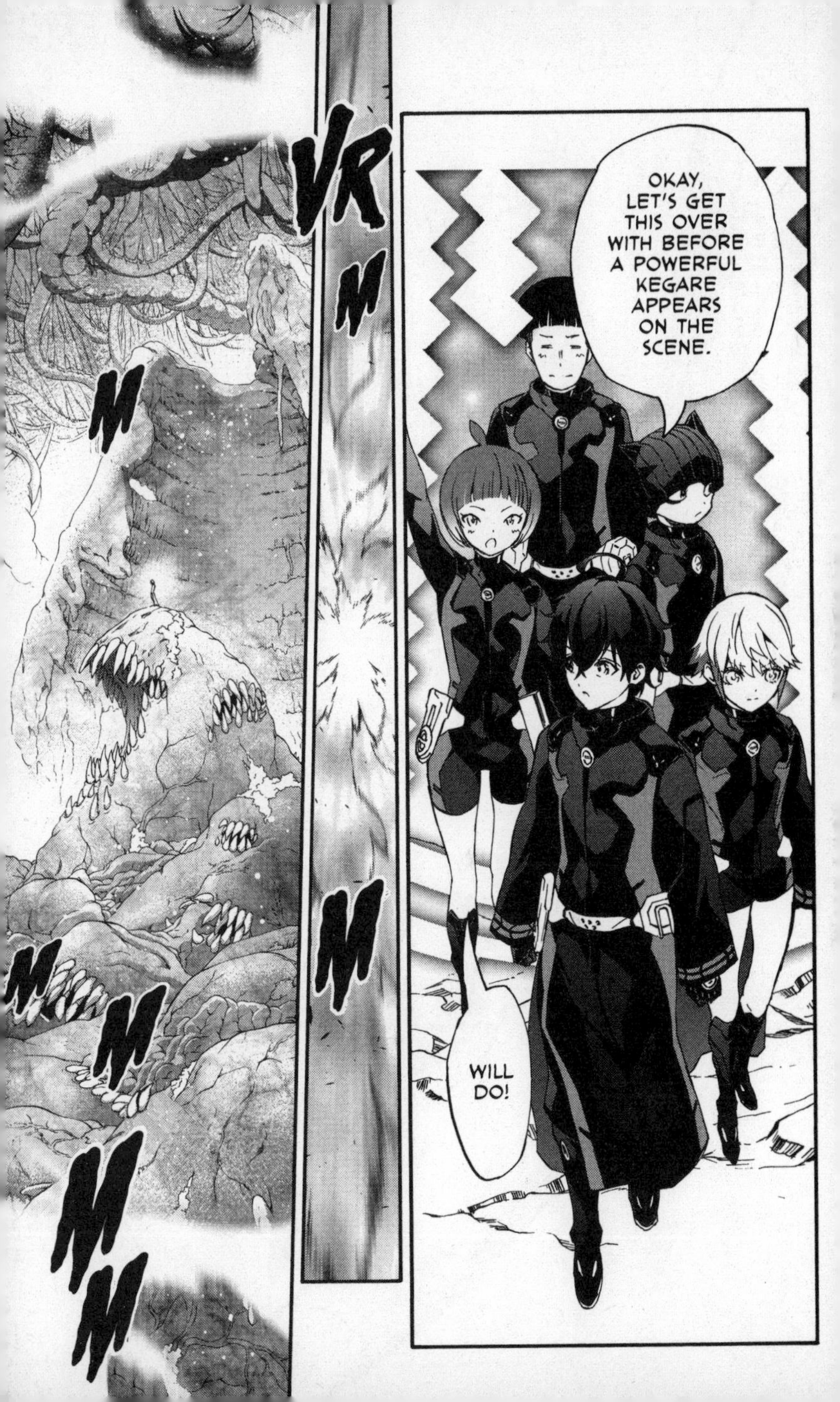
OKAY, LET'S GET THIS OVER WITH BEFORE A POWERFUL KEGARE APPEARS ON THE SCENE.
WILL DO!
VRMM
MMMMMM

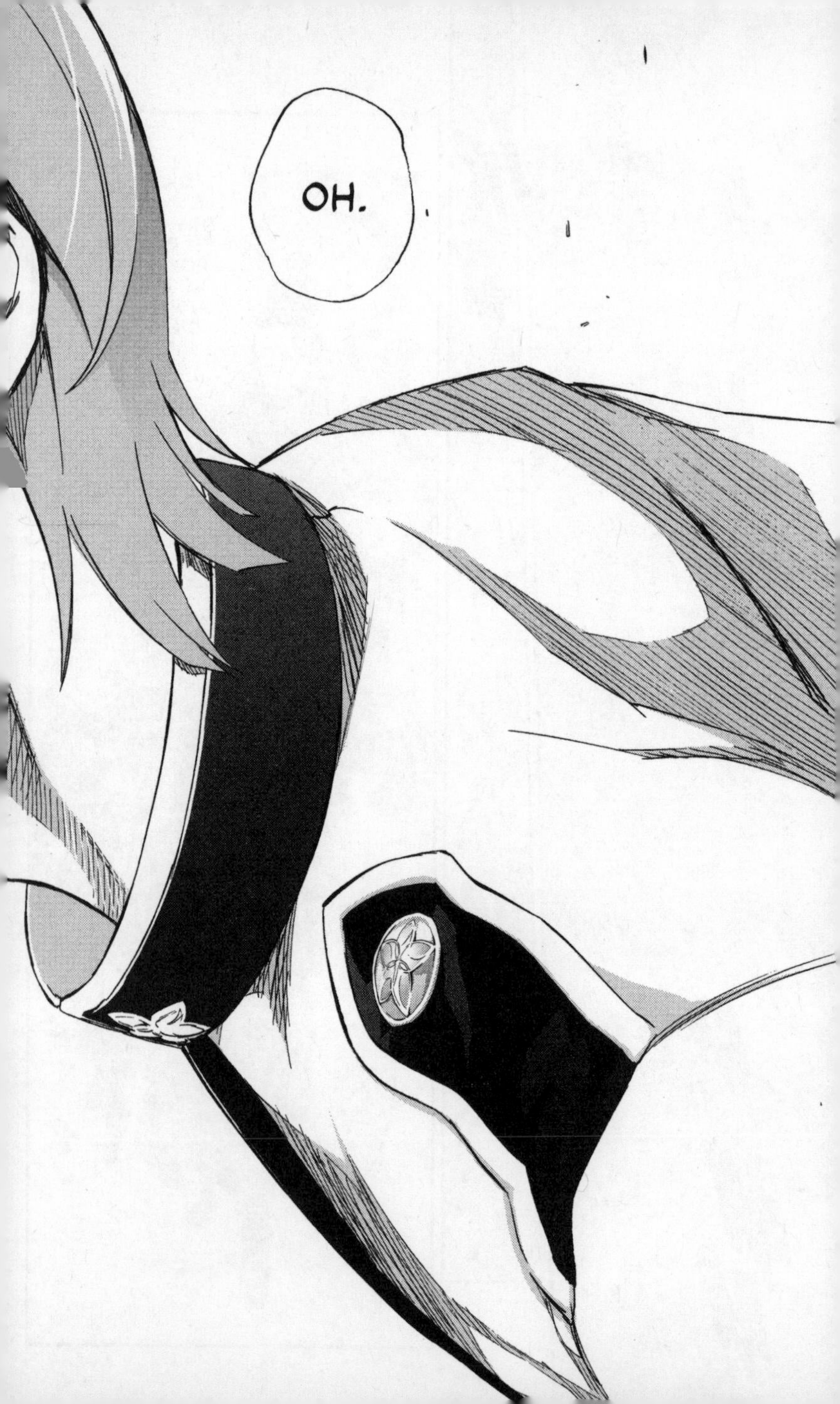
OH.

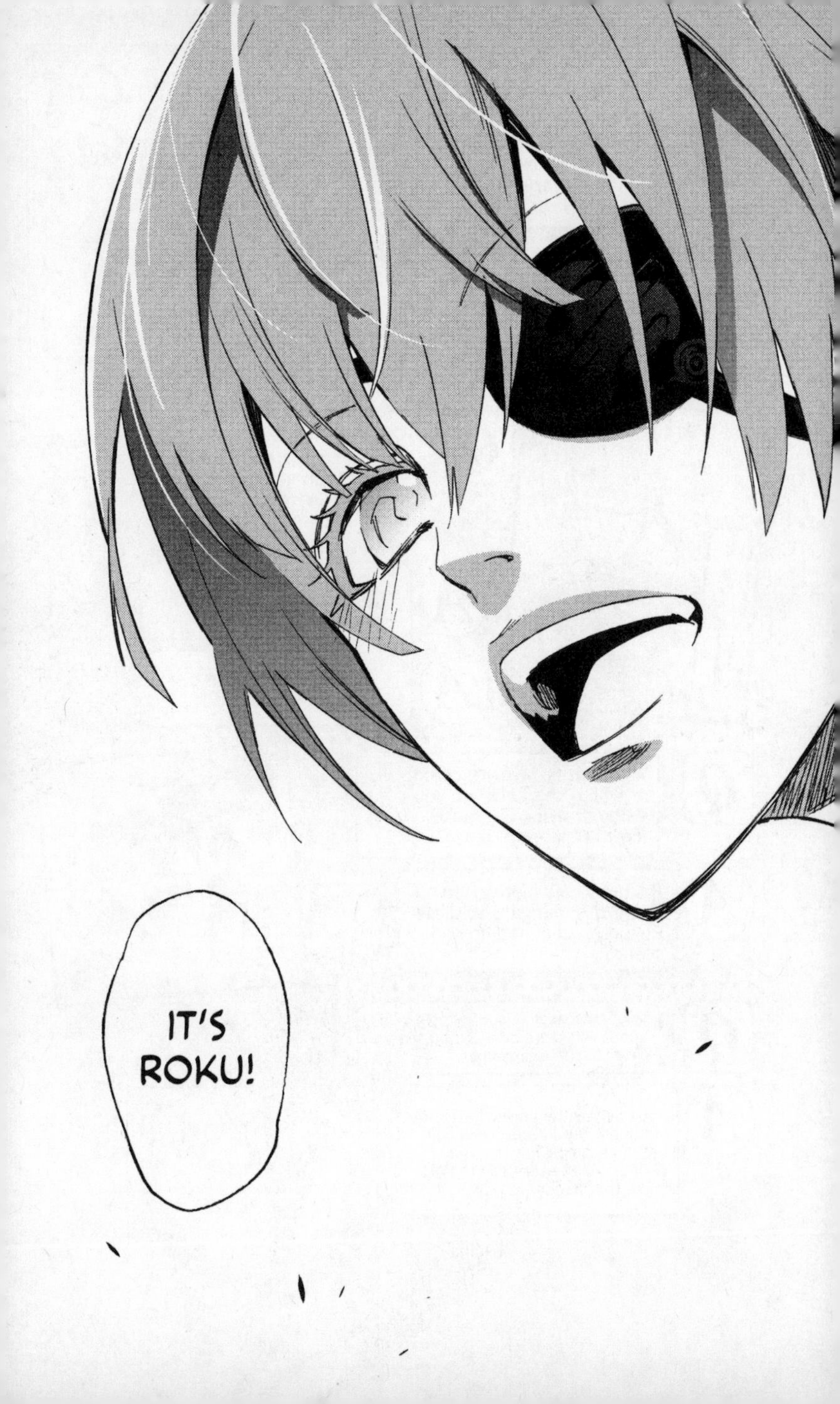
IT'S ROKU!

Q Q nyoritsuryo!

Question Corner

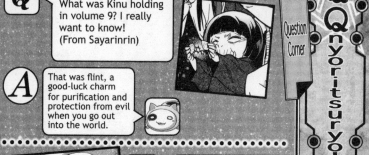

Q What was Kinu holding in volume 9? I really want to know! (From Sayarinrin)

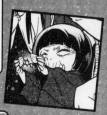

A That was flint, a good-luck charm for purification and protection from evil when you go out into the world.

Q How strong is Arima compared to a member of the Twelve Guardians? (From Kunio Tomura)

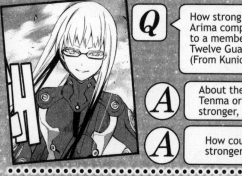

A About the same as Tenma or maybe a little stronger, I suspect.

A How could anyone be stronger than me?!

Q Who is your favorite character, or which character do you enjoy drawing the most? (From Hinappe)

A Rokuro.☆ My motivation for doing this manga is to draw Rokuro in cool and comedic scenes.

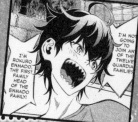

I'M NOT GOING TO JOIN AN OF THE TWELVE GUARDIAN FAMILIES
I'M ROKURO ENMADO, THE FIRST FAMILY HEAD OF THE ENMADO FAMILY!

Q The first season of the anime has finished. Will there be a second season? (From Kazuki Shiroyama)

A I don't have the power to decide anything, but I hope there will be! I'm working hard on the graphic novel every day to help make that happen.

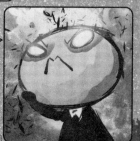

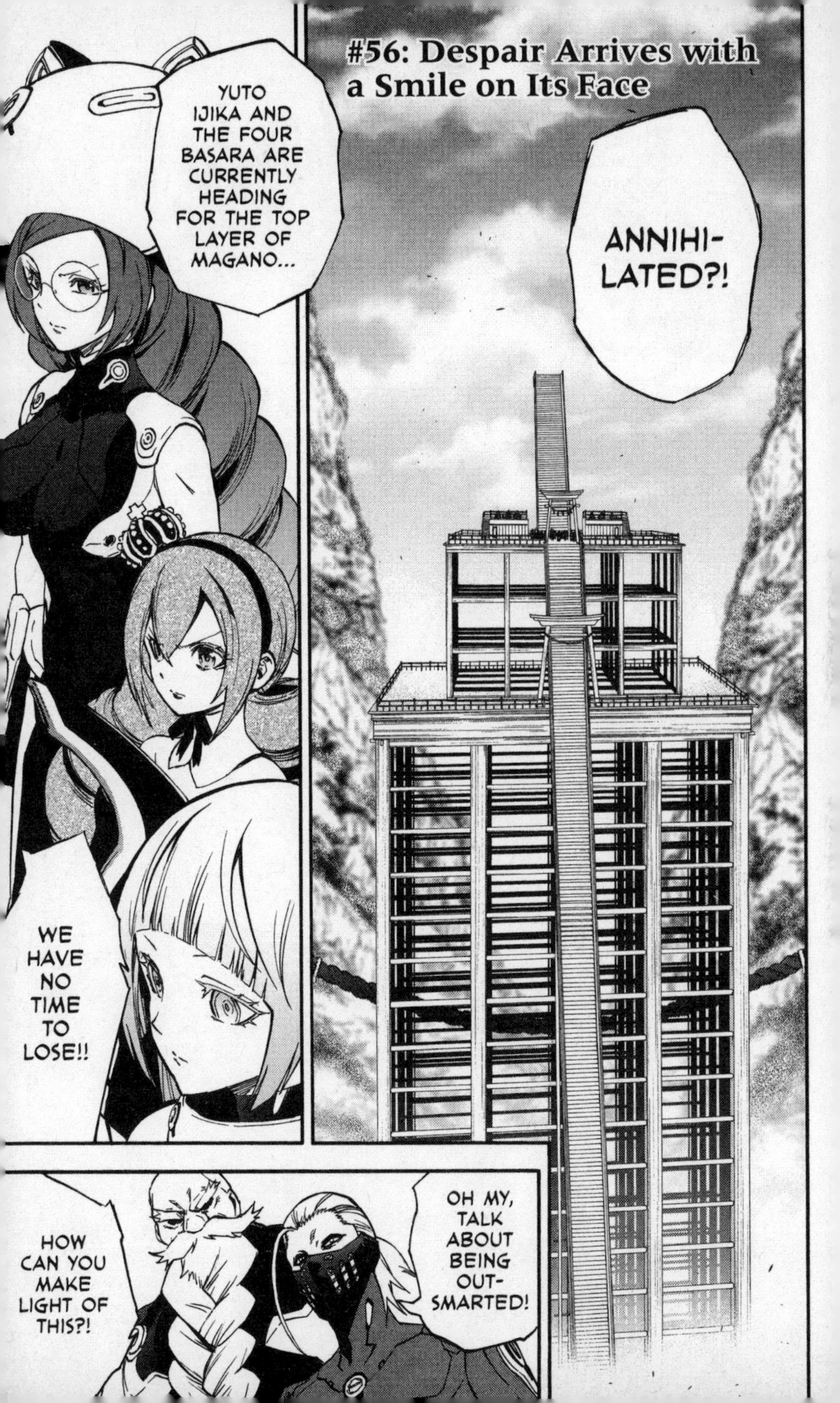
#56: Despair Arrives with a Smile on Its Face
ANNIHI-LATED?!
YUTO IJIKA AND THE FOUR BASARA ARE CURRENTLY HEADING FOR THE TOP LAYER OF MAGANO...
WE HAVE NO TIME TO LOSE!!
OH MY, TALK ABOUT BEING OUT-SMARTED!
HOW CAN YOU MAKE LIGHT OF THIS?!

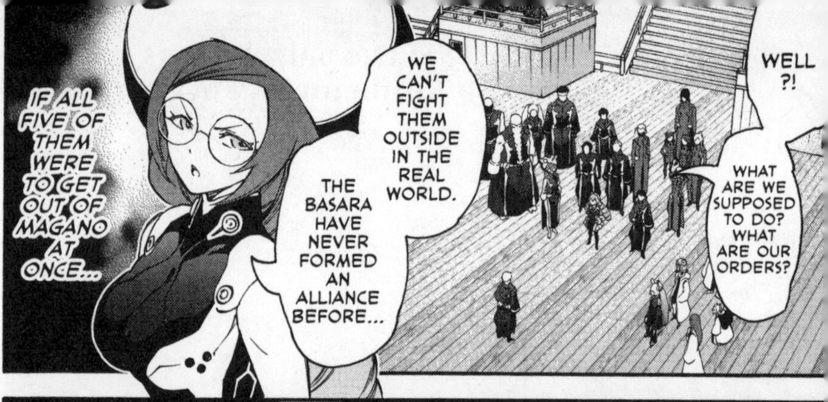
WELL ?!
WHAT ARE WE SUPPOSED TO DO? WHAT ARE OUR ORDERS?
WE CAN'T FIGHT THEM OUTSIDE IN THE REAL WORLD.
THE BASARA HAVE NEVER FORMED AN ALLIANCE BEFORE...
IF ALL FIVE OF THEM WERE TO GET OUT OF MAGANO AT ONCE...

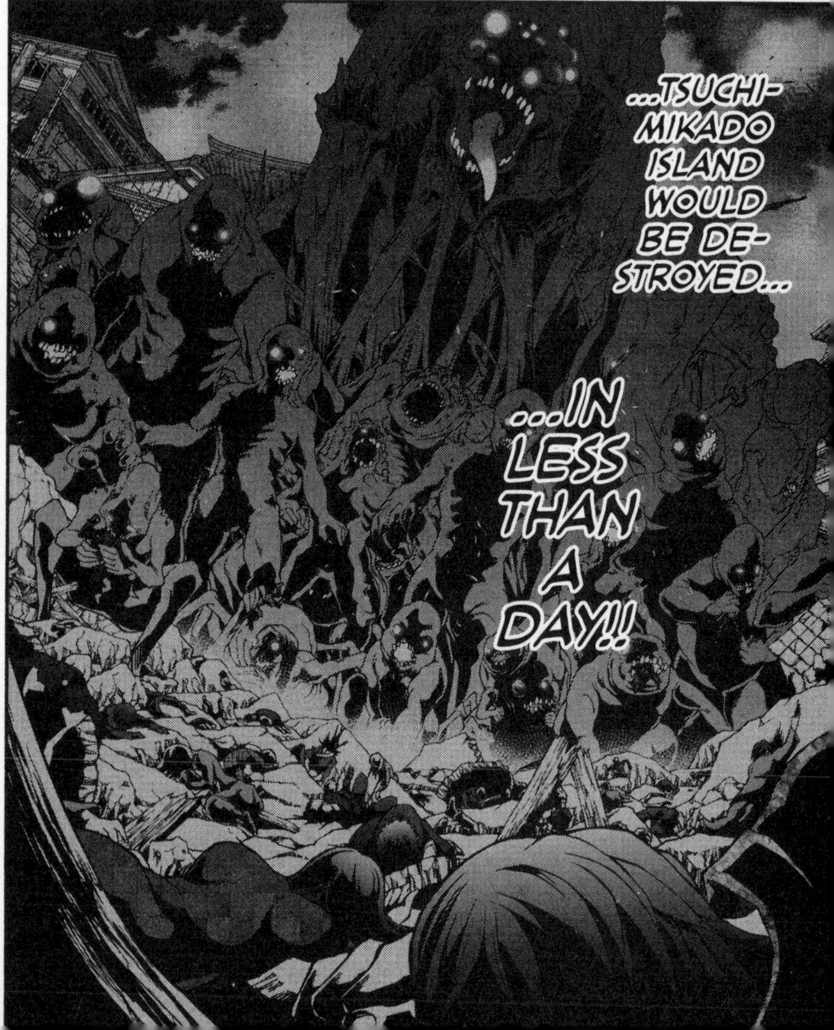
...TSUCHI-MIKADO ISLAND WOULD BE DE-STROYED...
...IN LESS THAN A DAY!!

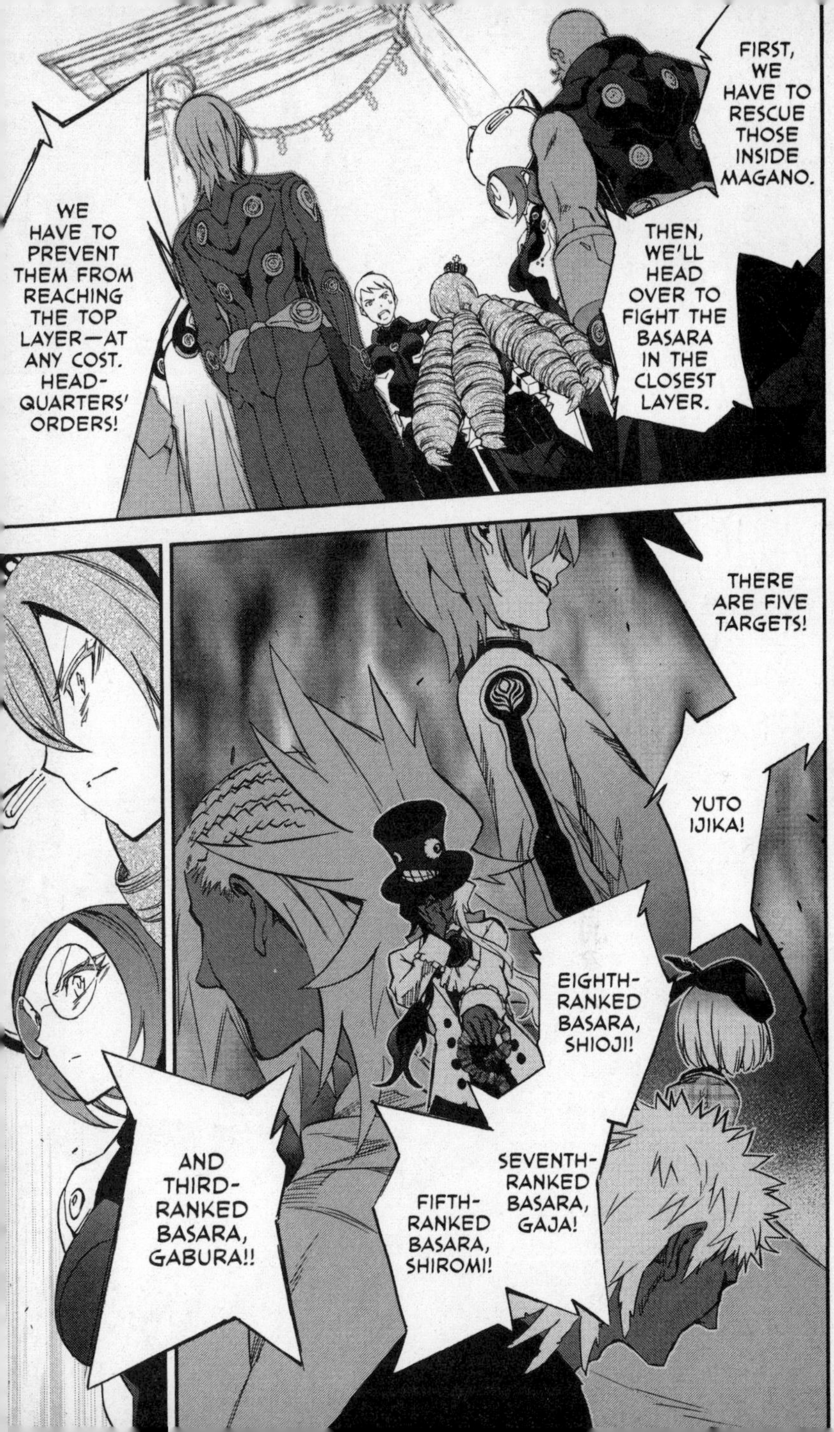
FIRST, WE HAVE TO RESCUE THOSE INSIDE MAGANO.
THEN, WE'LL HEAD OVER TO FIGHT THE BASARA IN THE CLOSEST LAYER.
WE HAVE TO PREVENT THEM FROM REACHING THE TOP LAYER—AT ANY COST. HEAD-QUARTERS' ORDERS!
THERE ARE FIVE TARGETS!
YUTO IJIKA!
EIGHTH-RANKED BASARA, SHIOJI!
SEVENTH-RANKED BASARA, GAJA!
FIFTH-RANKED BASARA, SHIROMI!
AND THIRD-RANKED BASARA, GABURA!!

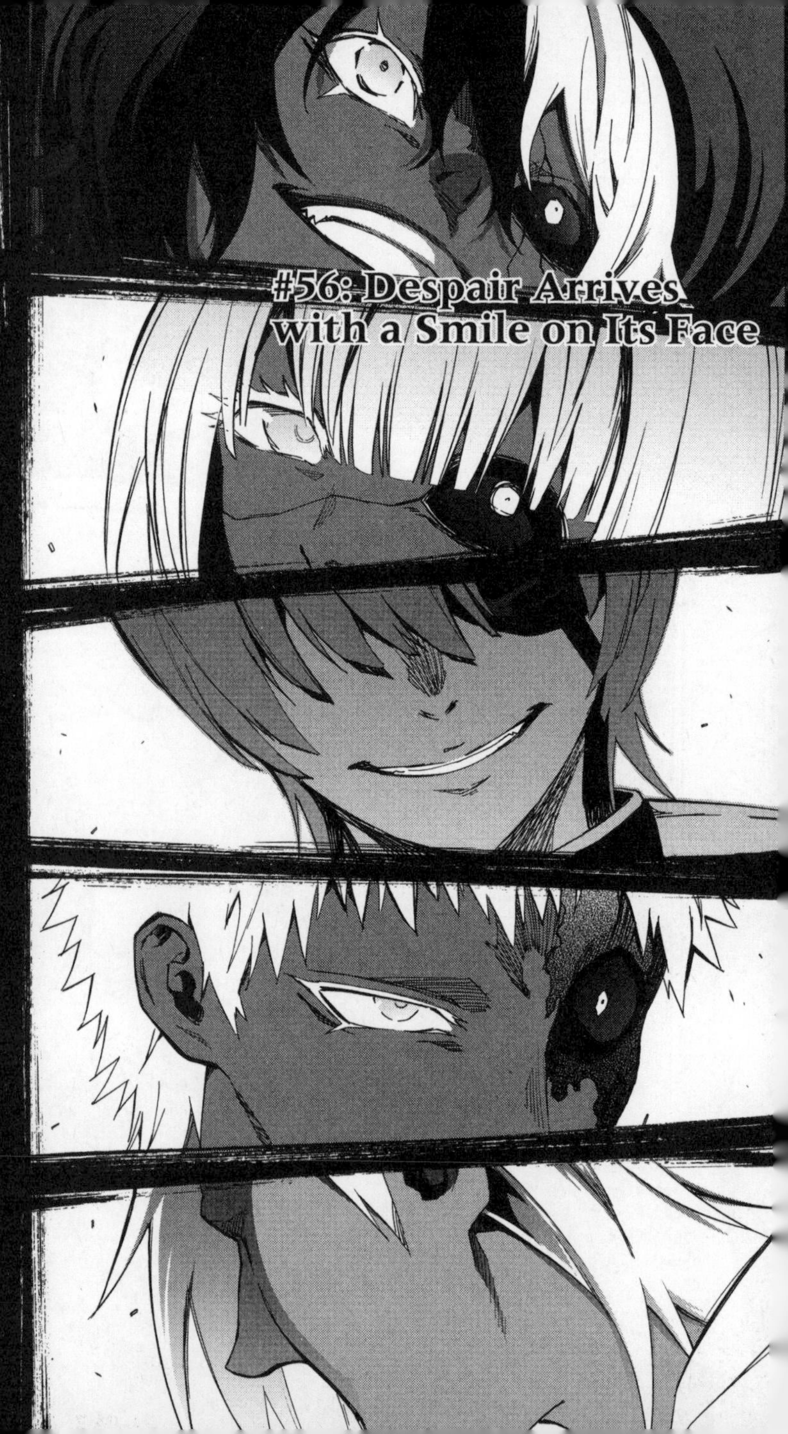
#56: Despair Arrives with a Smile on Its Face

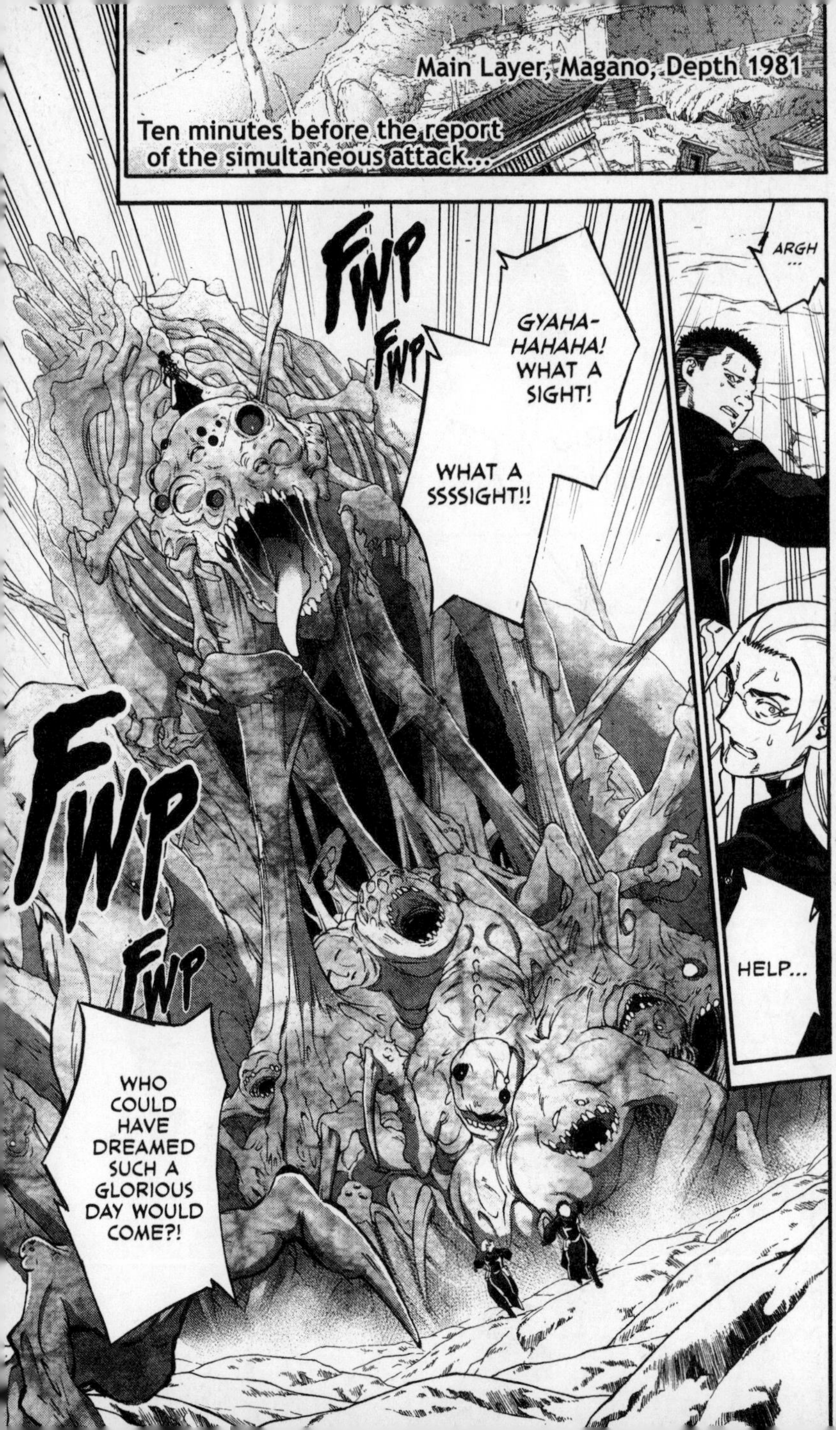
Main Layer, Magano, Depth 1981
Ten minutes before the report of the simultaneous attack...
ARGH...
HELP...
FWP
FWP
GYAHA-HAHAHA! WHAT A SIGHT!
WHAT A SSSSIGHT!!
FWP
FWP
WHO COULD HAVE DREAMED SUCH A GLORIOUS DAY WOULD COME?!

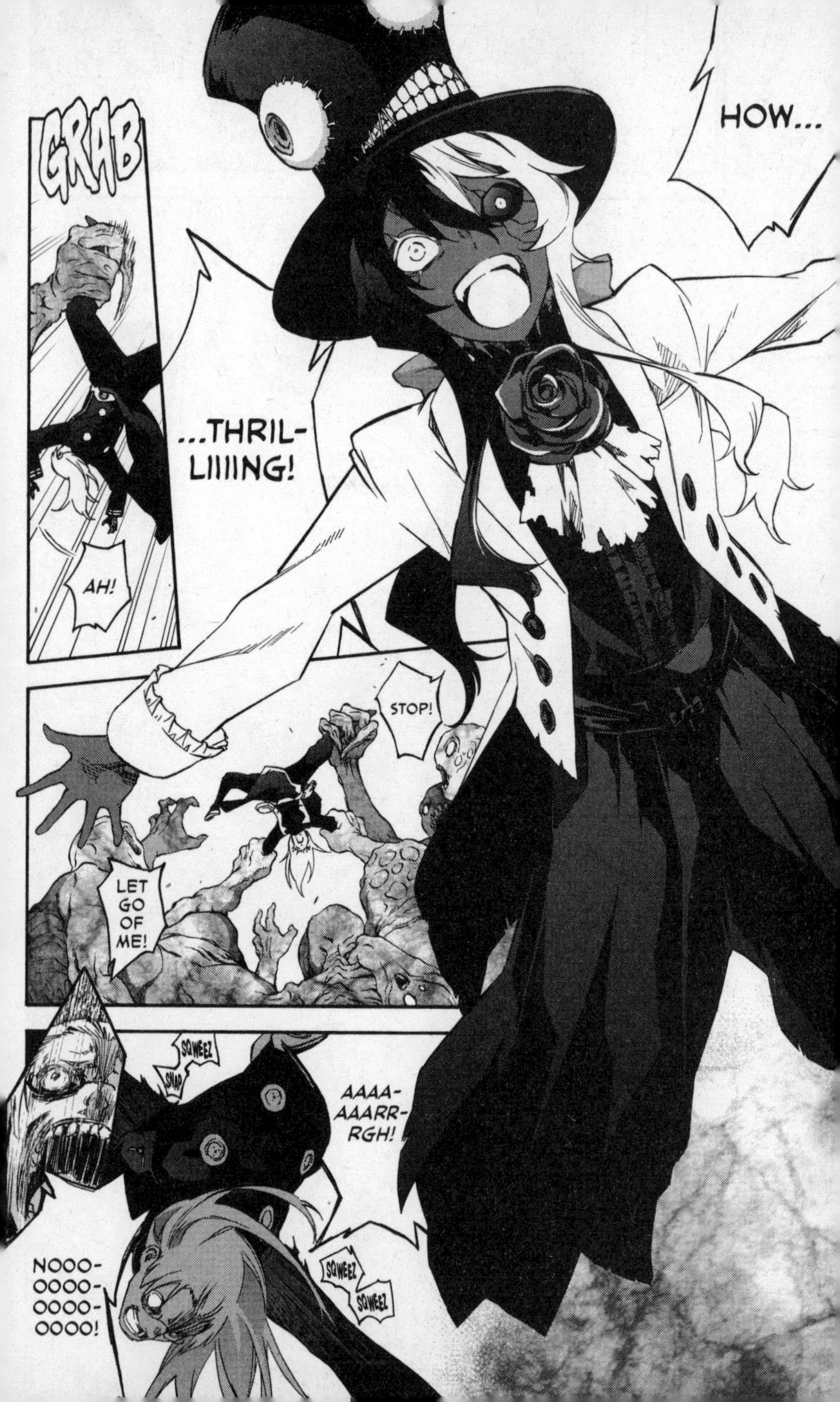
HOW...
...THRIL-LIIIING!
GRAB
AH!
STOP!
LET GO OF ME!
AAAA-AAARR-RGH!
SQWEEZ
SNAP
SQWEEZ
SQWEEZ
NOOO-OOOO-OOOO-OOOO!

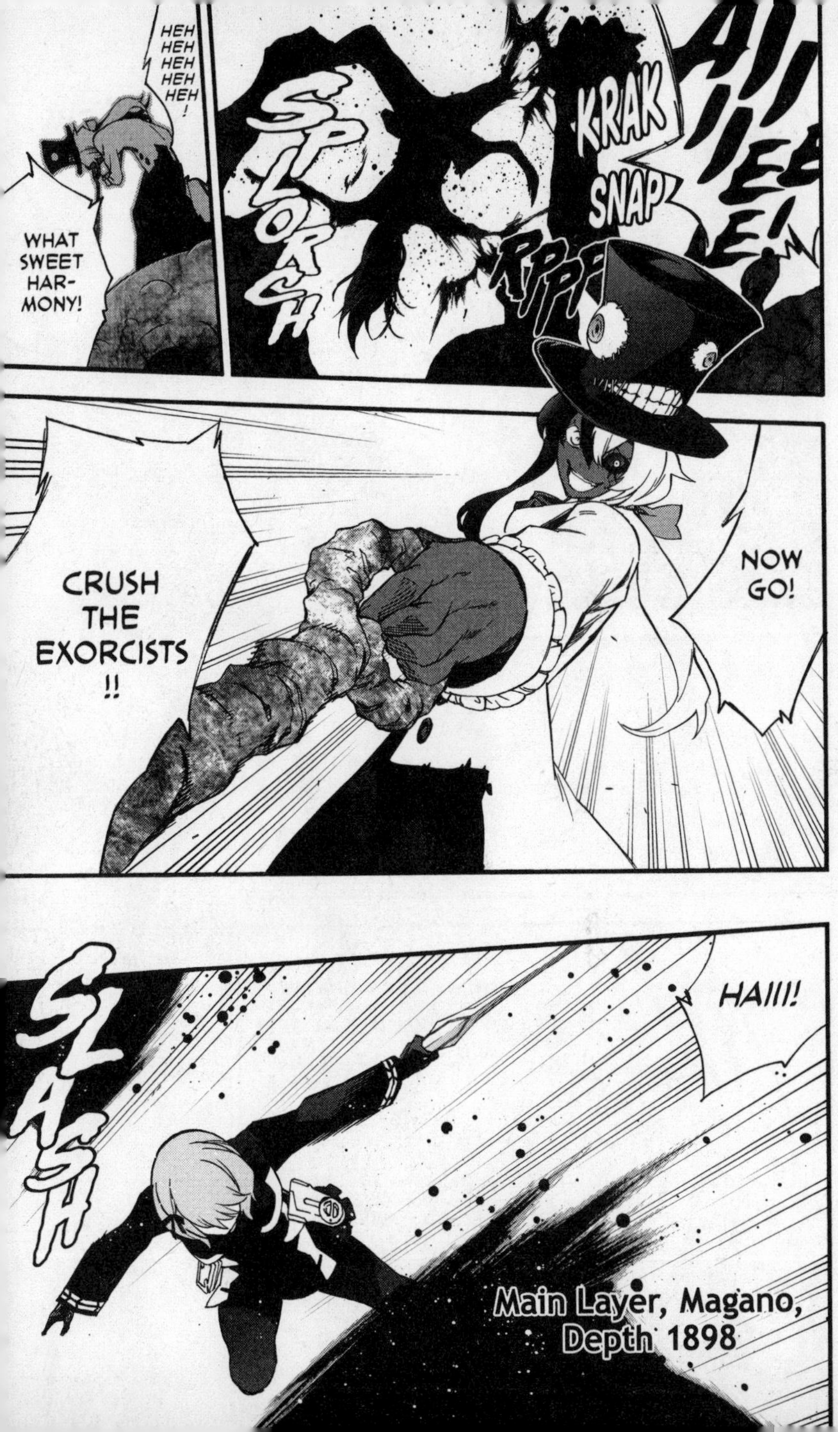
AIIIIEEEE!
KRAK
SNAP
RIPPP
SPLORCH
HEH HEH HEH HEH HEH!
WHAT SWEET HAR-MONY!
NOW GO!
CRUSH THE EXORCISTS!!
HAIII!
SLASH
Main Layer, Magano, Depth 1898

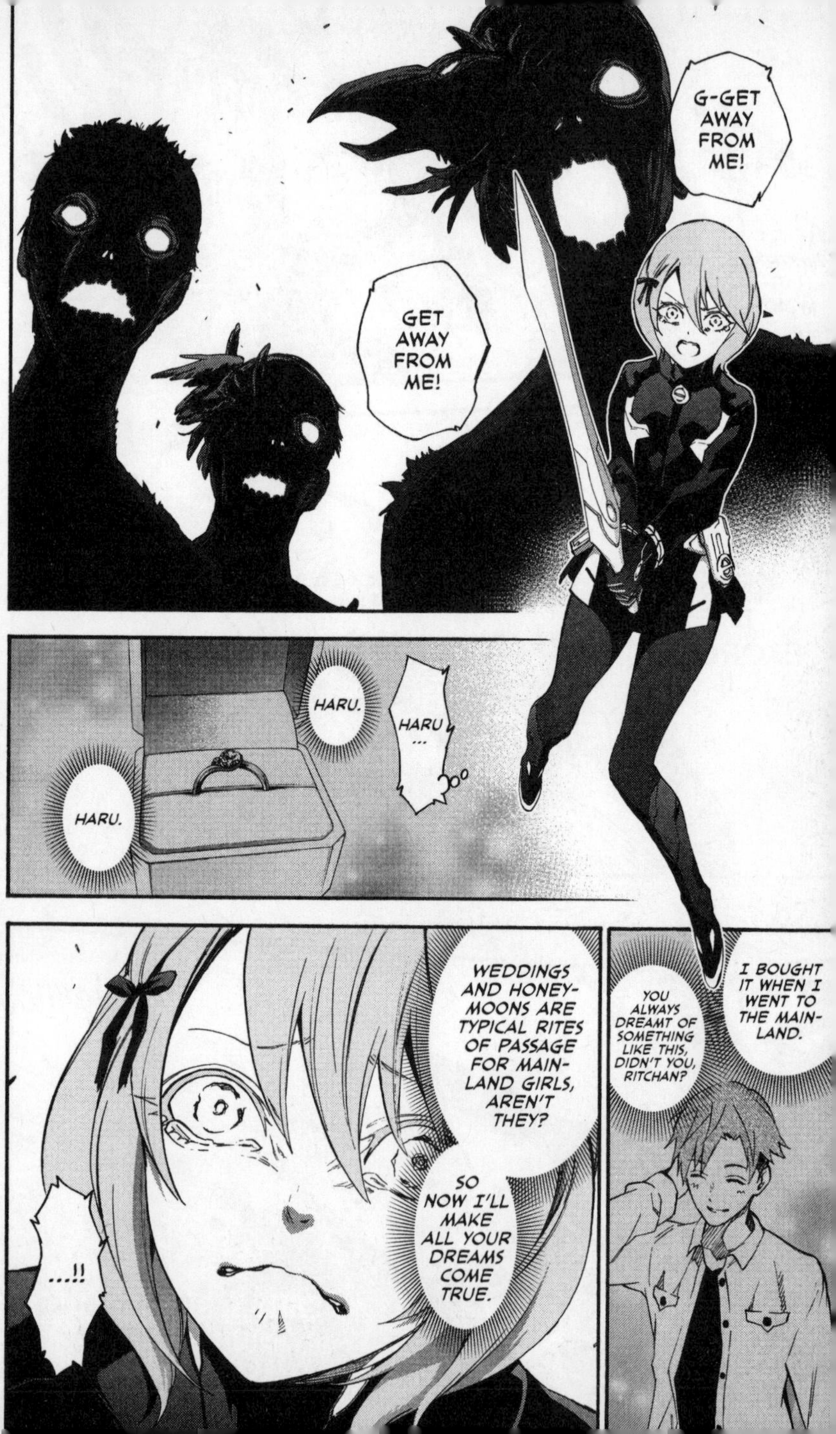
G-GET AWAY FROM ME!
GET AWAY FROM ME!
HARU...
HARU.
HARU.
I BOUGHT IT WHEN I WENT TO THE MAIN-LAND.
YOU ALWAYS DREAMT OF SOMETHING LIKE THIS, DIDN'T YOU, RITCHAN?
WEDDINGS AND HONEY-MOONS ARE TYPICAL RITES OF PASSAGE FOR MAIN-LAND GIRLS, AREN'T THEY?
SO NOW I'LL MAKE ALL YOUR DREAMS COME TRUE.
...!!

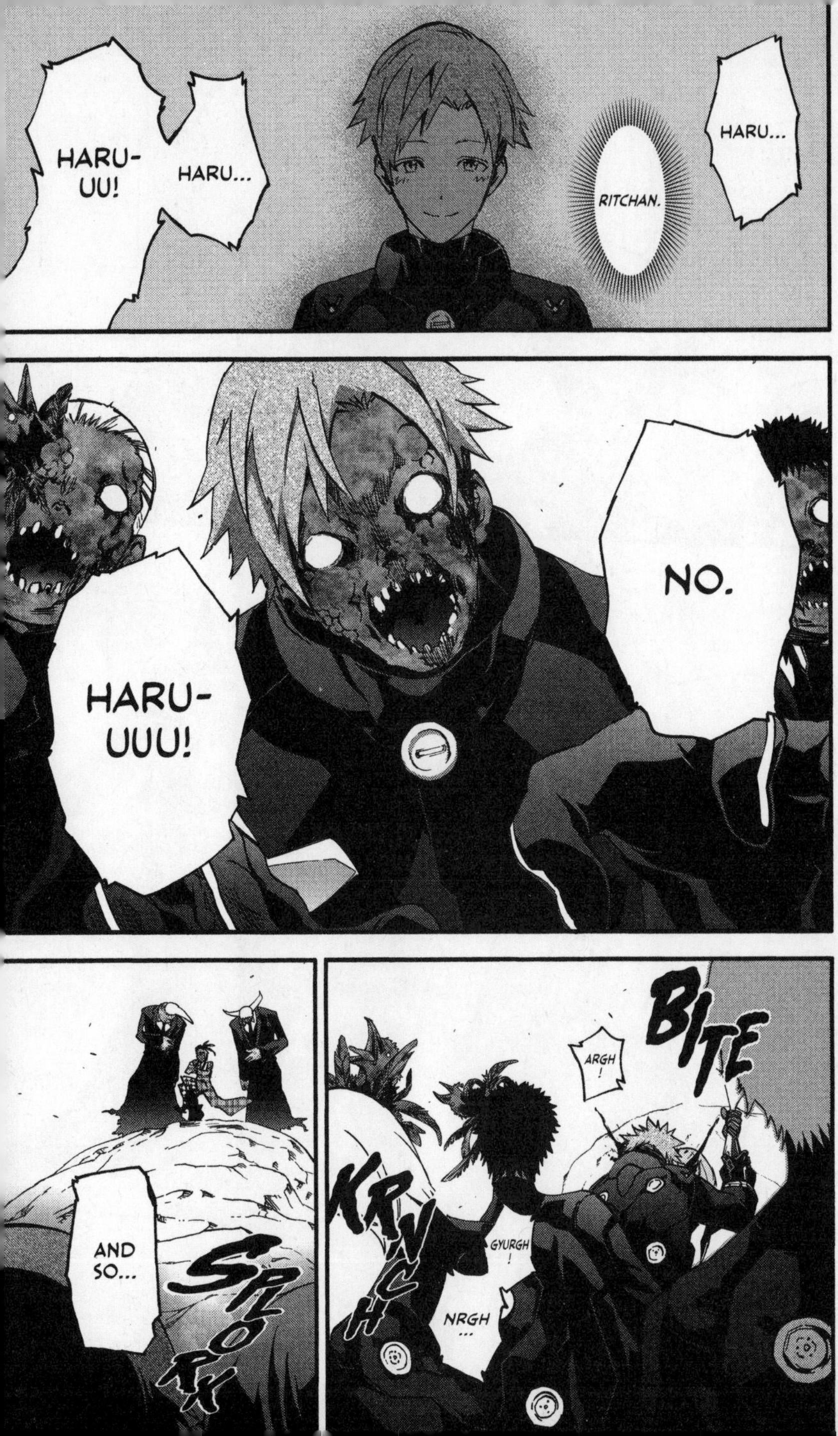
HARU...
RITCHAN.
HARU...
HARU-UU!
NO.
HARU-UUU!
BITE
ARGH!
GYURGH!
KRUNCH
NRGH...
SPLORK
AND SO...

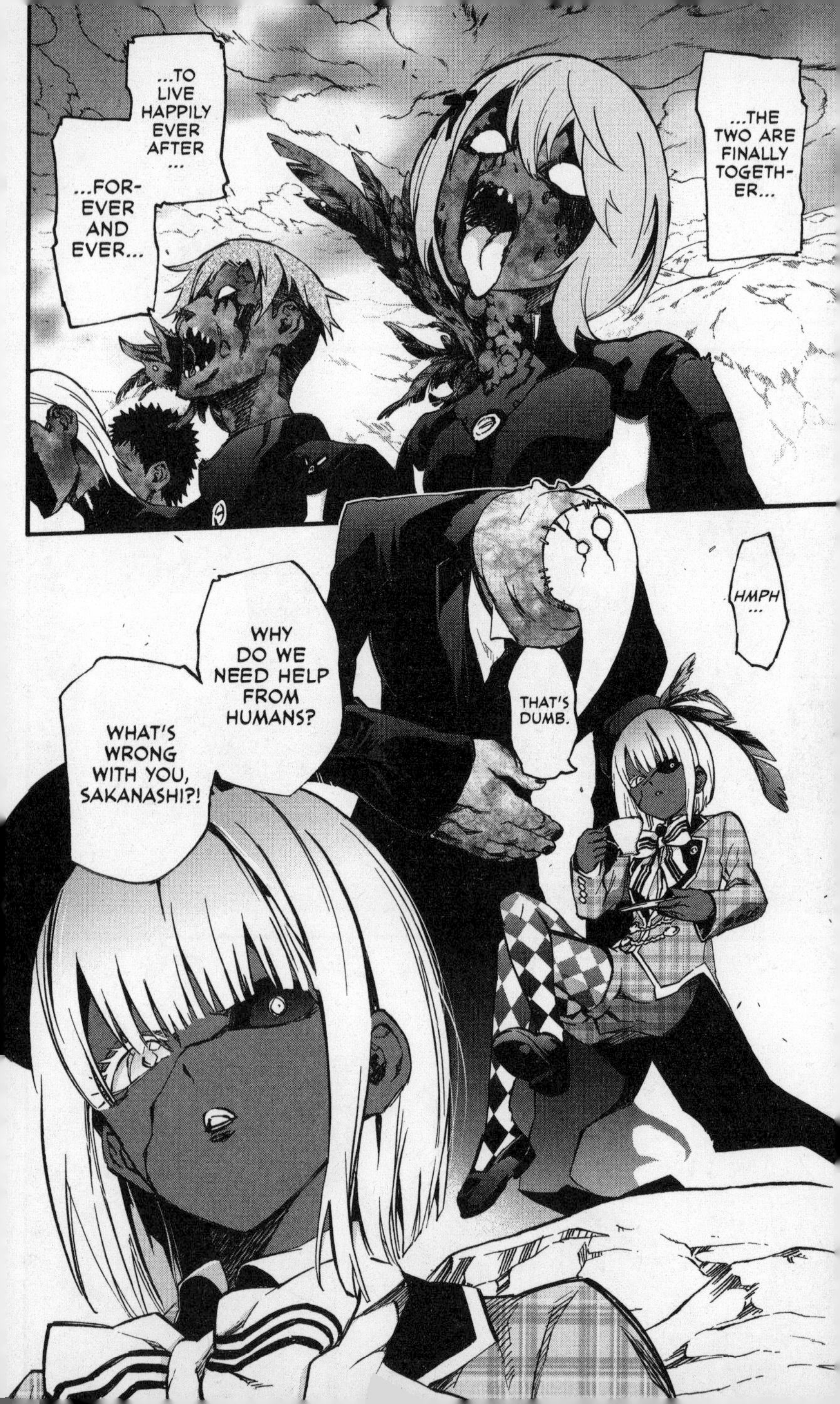
...THE TWO ARE FINALLY TOGETH-ER...
...TO LIVE HAPPILY EVER AFTER...
...FOR-EVER AND EVER...
HMPH...
THAT'S DUMB.
WHY DO WE NEED HELP FROM HUMANS?
WHAT'S WRONG WITH YOU, SAKANASHI?!

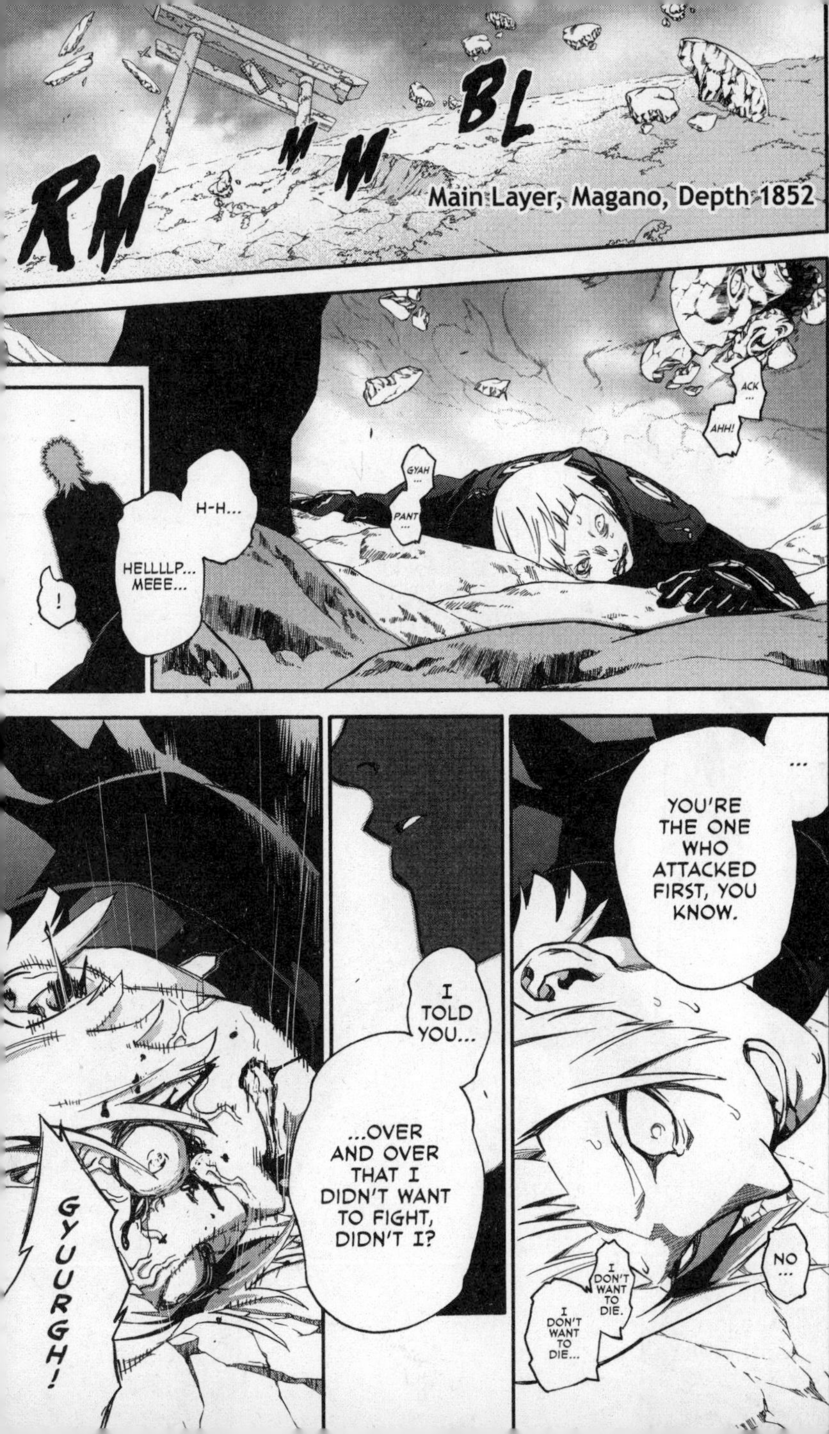
RMMMBL
Main Layer, Magano, Depth 1852
ACK... AHH!
GYAH...
PANT...
H-H...
HELLLLP... MEEE...
!
...
YOU'RE THE ONE WHO ATTACKED FIRST, YOU KNOW.
NO...
I DON'T WANT TO DIE.
I DON'T WANT TO DIE...
I TOLD YOU...
...OVER AND OVER THAT I DIDN'T WANT TO FIGHT, DIDN'T I?
GYUURGH!

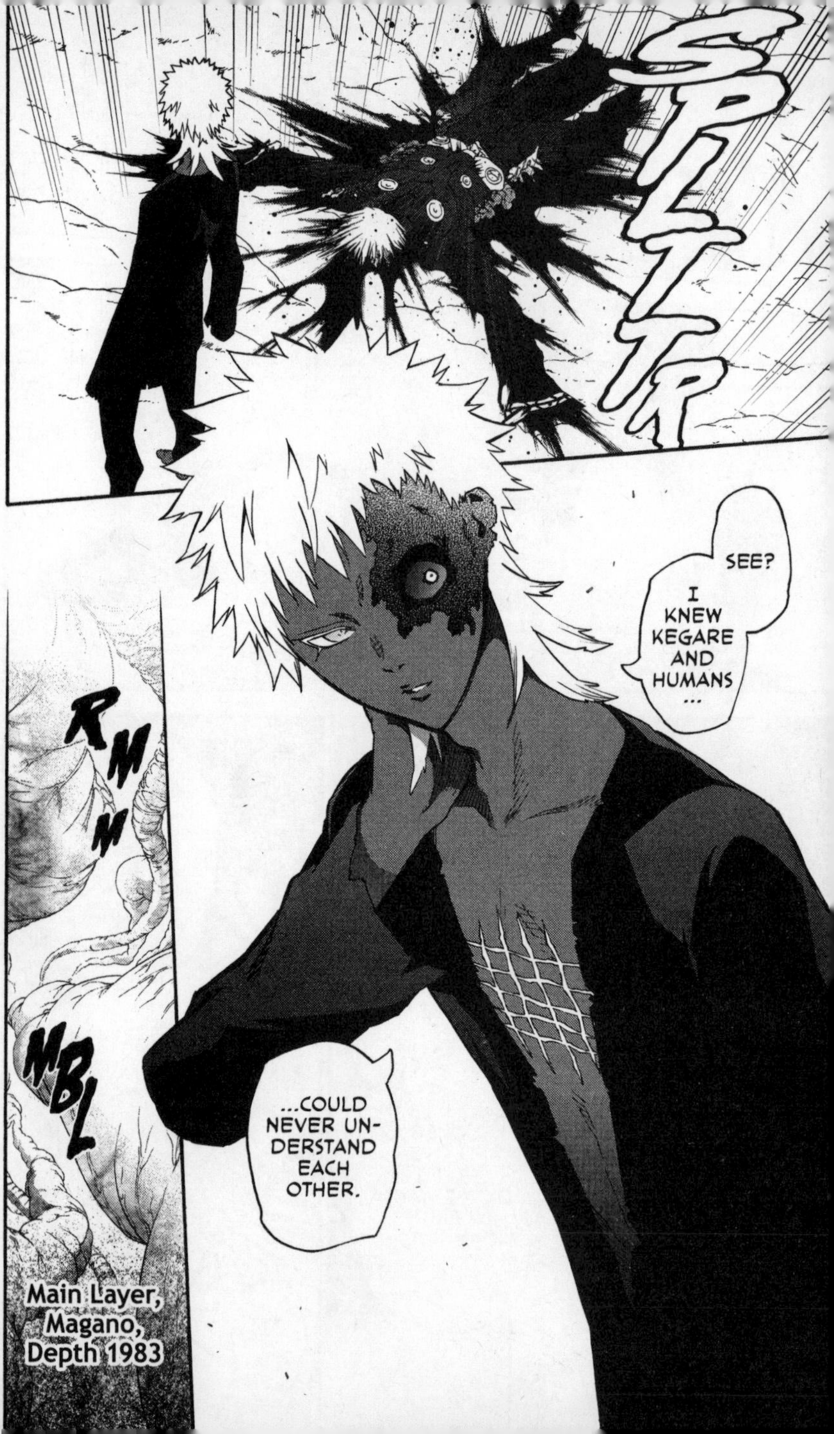
SPLITR
SEE? I KNEW KEGARE AND HUMANS ...
...COULD NEVER UN-DERSTAND EACH OTHER.
RMMM
NBL
Main Layer, Magano, Depth 1983

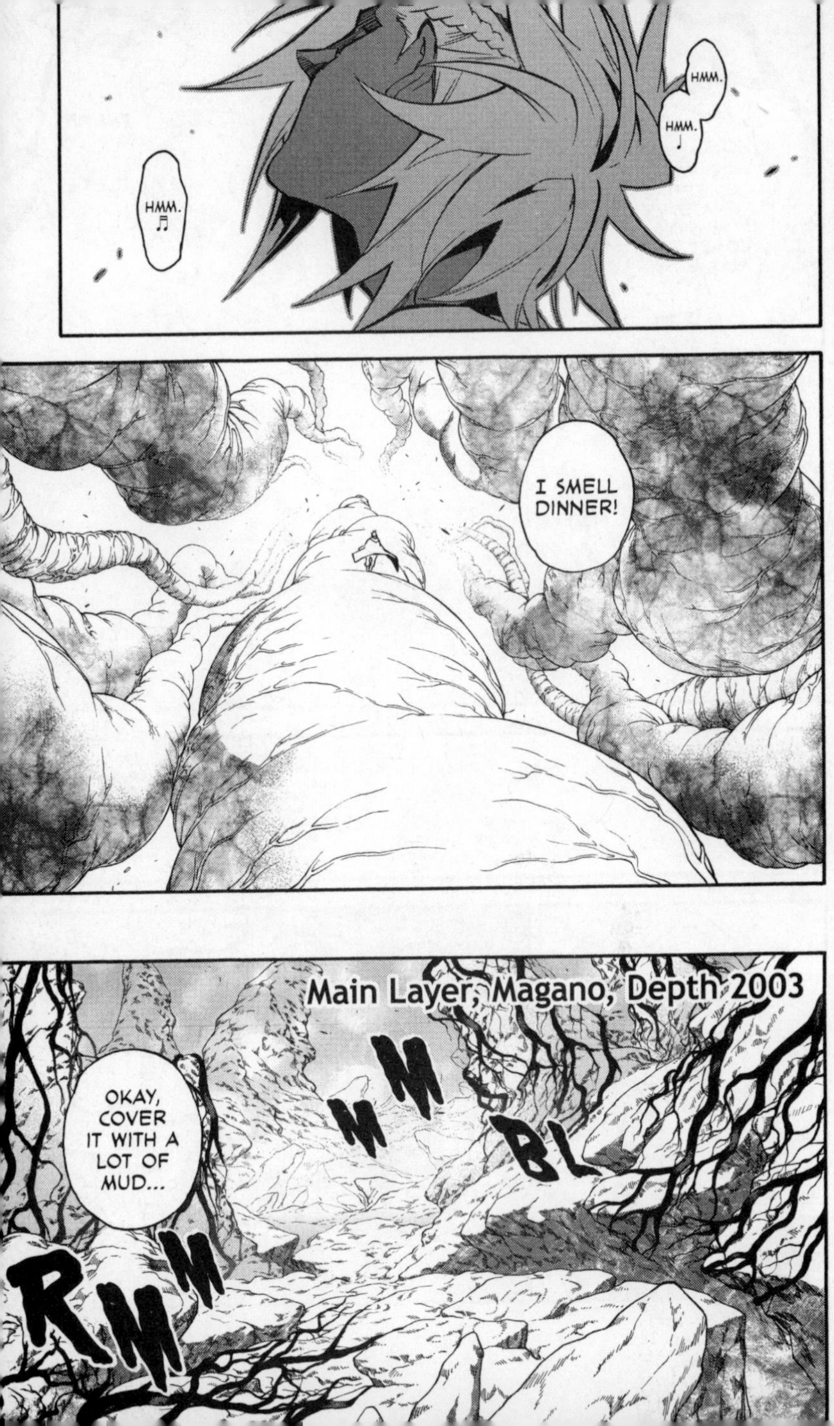
HMM.
HMM. ♩
HMM. ♬
I SMELL DINNER!
Main Layer, Magano, Depth 2003
MMBL
OKAY, COVER IT WITH A LOT OF MUD...
RMM

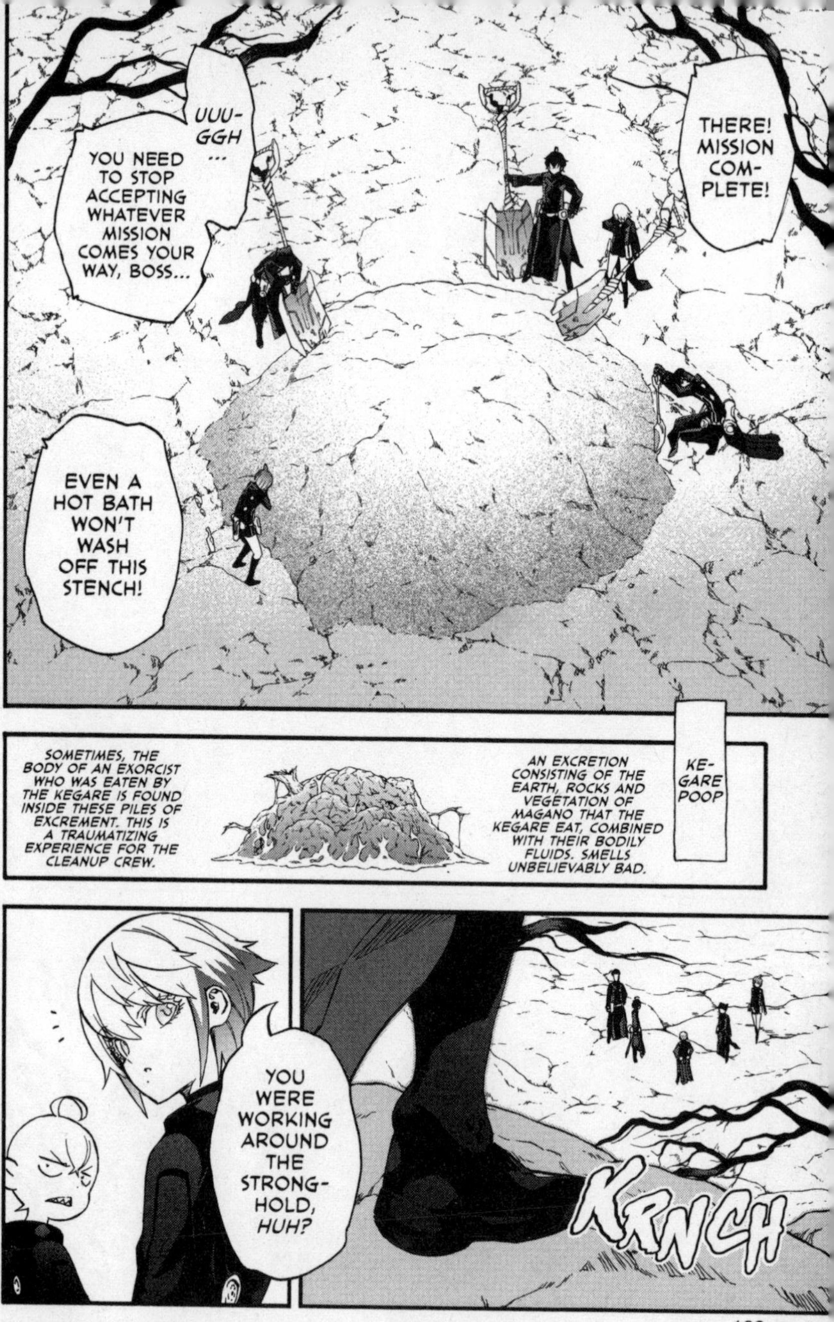
THERE! MISSION COM-PLETE!
UUU-GGH...
YOU NEED TO STOP ACCEPTING WHATEVER MISSION COMES YOUR WAY, BOSS...
EVEN A HOT BATH WON'T WASH OFF THIS STENCH!
KE-GARE POOP
AN EXCRETION CONSISTING OF THE EARTH, ROCKS AND VEGETATION OF MAGANO THAT THE KEGARE EAT, COMBINED WITH THEIR BODILY FLUIDS. SMELLS UNBELIEVABLY BAD.
SOMETIMES, THE BODY OF AN EXORCIST WHO WAS EATEN BY THE KEGARE IS FOUND INSIDE THESE PILES OF EXCREMENT. THIS IS A TRAUMATIZING EXPERIENCE FOR THE CLEANUP CREW.
KRNCH
YOU WERE WORKING AROUND THE STRONG-HOLD, HUH?

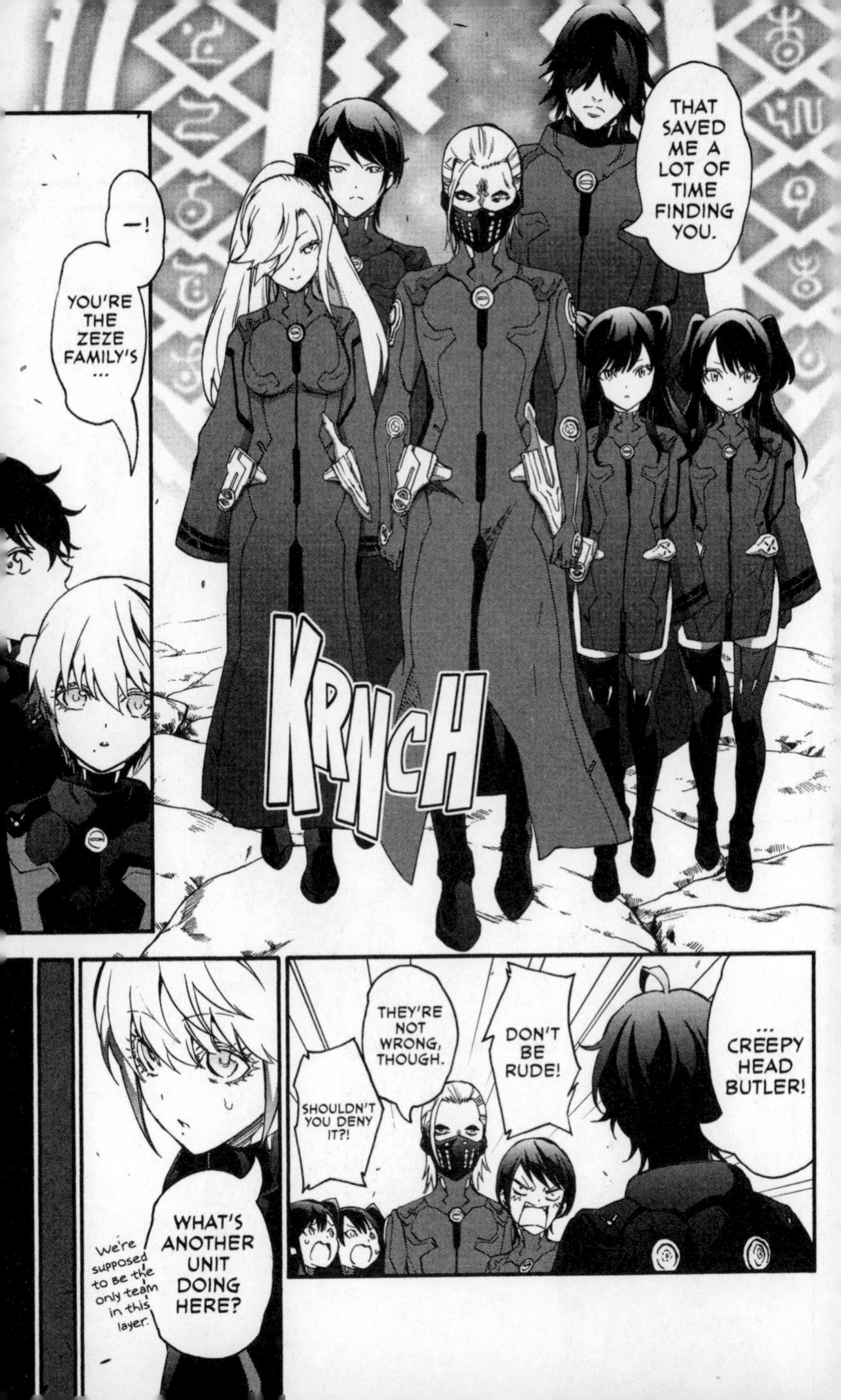
THAT SAVED ME A LOT OF TIME FINDING YOU.
KRNCH
—!
YOU'RE THE ZEZE FAMILY'S ...
... CREEPY HEAD BUTLER!
DON'T BE RUDE!
THEY'RE NOT WRONG, THOUGH.
SHOULDN'T YOU DENY IT?!
WHAT'S ANOTHER UNIT DOING HERE?
We're supposed to be the only team in this layer.

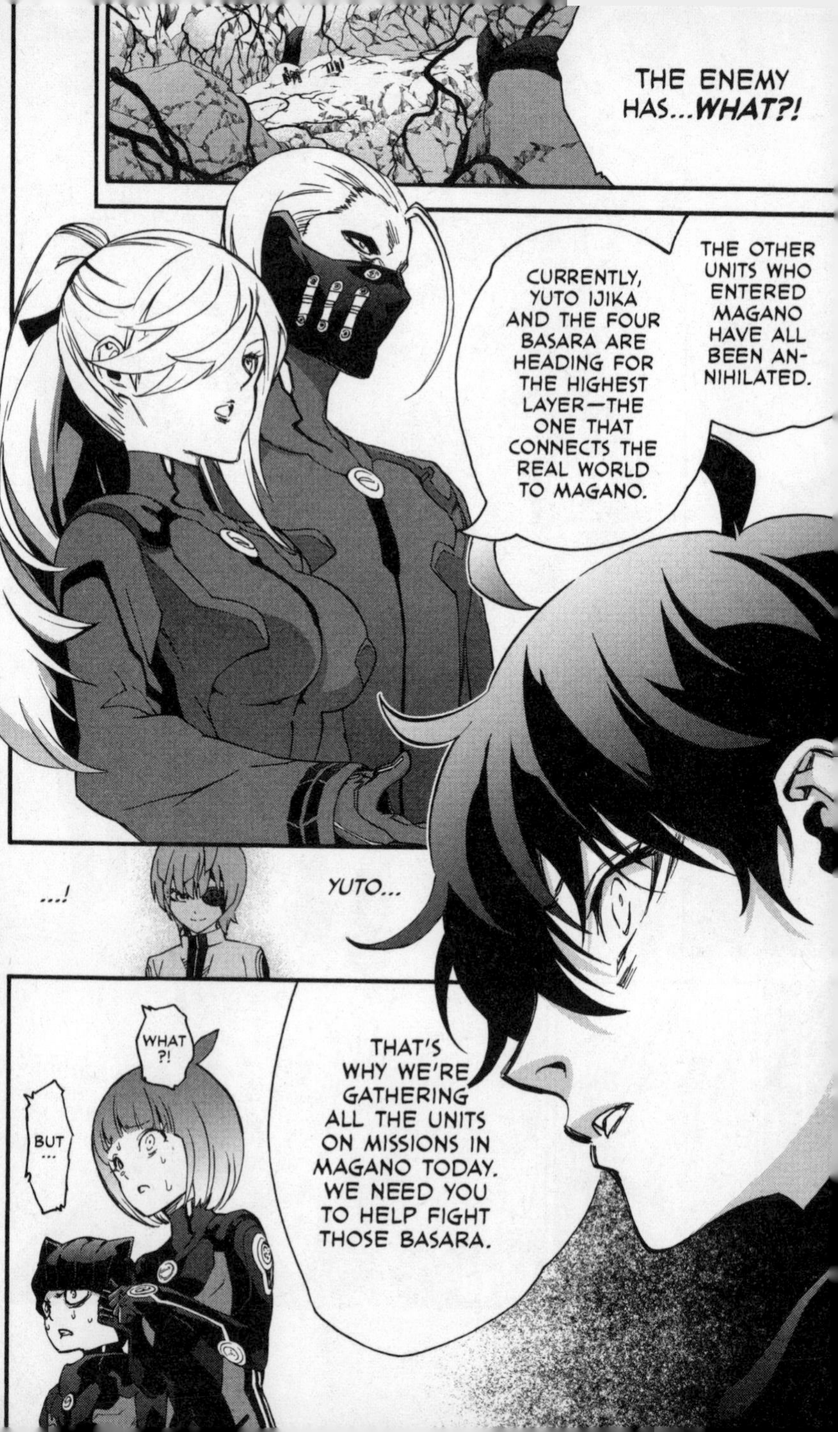
THE ENEMY HAS...WHAT?!
THE OTHER UNITS WHO ENTERED MAGANO HAVE ALL BEEN AN-NIHILATED.
CURRENTLY, YUTO IJIKA AND THE FOUR BASARA ARE HEADING FOR THE HIGHEST LAYER—THE ONE THAT CONNECTS THE REAL WORLD TO MAGANO.
YUTO...
...!
THAT'S WHY WE'RE GATHERING ALL THE UNITS ON MISSIONS IN MAGANO TODAY. WE NEED YOU TO HELP FIGHT THOSE BASARA.
WHAT ?!
BUT ...

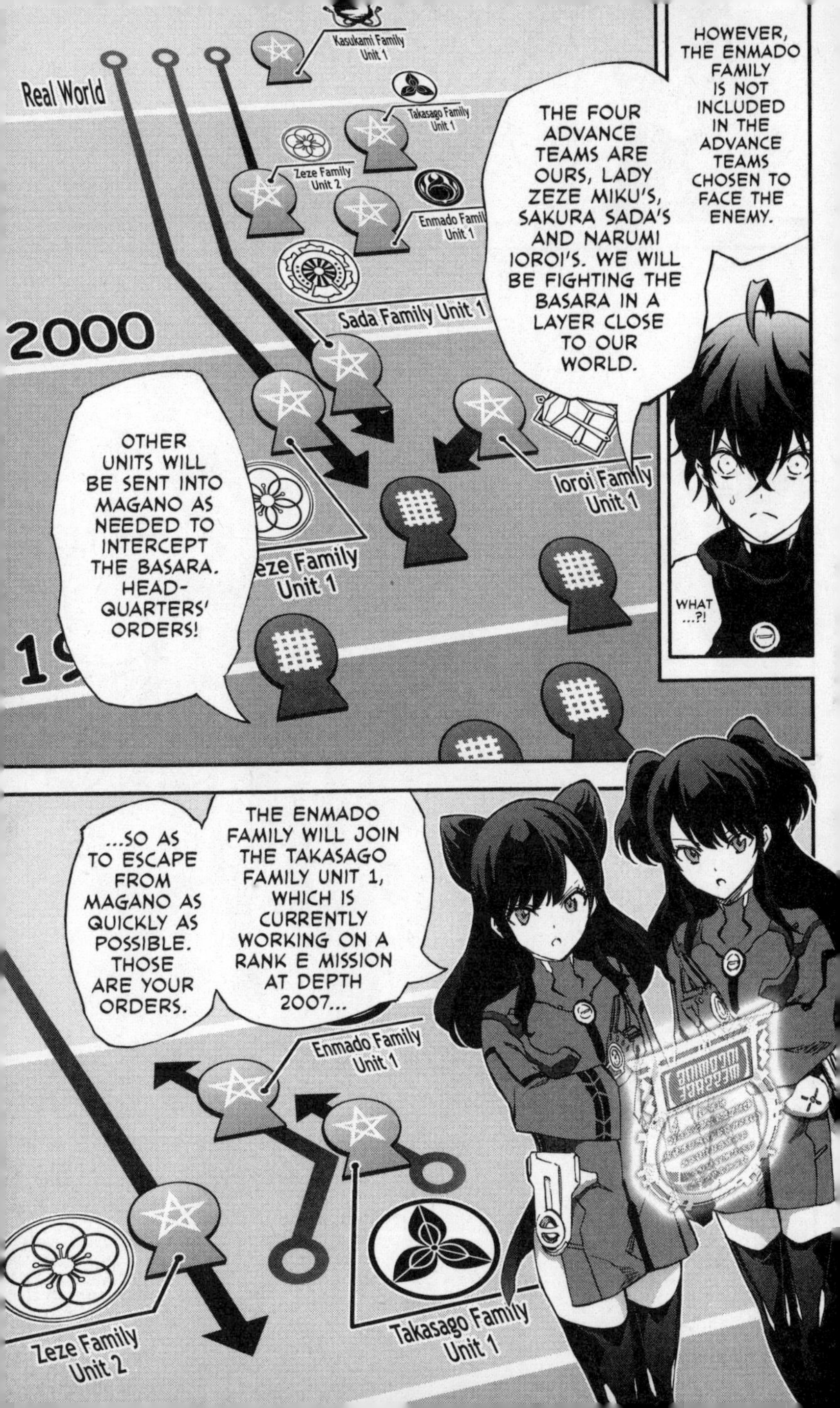
THE FOUR ADVANCE TEAMS ARE OURS, LADY ZEZE MIKU'S, SAKURA SADA'S AND NARUMI IOROI'S. WE WILL BE FIGHTING THE BASARA IN A LAYER CLOSE TO OUR WORLD.
OTHER UNITS WILL BE SENT INTO MAGANO AS NEEDED TO INTERCEPT THE BASARA. HEAD-QUARTERS' ORDERS!
Real World
Kasukami Family Unit 1
Takasago Family Unit 1
Zeze Family Unit 2
Enmado Famil Unit 1
Sada Family Unit 1
2000
Ioroi Family Unit 1
eze Family Unit 1
19
HOWEVER, THE ENMADO FAMILY IS NOT INCLUDED IN THE ADVANCE TEAMS CHOSEN TO FACE THE ENEMY.
WHAT ...?!
THE ENMADO FAMILY WILL JOIN THE TAKASAGO FAMILY UNIT 1, WHICH IS CURRENTLY WORKING ON A RANK E MISSION AT DEPTH 2007...
...SO AS TO ESCAPE FROM MAGANO AS QUICKLY AS POSSIBLE. THOSE ARE YOUR ORDERS.
Enmado Family Unit 1
Takasago Family Unit 1
Zeze Family Unit 2

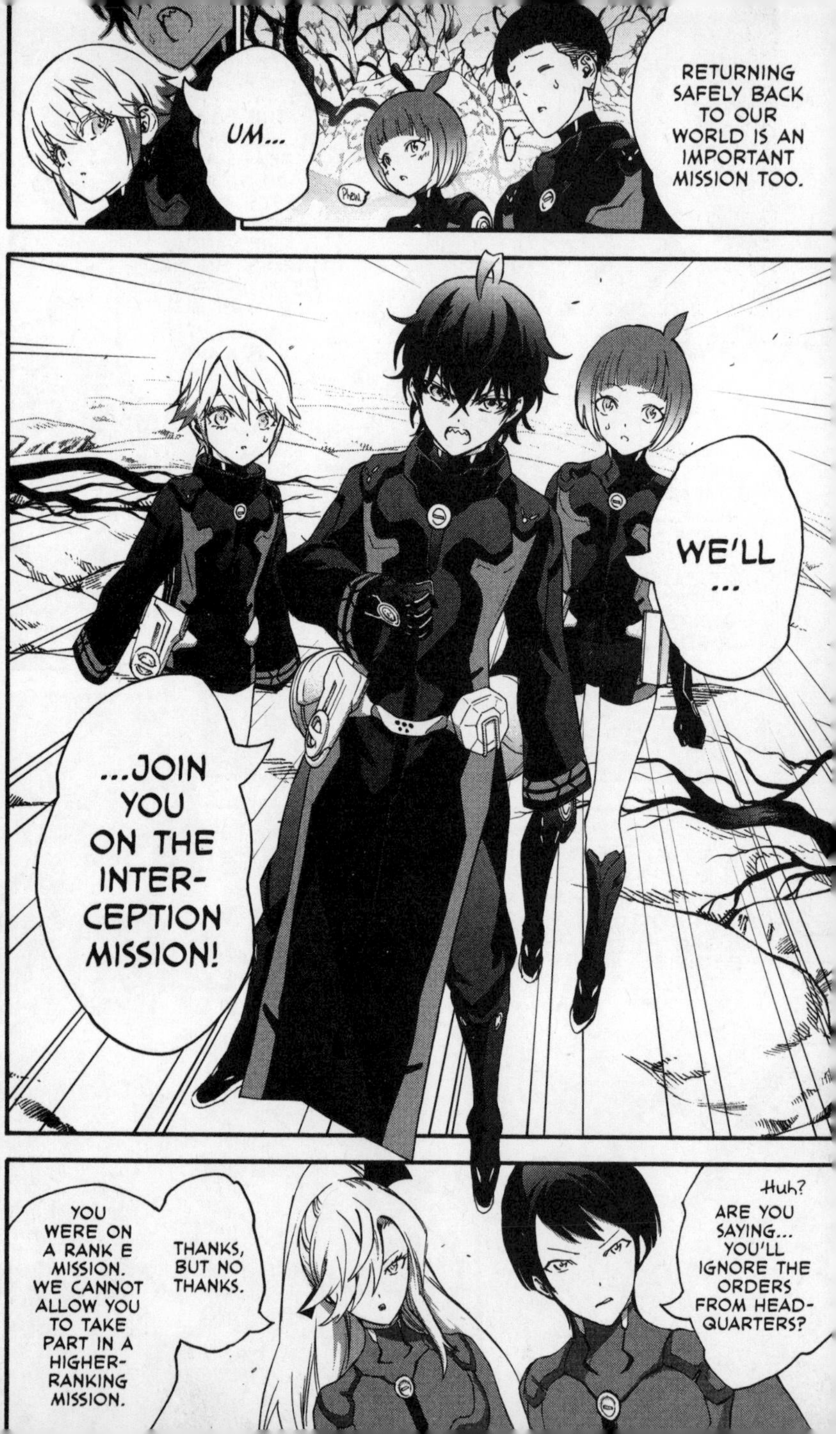
RETURNING SAFELY BACK TO OUR WORLD IS AN IMPORTANT MISSION TOO.
PHEW
UM...
WE'LL ...
...JOIN YOU ON THE INTER-CEPTION MISSION!
Huh?
ARE YOU SAYING... YOU'LL IGNORE THE ORDERS FROM HEAD-QUARTERS?
THANKS, BUT NO THANKS.
YOU WERE ON A RANK E MISSION. WE CANNOT ALLOW YOU TO TAKE PART IN A HIGHER-RANKING MISSION.

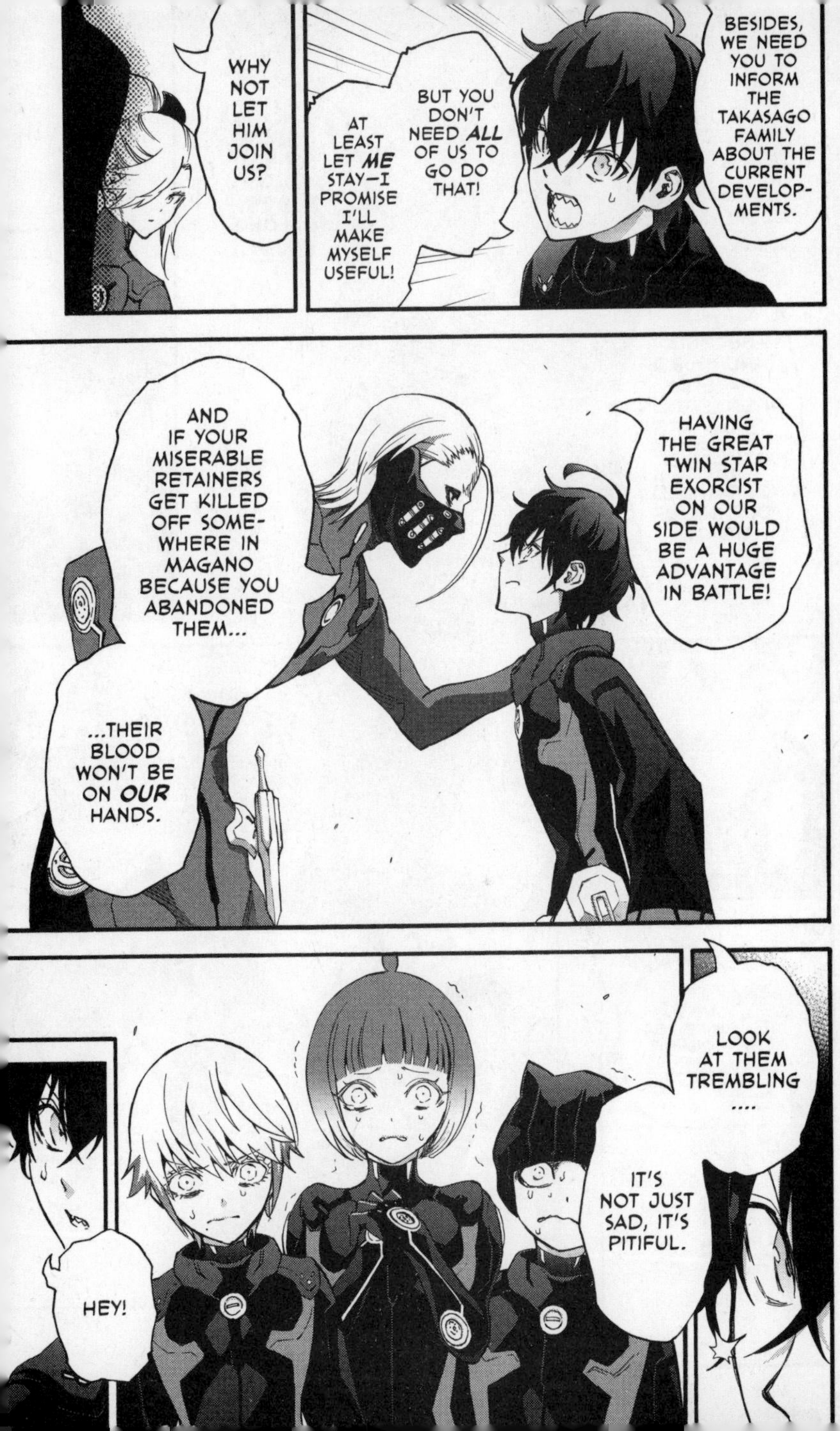
BESIDES, WE NEED YOU TO INFORM THE TAKASAGO FAMILY ABOUT THE CURRENT DEVELOPMENTS.
BUT YOU DON'T NEED *ALL* OF US TO GO DO THAT!
AT LEAST LET *ME* STAY—I PROMISE I'LL MAKE MYSELF USEFUL!
WHY NOT LET HIM JOIN US?
HAVING THE GREAT TWIN STAR EXORCIST ON OUR SIDE WOULD BE A HUGE ADVANTAGE IN BATTLE!
AND IF YOUR MISERABLE RETAINERS GET KILLED OFF SOME-WHERE IN MAGANO BECAUSE YOU ABANDONED THEM...
...THEIR BLOOD WON'T BE ON *OUR* HANDS.
LOOK AT THEM TREMBLING....
IT'S NOT JUST SAD, IT'S PITIFUL.
HEY!

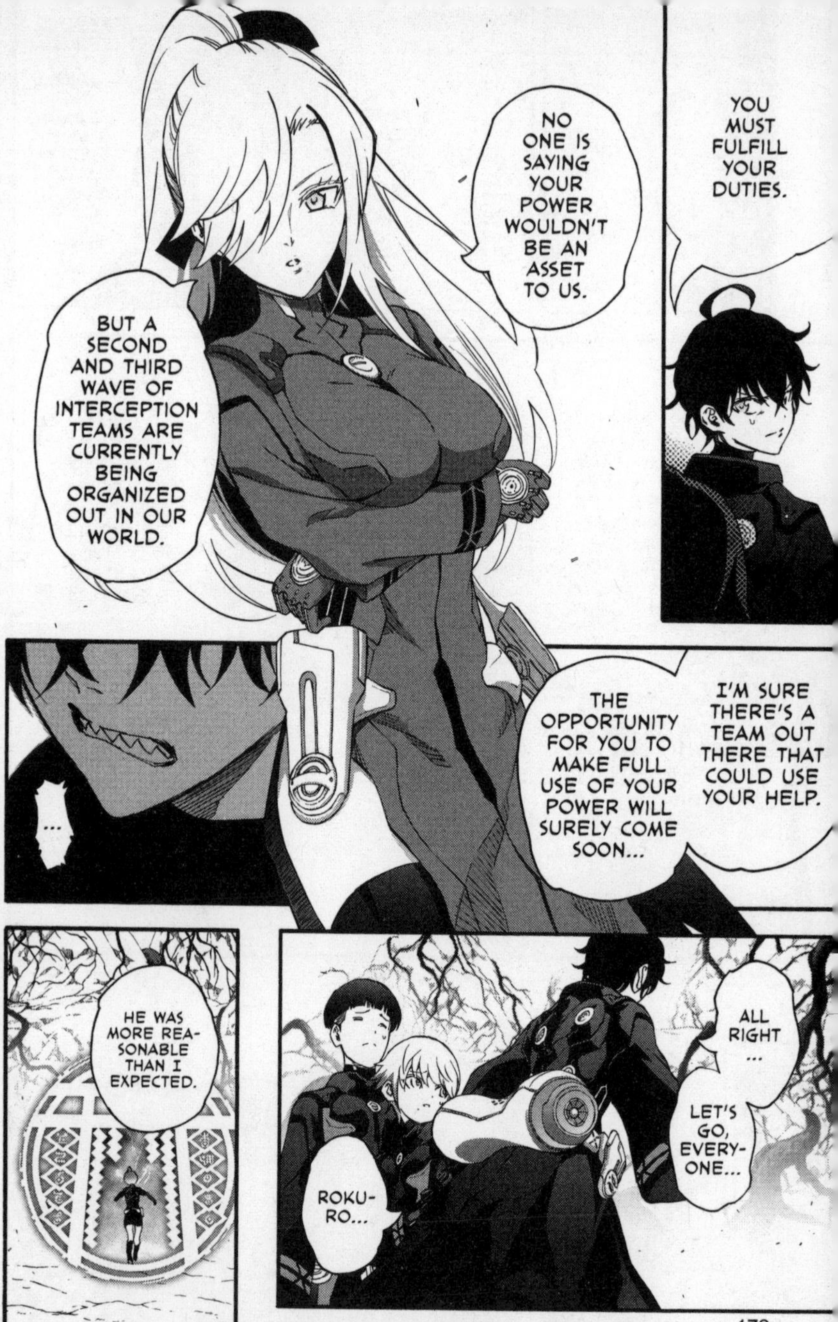
YOU MUST FULFILL YOUR DUTIES.
NO ONE IS SAYING YOUR POWER WOULDN'T BE AN ASSET TO US.
BUT A SECOND AND THIRD WAVE OF INTERCEPTION TEAMS ARE CURRENTLY BEING ORGANIZED OUT IN OUR WORLD.
I'M SURE THERE'S A TEAM OUT THERE THAT COULD USE YOUR HELP.
THE OPPORTUNITY FOR YOU TO MAKE FULL USE OF YOUR POWER WILL SURELY COME SOON...
...
ALL RIGHT...
LET'S GO, EVERY-ONE...
ROKU-RO...
HE WAS MORE REA-SONABLE THAN I EXPECTED.

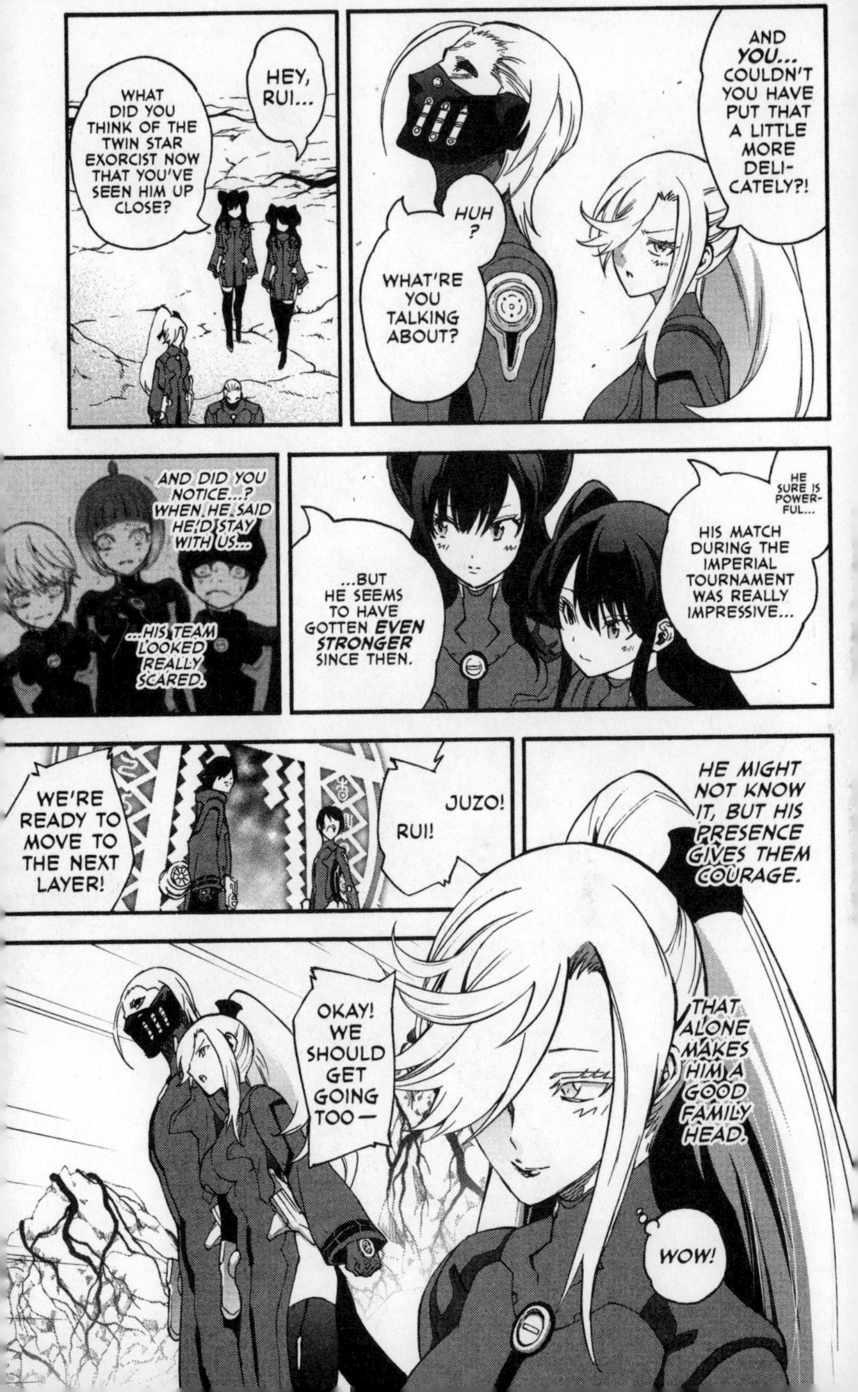
AND YOU... COULDN'T YOU HAVE PUT THAT A LITTLE MORE DELI-CATELY?!
HUH?
WHAT'RE YOU TALKING ABOUT?
HEY, RUI...
WHAT DID YOU THINK OF THE TWIN STAR EXORCIST NOW THAT YOU'VE SEEN HIM UP CLOSE?
HE SURE IS POWER-FUL...
HIS MATCH DURING THE IMPERIAL TOURNAMENT WAS REALLY IMPRESSIVE...
...BUT HE SEEMS TO HAVE GOTTEN EVEN STRONGER SINCE THEN.
AND DID YOU NOTICE...? WHEN HE SAID HE'D STAY WITH US...
...HIS TEAM LOOKED REALLY SCARED.
HE MIGHT NOT KNOW IT, BUT HIS PRESENCE GIVES THEM COURAGE.
JUZO!
RUI!
WE'RE READY TO MOVE TO THE NEXT LAYER!
THAT ALONE MAKES HIM A GOOD FAMILY HEAD.
OKAY! WE SHOULD GET GOING TOO—
WOW!

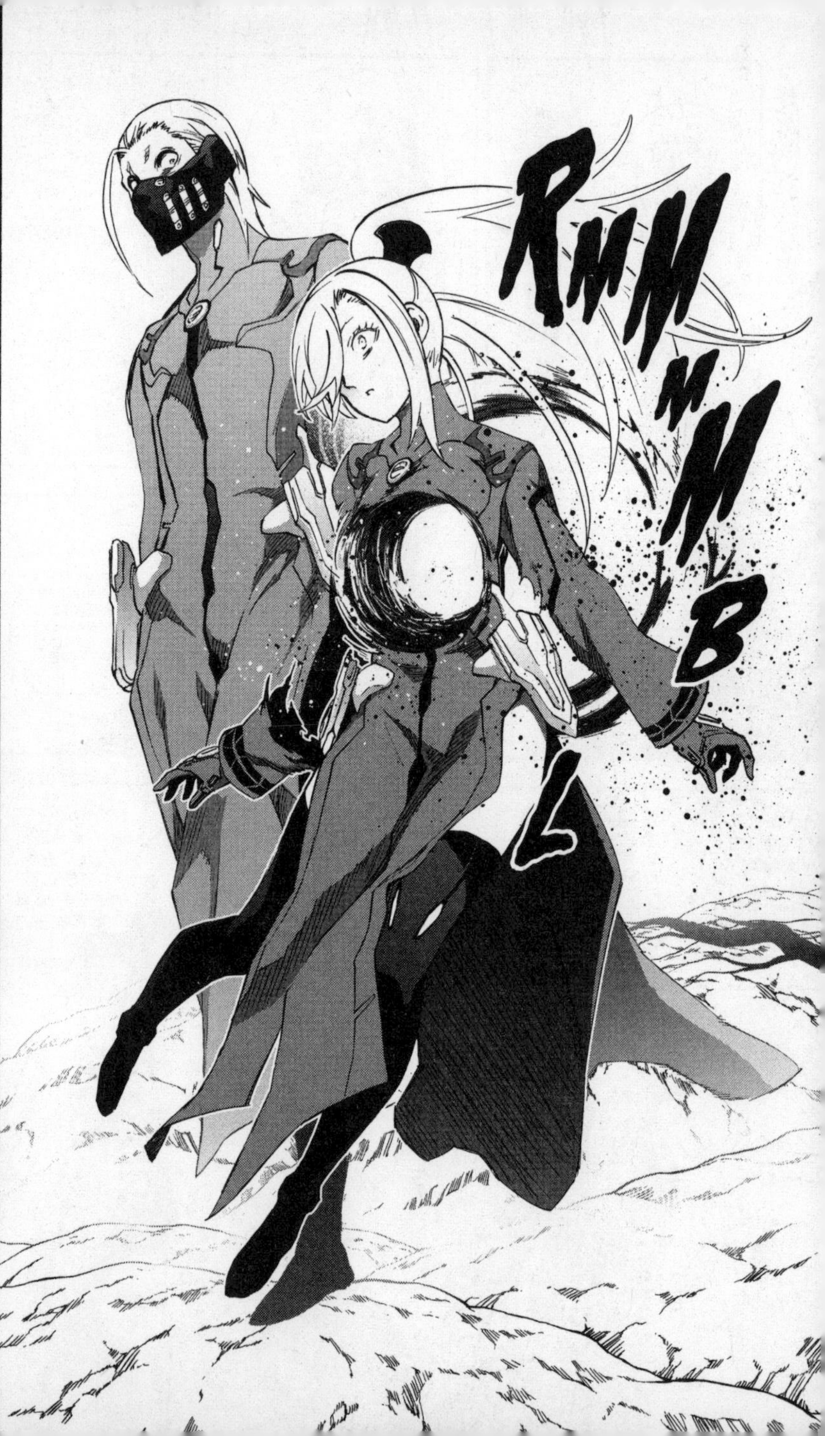
RMMMMBL

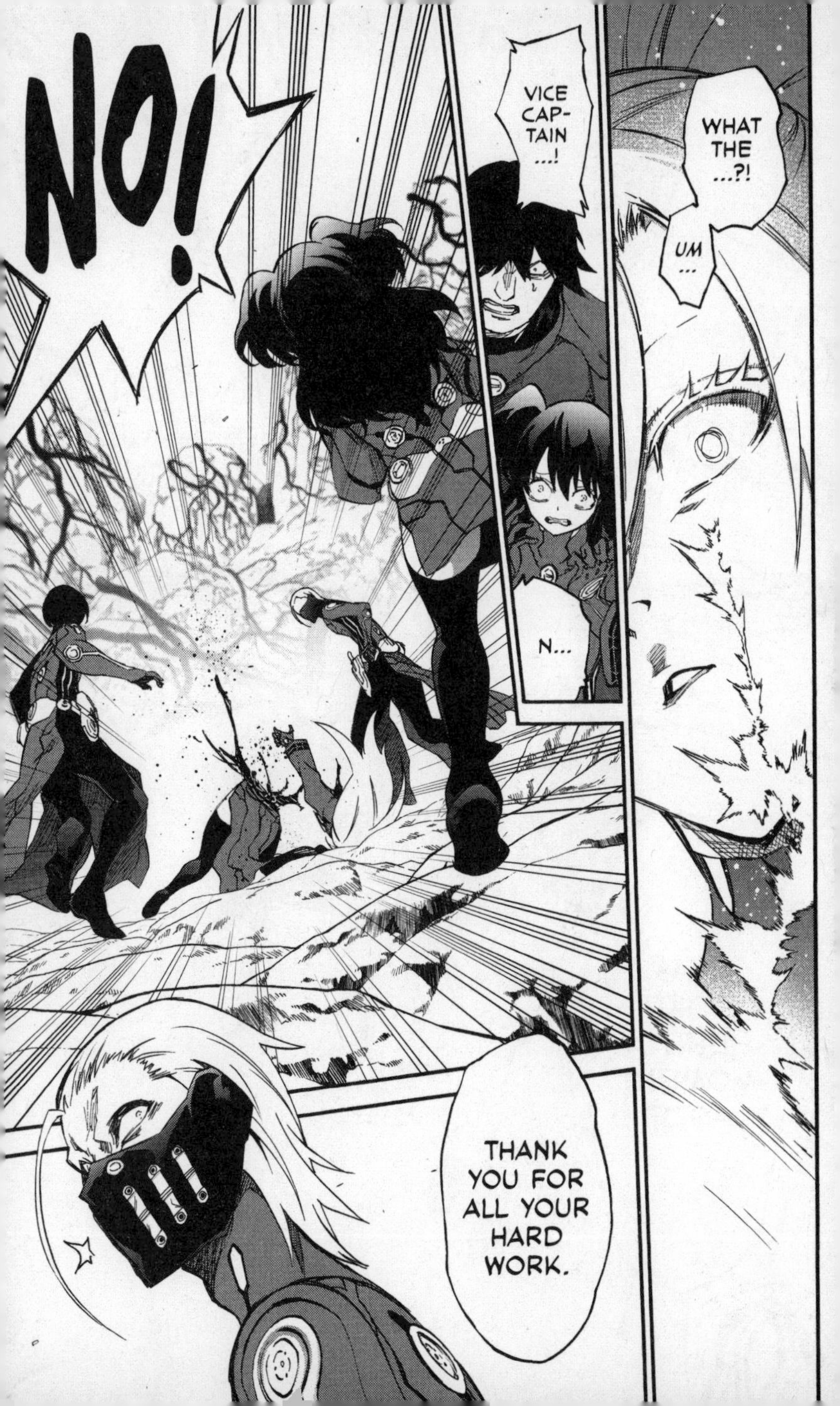
WHAT THE ...?!
UM ...
VICE CAP-TAIN ...!
N...
NO!
THANK YOU FOR ALL YOUR HARD WORK.

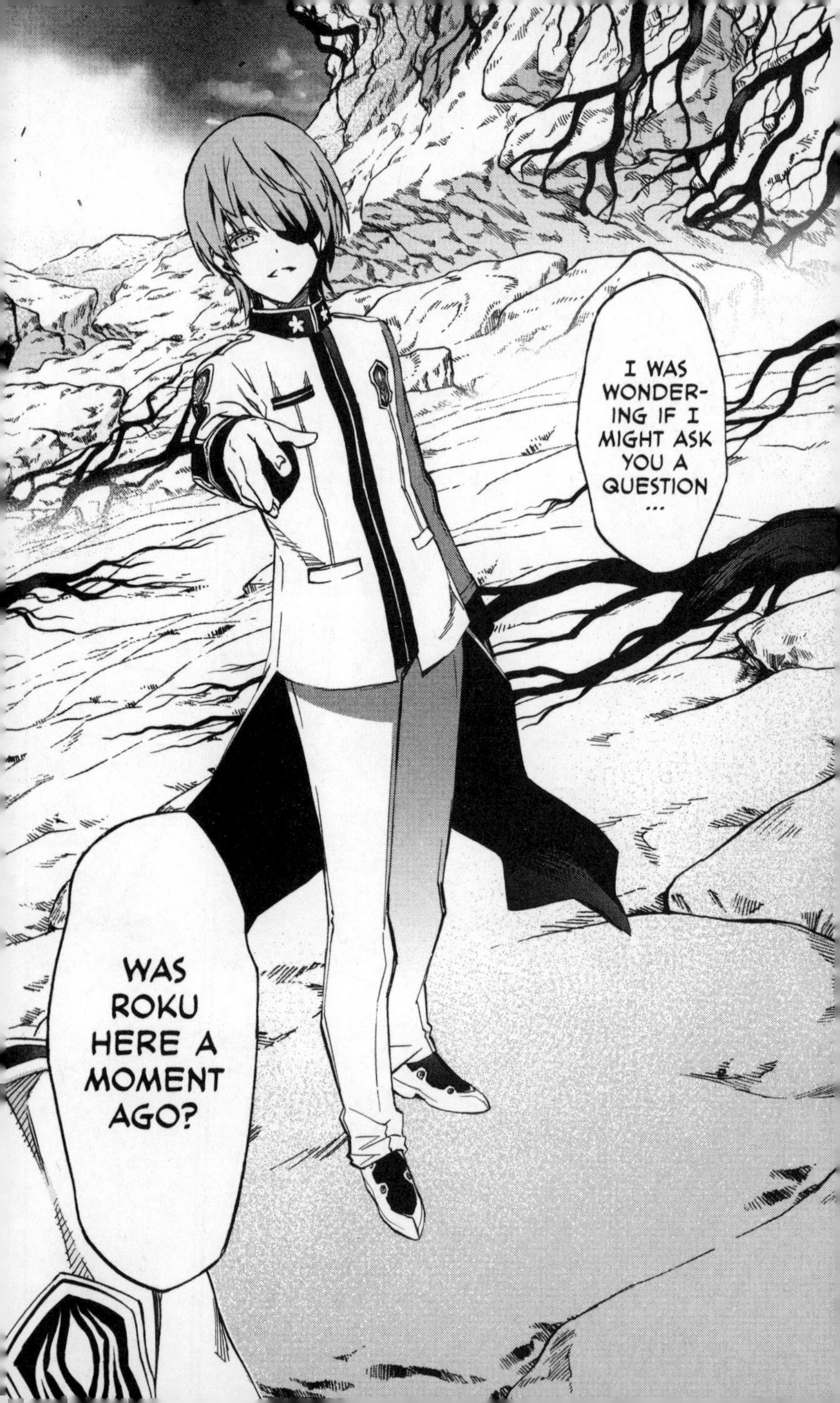
I WAS WONDERING IF I MIGHT ASK YOU A QUESTION ...
WAS ROKU HERE A MOMENT AGO?

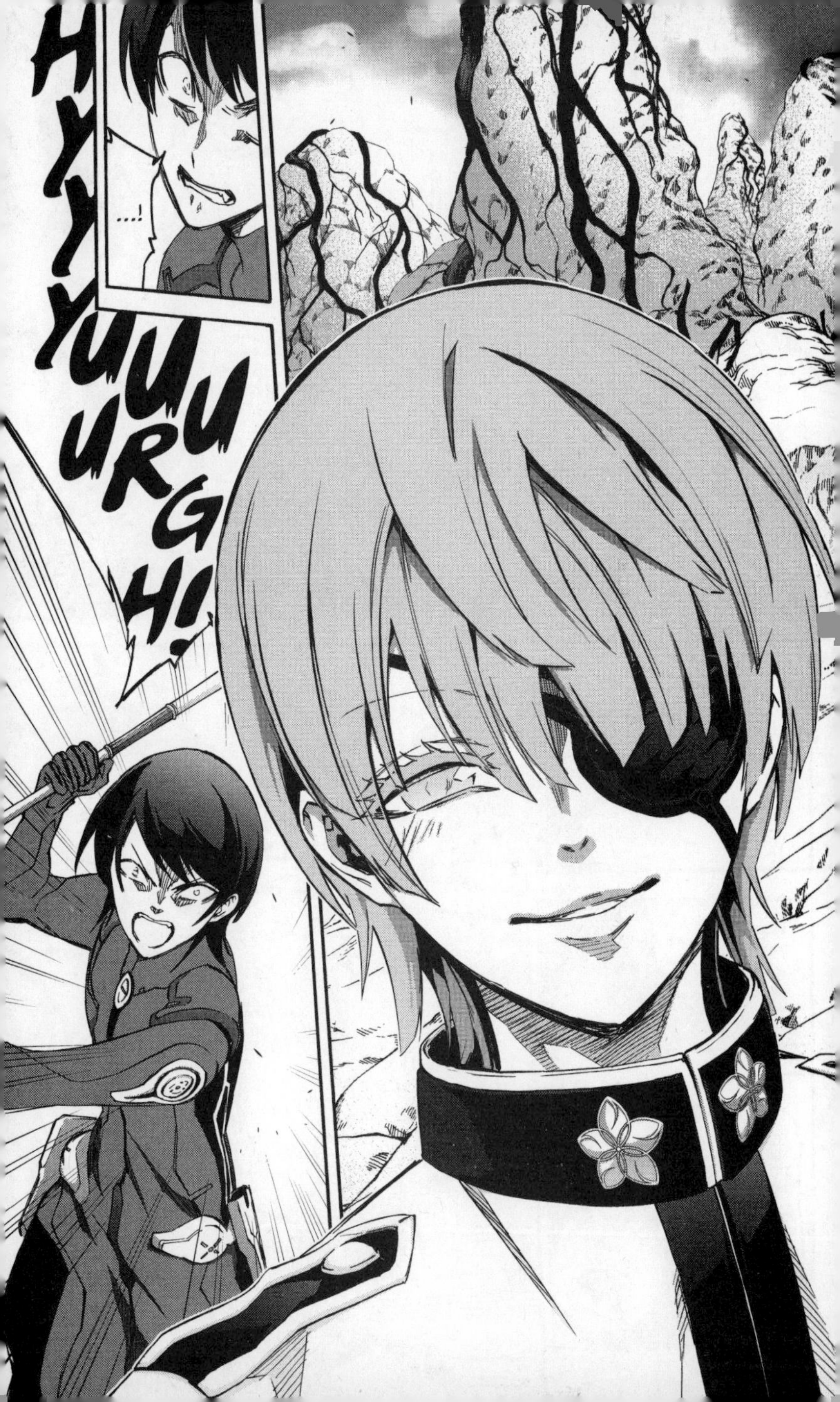
...!
HYYYYUUUURGH!

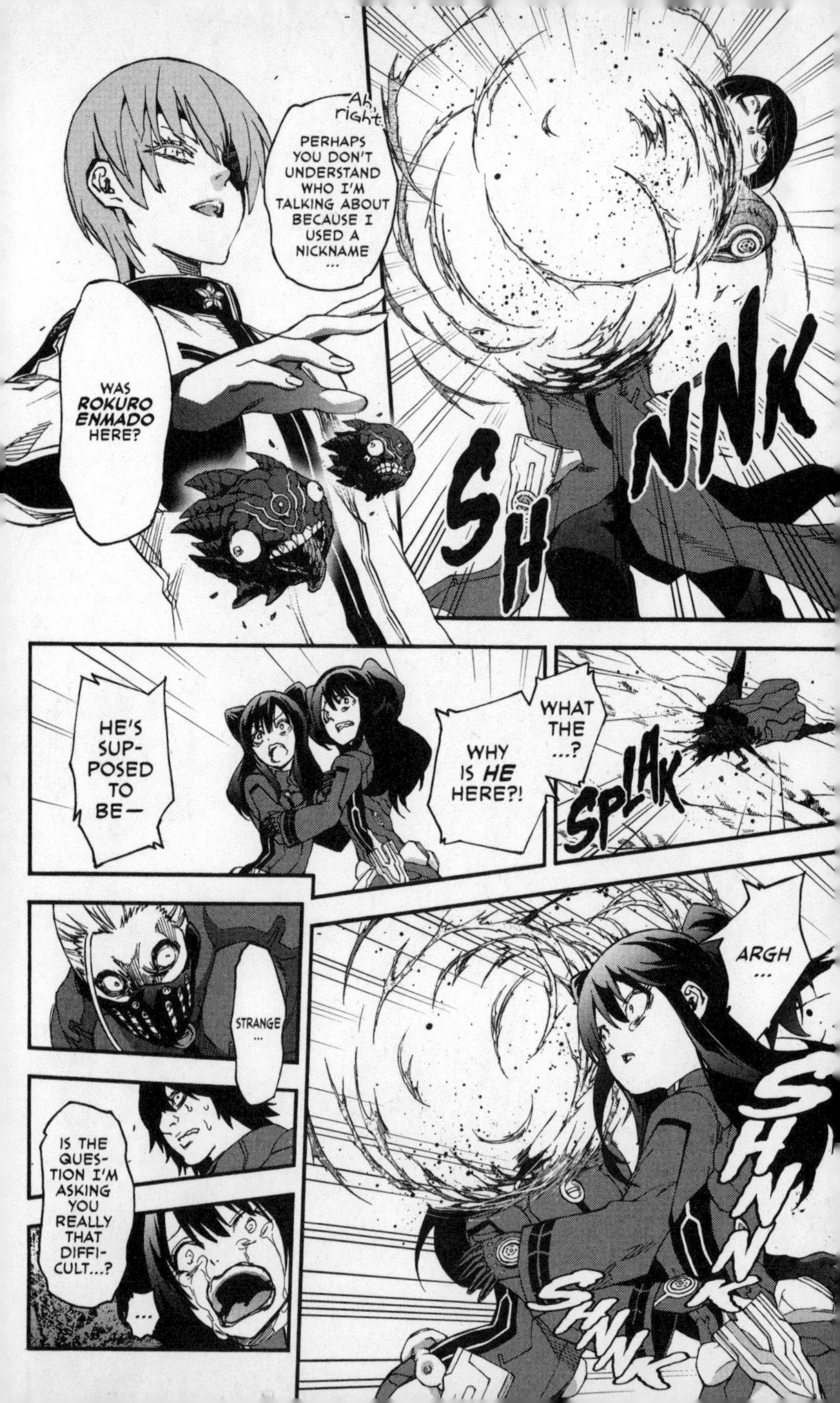
SHNNK
Ah, right.
PERHAPS YOU DON'T UNDERSTAND WHO I'M TALKING ABOUT BECAUSE I USED A NICKNAME ...
WAS *ROKURO ENMADO* HERE?
WHAT THE ...?
SPLAK
WHY IS *HE* HERE?!
HE'S SUP-POSED TO BE—
ARGH ...
SHNNK
SHNNK
STRANGE ...
IS THE QUES-TION I'M ASKING YOU REALLY THAT DIFFI-CULT...?
...

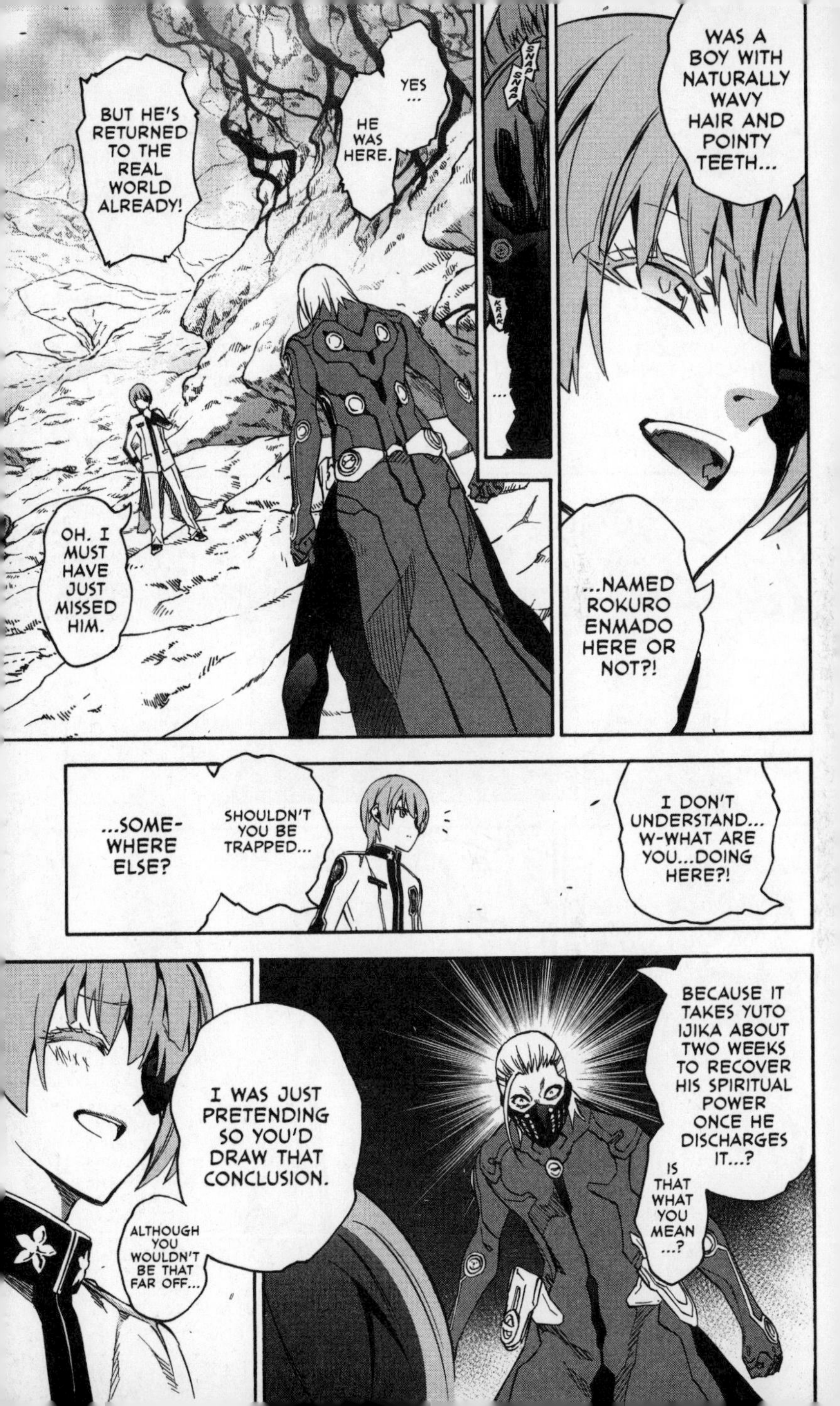
WAS A BOY WITH NATURALLY WAVY HAIR AND POINTY TEETH...
...NAMED ROKURO ENMADO HERE OR NOT?!
SNAP SNAP
KRAK
...
YES ... HE WAS HERE.
BUT HE'S RETURNED TO THE REAL WORLD ALREADY!
OH. I MUST HAVE JUST MISSED HIM.
I DON'T UNDERSTAND... W-WHAT ARE YOU...DOING HERE?!
SHOULDN'T YOU BE TRAPPED...
...SOME-WHERE ELSE?
BECAUSE IT TAKES YUTO IJIKA ABOUT TWO WEEKS TO RECOVER HIS SPIRITUAL POWER ONCE HE DISCHARGES IT...?
IS THAT WHAT YOU MEAN ...?
I WAS JUST PRETENDING SO YOU'D DRAW THAT CONCLUSION.
ALTHOUGH YOU WOULDN'T BE THAT FAR OFF...

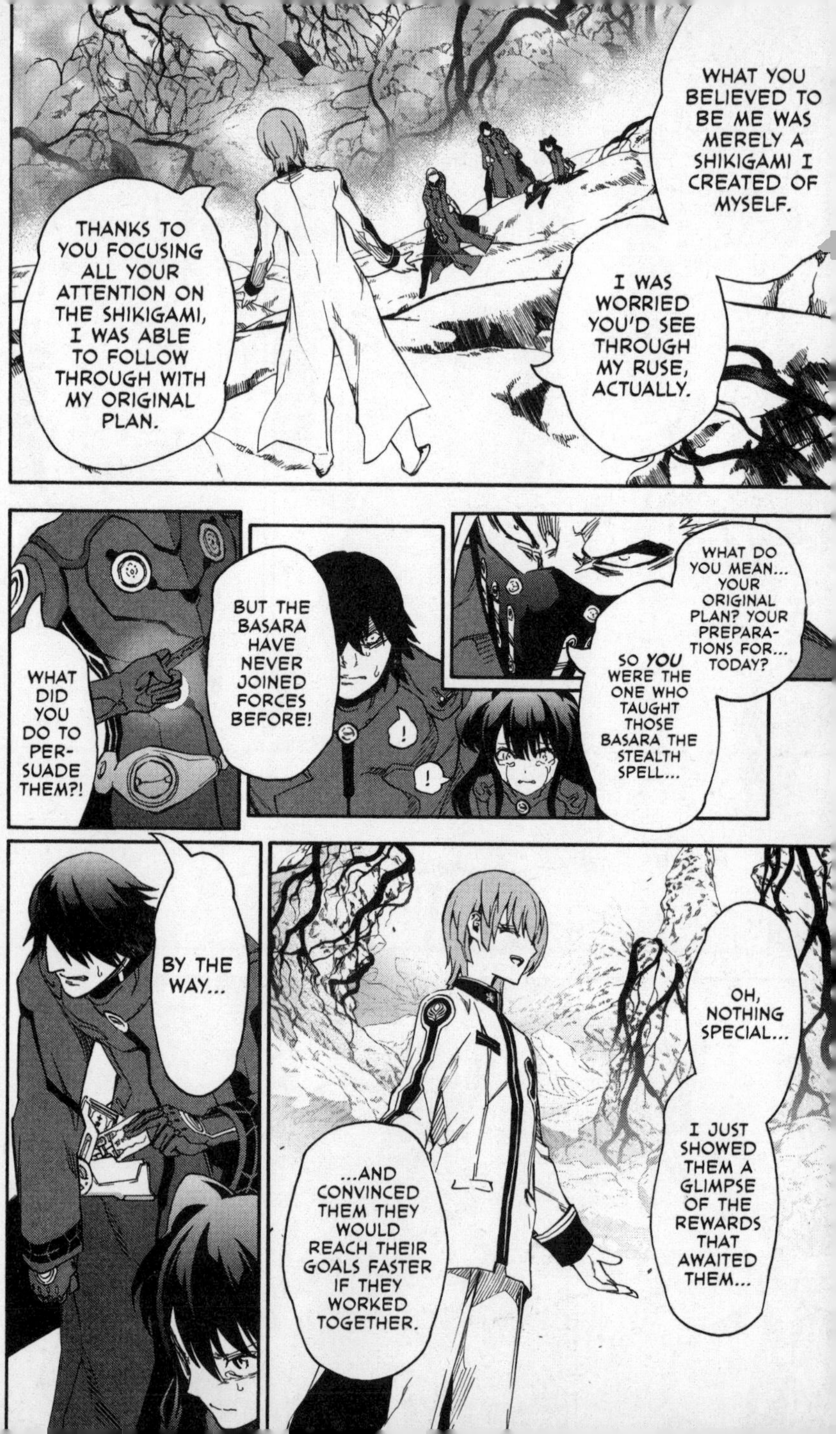

WHAT YOU BELIEVED TO BE ME WAS MERELY A SHIKIGAMI I CREATED OF MYSELF.
I WAS WORRIED YOU'D SEE THROUGH MY RUSE, ACTUALLY.
THANKS TO YOU FOCUSING ALL YOUR ATTENTION ON THE SHIKIGAMI, I WAS ABLE TO FOLLOW THROUGH WITH MY ORIGINAL PLAN.
WHAT DO YOU MEAN... YOUR ORIGINAL PLAN? YOUR PREPARATIONS FOR... TODAY?
SO *YOU* WERE THE ONE WHO TAUGHT THOSE BASARA THE STEALTH SPELL...
BUT THE BASARA HAVE NEVER JOINED FORCES BEFORE!
!
!
WHAT DID YOU DO TO PERSUADE THEM?!
OH, NOTHING SPECIAL...
I JUST SHOWED THEM A GLIMPSE OF THE REWARDS THAT AWAITED THEM...
...AND CONVINCED THEM THEY WOULD REACH THEIR GOALS FASTER IF THEY WORKED TOGETHER.
BY THE WAY...

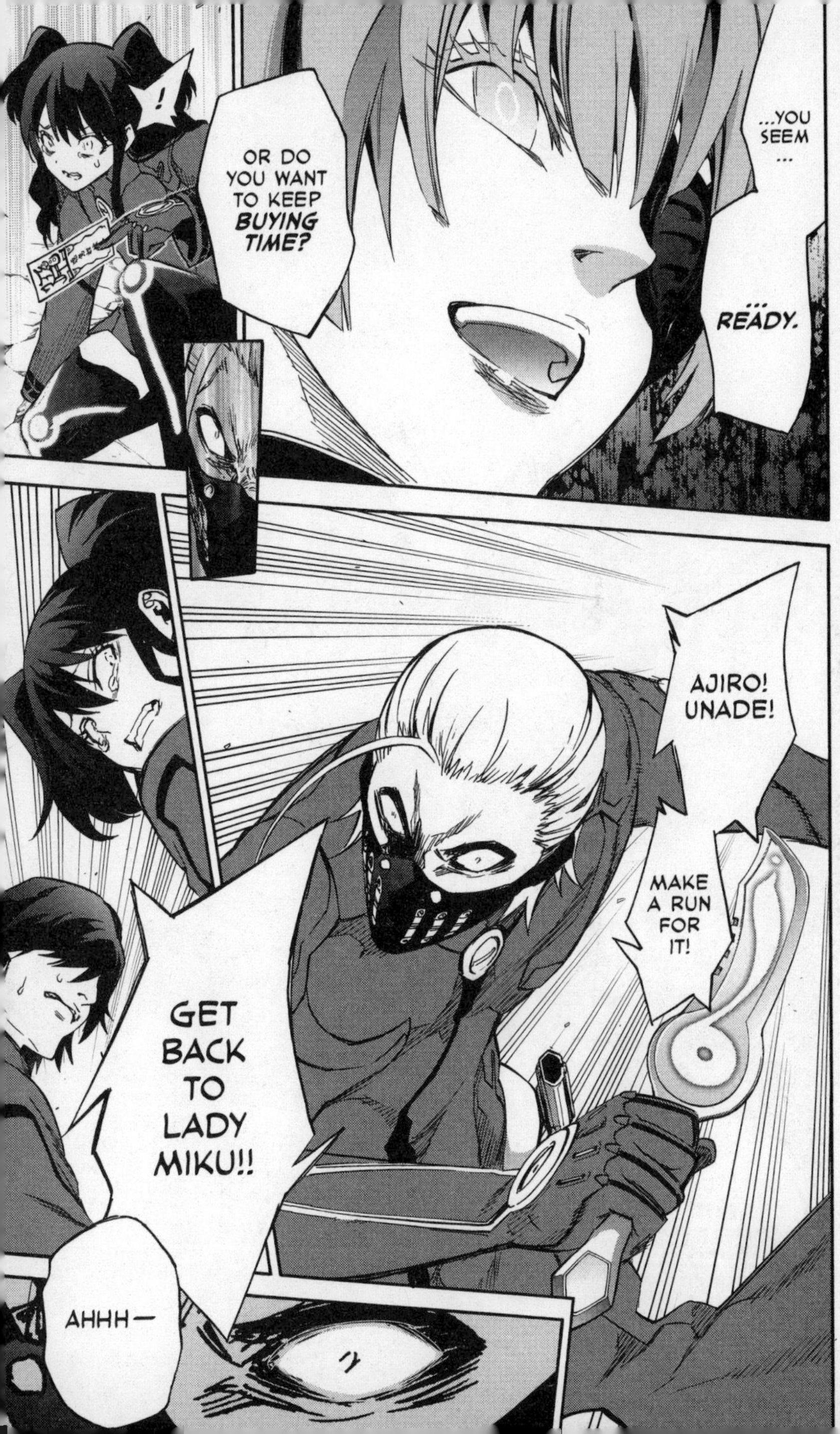
...YOU SEEM ...
... READY.
OR DO YOU WANT TO KEEP BUYING TIME?
!
AJIRO! UNADE!
MAKE A RUN FOR IT!
GET BACK TO LADY MIKU!!
AHHH—

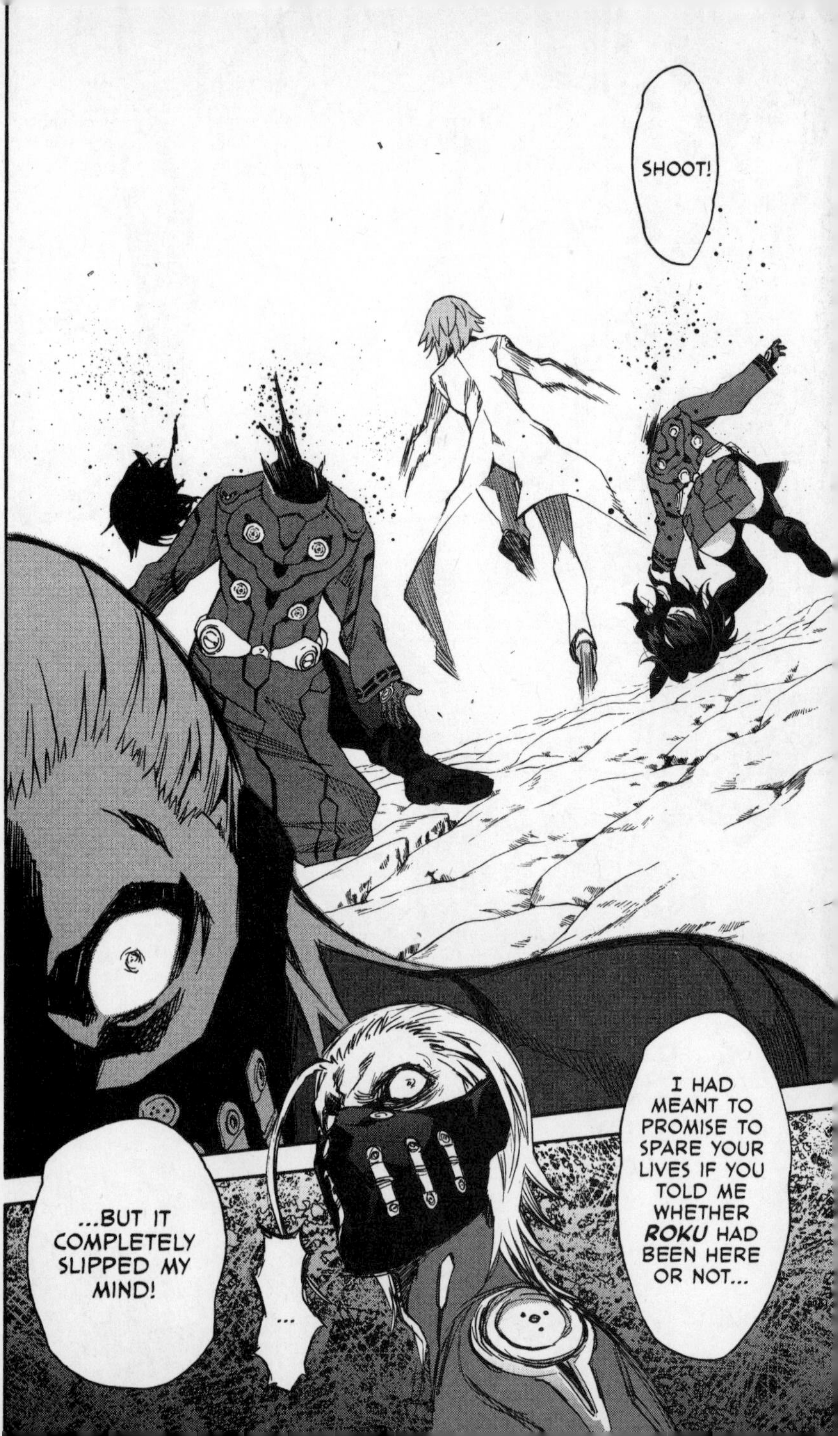
SHOOT!
I HAD MEANT TO PROMISE TO SPARE YOUR LIVES IF YOU TOLD ME WHETHER *ROKU* HAD BEEN HERE OR NOT...
...
...BUT IT COMPLETELY SLIPPED MY MIND!

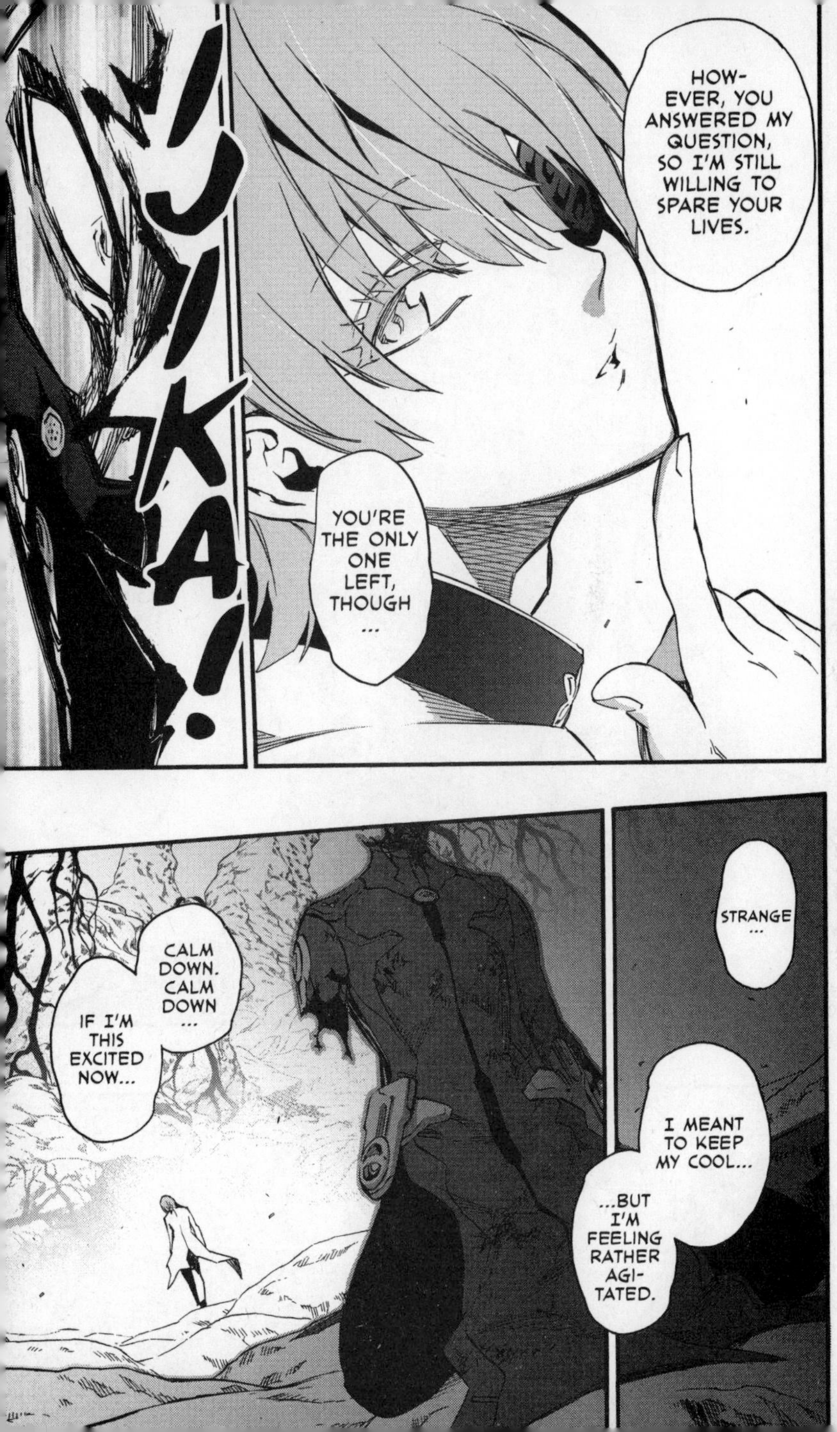
HOW-EVER, YOU ANSWERED MY QUESTION, SO I'M STILL WILLING TO SPARE YOUR LIVES.
YOU'RE THE ONLY ONE LEFT, THOUGH...
JIKA!
STRANGE...
I MEANT TO KEEP MY COOL...
...BUT I'M FEELING RATHER AGI-TATED.
CALM DOWN. CALM DOWN...
IF I'M THIS EXCITED NOW...

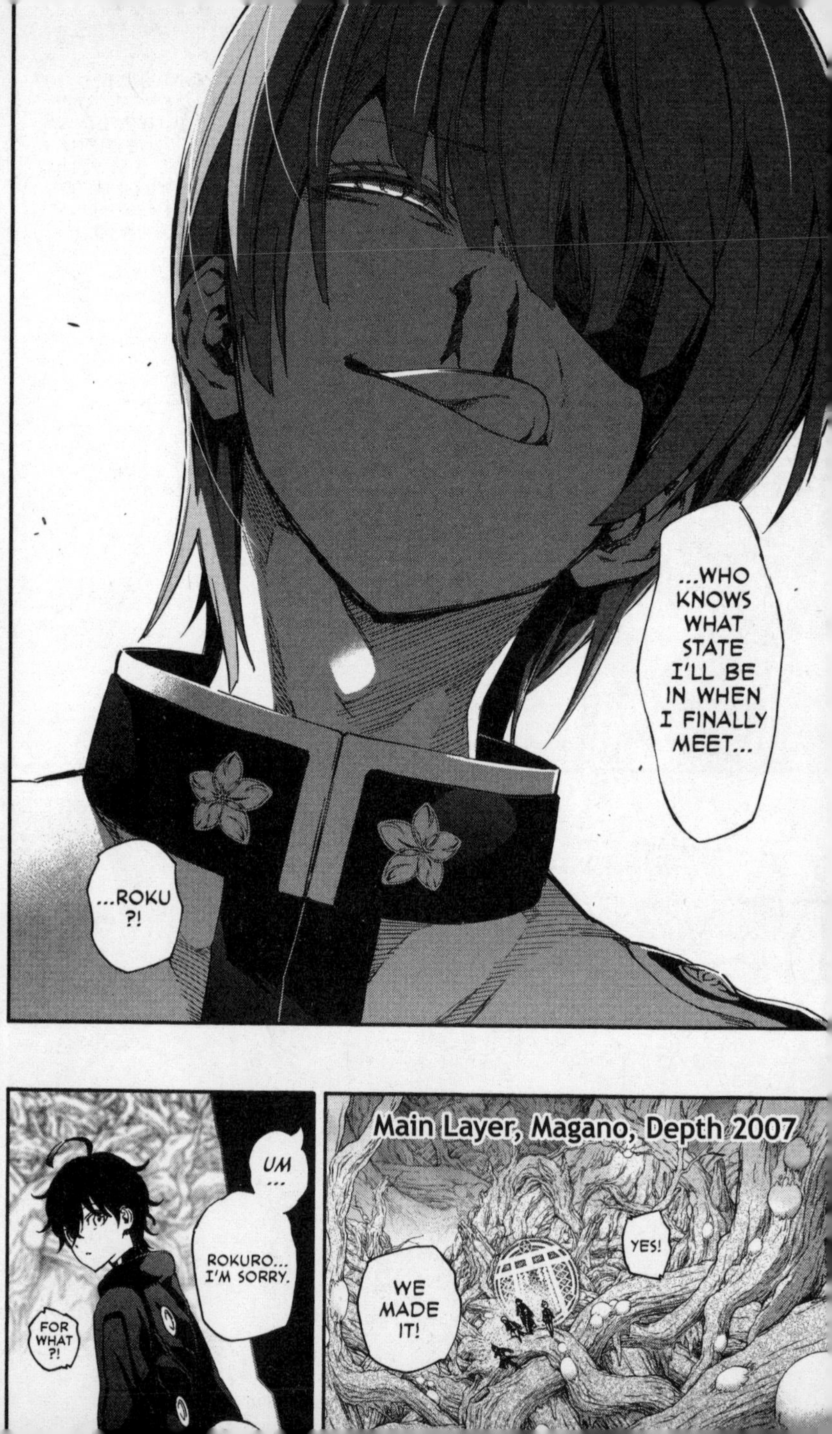
...WHO KNOWS WHAT STATE I'LL BE IN WHEN I FINALLY MEET...
...ROKU ?!
Main Layer, Magano, Depth 2007
YES!
WE MADE IT!
UM ...
ROKURO... I'M SORRY.
FOR WHAT ?!

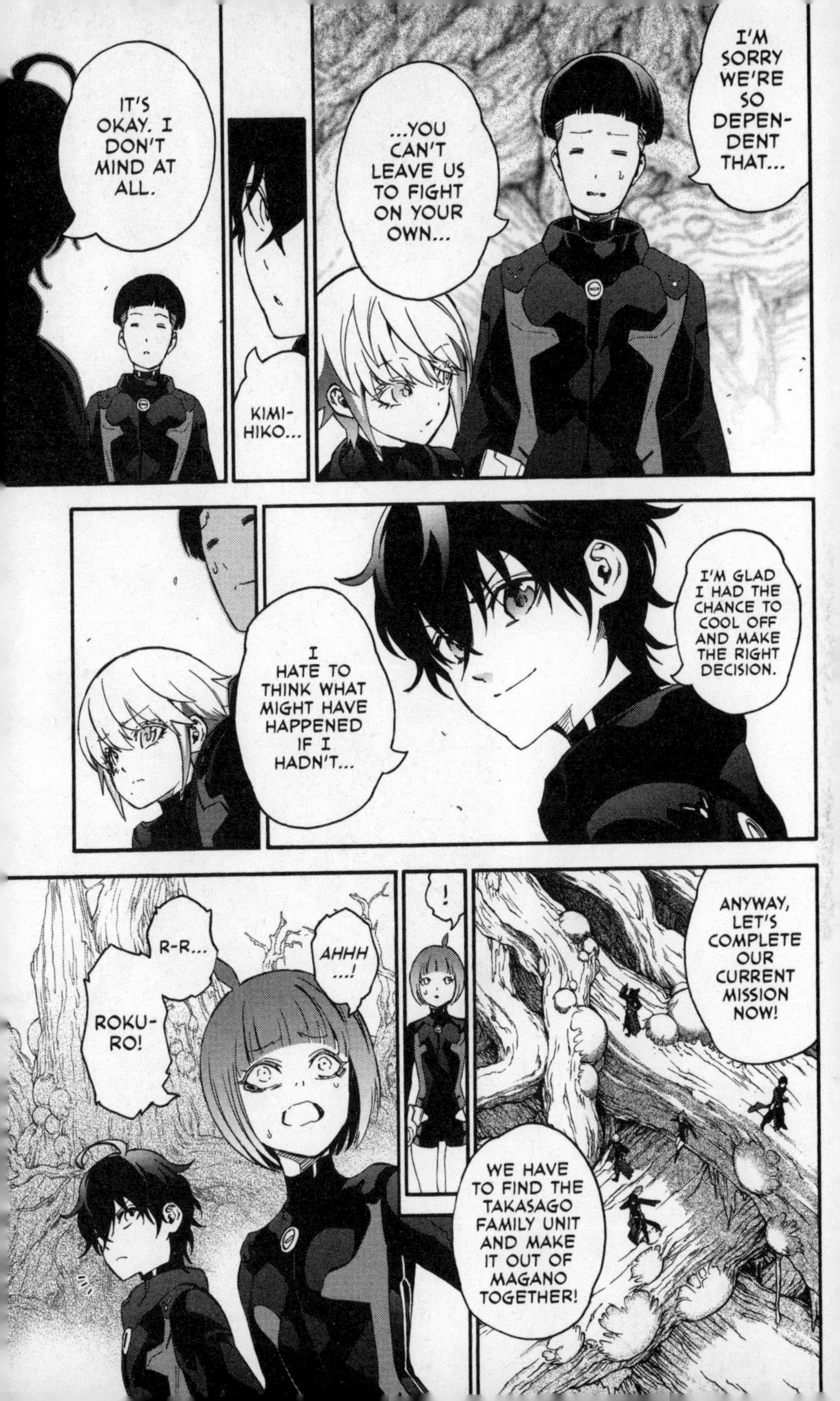
I'M SORRY WE'RE SO DEPENDENT THAT...
...YOU CAN'T LEAVE US TO FIGHT ON YOUR OWN...
KIMIHIKO...
IT'S OKAY. I DON'T MIND AT ALL.
I'M GLAD I HAD THE CHANCE TO COOL OFF AND MAKE THE RIGHT DECISION.
I HATE TO THINK WHAT MIGHT HAVE HAPPENED IF I HADN'T...
ANYWAY, LET'S COMPLETE OUR CURRENT MISSION NOW!
WE HAVE TO FIND THE TAKASAGO FAMILY UNIT AND MAKE IT OUT OF MAGANO TOGETHER!
!
AHHH ...!
R-R...
ROKURO!

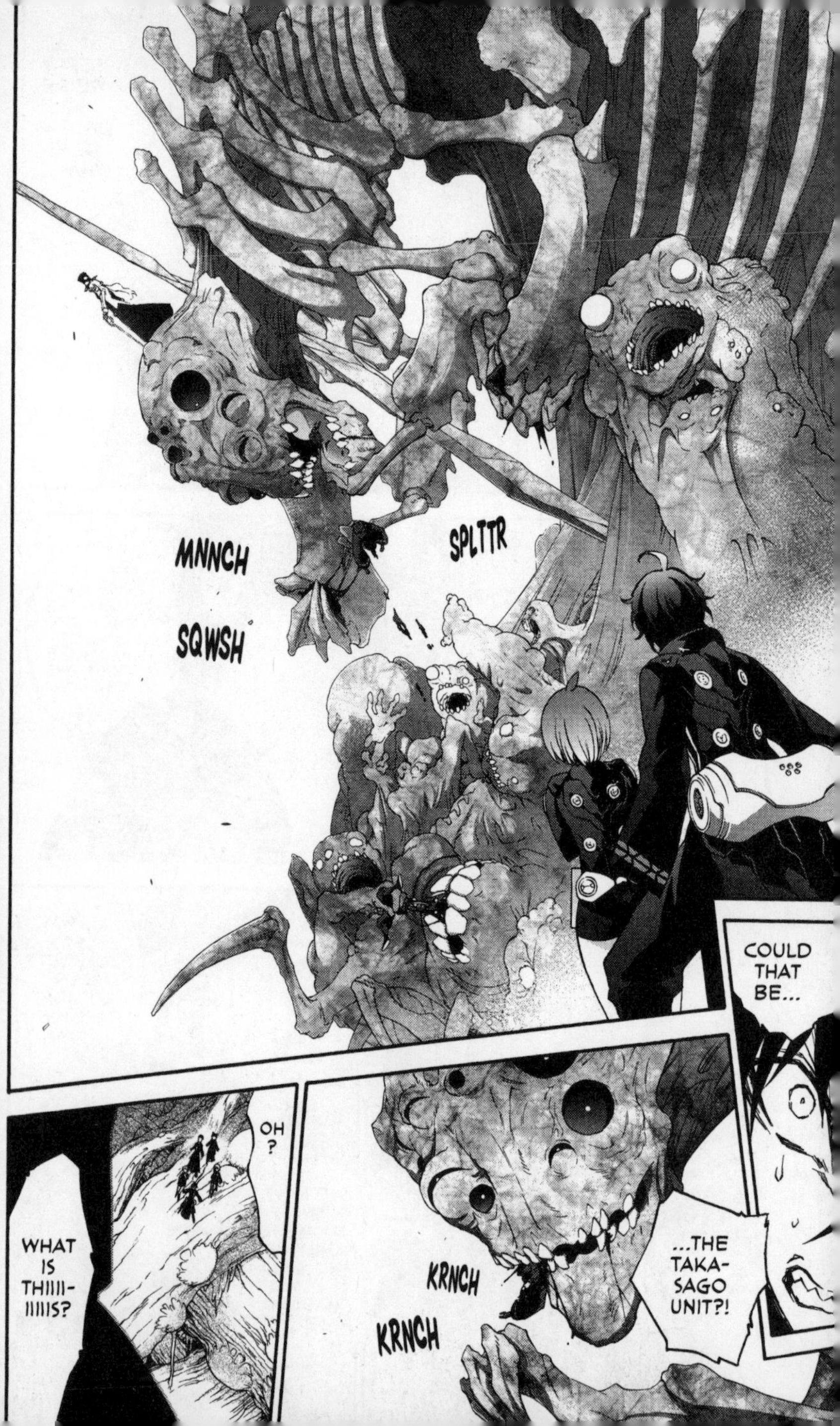
SPLTTR
MNNCH
SQWSH
COULD THAT BE...
...THE TAKA-SAGO UNIT?!
KRNCH
KRNCH
OH?
WHAT IS THIIIII-IIIIIS?

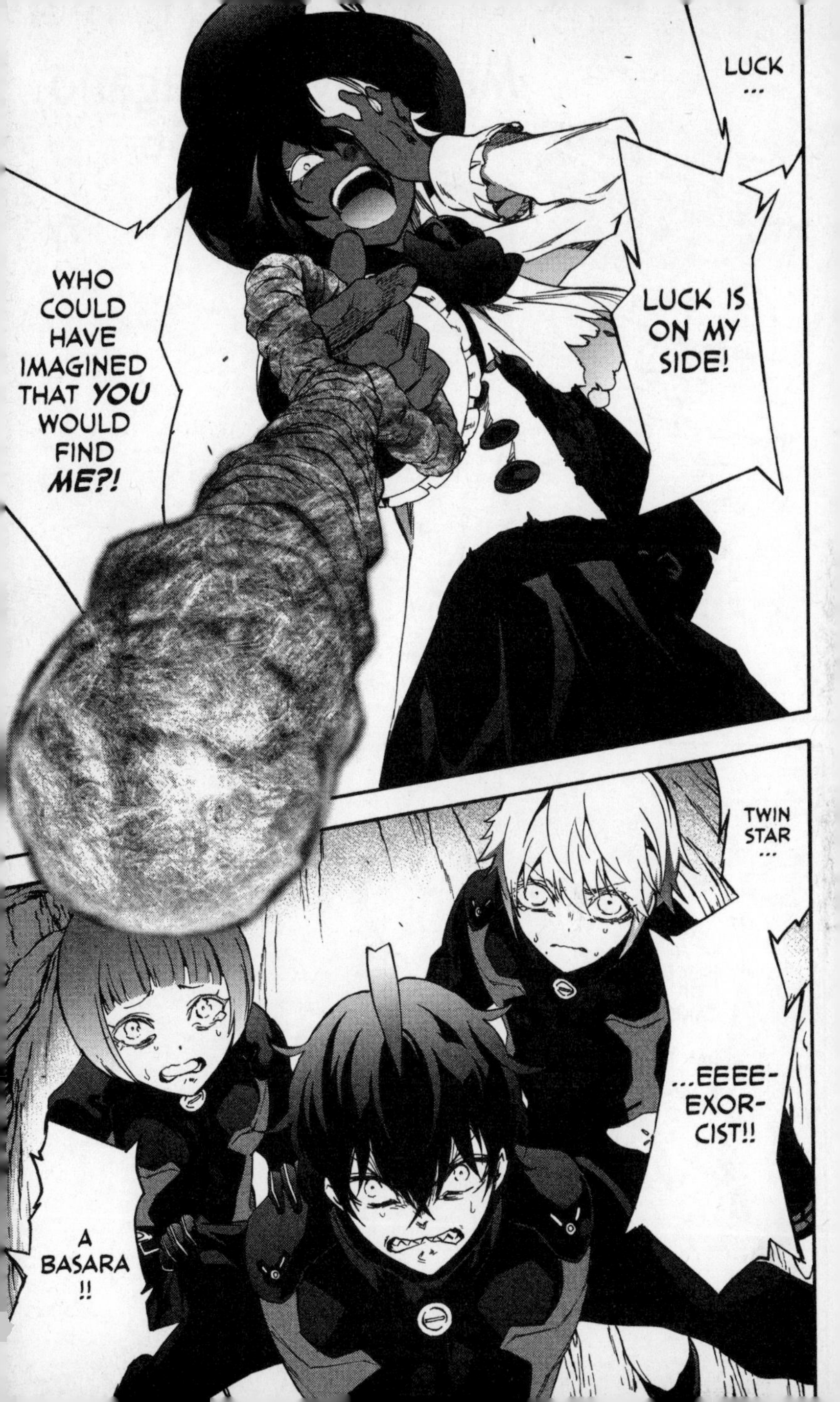
LUCK ...
LUCK IS ON MY SIDE!
WHO COULD HAVE IMAGINED THAT *YOU* WOULD FIND *ME?!*
TWIN STAR ...
...EEEE-EXOR-CIST!!
A BASARA !!

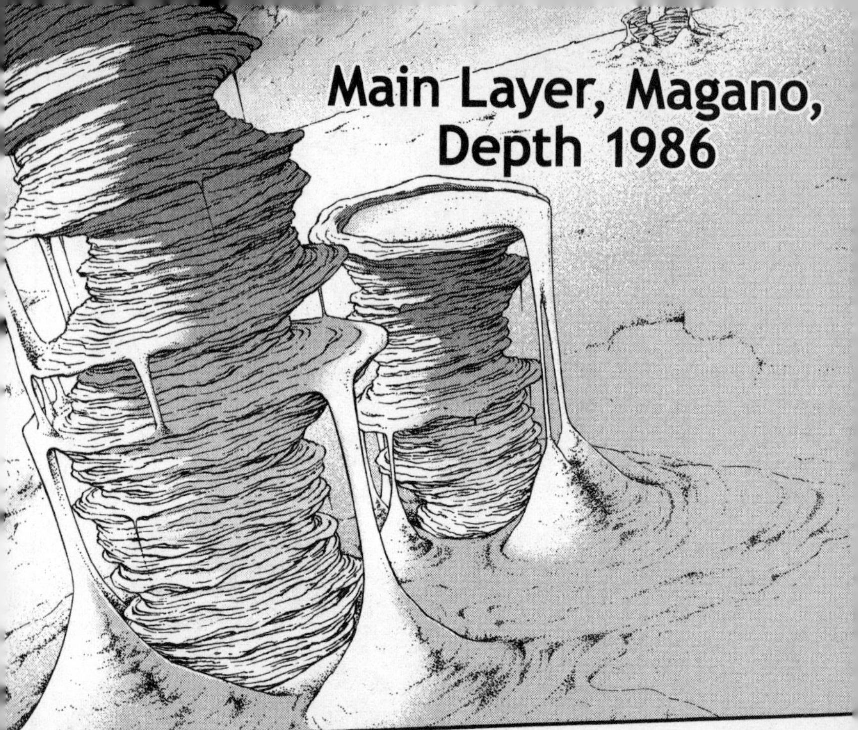
Main Layer, Magano, Depth 1986

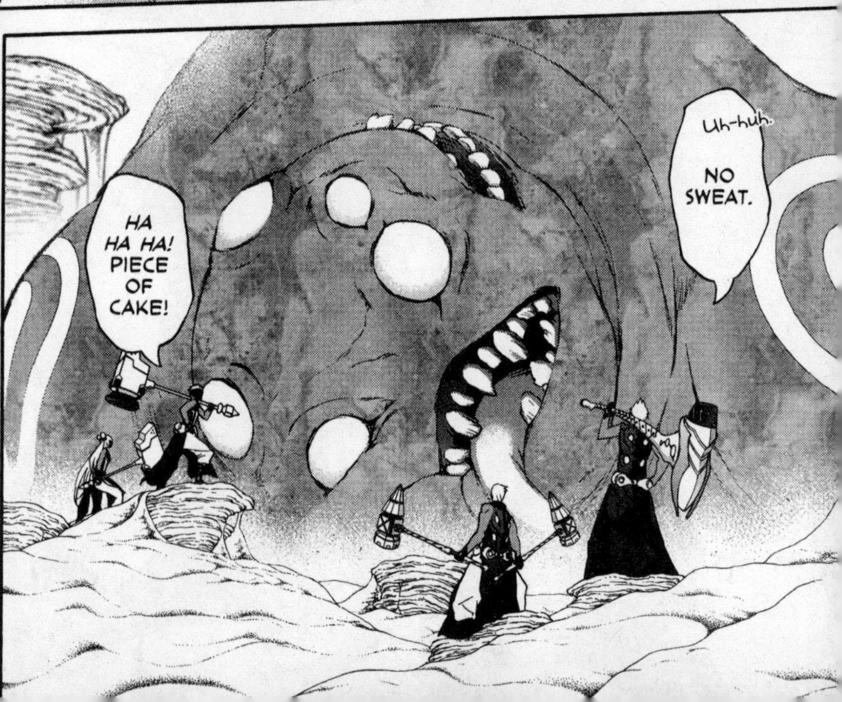
Uh-huh.
NO SWEAT.
HA HA HA! PIECE OF CAKE!

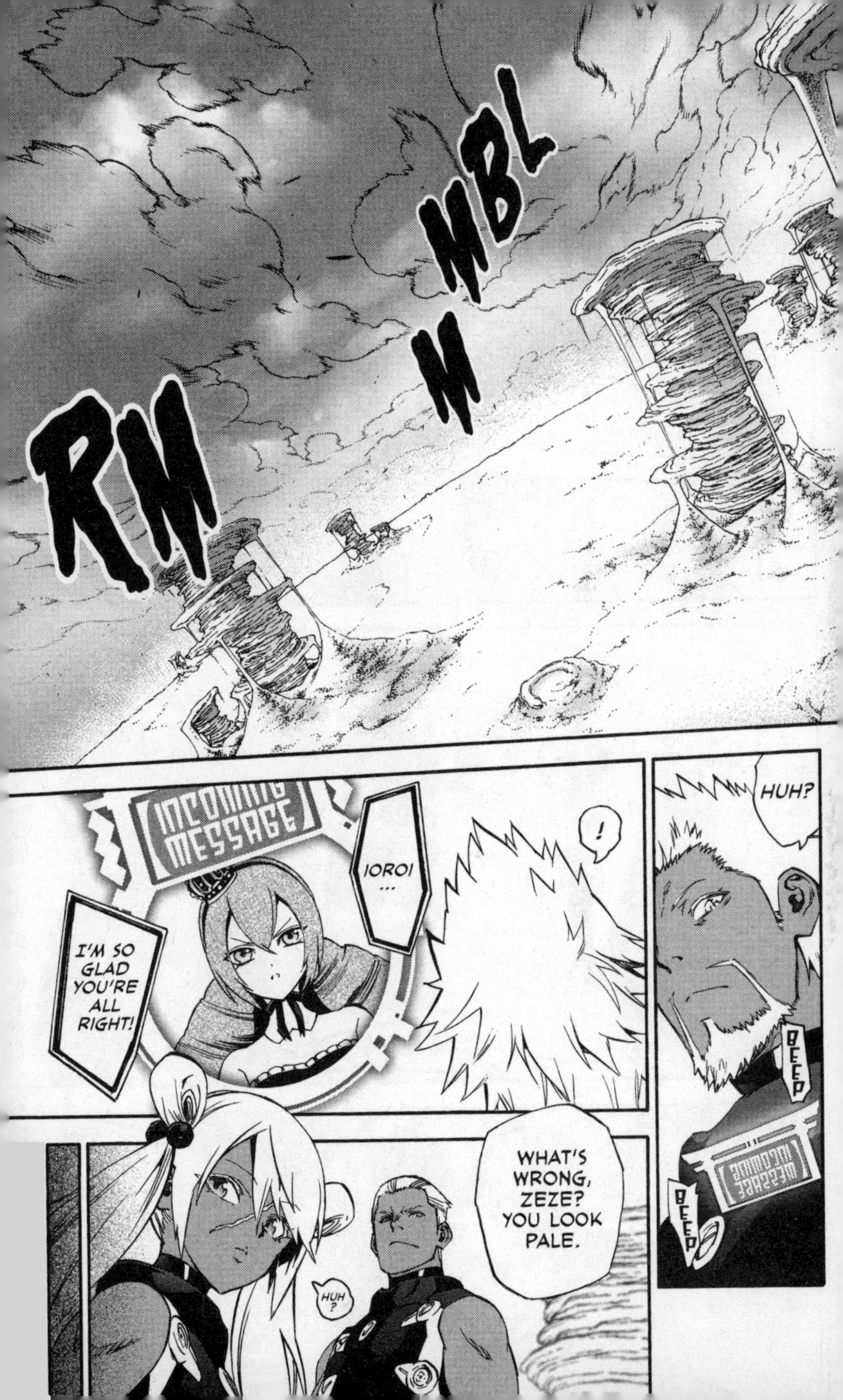
RM
M
MBL
HUH?
BEEP
BEEP
!
IOROI ...
INCOMING MESSAGE
I'M SO GLAD YOU'RE ALL RIGHT!
WHAT'S WRONG, ZEZE? YOU LOOK PALE.
HUH?

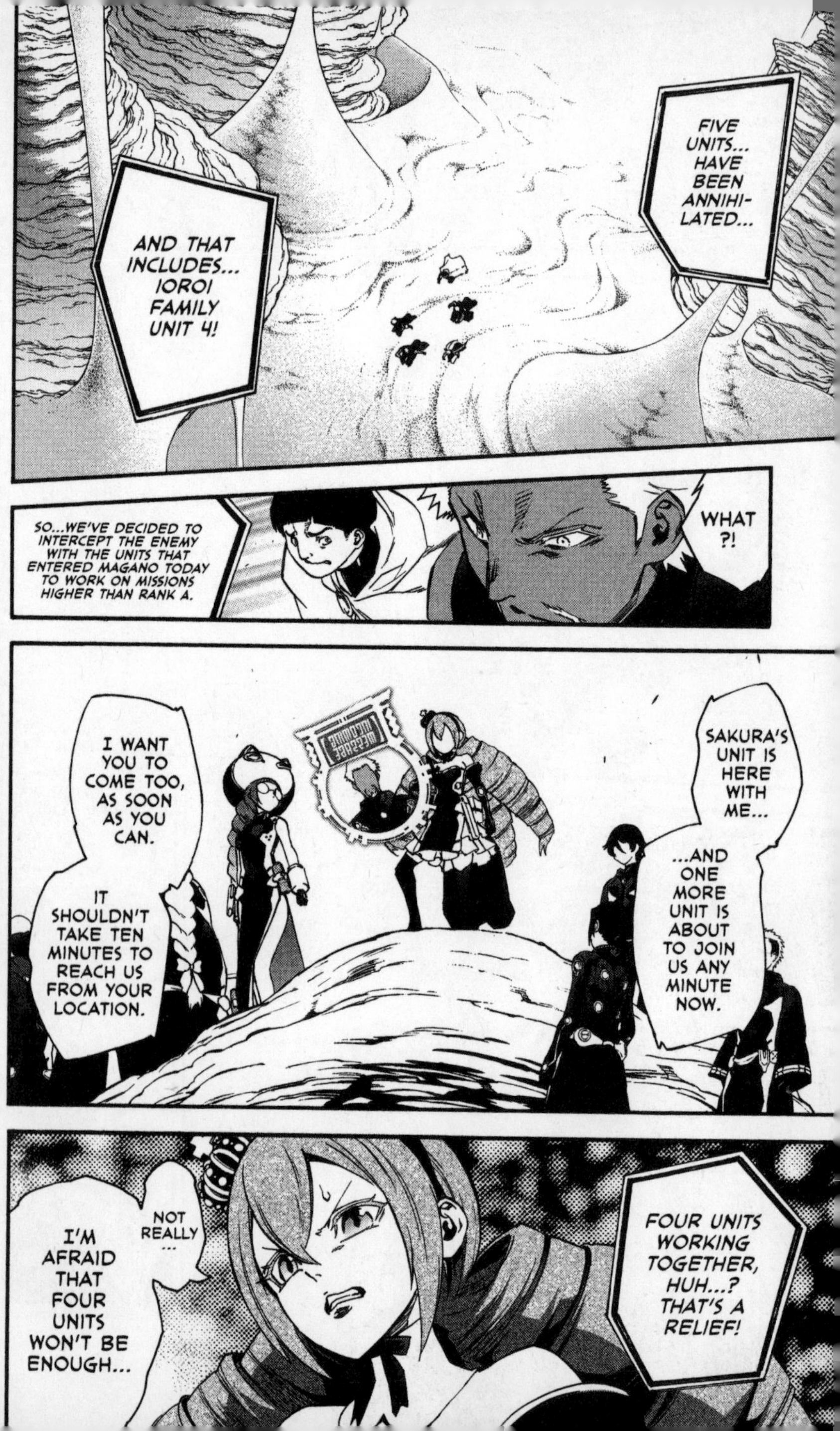
FIVE UNITS... HAVE BEEN ANNIHILATED...
AND THAT INCLUDES... IOROI FAMILY UNIT 4!
WHAT ?!
SO...WE'VE DECIDED TO INTERCEPT THE ENEMY WITH THE UNITS THAT ENTERED MAGANO TODAY TO WORK ON MISSIONS HIGHER THAN RANK A.
SAKURA'S UNIT IS HERE WITH ME...
...AND ONE MORE UNIT IS ABOUT TO JOIN US ANY MINUTE NOW.
I WANT YOU TO COME TOO, AS SOON AS YOU CAN.
IT SHOULDN'T TAKE TEN MINUTES TO REACH US FROM YOUR LOCATION.
FOUR UNITS WORKING TOGETHER, HUH...? THAT'S A RELIEF!
NOT REALLY...
I'M AFRAID THAT FOUR UNITS WON'T BE ENOUGH...

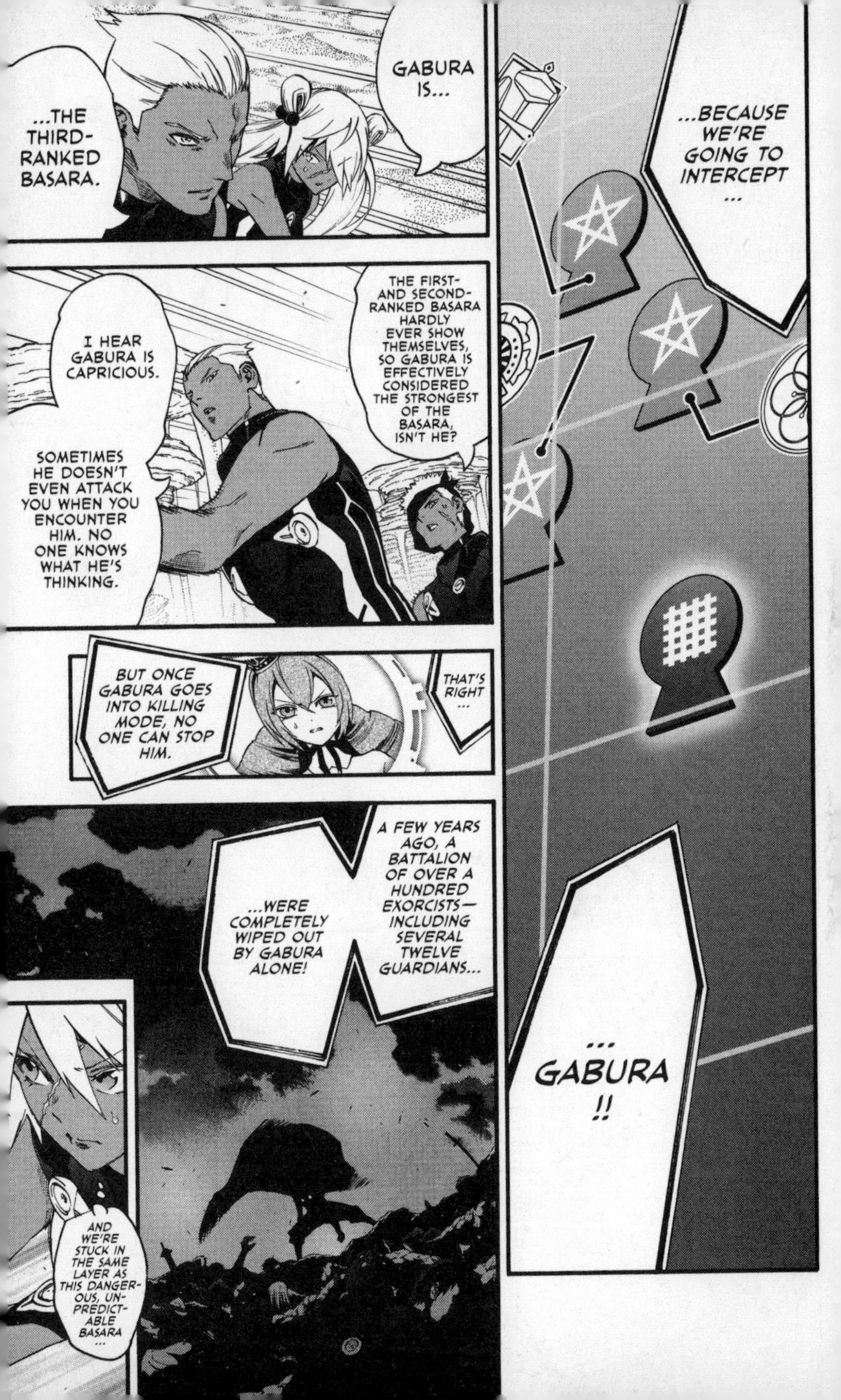
...BECAUSE WE'RE GOING TO INTERCEPT ...
... GABURA !!
GABURA IS...
...THE THIRD-RANKED BASARA.
THE FIRST- AND SECOND-RANKED BASARA HARDLY EVER SHOW THEMSELVES, SO GABURA IS EFFECTIVELY CONSIDERED THE STRONGEST OF THE BASARA, ISN'T HE?
I HEAR GABURA IS CAPRICIOUS.
SOMETIMES HE DOESN'T EVEN ATTACK YOU WHEN YOU ENCOUNTER HIM. NO ONE KNOWS WHAT HE'S THINKING.
THAT'S RIGHT ...
BUT ONCE GABURA GOES INTO KILLING MODE, NO ONE CAN STOP HIM.
A FEW YEARS AGO, A BATTALION OF OVER A HUNDRED EXORCISTS—INCLUDING SEVERAL TWELVE GUARDIANS...
...WERE COMPLETELY WIPED OUT BY GABURA ALONE!
AND WE'RE STUCK IN THE SAME LAYER AS THIS DANGEROUS, UNPREDICTABLE BASARA ...

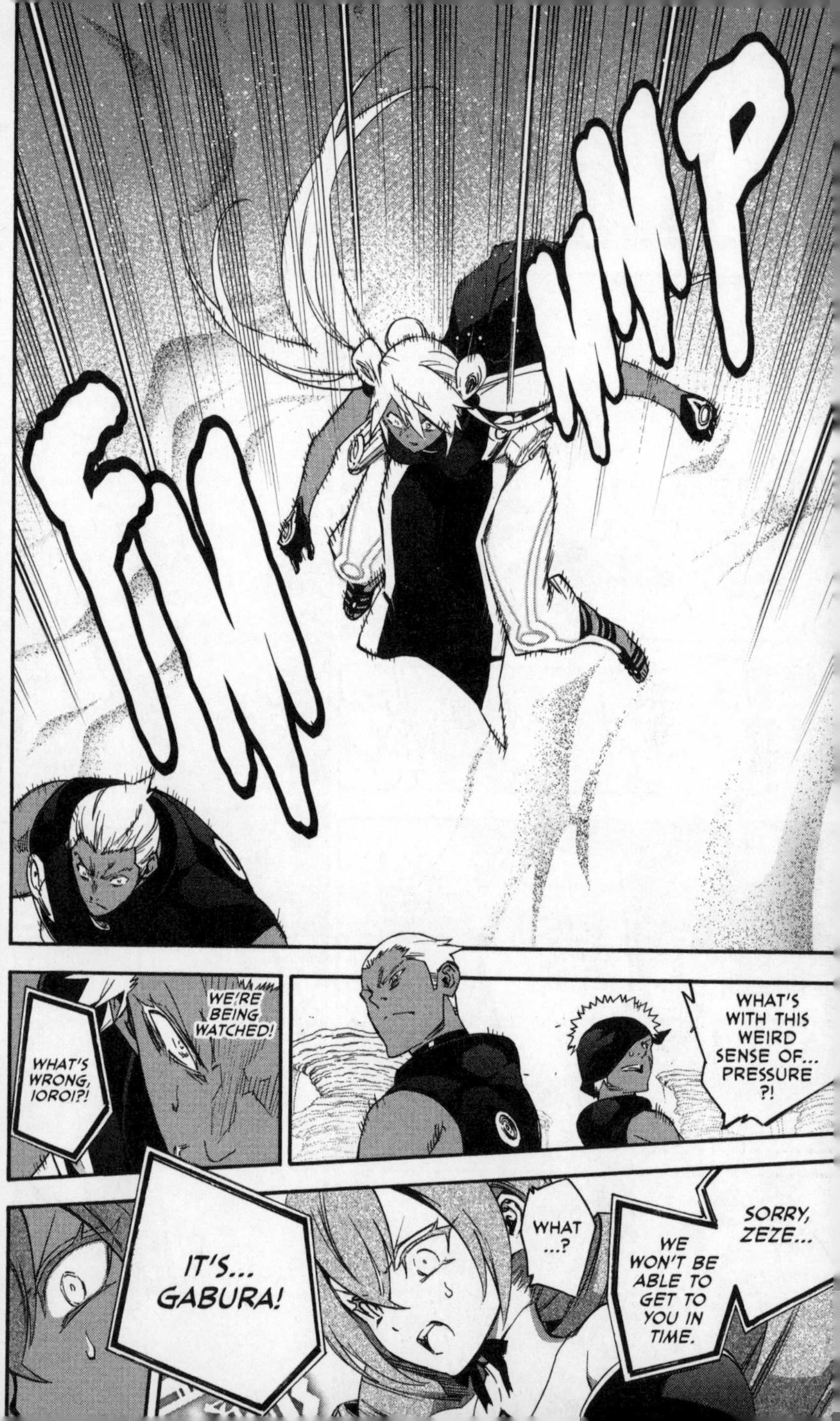

WHAT'S WITH THIS WEIRD SENSE OF... PRESSURE ?!
WE'RE BEING WATCHED!
WHAT'S WRONG, IOROI?!
SORRY, ZEZE...
WE WON'T BE ABLE TO GET TO YOU IN TIME.
WHAT ...?
IT'S... GABURA!

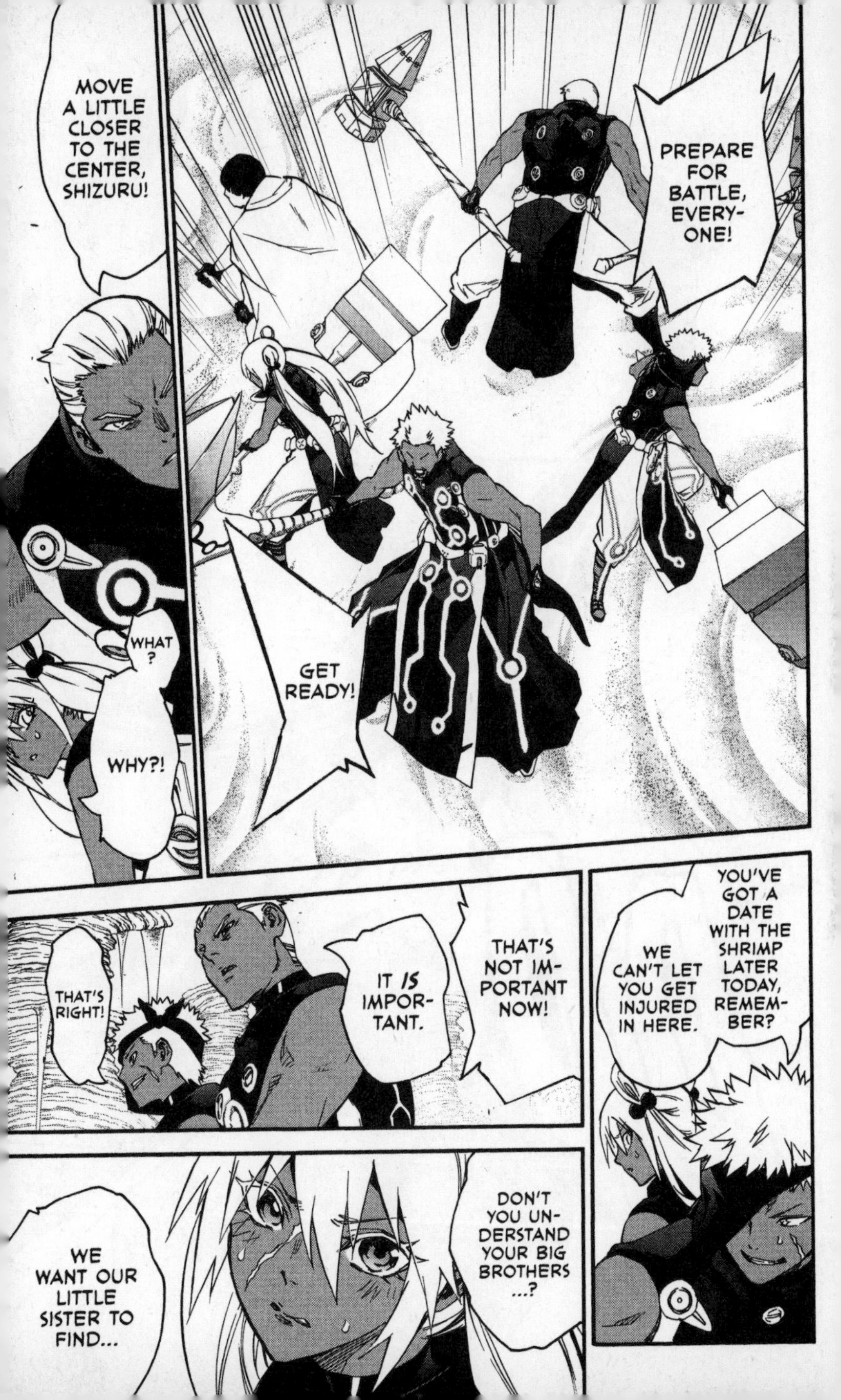
PREPARE FOR BATTLE, EVERY-ONE!
GET READY!
MOVE A LITTLE CLOSER TO THE CENTER, SHIZURU!
WHAT?
WHY?!
YOU'VE GOT A DATE WITH THE SHRIMP LATER TODAY, REMEMBER?
WE CAN'T LET YOU GET INJURED IN HERE.
THAT'S NOT IM-PORTANT NOW!
IT *IS* IMPOR-TANT.
THAT'S RIGHT!
DON'T YOU UN-DERSTAND YOUR BIG BROTHERS ...?
WE WANT OUR LITTLE SISTER TO FIND...

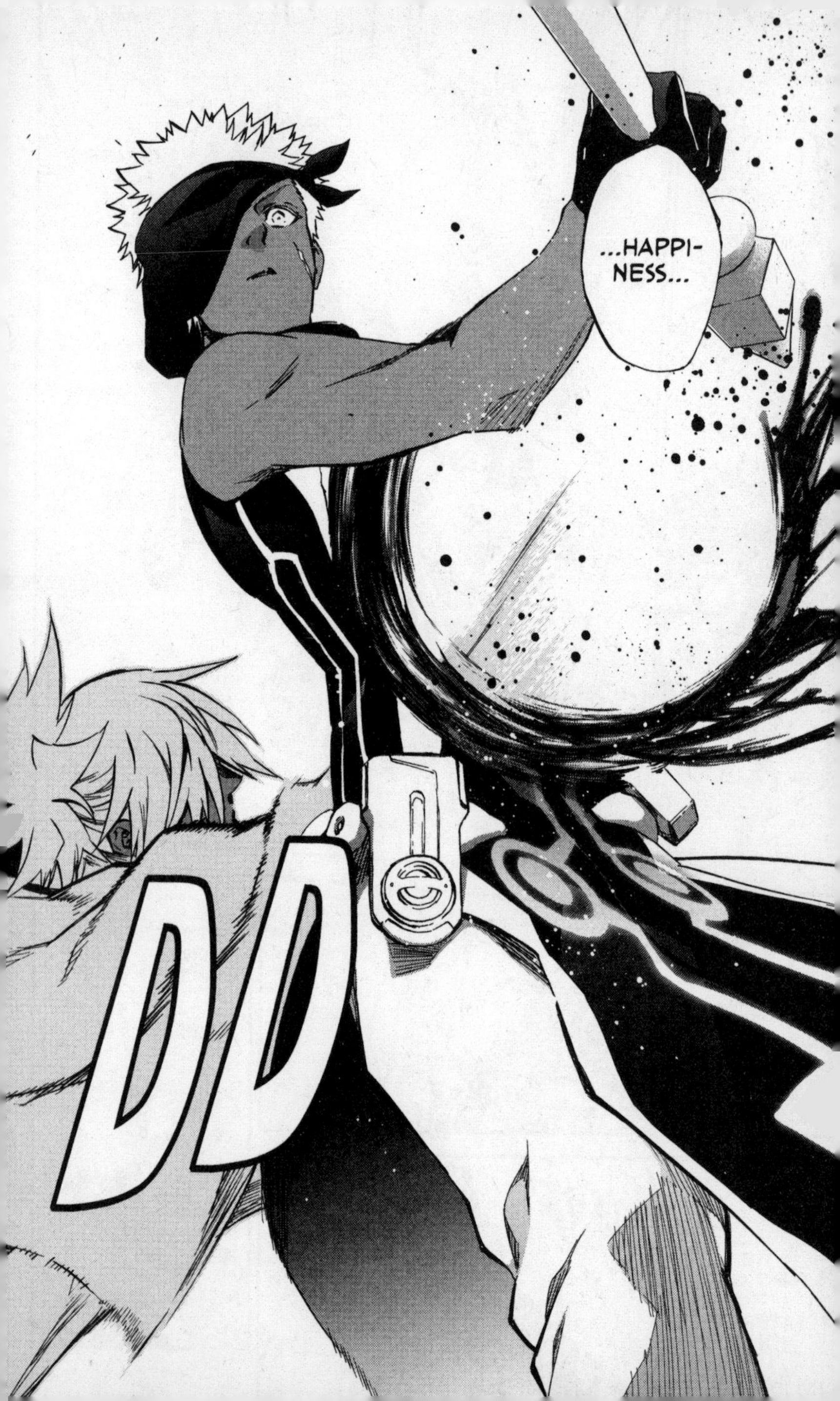
...HAPPI-
NESS...
DD

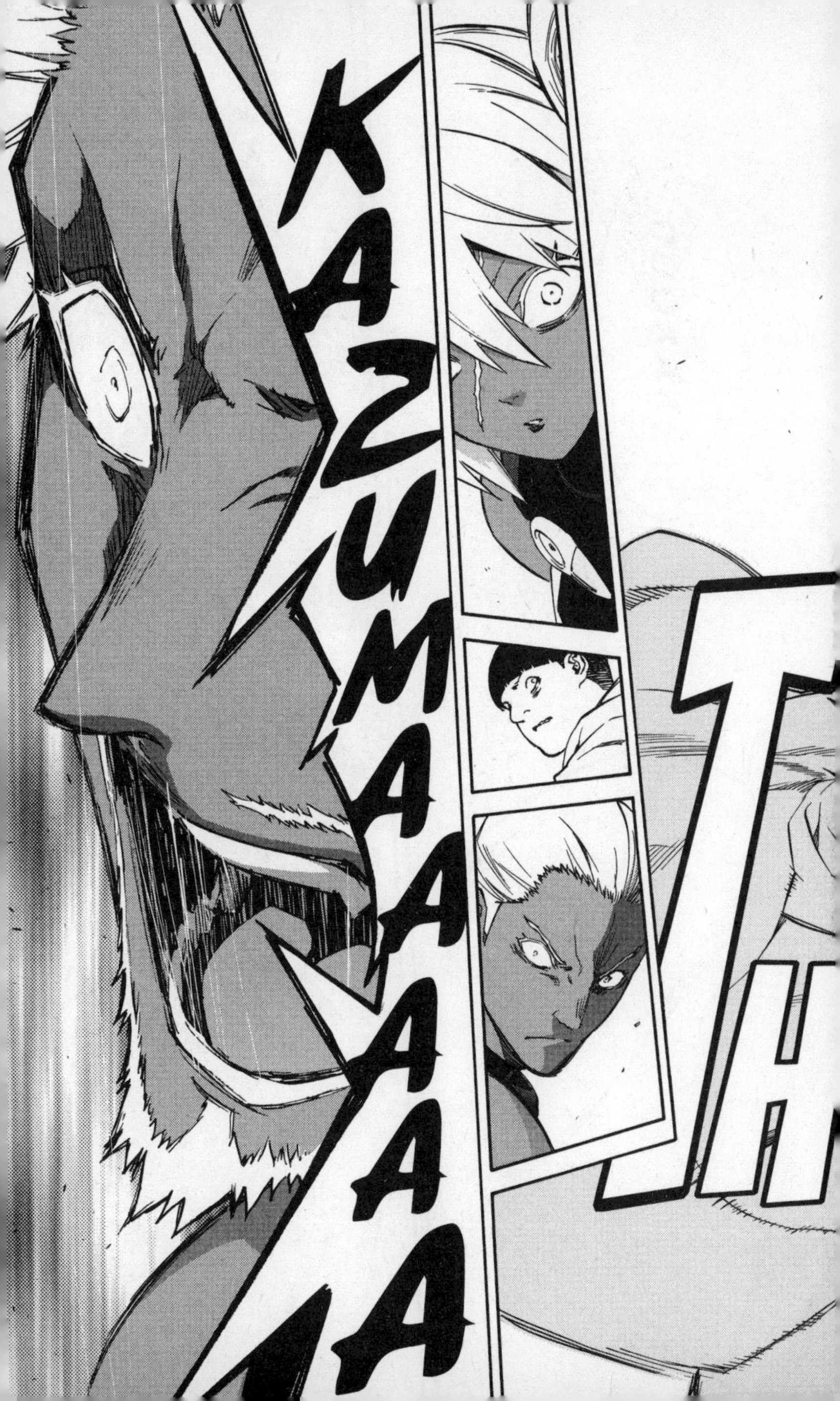
KAZUMAAAAAAA
TH

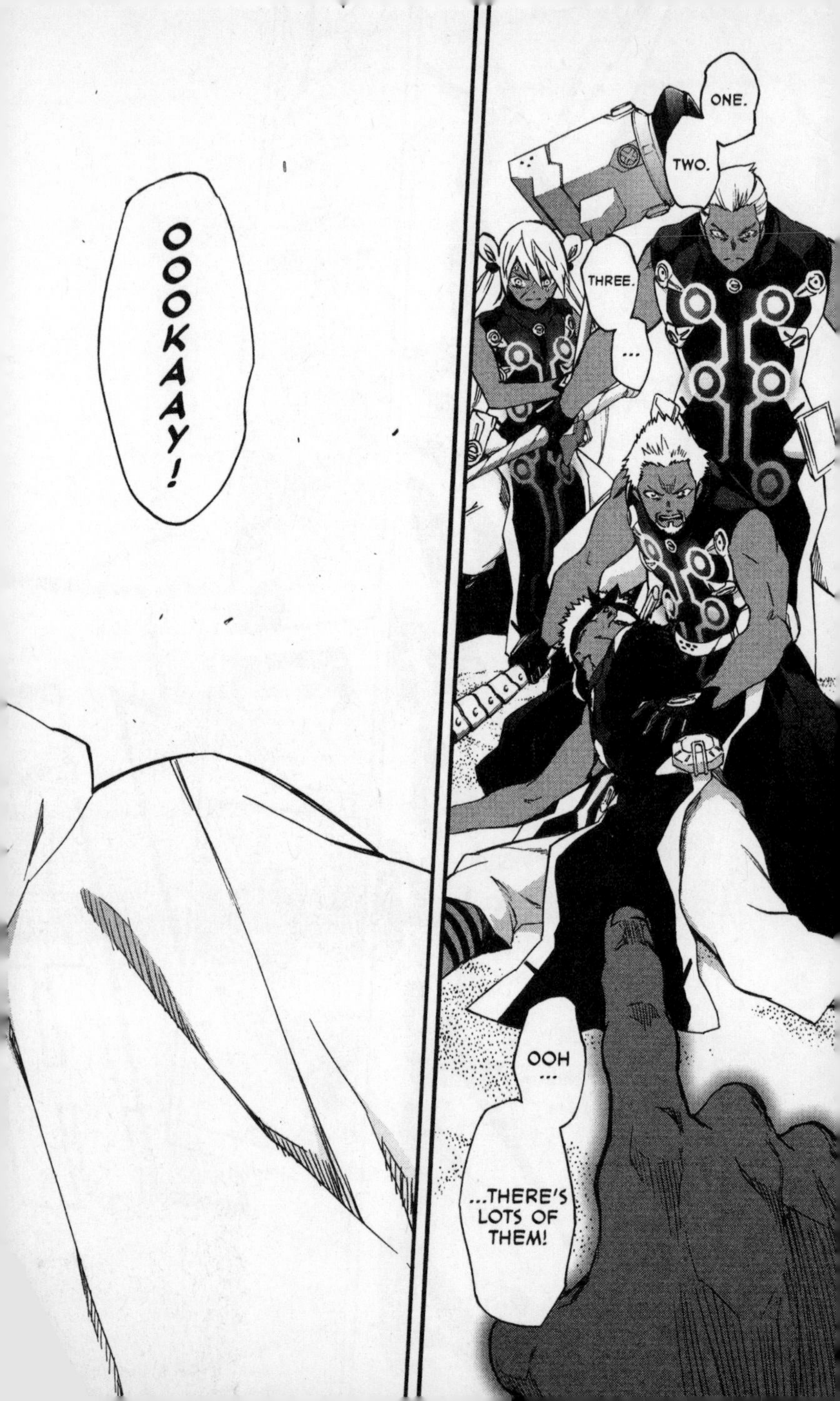
ONE.
TWO.
THREE.
...
OOH ...
...THERE'S LOTS OF THEM!
OOOKAAY!

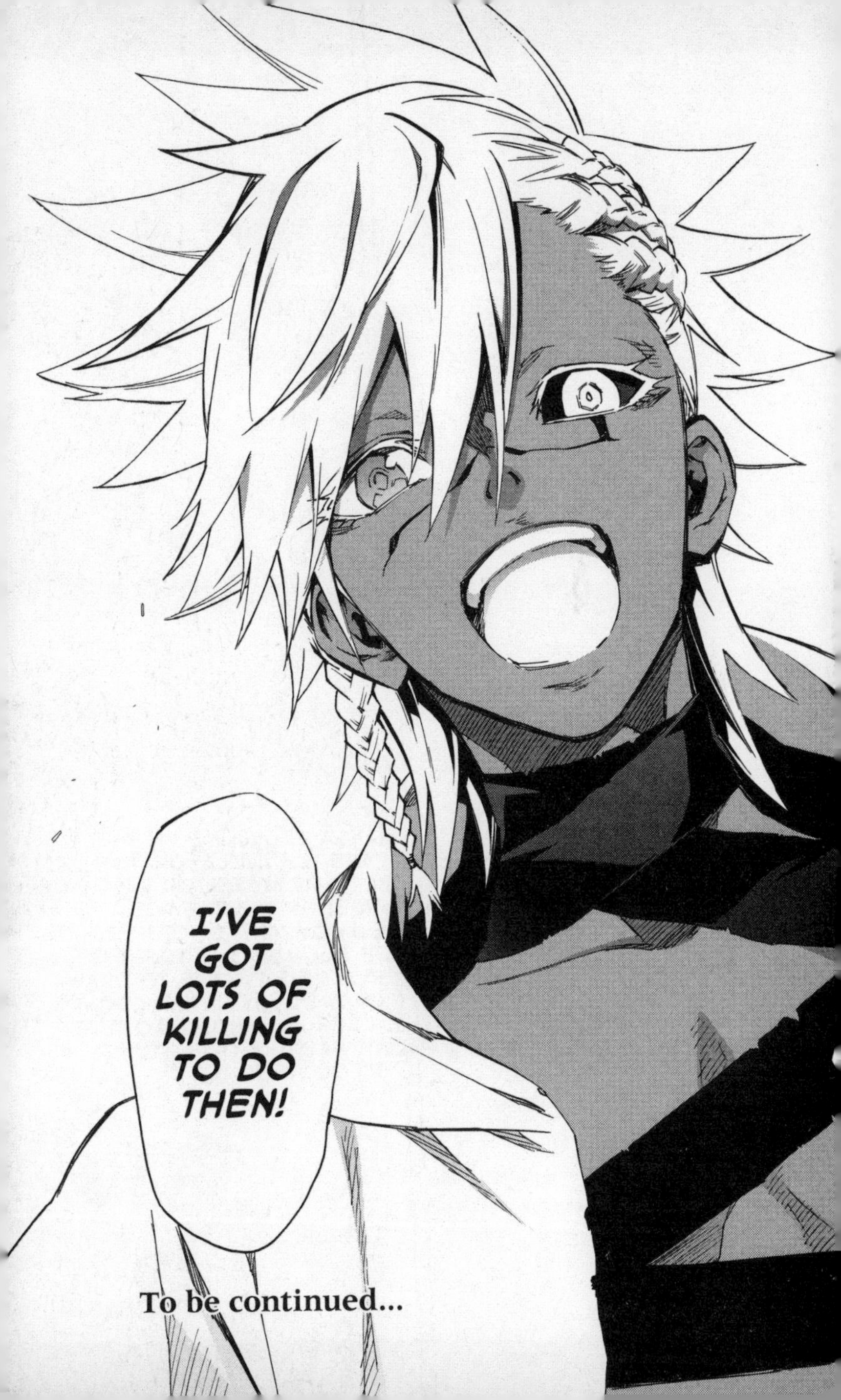
I'VE GOT LOTS OF KILLING TO DO THEN!
To be continued...

THE MANGA BEGINNING ON THE
NEXT PAGE IS A COLLABORATIVE
PROJECT THAT MY EDITOR KASAI
ARRANGED WITH AIRWEAVE, A
MATTRESS COMPANY. I ACCEPTED
THE JOB BECAUSE I THOUGHT IT
WOULD GIVE ME A CHANCE TO DRAW
SOME (LOVEY-DOVEY) INTERACTIONS
BETWEEN ROKURO AND BENIO THAT
I HADN'T HAD THE OPPORTUNITY
TO DO RECENTLY. ☆

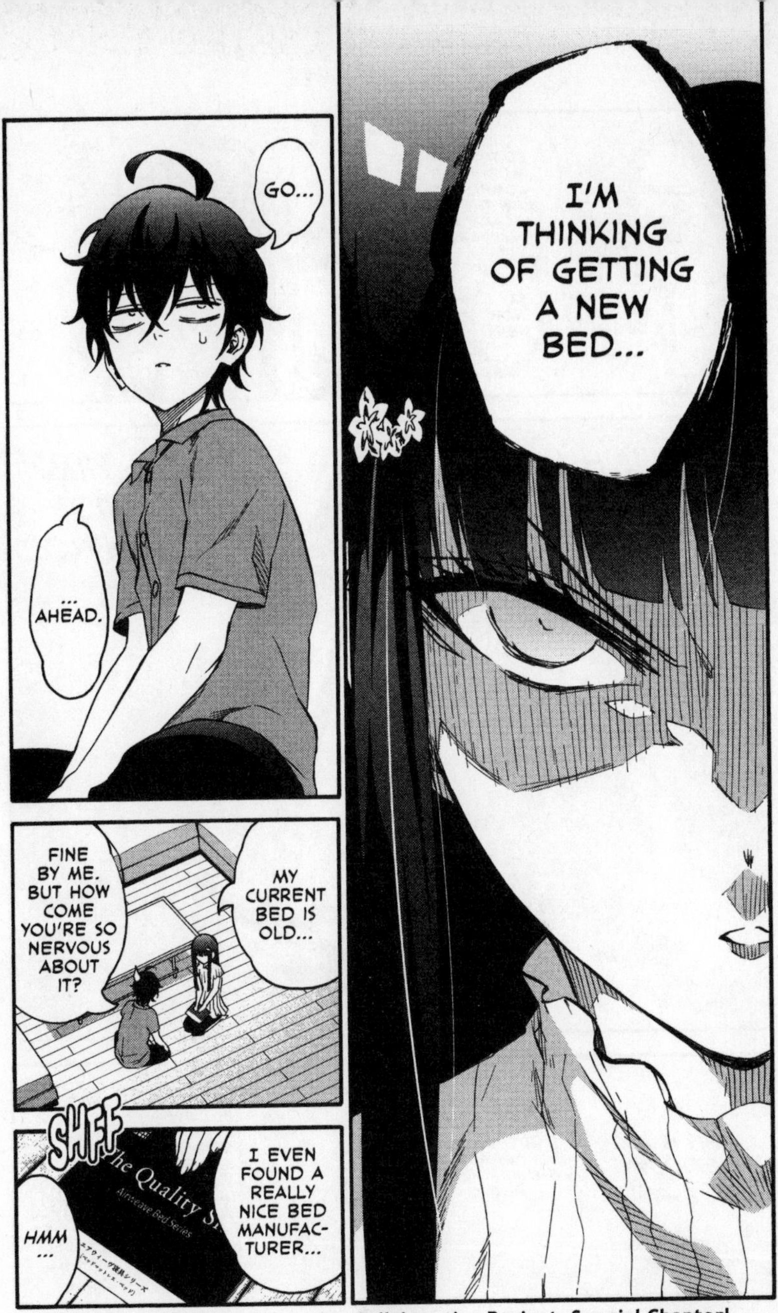
I'M THINKING OF GETTING A NEW BED...
GO...
...AHEAD.
MY CURRENT BED IS OLD...
FINE BY ME. BUT HOW COME YOU'RE SO NERVOUS ABOUT IT?
SHFF
I EVEN FOUND A REALLY NICE BED MANUFAC-TURER...
HMM...

Shueisha Jump SQ × Airweave Collaborative Project, Special Chapter!

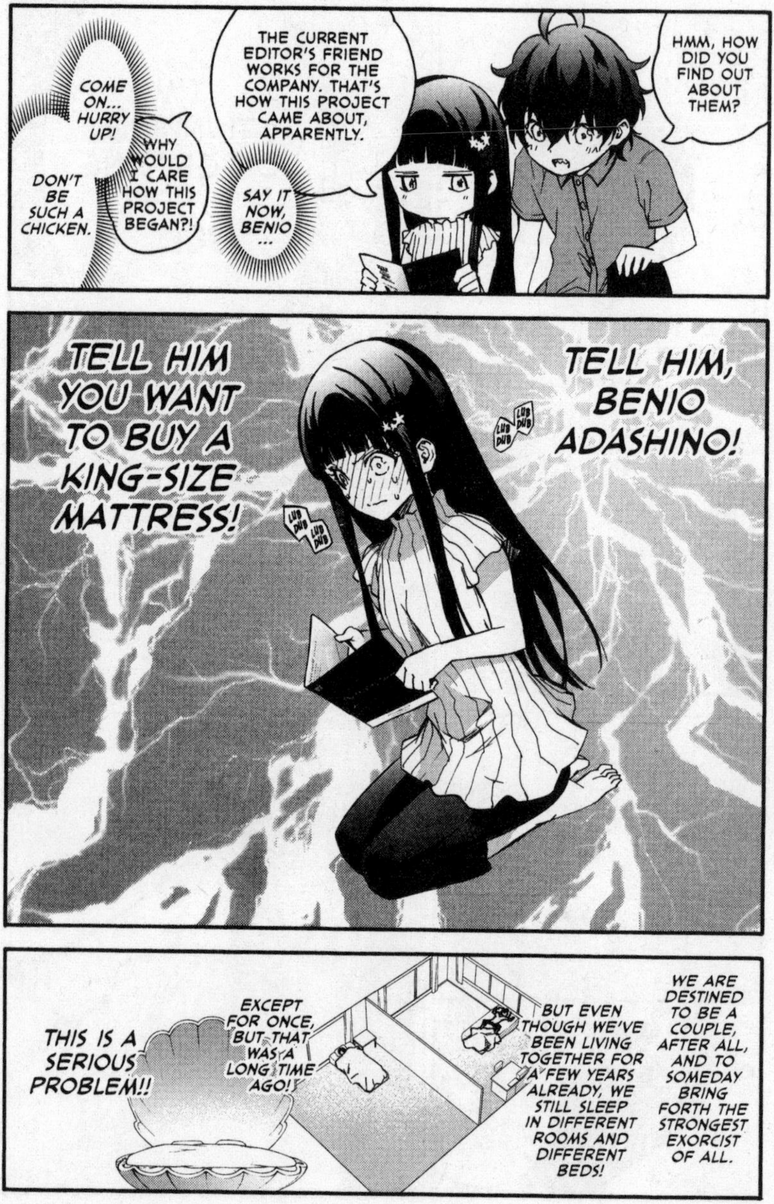
HMM, HOW DID YOU FIND OUT ABOUT THEM?
THE CURRENT EDITOR'S FRIEND WORKS FOR THE COMPANY. THAT'S HOW THIS PROJECT CAME ABOUT, APPARENTLY.
SAY IT NOW, BENIO ...
WHY WOULD I CARE HOW THIS PROJECT BEGAN?!
COME ON... HURRY UP!
DON'T BE SUCH A CHICKEN.
TELL HIM, BENIO ADASHINO!
LUB DUB LUB DUB
TELL HIM YOU WANT TO BUY A KING-SIZE MATTRESS!
LUB DUB LUB DUB
WE ARE DESTINED TO BE A COUPLE, AFTER ALL, AND TO SOMEDAY BRING FORTH THE STRONGEST EXORCIST OF ALL.
BUT EVEN THOUGH WE'VE BEEN LIVING TOGETHER FOR A FEW YEARS ALREADY, WE STILL SLEEP IN DIFFERENT ROOMS AND DIFFERENT BEDS!
EXCEPT FOR ONCE, BUT THAT WAS A LONG TIME AGO!
THIS IS A SERIOUS PROBLEM!!

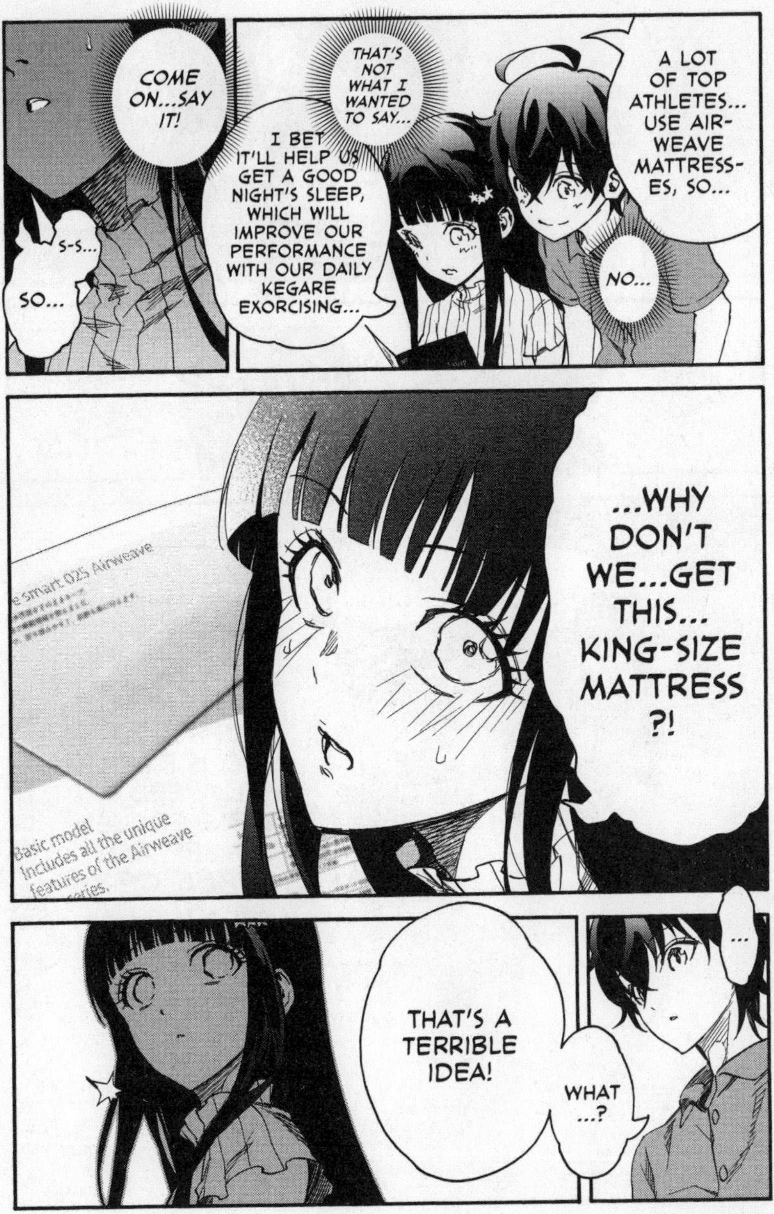

A LOT OF TOP ATHLETES... USE AIR-WEAVE MATTRESS-ES, SO...
NO...
THAT'S NOT WHAT I WANTED TO SAY...
I BET IT'LL HELP US GET A GOOD NIGHT'S SLEEP, WHICH WILL IMPROVE OUR PERFORMANCE WITH OUR DAILY KEGARE EXORCISING...
COME ON...SAY IT!
S-S...
SO...
...WHY DON'T WE...GET THIS... KING-SIZE MATTRESS ?!
smart 025 Airweave
Basic model
Includes all the unique
features of the Airweave
...
THAT'S A TERRIBLE IDEA!
WHAT ...?

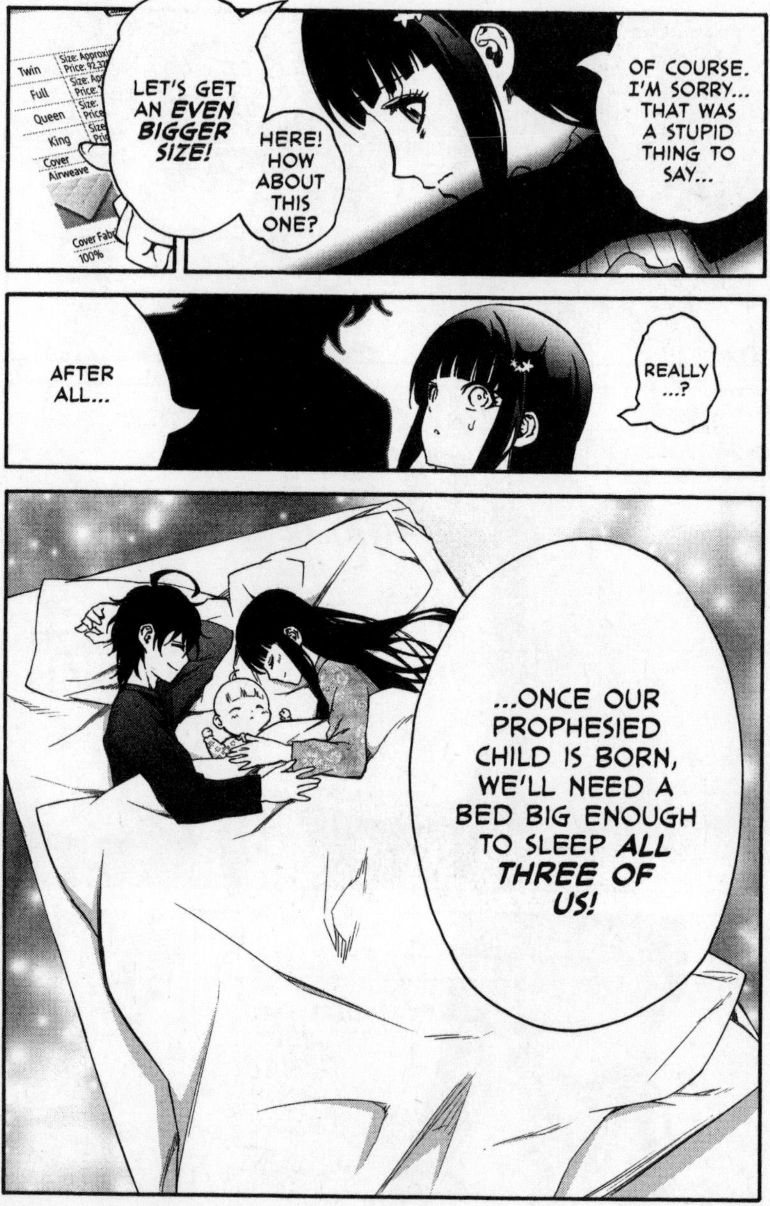
OF COURSE. I'M SORRY... THAT WAS A STUPID THING TO SAY...
HERE! HOW ABOUT THIS ONE?
LET'S GET AN *EVEN BIGGER SIZE!*
Twin
Full
Queen
King
Cover
Airweave
100%
REALLY ...?
AFTER ALL...
...ONCE OUR PROPHESIED CHILD IS BORN, WE'LL NEED A BED BIG ENOUGH TO SLEEP *ALL THREE OF US!*

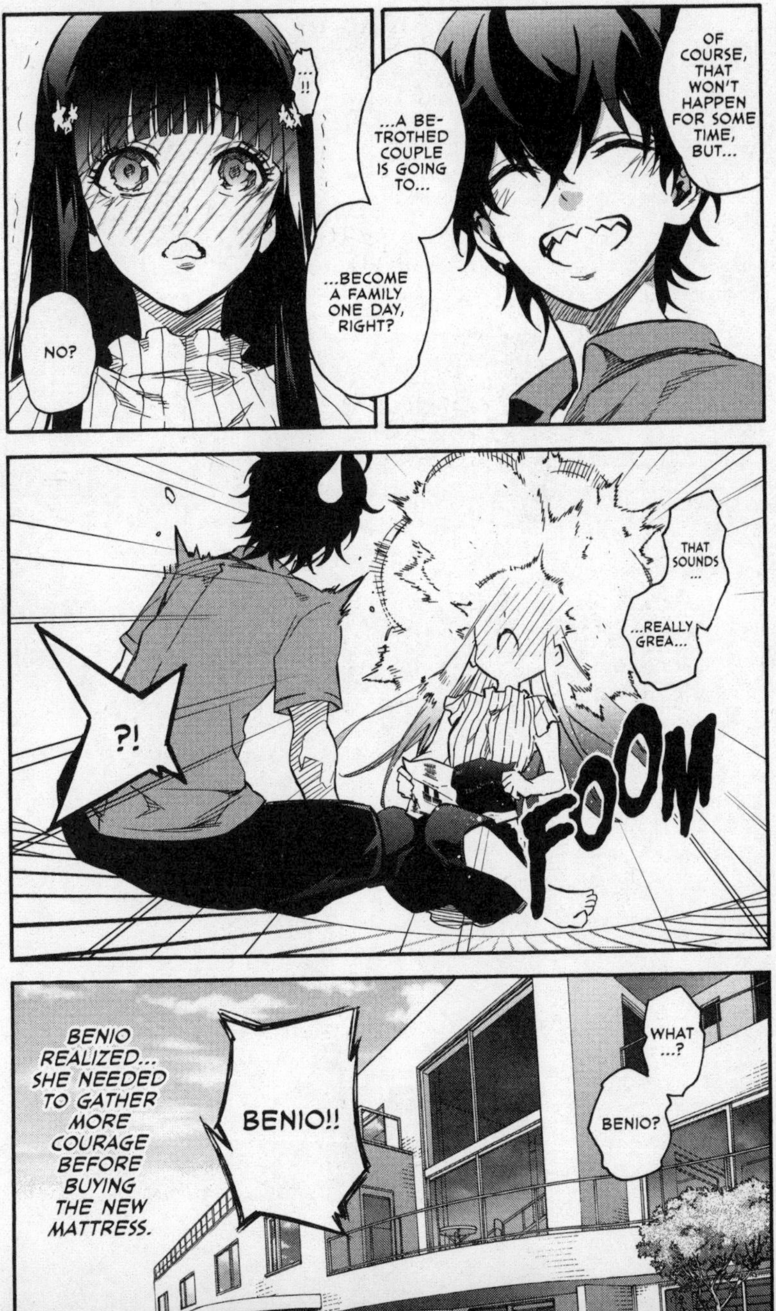
OF COURSE, THAT WON'T HAPPEN FOR SOME TIME, BUT...
...A BE-TROTHED COUPLE IS GOING TO...
...BECOME A FAMILY ONE DAY, RIGHT?
...!!
NO?
THAT SOUNDS...
...REALLY GREA...
FOOM
?!
WHAT...?
BENIO?
BENIO!!
BENIO REALIZED... SHE NEEDED TO GATHER MORE COURAGE BEFORE BUYING THE NEW MATTRESS.

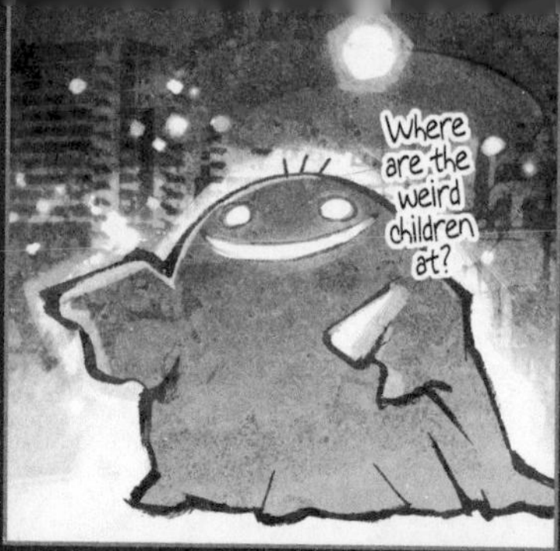
Where are the weird children at?

Benio's story in this volume and the previous one was serialized for one year in the seasonal magazine *Jump SQ CROWN* (which changed to *Jump SQ RISE* midway). It was the first time I worked on a series that was being published simultaneously in two different magazines. I was apprehensive, but it turned out to be a fulfilling experience. I'll create something like that again for another character. It'll be like a spin-off.

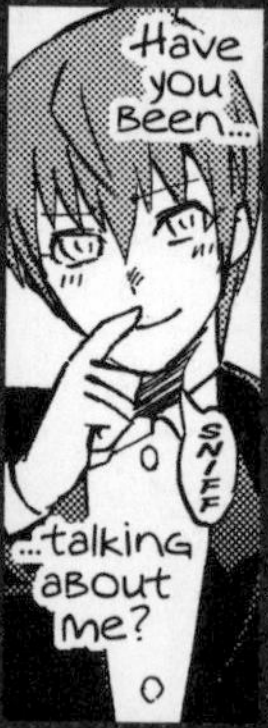
Have you been...
SNIFF
...talking about me?

YOSHIAKI SUKENO was born July 23, 1981, in Wakayama, Japan. He graduated from Kyoto Seika University, where he studied manga. In 2006, he won the Tezuka Award for Best Newcomer Shonen Manga Artist. In 2008, he began his previous work, the supernatural comedy *Binbougami ga!*, which was adapted into the anime *Good Luck Girl!* in 2012.

The Stairway to the Great Black Torii

The Plateau of the Starry Heavens

• There are several relatively large rest areas en route to the top level. They are commonly known as follows:

1. Plateau of Courage

2. Plateau of Trembling

3. Plateau of Reconsideration

4. Plateau of Regret

5. Plateau of Grief

Each plateau represents a stage of anxiety of the exorcists about to enter Magano.

• You can summit in 20 to 30 minutes walking at a slow pace, but you can reach the top in less than a minute with an elevator shikigami called the Spider Bus. (However, you will suffer from severe motion sickness.)

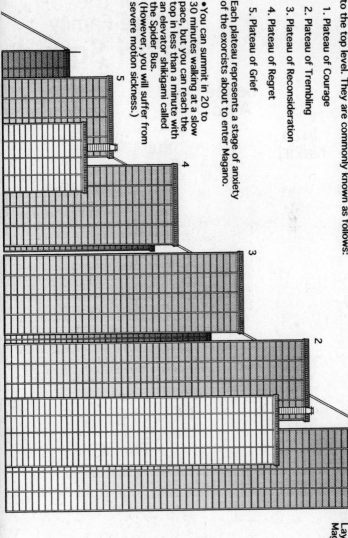

Great Black Torii (Entrance to the Main Layer of Magano)

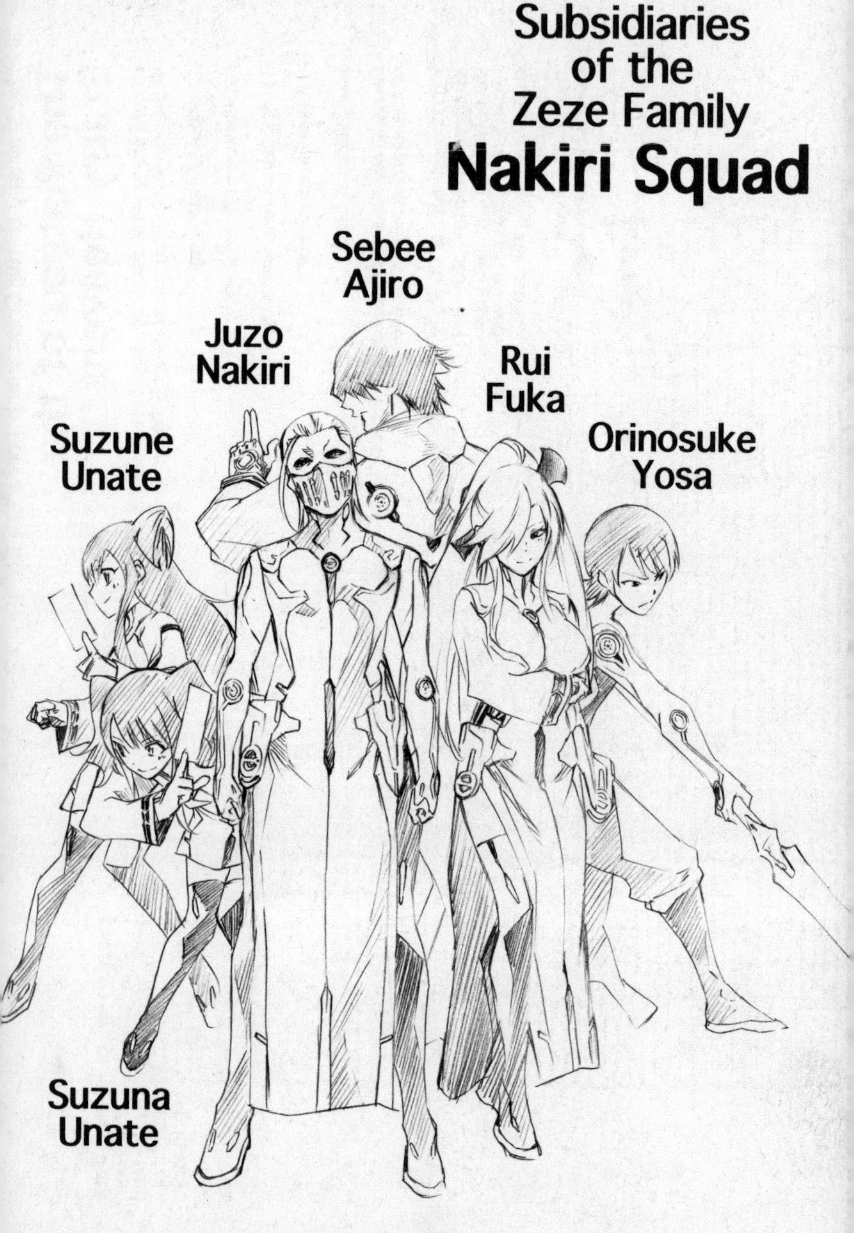

Subsidiaries of the Zeze Family
Nakiri Squad
Sebee Ajiro
Juzo Nakiri
Rui Fuka
Suzune Unate
Orinosuke Yosa
Suzuna Unate

Twin Star Exorcists
ONMYOJI

15

—SHONEN JUMP Manga Edition—

STORY & ART **Yoshiaki Sukeno**

TRANSLATION **Tetsuichiro Miyaki**
ENGLISH ADAPTATION **Bryant Turnage**
TOUCH-UP ART & LETTERING **Stephen Dutro**
DESIGN **Shawn Carrico**
EDITOR **Annette Roman**

SOUSEI NO ONMYOJI © 2013 by Yoshiaki Sukeno
All rights reserved.
First published in Japan in 2013 by SHUEISHA Inc., Tokyo.
English translation rights arranged by SHUEISHA Inc.

The stories, characters and incidents mentioned in this
publication are entirely fictional.

Printed in the U.S.A.

Published by VIZ Media, LLC
P.O. Box 77010
San Francisco, CA 94107

10 9 8 7 6 5 4 3 2 1
First printing, May 2019

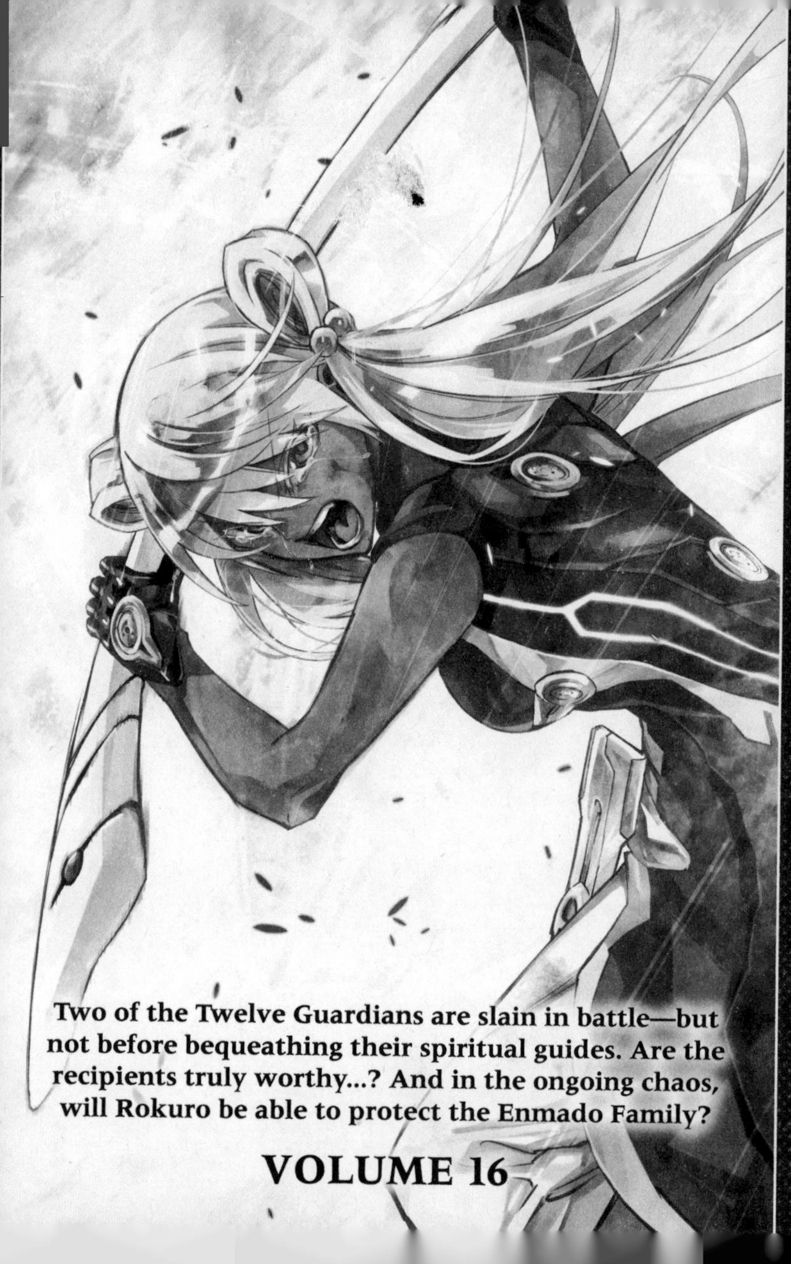
Two of the Twelve Guardians are slain in battle—but not before bequeathing their spiritual guides. Are the recipients truly worthy...? And in the ongoing chaos, will Rokuro be able to protect the Enmado Family?
VOLUME 16